Great Canadian War Stories

Great Canadian War Stories

Edited by
Muriel Whitaker

With a foreword by
Peter Stursberg

The University of Alberta Press

Published by
The University of Alberta Press
Ring House 2
Edmonton, Alberta T6G 2E1
Copyright this volume © Muriel Whitaker 2001
Copyright for individual stories remains with their rights holders; see page xii
for details.

National Library of Canada Cataloguing in Publication Data

Main entry under title:
  Great Canadian war stories

    ISBN 0-88864-383-7

    1. War stories, Canadian (English)* 2. Canadian fiction
(English)—20th century*. I. Whitaker, Muriel, 1923–
PS8323.W37G73 2001   C813'.0108358   C2001-911404-4
PR9197.35.W37G73 2001

Printed and bound in Canada by Kromar Printing Ltd., Winnipeg, Manitoba.
5 4 3 2 1
∞ Printed on acid-free paper.
Book design by Carol Dragich.
Proofreading by Kate Hole and Tara Taylor.

The University of Alberta Press acknowledges the financial support of the
Government of Canada through the Book Publishing Industry Development
Program for its publishing activities. The Press also gratefully acknowledges the
support received for its program from the Canada Council for the Arts.

THE CANADA COUNCIL | LE CONSEIL DES ARTS
FOR THE ARTS | DU CANADA
SINCE 1957 | DEPUIS 1957

To the memory of
my father Howard McDiarmid,
who served with the Royal Flying Corps in the Great War,

my brother Bill,
a Flying Officer in #159 Squadron RCAF *and #355 Squadron* RAF,

and my brother Jim,
a member of the Canadian Parachute Corps in the Second World War

Contents

Peter Stursberg • *Foreword*   IX

Acknowledgements   XIII

Muriel Whitaker • *Introduction: Inheritors of Glory:*
Twentieth-Century Canadian War Stories   XV

Timothy Findley • Bird Song   1

Charles Yale Harrison • The Sniper   11

Will R. Bird • Sunrise for Peter   19

Peregrine Acland • Zero Hour   35

Anonymous • Hard Lines!   43

Thomas H. Raddall • Winter's Tale   49

J.G. Sime • Munitions!   69

George Reid Clifford • George and the Red Baron   77

Greg Clark • The Bully   85

Louis Caron • The Draft Dodger   89

Hugh Garner • The Stretcher-Bearers   105

Max Braithwaite • The Porpoise that Couldn't Swim   113

Edward Meade • A Moonless Night   127

Joy Kogawa • Obasan   135

Agnes Newton Keith • Getting Rid of Proudery and Arrogance   143

Andrew Campbell Ballantine • Lion-taming for Beginners   163

D.A. MacMillan • The Newspaper Writer   169

Colin McDougall • The Firing-Squad   175

Ralph Allen • The Landing   193

Earle Birney • Turvey is Considered for Knighthood   213

Roch Carrier • Son of a Smaller Hero   231

Henry Kreisel • Homecoming: A Memory of Europe After the Holocaust   237

Foreword

WE KNEW WE WERE AT WAR WHEN WE LISTENED
to the British Prime Minister, Neville Chamberlain, on the radio that
late Saturday night, early Sunday morning, September 3, 1939, in
Victoria, BC. The dance bands on the networks had been interrupted:
"Now we bring you London," and there was his voice saying that all his
efforts at peace had failed. It was no clarion call to arms; it was more like
a mournful epitaph. The next day was another quiet Sunday with all
stores closed. There were no flags flying, no crowds cheering and
singing "Rule Britannia," no bands playing, as there were in 1914—just
an awful realization and, within time, a grim determination to go to war.

The Second World War was said to be the continuation of the First
World War, the Great War, "the war to end all wars," but there were
marked differences. For one thing, while the Blitzkrieg sputtered out,
there were staged battles and heavy casualties on both sides, but the
armies never got bogged down as they did the time before, and the
troops never suffered the dreadful conditions of trench warfare that
went on for so long, the horror and indignity of having to fight and live
in slime and filth. Then, flying, which was in its infancy in 1914–18,
some twenty years later bore out Tennyson's vision, "and there rained a
ghastly dew from the nations' airy navies grappling in the central flue":
cities and civilians were bombed, without any mercy or restraint.

Another distinguishing factor was the number of landings which were combined operations of all three services. The Canadians had five of them, the disastrous Dieppe raid, the invasion of Sicily (which was the first time the Canadians were really in action), crossing the Straits of Messina into Italy, and the greatest of all, the landing on the beaches of Normandy, which became known as "D-Day." The fifth, the invasion of Southern France, had a small Canadian component in the troops of the combined American-Canadian Special Service Force. My friend Ralph Allen's story, "The Landing," is about D-Day.

The Canadian troops in Italy resented the way that D-Day had been "expropriated" and applied only to the June 6, 1944 cross-channel operation. Their D-Day was almost a year earlier, the July 10, 1943 landing in Sicily. And I should point out that almost half the Canadian army was in Italy. At the insistence of Ottawa, in a move that was deplored by military historians, the First Canadian Army was split in two, with the First Corps being sent to Italy at the end of 1943. It fought there through 1944, and only returned to the fold in March 1945. Its last task was the liberation of Holland.

When the notorious Lady Astor referred, perhaps jokingly, to the Allied troops in Italy as the "D-Day Dodgers," there was anger. But just as the British troops in the First World War called themselves "the Old Contemptibles," turning the Kaiser's scorn into a badge of honour (he described the British Expeditionary Force as "that contemptible little army"), so the Canadian soldiers in Italy accepted that snide epithet and called themselves the D-Day Dodgers. There is a D-Day Dodgers association in Canada, D-Day Dodgers caps and badges, even a D-Day Dodgers medal, and a comprehensive history of the Canadian corps in Italy is entitled *The D-Day Dodgers*.

By 1943, it was becoming apparent that the main force defeating the Nazis was the Americans and the Russians. The U.S. Second Corps, which had helped the American Fifth Army liberate Rome, hung a huge banner on the Colosseum bearing the slogan "Follow the Blue to Speedy Two / Rome, Berlin and Tokyo Too." Most people were amused by the vulgarity of the "Yanks" turning this ancient monument into an advertising board, but some Romans considered it boorish and an affront, and one muttered to me, "Europe is being overrun by the barbarians from the East *and* the West."

The Second World War was a much bigger war: it was everywhere on almost every land and sea, whereas the First World War was confined mostly to Europe and its environs. The stories in this book reflect this; they are from Canada and England, North Africa and Italy, France and Spain. They include Hugh Garner's piece, a vignette of the Spanish Civil War, the "ante-room to Armageddon" and the prelude to the world war; and Agnes Newton Keith's moving account of being a prisoner of the Japanese. The campaign in the Pacific got much less attention, certainly in Canada, than the fighting in Europe. They had different endings. Almost everyone knows that VE Day is May 8, but who knows the date of VJ Day? There happen to be two, according to the calendar of events: August 14 and September 2.

Greg Clark was a link between the wars. I knew him as a war correspondent, but he had had a distinguished career as an infantry officer in the First World War. His story of how he met the hated bully of his boyhood days on the battlefield of Vimy Ridge and they became comrades in arms will strike a chord with many veterans. Although different, Greg's story somehow reminded me of my encounter with Jack Mahony. I did some work with him in New Westminster and found him to be a mild-mannered, gentle, almost timid fellow. The next time I saw him, now Major J.K. Mahony, was in Italy when I rushed to get an interview with him as he had won the Victoria Cross in the battle for Rome.

Most of the surviving veterans of the Second World War remember it as a time of adventure and excitement, of fun and freedom from domestic ties, of self-indulgence and camaraderie. Moreover, it was when they were young. They have forgotten, or closed their minds to, all the death and destruction, the long stretches of enervating boredom, and moments of morale-destroying terror. One of the contemporaries of the First World War recalled all its ghastly slaughter and yet spoke of it as being "also exciting," and another said, "We are living at a time when days and weeks have the fullness and significance of years and decades." The stories in this book seem to bear out these paradoxes.

—Peter Stursberg

Acknowledgements

THE UNIVERSITY OF ALBERTA PRESS ACKNOWLEDGES the following sources for the materials in this volume. We thank those who have granted their permission for reprinting. The Press has made every effort to contact the rights-holders; should you have any additional information, please contact our office.

Excerpt from *The Wars* by Timothy Findley. Copyright © 1979 by Timothy Findley. Reprinted by permission of Penguin Books Canada Limited.

"The Sniper" by Charles Yale Harrison from *Generals Die in Bed* copyright © 1975 by Potlatch Publications. Reprinted by permission of Potlatch Publications.

"Sunrise for Peter" from *Sunrise for Peter and Other Stories* by Will R. Bird, copyright © 1946. Used by permission of the copyright holder.

"Zero Hour" from *All Else Is Folly: A Tale of War and Passion* by Peregrine Acland, copyright © 1929.

"Hard Lines!" from *Letters from the Little Blue Room: By The Elder Sister to her Brother Who Came over with the First Canadian Contingent to Serve in the War to End War*, copyright © 1917.

"Winter's Tale" by Thomas H. Raddall is reprinted with permission of Dalhousie University.

"Munitions!" from *Sister Woman* by J.G. Sime, copyright © 1919. Used by permission of the copyright holder.

Inheritors of Glory

TWENTIETH-CENTURY
CANADIAN WAR STORIES

"I SING OF ARMS AND THE MAN"—*arma virumque cano.* So begins Virgil's epic about Aeneas, the survivor of the Trojan Wars who founded Rome. For at least three millennia, the idea of hero has incorporated the role of warrior. In the nineteenth century the medieval knight, who represented order, service, courtesy, piety, protection of the weak and devotion to a monarch, was the model of a gentleman. Honour was a virtue to be prized. Patriotic and chivalric ideas spread throughout the empires. The first selection in *The Fourth Canadian Reader* used in the schools of British Columbia, Alberta, Saskatchewan, Manitoba, New Brunswick and Prince Edward Island in the 1920s and 1930s was the Duke of Argyll's "Dominion Hymn" which ended with these words:

> Inheritors of glory
> Oh! countrymen! we swear
> To guard the flag that o'er ye
> Shall onward victory bear.
> Where'er through earth's far regions
> Its triple crosses fly,
> For God, for home, our legions
> Shall win, or fighting, die!

When the murder of an Austrian archduke in Sarajevo, Serbia on June 28, 1914 upset the balance of power in Europe, honour demanded and power politics contrived that the Austrian-Hungarian, German and subsequently Ottoman empires would engage in war against Serbia, Russia, France, Britain and her empire.

After a hundred years of prosperity without a major conflict, only a few people in Britain foresaw the coming collapse of European civilization. One who did was novelist Henry James, who wrote that the approaching war was a "grand Niagara," a "black and hideous" tragedy that would undo "everything that was ours in the most horrible retroactive way." Eighty-five years later the eminent military historian John Keegan considered the reasons that had induced the civilized, optimistic European states at the height of their cultural achievements to risk it all in a war that became world wide. He could only answer, "It is a mystery."

Britain's declaration of war on August 4, 1914 automatically included Canada. Fishermen, farmers, loggers, cowboys, miners, railway workers, small-town storekeepers, clerks, teachers, nurses and students enlisted in defence of "God, King and Country." Half the army recruits came from western Canada, many of them recent British immigrants who had seen in the land-rich prairie provinces and the fertile valleys of British Columbia an opportunity of exchanging polluted cities, class-ridden social conventions and unemployment for an earthly paradise. A remarkable but not unique example of those willing to postpone their hopes and dreams is associated with Walhachin, British Columbia. In 1908, thirty-five miles west of Kamloops on the flats above the Thompson River, a British colonizing company had established a townsite. The settlers oversaw the planting of 16,000 fruit trees, built comfortable homes and stables, a hotel where a barrel of whiskey with attached cup was on offer in the lobby, a townhall containing Paderewski's piano, stores, tennis courts, a cricket pitch and an irrigation system. When war was declared, the settlement's one hundred and seven men rushed to the recruiting centre with such speed that only three weeks later ninety-seven of them were on their way to Salisbury Plain in England. One of them, Lieutenant G.M. Flowerdew, gained the Victoria Cross and his death wound while leading a Canadian cavalry charge on March 30, 1918—flashing swords opposed to machine guns. Few settlers returned. The wooden flumes rotted. The fruit trees died.

We cannot visualize the action of many Great War stories without understanding the layout of the Western Front, a line of opposing trenches that stretched from Nieuport on Belgium's North Sea coast to the Swiss Alps. It zigzagged along rivers, across villages and towns, through wheatfields on rolling chalk downs, into vineyards and orchards—12,000 miles of Allied trenches and 13,000 miles for the Central Powers. The Germans, having established themselves on higher ground, had look-out posts surveying the countryside, strongholds, artillery emplacements and underground galleries filled with reserve troops. During an attack, the Allied soldiers had to cross open ground in broad daylight (the British generals' strategy), traverse the barbed wire entanglements of No Man's Land under continuous fire and sometimes, as the Canadians did at the Battle of the Somme and Vimy Ridge, climb a slope while heavily loaded with equipment.

The front line was a ditch six or eight feet deep with "funk holes" dug into the sides. On the enemy side it was protected with a parapet of sandbags over which soldiers fired, lobbed grenades or climbed to charge the enemy. The raised fire-step on which they stood also served as a bed, food-board, seat and shelf. Several hundred yards back was a second trench holding support troops and behind that again the reserve line. At right angles ran communication trenches marked by such descriptive signs as Hellfire Corner, the Crab Crawl, Death Valley and Bury Ave. Along these, troops moved in single file, passing recesses where manoeuvres were planned, telephones and telegraphs were operated and supplies were stored.

The Allied trenches were wet, cold and foul-smelling because of the latrines, the coke gas used for cooking, the garbage and the rotting corpses which shelling brought to the surface. Greg Clark, who wrote "The Bully," called them stealth zones—"squeaking and squealing with these huge, monstrous rats living on this garbage." Will Bird, another Canadian author, fought in the Ypres Salient where the endless rains turned the land to mud and slime that gripped like glue, drowning not only the artillery horses but also the men who slipped off duckboard walks or were hit by shells. Donald Fraser, a Scottish immigrant who was a private in the 31st (Alberta) Battalion, kept a daily diary from September 17, 1915 to August 24, 1917. Published as *The Journal of Private Fraser*, ed. Reginald H Roy (1985), it records the reality of a trench life even more horrible than the fictionalized versions. At the St. Eloi Craters, where Timothy Findley sets Robert Ross in 1916, Fraser saw comrades buried under earthworks, blown to pieces, dying of blood loss before the stretcher-bearers could move them, decapitated, concussed, shorn of arms and legs, and splattered with rotted flesh. When they finally captured some German trenches, Canadian soldiers found infinitely superior accommodations with electric lights, proper beds, wallpaper, curtains, bookshelves, kitchens well supplied with food and liquor, and signs of female visitors.

In 1917 John Masefield, an English poet-laureate, published *The Old Front Line* to describe its appearance as it was during the Battle of the Somme because "when the trenches are filled in, and the plough has gone over them, the ground will not long keep the look of war. One summer with its flowers will cover most of the view that man can make." But more than eighty years after the Great War ended, the fields are still marked by the pattern of trenches and exploded earth, still lethal from rusty shells and gas canisters, still whitened with bones beneath and crosses above.

Censorship protected people at home from knowing the worst. The official letter from the Minister of Militia and Defence for Canada expressed "my very sincere sympathy in the recent decease of your son." It praised the sacrifice of life that had "rendered the highest services of a worthy citizen." And it assured the bereaved that their depressing loss would be "redeemed by the knowledge that the brave comrade for whom we mourn performed his duties fearlessly and well as became a good soldier, and gave his life for the great cause of Human Liberty and the Defence of the Empire." In truth, the international reputation of Canada's soldiers was confirmed on August 10, 1942 when *Time* magazine's cover picture of General Andrew McNaughton was accompanied by a text that read in part:

> The world's memories of Canadians in battle is a bright
> memory. The Canadians of World War I seemed to shine
> out of the blood and muck, the dreary panorama of trench
> warfare. They seemed to kill and to die with a special dash
> and lavishness. In a war and at a time when glory had
> already lost its meaning the Canadians in France kept the
> sheen of glory.

Sixty thousand, six hundred and sixty-one Canadians died in the Great War, operating under British command. Thousands more returned home blinded, deafened, gassed, maimed, shell-shocked, disillusioned and exhausted. On the death of Sir Arthur Currie, the first Canadian appointed to command the Canadian Corps, the Toronto *Globe's* report of his funeral (December 6, 1933) included this sentence: "Fifteen years ago war-weary veterans returned from the European holocaust, their whole being in revolt against the atrocities they had witnessed and in which they had been required to take part, and they vowed that no more would they lend themselves to recalling the hideous thing they had called duty." The legacy of the Great War was revolution, civil war, the collapse of empires, Communism, Nazism, Fascism, the Second World War, the Holocaust, nuclear weaponry and the threat of nuclear war.

During the 1930s, the Great Depression and prairie drought made Canada a bleak and bankrupt land. The rich wheatfields that had supported Canada's export economy were transformed into black, wind-borne clouds of dust. Jobless men rode the rails from one end of the country to the other, hanging out in hobo jungles near towns where they walked residential streets to exchange an hour's woodsplitting, coal shovelling or gardening for a cup of coffee and a fried egg sandwich. Germany's invasion of Poland on September 1, 1939 ended years of non-intervention in Britain and France, making it necessary to repeat the rituals of war only twenty years after the Treaty of Versailles had been signed. Canadian poet Milton Acorn wrote:

> This is where we came in; this has happened before
> Only the last time there was cheering.

As Canada was no longer a British colony, it was the Canadian Parliament that decided to support Britain and France against Nazi Germany by declaring war on September 10, 1939.

To some who enlisted in 1939–40, the defence of God, king and country and dislike of Fascistic aggressors were no more compelling than the prospect of food, shelter and regular pay. Recruits, perhaps, recalled their schoolday memorization of John McCrae's "In Flanders Fields": "If ye break faith with us who die / We shall not sleep, though poppies grow / In Flanders fields." The Second World War (1939–45) was truly global, leaving no continent unaffected. Even the most disillusioned veteran of the Great War could not have imagined the massive destruction that technology would spawn. Age-long impulses towards honour and decency such as those set out in the Hague Convention's prohibitions against "terrorizing the civilian population, destroying private property or injuring non-combatants" were ignored. In the Second World War the ideology of the chief aggressors, Germany and Japan, was based on racial hatred and a desire for revenge. The atrocities and stupidities of modern war refuted the nineteenth century's confidence in a moral and spiritual progress of the human race towards a higher state of being.

One Canadian issue that proved divisive during both wars was conscription. For many French-Canadians overseas service in Britain's wars symbolized New France's defeat on the Plains of Abraham in 1759. They were equally unwilling to fight for their cultural homeland, France. A character in Louis Caron's *The Draft Dodger* explains:

> When our ancestors were fighting to build the colony
> here, the French were happy to be bowing and scraping at
> the King's court! Then one fine day we lost the battle of
> the Plains of Abraham. Why? Because the French didn't
> even come and help us. Do you think we were about to go
> get ourselves killed for France! Especially since we stayed
> Catholic when the French wanted to throw out all their
> priests during the Revolution.

Out of 258 battalions in the Canadian Expeditionary Force raised by voluntary recruitment 13 were French-Canadian. After the disastrous Battle of Passchendaele (1917) in which 15,654 men out of a Canadian force of 20,000 were killed or wounded, conscription was inevitable.

At the beginning of World War Two, Prime Minster W.L. Mackenzie King promised that there would be no conscription for overseas service. After the fall of France in June 1940 The National Mobilization Act permitted conscription for home service only. The conscripts were popularly known as "zombies." Conscription became necessary in 1944; when volunteers no longer could replace casualties, 2500 home defence servicemen out of a total trained force of 70,000 finally reached the front.

The Second World War stories in this anthology reflect the war's global nature. They are set in English training camps where the First Canadian Army lingered for years waiting for the invasion of Europe, in a North African airfield where lions wandered in from the desert, in an Italian firing range overlooked by "a precise green line of cypresses." The decrepit garage in a dusty prairie town that has suddenly been transformed into HMCS *Porpoise* is contrasted with the powerful ship carrying troops to the Normandy beaches. Grey huts in Kootenay Valley ghost towns and fetid jungle prisoner-of-war camps reveal two sides of racial discrimination while a Polish town reduced by Germans and Russians to "heaps of rubble and bits of rugged slabs of wall set over the rubble heaps, marking them, like rough-hewn gravestones" conveys the extremes of hatred. Where one of the Great War's feisty Canadian pilots had battled the Red Baron and his squadron above the Allied trenches near Arras and Vimy, now in the airspace over Berlin, flashing with searchlights, flash flares and the guns of fighter planes, a Canadian bomber pilot uses his skills and brains to complete another Op in the Second World War.

Even though the majority of stories in this collection may be classified as fiction, with few exceptions they are based on the authors' own experiences. Memoir and fiction merge seamlessly through the technique of focussing on a single character who represents the author. The authenticity of voice is unmistakable. The untidiness of real life is shaped into story by providing a beginning, a middle and an end. The archetypal quest pattern of departure on a perilous journey, crucial confrontations with an opponent and return home—which Homer's epics the *Iliad* and the *Odyssey* anciently presented—becomes the usual structure of twentieth-century war literature. When the protagonist does not survive the conflict, the return may take the form of a vision. The superstitious Newfoundlander Peter Teale, like his friend Simon, characters in Will Bird's "Sunrise for Peter," experiences a premonitory dream that means "wonderful good luck." On the evening before his death he sees the sun rising behind the bald rock of Old Bear Bay and a dory going ashore. Edward Meade provides closure to O'Rourke's fictional life when the man dying at the Falaise Gap believes that a thundering train is carrying him across "the fabulous land, the vast and lonely land of the north" to home and Gerda waiting.

In the earlier stories, a psychological regression into disillusionment, anger and cynicism often parallels physical deterioration, as the authors filter their own emotions and attitudes through the *personae* that they have created. A sense of futility infuses Charles Yale Harrison's "The Sniper" and Hugh Garner's "The Stretcher-Bearers." Anger inspires the satiric attack on malingerers and war profiteers in "Hard Lines!" Irony is pervasive as the anticipated glory of fighting in a noble cause disappears when confronted by the reality of war. Second World War literature is more varied in mood, attitude and theme. It ranges from the moral problems examined in Joy Kogawa's "Obasan," Colin McDougall's "The Firing-Squad," Agnes Newton Keith's "Getting Rid of Proudery and Arrogance" and Henry Kreisel's "Homecoming: A Memory of Europe After the Holocaust" to the zaniness of Max Braithwaite's "The Porpoise That Couldn't Swim," Andrew Campbell Ballantine's "Lion-taming for Beginners" and Earl Birney's "Turvey is Considered for Knighthood." What Northrop Frye calls ironic comedy seems the only possible response to the absurd irrationality of modern war.

Paul Fussell's *The Great War and Modern Memory* (1975) makes the point that British soldiers relied on English literature, particularly the *Oxford Book of English Verse* and chivalric romances, to provide a language for expressing the demonic present and a contrasted pastoral past. In Canadian war literature, however, it is wilderness imagery that, through flashback, memory or dream, most often acts as an escape mechanism. Instead of springtime gardens, sheep in hedged fields, roses and nightingales, our pastoral imagery draws on the spacious, untrammelled and elemental. Waiting to attack during the Battle of the Somme, Peregrine Acland's hero Falcon recalls nights before the war when he heard "the thudding of hoofs on the soft turf of the prairie .... the sound of swift waters swirling around rocks." During four years as a prisoner of the Japanese in tropical Borneo, starved, beaten, overworked, sick, Agnes Newton Keith aches "to sit quietly in the long Canadian twilight over a simple meal" and when, early in 1945, she returns with her husband and child to their home in Victoria, British Columbia, the sight of grey trees standing against grey skies bare of all foliage in place of lush, strangling, equatorial vines signifies peace and recovery. Although Naomi's desired home is only a few hundred miles away, her Japanese family's enforced move from the West Coast produces a homesickness no less painful than that of soldiers thousands of miles from home. The shape of a crude bridge over a creek is a device for retaining the memory of "the curved bridge over the goldfish pond at Obasan's house, and the bridges that Stephen and I made in the sand to the desolate sound of the sea, and the huge Lion's Gate Bridge in Stanley Park, and the terrifying Capilano swinging bridge that trembled as we crossed it high up in the dangerous air."

Snow and cold are an integral part of Canadian experience and a defining imagery in our literature. (During the bitter winter of 1916–17 familiarity made our soldiers on the Western Front better able to endure the weather than their allies from Britain, France and Australia.) Robert Ross, after the gas attack, rolls over with his arms stuck out above his head "like a child about to make 'an angel' in the snow." Peter Teale's ideal companion at the front was Simon "who could sense his way in the winter through dense stunted spruce where the windfalls of ages made countless pitfalls hidden under light snow coverings." The snow of Nazaire's "great black misery of winter" is both a protector and a betrayer, making martyrs of the deserters, in the narrator's words. In the aftermath of the Halifax explosion, with the snow blowing onto the frozen corpses laid out in the school basement and the wind gusting into his wrecked home, "like invisible fingers of ice," fourteen-year-old James Gordon fears that "the world had come to a dark end and the sun would never come back again."

A uniquely Canadian social scene covering almost half a century emerges from these war stories. The school routine described in "Winter's Tale" could have been found anywhere in Canada from the turn of the century to the 1950s. J.G. Simes' "Munitions!" illustrates that women could escape from the Upstairs-Downstairs structure of urban life into the free-wheeling camaraderie of factories. Disparate regional attitudes in an enormous land are mirrored by juxtaposing a down-east naval officer's allusion to the "godforsaken, drought-ridden prairies" and the ocean-going dream of a prairie boy who "had never seen a body of water larger than a slough." As the ship carries Canadian troops towards Normandy in Ralph Allen's "The Landing," Rinowski's high-pitched monologue (his defence against fear) recreates an ordinary Canadian's Toronto scene during the 1930s: courting a girl who works at Eaton's, going to the bowling rink and drugstore, drinking beer, making fifteen-cent bets and entering a marriage where the bride's family outranks the groom's. The pervasive influence of the Roman Catholic church permeates the stories set in rural Quebec.

The Great War was an unmitigated disaster for the embattled nations. It reversed their physical, economic, moral and spiritual progress. The

Second World War caused the death or injury of 78 million people, more of them civilians than combatants. Canada's service in both wars established as part of our national identity the virtues of courage, loyalty, diligence, resourcefulness, decency and generosity.

★★★

This anthology is not intended to provide a political, social, economic or military history of Canada at war. The introductions to individual stories provide only the information needed for comprehension. Major-General Lewis Mackenzie, the first United Nations commander in Sarajevo, has said, "Wars are best understood by studying the actions of individuals, not the large formulations to which they belong." These are stories of individuals, generally taking the form of fiction based on personal experience. There are women and children who lost their homes and men who lost their dreams and lives. There are strangers brought together by the accident of war to be bound in loyalty and a kind of love. There are adventurers who like the young RCAF pilot "slipped the surly bonds of earth and danced the skies on laughter-silvered wings" and the disillusioned volunteers who exchanged heroic anticipations for victimization. There are the weak whom conviction made strong. For most of the individuals who took part in those wars, the paths of glory have already led to the grave. We must not forget them.

Timothy Findley

TIMOTHY FINDLEY (1930–), who was born in Toronto, began his professional life as an actor, performing in the Stratford (Ontario) Shakespeare Festival productions under Tyrone Guthrie and in the American and British tours of a Thornton Wilder play. In 1962 he gave up acting as a career to devote himself to writing. "Bird Song" is selected from Findley's novel *The Wars* (1977), which won the Governor General's Award for fiction. Unlike other authors in this collection, Findley had no personal experience of war's violence. His war scenes are influenced by letters which his uncle and godfather, Thomas Irving Findley (Uncle Tif), wrote during the Great War from the battlefields of Flanders. As his uncle did not die until 1933, the author has childhood memories of the old soldier. "I know he sacrificed his youth, his health, his leg and finally his life for his country … I am grateful that he had his own life. I am grateful … that he is in my memory," Findley later commented.

The central character in *The Wars* is a young Canadian artillery officer, Robert Ross, who is engaged in battles on the Western Front. On April 22, 1915 in the Ypres Salient where forty-two German battalions faced twenty-one Allied battalions, twelve of them Canadian, the Germans launched the first-ever chlorine gas attack, directing it against unprotected French and Canadian troops. On February 21, 1916 at Verdun the enemy initiated the stupidly costly battles of attrition that made 1916 the most bloodstained year in history. The following episode in Findley's fictional account of that battle front takes place on February 28, 1916, the beginning of a six-day battle in which 30,000 men would die and not an inch of ground be taken.

After a heavy bombardment, Robert has been sent out with Corporal Bates and six men to set up four trench mortars in No Man's Land close to the German lines. By timing the actions so precisely, Findley presents the narrator as an eye witness who is documenting the events as they occur, thus providing a sense of historical reality. The gas masks used at this time were described by artist-poet David Jones as "ghastly to wear for very long, especially if one was exerting oneself—they became a filthy mess of condensation inside and you couldn't see out of the misted-over talc of the eye-vents."

In 1983 *The Wars* was made into a film directed by Robin Phillips, starring Brent Carver with music performed by Glenn Gould. Another award-winning novel, *Famous Last Words* (1981), is set during the Second World War, as is the title story in a collection *Stones* (1988), describing the effect on a family of the father's participation in the Dieppe raid, August 19, 1942.

Bird Song

8:50 a.m.

Four men were digging. A second shelf had been begun six or seven yards to the left of the first, where Robert was sitting. No one spoke, Robert looked down and saw that one of the gunners was throwing clods of earth into the pool below—like a child in High Park on a Sunday afternoon.

He got his notebook out and a broken stub of pencil and, gauging the angle of the crater's edge, he began his calculations. He became so engrossed he was barely aware of the fact the barrage had ceased. He was halfway through his geometry when his ears popped and the silence poured in.

The gunner down below had already thrown another lump of clay. It landed in the water like a bomb. Everyone stood still, except that each man leaned in automatically against the earth at his shoulder. The silence could only mean one thing. The Germans were going to attack. All at once—a bird sang over their heads. Someone swore, as if the bird had given them away.

Robert gazed upward. The sky beyond the crater's rim was patched with blue. The flat, steel-coloured clouds were breaking up and easing apart. This was dangerous. The smoke had begun to drift. It was dispersing back towards their own lines. Their cover was being destroyed. Robert carefully put the notebook and pencil away and drew his automatic. He felt in his pockets for his reserve of clips. There were only seven of these. He fingered them—counting and recounting. Each clip had seven cartridges. *Seven. Seven. Seven times seven. Is forty-nine. Plus seven. Is fifty-six.* If he hadn't fired the gun—but he couldn't remember that. He'd fired it at a peach can. When?

"Sir?" said one of the men who was with him on the ledge.

"Be quiet!" said Robert. Both of them were whispering.

"But sir ..."

The man pointed.

Robert looked.

Slithering over the crater's rim—a pale blue fog appeared. Like a veil his mother might've worn.

Robert blinked.

It tumbled over the edge and began to spread out over their heads—drifting on a layer of cold, dank air rising from the pool below them.

Jesus.

Gas.

Bates had scrabbled up to the ledge.

"Put on your masks," Robert whispered. The air seemed to be alive with sibilance. The canisters were that close.

Bates just stared.

"Put your mask on, Corporal Bates!"

"I can't," said Bates.

"What the hell do you mean?" Robert turned and shouted hoarsely to the men below him. "Put your masks on!"

"We *can't* sir," said Bates. "They sent us up so quick that none of us was issued masks."

"*Every* man is issued a mask!" Robert shouted out loud. (It was like being told that none of the men had been issued boots.)

"No, sir," said Bates. "It ain't true." He was shaking. Shivering. His voice was barely audible. Robert might as well have yelled at God, for all the good it would do. He looked at the weaving strands of gas. They were spreading further out—like a spider's web above the crater—reaching for the other side. Some of it was spilling down towards them.

Robert didn't even think. He just yelled: "Jump!" and leapt into the air.

Looking back at the gas and seeing nothing else was to be done, one by one the others also jumped. Some landed short and tumbled the rest of the way but most landed helter skelter on top of one another in the water.

In seconds there was nightmare. All too quickly they discovered they could not touch bottom. Three of the men could not swim. One man had broken both his legs in the fall. Two or three corpses that had lain nearby against the sides of the crater, slid down after them and sank like stones. But in moments they floated to the surface and when Robert and Bates began to struggle to the edge with the men who could not swim, Robert found he was saving a man who was already dead. He pushed the corpse back in the water but it wouldn't sink this time and he had to kick its hands away from his boots. Silence—and every other safety precaution was thrown to the winds. For a moment they ceased to be soldiers and became eight panic-stricken men who were trapped in the bottom of a sink hole, either about to be drowned or smothered to death with gas. Eight men and one mask. Robert had to fight to keep it and he ended up kicking both the living and the dead. At last, lying flat on his back, he managed to get the automatic out of his pocket and using both hands he pointed it straight at Bates. "Tell them to back off," he said; "or by Jesus I'll fire!"

"Back off," said Bates.

Robert sat—and used his knee to support the gun. He was shaking so violently the air was filled with drops of water spraying off his head. He swallowed hard and looked at the gas. "All right," he said, "you sons-of-bitches do exactly what I say." One of the men began to run. Robert fired. The man fell down but was not hit, Robert having missed him on purpose. "Now," he said. "If you want to live you have about twenty seconds. Get out your handkerchiefs."

"We got no handkerchiefs," said Bates.

"Then tear the tails off your God damned shirts!"

To a man—like chastised children—they reached around and tore the tails from their shirts. The man with the broken legs was lying by the water's edge. He was already the colour of death. His hands were full of clay. He didn't utter a word. He'd bitten his lips until they'd bled and his teeth had gone through the flesh. Robert threw the gas mask at Bates. "Put that over his face. And remember this gun is pointed right at your back." Bates obeyed—crawling to the man on his hands and knees.

The rest of the men were waiting numbly, holding torn pieces of cloth in their hands—staring at Robert with their mouths open. "What are we s'posed to do?" one of them asked. "These won't save us. Not if it's chlorine."

"Piss on them," said Robert.

"Unh?"

"Piss on them!!!"

The men all looked at Bates, who had turned again, having put the gas mask over the injured man's face. He looked at Robert and shrugged. He nodded at the men. Then he knelt and began to fumble with his flies. He was quite convinced that Robert had lost his reason—but you have to obey a man with a gun—mad or sane. Here was the terror. Bates was so afraid that he collapsed backward and sat like a child in the sand and dug in his underwear for his penis. It had shrunk with fear. The gas was reaching down towards them—six feet—five feet—four. Bates was certain he would defecate. His bowels had turned to water. He fell on his side. At last his fingers took hold. He closed his eyes. He prayed: *dear Jesus, let me piss*. But he couldn't. Neither could one of the other men and this other man began to weep, till Robert shouted at him: "Damn you! *Damn you!* Give it to me!" and he ripped the shirt tail away from the man and urinated on it himself. Then, with it dripping like a dishcloth, he thrust it back at the other man and said to him: "Put it over your face." But the poor daft crazy was so afraid and so confused that he put the cloth on top of his head and Robert had to grab it again and slap it on the man's face so that it covered him from eyes to chin. Then Robert said: "All you others do the same thing and lie down flat with your faces in your hands." They did. Without a word. The gas was now two feet above their heads. Finally, Bates let go. His muscles gave away like bits of yarn and he fouled himself as he peed. How could it matter? They were all going to die. He flattened the wettened tail of his shirt across his face and rolled to his stomach, pressing his face in the mud. His father's image deserted him. His mind was white.

In the meantime, Robert dribbled all that was left in his bladder into his handkerchief and he too lay down—like a pilgrim in the clay.

9:30 a.m.

They waited.

What would save them—if it did—was an image that had come unbidden into Robert's mind from a dull winter classroom long ago. It was an image clear and definite as the words themselves: *two tiny bottles poised side by side.* Crystals forming in the air. *Ammonium-chloride*—a harmless dusty powder blown off the back of someone's hand.

Chloride in one tiny bottle—but what was the other? Clear as a bell—in fact, so clear he thought he'd heard it aloud—came the sound of Clifford Purchas, all of twelve years old, giggling and poking at Robert's ribs. *"Piss,"* he'd said—and been dismissed from class for saying it. Now that one word might save them. The ammonia in their urine would turn the chlorine into harmless crystals that could not be breathed.

10:30 a.m.

Still, they waited.

The gas had begun to dissipate. More breeze had sprung up. More and more clouds were leaving the sky. It became very cold. But Robert and the men dared not move. At any moment the Germans would appear, for surely the gas had been the prelude to their attack. And if the Germans came, their only hope was to play dead and pray.

12:15 p.m.

The sun—at its zenith—died.

The crows began to call to one another.

It also began to snow.

1 p.m.

Robert slowly tilted his head to one side. He had lain completely still for three hours. The back of his neck was numb. He slid his hand up under his cheek. The glove made it feel like a stranger's hand. His hair was frozen into points that hung down over his eyes.

"Bates?"

There was no answer.

"Bates?" A little louder.

"Yes sir?" Somewhere to his left.

"I'm going to roll over now. Onto my back. I don't want anybody else to move."

"Yes sir."

Robert eased himself onto his side. So far—so good. There wasn't a sound. Then he rolled over with his arms stuck out above his head. He looked like a child about to make "an angel" in the snow. The handkerchief was frozen to his left glove. Looking back, he could see it way off down his arm in another country. A bird sang, something like a white-throated sparrow: one long note descending; three that wavered. This was the bird that had sung before. He waited for it to sing again. It didn't. Robert tried to focus every inch of the rim within his range. The bird had made him extremely nervous. *Rob the Ranger* always whistled like a white-throat if he saw an Indian moving in the woods. And the Indians hooted like owls and howled and barked and yipped like wolves. Robbers could *meow* like cats. Anyone in hiding was an imitation animal.

Once he'd rolled over, Robert was the only brown figure in the landscape. That could only mean one thing. He was alive. All the others, playing dead, were covered with snow. Robert thought: well—no one's shot at me yet. Surely if anyone's watching they'd have killed me by now.

Snow was still falling. It filled his lashes and turned them white. He could taste it on his lips. He could feel a single flake on the tip of his nose. He sat up, resting on his elbows, sweeping his arms to his sides and his right hand into contact with the Webley.

He lifted his gaze to the rim.

Nothing.

He angled his head to the left.

The bird sang.

Robert froze.

There was a German soldier with a pair of binoculars staring right at him.

Robert stared back—unmoving.

The German—who was lying down at the very edge of the crater—lowered the binoculars. Robert could see his eyes. He was very young.

Maybe eighteen. He was not an officer and he wore no hat. He did not even wear a helmet. His hair was frozen like Robert's, but blond. He wore a pair of woolen mitts that had no fingers.

Robert could see him so clearly he could see him swallow, as if he was nervous.

Bates said "Sir?"

Robert tried to speak without moving his lips. "Don't move," he said. "There's somebody there."

Bates did not reply but Robert heard one of the other men cursing in the mud. "Be quiet," he said and, as he said it, he saw in front of them the dreadful phenomenon that could give them all away. His breath. He muttered: "Don't anybody raise his head. Keep on breathing into the ground."

All this time, Robert had not moved. All this time, the German had watched him. Robert thought: there has to be a reason.

He sat up.

Nothing happened.

The German went on staring at Robert—not even using the binoculars. He seemed to be waiting for Robert to take the initiative.

Robert thought: he isn't armed. That's what it is. He isn't armed. He hasn't caught us—we've caught him. He's afraid to move.

Very slowly, Robert drew the Webley and held it in such a way that the German could not but help see it. He didn't want to point it at him yet. He waited to see what reaction the gun itself would get. The German raised his binoculars. Then he lowered them—but that was all.

Robert said: "Bates? Don't be afraid. There's only one and I don't think he has a gun. Try rolling over and see what happens. I've got him covered."

Bates rolled over.

The German shifted his gaze—saw that Bates had moved and then looked back at Robert. He nodded. It was astounding. He nodded!

Robert did not quite understand at first and then the German lifted his head as much as to say: *get up.*

"Get up," Robert said to Bates. "Stand right up. He isn't going to shoot."

Bates had been watching the German too. He stood up. "Now what?" he said.

"Go to the top," said Robert. "Go the way we came. Just go. But go slowly. Don't alarm him."

Bates went around behind Robert—out of his sight lines—but Robert could hear him scrambling and squelching through the mud and then the sound of falling debris as he clambered up the face of the crater. Robert didn't take his eyes off the German for a second and the German didn't take his eyes off Bates. The tilt of his head was like a mirror. It showed Bates' progress all the way to the top. And when Bates had arrived and was safe the German looked back down at Robert—smiling.

Robert stood up. He waved acknowledgement. Whatever his reasons— the German obviously intended them all to go free.

"I want everyone of you to go and join Bates," Robert said.

"Don't stop and don't look back. Go as far as you can with your hands in the air, so he'll know you're not armed. Maybe he's crazy—but he isn't going to kill us."

One by one, four of the men began to stumble to the Lewis gun. "Get up," Robert said to the fifth, whom he thought must have fallen asleep. When the man did not respond, Robert went across to him and turned him over with the toe of his boot. It was the man who had wept and become hysterical. Dead. His eyes wide and staring. He had strangled on his shirt tail.

Robert rolled him back, face down in the mud, and went to the man with the broken legs. All this while the German was watching him but Robert felt entirely safe. He crouched by the water's edge and was amazed to see it was solid. In the three hours they had lain there it had got that cold. This man was also dead. Probably of shock. Robert could not see his eyes. The vapour inside the gas mask had frozen. The man's last breath was a sheet of ice.

It was now Robert's turn to climb.

He would have to turn his back on the German.

Well. There was no other way.

He began.

It was the sort of climb you have in dreams. Every step forward, he slid back two. He almost dropped the gun. His knees were in agony. Harris's scarf got caught on the Lewis gun and Robert had to tear it away. He kept falling forward, sliding in the snow. Once he looked up and could see Bates waiting—watching the German. The others could not be seen. They were over the lip and safe in the trench. Robert had about six feet to go.

All of a sudden Bates shouted: "Sir."

What happened next was all so jumbled and fast that Robert was never to sort it out. He fell. He turned. He saw the German reaching over the lip of the crater. Something exploded. The German gave a startled cry and was suddenly dead, with his arms dangling down.

The shot that had killed him rang around and around the crater like a marble in a bowl. Robert thought it would never stop. He scrambled for the brink only in order to escape it and Bates had to pull him over the edge, falling back with Robert on top of him. The warmth of Bates's body was a shock and the two men lay in one another's arms for almost a minute before Robert moved. He couldn't breathe. He couldn't speak. He could barely see. He sat with his head between his knees. He didn't even know the gun was still in his hand until he reached with it to wipe the mud from his face. It smelt of heat and oil. He turned around and crawled to the edge of the fold where, hours ago, he and Bates had first looked out and seen the crater. He could barely see. He sat with his head between his knees. He wanted to know what had happened and why the German had so suddenly moved against him after letting all the others escape.

He raised his field glasses and the first thing he saw was their counterpart lying in the mud about a foot from the young man's hand. Binoculars. He had only been reaching for his binoculars.

Robert sagged against the ground. It was even worse than that. Lying beside the German was a modified Mauser rifle of the kind used by snipers. He could have killed them all. Surely that had been his intention. But he'd relented. Why?

The bird sang.

One long note descending: three that wavered on the brink of sadness.

That was why.

It sang and sang and sang, till Robert rose and walked away. The sound of it would haunt him to the day he died.

When they made their way back through the trench there was no one there alive. They had all been gassed or had frozen to death. Those who lay in water were profiled in ice. Everything was green: their faces—and their fingers—and their buttons. And the snow.

Charles Yale Harrison

CHARLES YALE HARRISON (1898–1954) was born in Philadelphia, USA in 1914. Still in his teens, he took a job with the *Montreal Star* but soon gave it up to join the Royal Montreal Regiment. As a machine-gunner, Harrison participated in the terrible trench warfare on the Western Front and was wounded on August 8, 1918 during the Battle of Amiens. His brilliant and bitter war novel, *Generals Die In Bed*, first published in England in 1930 and soon translated into Spanish, French, German and Russian, is dedicated "To the bewildered youths—British, Australian, Canadian and German—who were killed in that wood a few miles beyond Amiens on August 8th 1918." The Royal Montreal Regiment fought in the Ypres Salient in 1915. In a battle there on May 18, it was reported that "the Canadians are all blown to hell. There is terrible murder up there." This regiment was also responsible for capturing Arras in 1918, one of the set-piece incidents of plot in Harrison's novel.

Harrison uses the technique of first-person narration to create a shocking sense of immediacy. The eighteen-year-old recruit who provides the point of view is nameless because he represents the common experience of the Canadian private soldier in France. Most of his companions are under twenty, with tanned weather-beaten faces and "that aged look which the trench gives us." The narrator's friend Brown, a farmer's son from Prince Edward Island, had been married for only two weeks before the battalion left Montreal. By the time "The Sniper" occurs, early in the novel, the young soldiers have already learned who their enemies are: "the lice, some of our officers and Death." Failing to find justification for the human misery and degradation, the narrator concludes that it is better to live like an unreasoning animal than seek for answers to the lottery of war.

The Sniper

SIX DAYS IN RESERVE NEAR THE LIGHT ARTILLERY, six days in supports, six days in the front trenches—and then out to rest. Five or six days out on rest and then back again; six days, six days, rest.

Endlessly in and out. Different sectors, different names of trenches, different trenches, but always the same trenches, the same yellow, infested earth, the same screaming shells, the same comet-tailed "minnies" with their splintering roar. The same rats, fat and sleek with their corpse-filled bellies, the same gleaming gimlet eyes. The same lice which we carry with us wherever we go. In and out, in and out, endlessly, sweating, endlessly, endlessly .... Somewhere it is summer, but here are the same trenches. The trees here are skeletons holding stubs of stark, shell-amputated arms towards the sky. No flowers grow in this waste land.

This is our fifth day in the front line, one more day and out we go back to rest.

For the past few days it has been raining ceaselessly. We are soaked and chilled.

It is near dawn.

As the smudge of grey appears in the east, the odors of the trenches rise in a miasmal mist on all sides of us. The soaked earth here is nothing but a thin covering for the putrescence which lies underneath; it smells like a city garbage dump in mid-August. We are sunk in that misery which men fall into through utter hopelessness.

We are in a shallow trench and last night the enemy trench mortars blew away part of the parapet, so that now we are exposed to enfilade fire from our left.

We will have to wait until nightfall to repair it.

They are sniping at us.

About two hundred yards from us there is a little wood, and in this wood there are snipers hidden somewhere among the trees.

The broken parapet does not hide us and we have to crawl around on our hands and knees because the sniper can shoot *down the length of our trench*.

We remember what the instructor in trench warfare told us at the base. "Enfilade fire is fire directed down the length of a line or trench. It is fire coming from the flanks. Keep low."

But the instructor is at the base, safe and comfortable, and we are here in this muddy trench.

Six short days in a trench!

It is nothing, it seems; less than a week but it seems like an eternity as we wait for night when we shall be relieved.

The dugouts here are filled with water and we live in hastily constructed funk-holes, holes burrowed into the side of the parapet or parados. We are wet to the skin.

Why do we crawl about here?

It would be better, it seems, to dash into No Man's Land and chance death, or down the communication trench to temporary safety—and a firing squad. But we are disciplined. Months of training on the rolling Sussex downs, at the base, in the periods of rest, have stiffened us. We must carry on, carry on ....

In a thousand ways this has been drilled into our heads. The salute, the shining of our brass buttons, the correct way to twist a puttee and so on. A thousand thundering orders! A thousand trivial rules, each with a penalty for an infraction, has made will-less robots of us all. All, without exception ....

Half a mile from our partly exposed trench, hidden in the hollow of a tree, sits a sniper holding an oiled, perfect rifle.

Every night they bring him his rations, maybe with a little extra schnapps, for I know our snipers get an extra rum ration.

Sooner or later this German sniper, who keeps us cowering in cold fear, will be caught in an advance by our troops.

We will fall upon him and bayonet him like a hapless trench rat. He will crawl out of his hiding-place as the first wave swarms about him menacingly. He will hold his trembling hands on high and stammer the international word for compassion and mercy. He will say that beautiful word *comrade*, a word born in suffering and sorrow, but we will stab him down shouting to one another, "Hey, look, we found a sniper!" And our faces will harden, our inflamed eyes will become slits and men will stab futilely at his prostrate body.

But now they bring him his little extra rations.

His rifle is fitted with telescopic sights so that we are brought quite close to him. Slowly he elevates his weapon, looks through the glass and sees his target as though it is but a few feet away. Then he pulls the trigger and one of us drops out of sight.

In our shattered trench we move about almost doubled over in two, much as a man does who is suffering with abdominal pains. Sometimes to get relief we crawl, like babies, on all fours.

The sniper's rifle cracks and we flop down groveling in the muddy bottom of the trench. Minutes pass before we move. No one is dead and slowly we face each other with grey, sheepishly smiling faces.

We lie cowering in the bottom of the trench.

There is nothing to do until rations come up, and we talk in whispers.

It is greying in the east.

The war sleeps.

No guns.

The machine gunners are quiet.

We talk.

"You'd think a guy would like to die living a life like this," says Fry. "But we flop just the same."

"How do you know you're gonna get killed for sure?" says Brown.

Anderson does not speak, he lies with his cheek glued to the ground. His lips move in prayer. He gives us the creeps.

"Maybe you'd only go blind or go batty or something."

"Yeah, that's it. How do you know you're gonna get killed?"

We all agree that a swift death would be a pleasant thing. At the crack of the distant rifle we cower lower in silent fear.

It is dawn now.

Soon a carrier will bring us our rations, and as soon as it is divided between us and we have filled our bellies, we will go to sleep and leave one man on sentry duty.

It is quiet. The guns are quiet. Even the sniper is quiet. It is half an hour since last his rifle sent us flopping into the mud.

Over the trench a few sparrows squabble and chirp with care-free energy. They swoop down on the sandbagged parapet and sit looking at us with perky heads cocked to one side.

We look at them in amazement.

They startle us with their noisy merriment, these foolish birds who may live in peaceful fields and forests and who come to look for food on a barren, waste battlefield.

They fly away suddenly towards the German lines.

"They're lost, I guess," Brown says.

The ration carrier crawls round the corner of the bay of the trench and dumps a hairy sandbag half-filled with grub on the firing-step. He says nothing and walks away. He is tired; he has been carrying food all night.

We take turns in sharing the food among ourselves. Today it is Brown's turn.

He spreads his rubber sheet along the firing-step. He bends low and empties the food into the sheet; a piece of yellow cheese, three large Spanish onions, a paper container of Australian jam labelled strawberry, but made of figs and artificially flavored with chemicals which we can taste but do not mind; some tea, sugar, condensed milk and a great hunk of grey war bread.

With hungry, grimy fingers he deftly cuts, slices, divides the food. We look on with greedy, alert eyes to see that justice is being done. From time to time he looks nervously over his shoulder in the direction of the concealed sniper in the distant woods. Our eyes follow his. His glance catches mine and he smiles faintly.

"Don't want to die before breakfast, eh?" he says.

I smile and nod and look at the food.

Anderson stands up to get a better view of the food. He leans over my shoulder.

Broadbent snarls a warning.

We are nervous.

The grub is soon divided into five equal parts. We each take our share and stuff it into our haversacks. We will eat it at leisure in the funk-hole after stand-down. The sun will soon rise and the immediate danger of an attack will be over.

Brown shakes the rubber sheet clean of breadcrumbs and bits of onion skin.

Now he will divide the sugar. Precious sugar with which we will sweeten the strong, hot tea that comes up at midnight in large thermos cans. Tea so bitter that it curls one's tongue. Strong tea, alive with tannic acid to soothe frayed, trench-shattered nerves, tea to still a thumping heart. Sugar to make it palatable. We watch him in silence.

The rusty spoon for dishing out sugar and such things is stuck between two sandbags in the parapet over his head.

Glad to straighten himself up for a second, Brown stands up to reach for it.

He turns to look in the direction of the woods to his left.

In that instant his head snaps back viciously from the impact of the bullet.

The report of the rifle fills our ears like the sound of a cannon.

He sags to the bottom of the sloppy trench.

His neck is twisted at a foolish, impossible angle.

Between his eyes, a little over the bridge of his nose, is a small neat hole. A thin, red stream runs from it.

No one moves.

On the parados to the rear of us a bit of slimy grey matter jiggles as it sticks to the hairy sacking of the sandbag.

At the crack of the sniper's rifle we crouched lower in the trench and looked with stupid amazement as Brown's body fell clumsily into our midst.

We look without resentment towards the woods. We are animated only by a biting hunger of safety. Safety ...

The sun is rising slowly now, it throws a pink pearly light on the parados behind us and colors the motionless bit of Brown's brains.

Everything is quiet.

It is stand-down along the whole front.

The sun warms us a little. We look towards the east, towards the German lines from whence came the swift bullet that had thrown Brown's body awkwardly among us; we look towards the east where the rising sun now slowly begins to climb into the heavens ...

We pull the heavy, limp body out of the mud. Its neck is twisted in such a manner that it seems to be asking a question of us.

We lay it on the firing-step and cover it with a grey woolen, regulation blanket. The blanket is short; it hides the head but reaches only to the ankles. The muddy boots stick out in V-formation.

The sugar is not yet divided. Some of it is spilled and dissolved in the bottom of the trench. Broadbent salvages as much of it as he can. Dispensing with the spoon he uses his hands. He scoops the remaining sugar into four, instead of five parts.

Soon a stretcher-bearer will come and take the body down to company headquarters. Broadbent takes the bread and cheese out of Brown's haversack and shares it with us.

"Anyway," he explains, "he can't eat any more ..."

Will R. Bird

WILLIAM R. BIRD (1891–1984) was born in East
Mapleton, Nova Scotia, a descendent of a Yorkshire family that had settled in
Cumberland County in 1774. He served as a corporal with the 42nd Battalion
(Royal Highlanders of Canada) in the Great War, winning the Military Medal.
His son, Captain Stephen Bird, was killed in the Second World War while leading
a company of the North Nova Scotia Highlanders. Will Bird's prolific writings—
novels, short stories, plays, history, biography and autobiography—include several
publications concerning the Great War: *And We Go On* (1930), republished as
Ghosts Have Warm Hands (1968), *The Story of Vimy Ridge* (1932), and *Private
Timothy Fergus Clancy* (1930). *Thirteen Years After* (1932) and *The Communication
Trench* (1933) record Canadian veterans' anecdotes of raids and battle actions,
statistical tables, poems and macabre jokes. In one preface Bird grumbles about
the difficulty of accessing military records in Ottawa that should be available now.
He prophesies that "within twenty years the veterans will have gone to their last
roll-call—then they can bury forever, with the spiders and stale tobacco, everything
regarding the Great War. It will then be of no interest to the existing generations."

During the two world wars Newfoundland was a separate British colony, not
part of Canada. The armies of the two countries sometimes fought side by side,
as at the Battle of the Somme in 1916 and at Masnieres in October 1917. In
"Sunrise for Peter" the central character, a Newfoundland fisherman, Private Peter
Teale, juxtaposes nostalgic images of home with the grisliness of the trenches, as
he awaits a letter from his wife. Handwritten letters were the lifeline connecting

servicemen to their families. In one week in December 1915, more than five million letters were delivered to the Allied forces in France.

"Sunrise for Peter" contains a powerful example of litotes (ironical understatement) when Peter muses, "Everyone had said that July, 1916, would be the turning point of the war. It had come but nothing great had happened." In fact, on July 1 the Royal Newfoundland Regiment, fighting near Beaumont Hamel, lost every officer within a half an hour together with 647 men. The total British casualties for the day were 57,470 men, making it the most wasteful battle in the history of British warfare. In Newfoundland July 1 is noted less as Canada Day than as a memorial day. Kevin Major's *No Man's Land* (1995) is a fictional account of the battle of Beaumont Hamel.

Sunrise for Peter

THE NEWFOUNDLANDERS WERE MOVING TO THE Somme. Three days "D" Company had marched through a sun-bathed, picturesque part of France, fragrant with flowers and fruit trees, pleasing to the eye. Peasant women in the fields had smiled at them, and children had clapped their hands and shouted *Bon chance*. The soldiers had feasted their eyes on homely, chalk-walled cottages nestled in backgrounds of deep verdure, grassy gay with buttercups and poppies, rich with clover in bloom. And now they were falling in for a night move, which meant that they were nearing the line.

A ceaseless, far-away, throaty grumble of gunfire was as impressive as the low-spoken comment of the veterans, and Private Peter Teale spoke quietly to the white-faced youth beside him.

"It'll take us th' night t' get there, and we won't be for it then."

The boy-like soldier looked up at him quickly, as if seeking a hope.

"But they'll shell us bad up there, won't they?" he blurted, and his voice was unsteady.

"It won't be cushy, that's sure," returned Peter, "but it'll not be too bad. There may be dugouts for the day."

The sergeant-major barked an order and the men stood stiffly at attention as their company commander took over. The latter was a tall man, slightly stooped, and his voice was kind, though tense, as he proceeded, after telling them to stand at ease, to read an order. It dealt with a contemplated attack. The battalion would take over a part of the line near Bus and the company would be in Pineapple Trench. The enemy would be shelled for two hours previous to the assault, and there would be an abundance of artillery support afterward. During the actual attack each man was to do his utmost to reach the objective—the German second trench—and no one was to pause to assist a wounded comrade. Every moment would count toward success or disaster.

Men shuffled uneasily, hitching at their equipment, and a course whisper was audible. "What a bloody hope we got."

The company moved out on the road and swung into rhythmical step. Just outside their billeting area an old curé stood by his church, peering at them as they passed, his head uncovered and bowed, a beautiful but ominous gesture. Peter felt melancholy, and a sort of homesickness banished all the thrill that had stirred him as they fell in; he felt incoherently sympathetic for all the blurred figures about him.

They marched into open country, and as the night deepened he watched the colour drain out of the landscape, leaving all contours vague and grey beneath a pallid starlight.

"Oh mademoiselle from Armentières, *parley-vous* ..."

The soldiers sang riotously, without attempts at harmony, seizing the song as an outlet for pent emotions. Peter did not join in. His melancholy muzzled him, and anyway he disliked the words. The doggerel ended and for a time there was only the thudding shuffle of hobnailed boots, the creak of equipment, and then someone started a sentimental ditty that drew mixed comment.

"... and another poor mother has lost her son."

It finished like a ribald defiance to the future.

They passed through another village. A door opened and a light gleamed, then a voice asked where they were going.

"The Somme, the Somme!" The challenge was unmistakable.

"Somme. Ah, *no bon*." The voice sounded hollow, hushed, seemed to drift in the damp air, ghostlike. "Ah, *no bon*."

It was disturbing, that sighing comment, but the marching men sang louder until they were exhausted. Then came a halt, and they fell out by the roadside and cigarettes glowed like fireflies. Peter sat by the youngster, and watched him loosen his belt and twist irritably at his haversack.

"It's cooler at nights," he offered, "and there's no marching to attention."

The youth twitched again. "My shoulders are raw," he complained. "I'll be glad when we're there."

Peter was carrying the boy's rifle and extra bandolier long before they reached the dark abyss of a communication trench that led to the front line, and in helping him he forgot for a time a worry that had gnawed at his heart. He had not, however, slumped on a chicken-wire bunk in the dugout to which they were assigned, before he remembered, and stirred about until he saw the sergeant.

"Has no mail come up?" he asked.

The non-com. grunted wearily. "I'll see," he said. "The limbers came behind us."

By the flickering light of a few candles the dugout looked a grisly cavern. Its roof timbers and jutting bunks made gloomy, shadow-ridden corners, and the sleeping men sprawled about as if they had been so stricken. Peter gazed at them with a return of his melancholy, and watched for the sergeant's return. Would there be a letter for him?

He glanced at the white, upturned face of Telfer, the youth, and realized that if there were a letter he must wake the lad. He could not wait until morning to have its message read. If only there had been one the previous night, when they had been rested and had had a good supper of stew and bread and hot tea. Then he would have had time to ponder each line, each phrase, like a tasty morsel, until he had imbibed the whole so thoroughly that it would have become a part of his memory.

It had been a snug billet, that overnight stopping place, very cooling and restful after marching over the hard, hot pavé. The big, stone-built barn held fresh clean straw, and in the rear were pollarded willows over-hanging a little river of bright water. The splashings of many bathers and the murmur of the men's voices had but added to the soothing qualities of the scene. Telfer had rested and slept like a child.

Peter wondered how many of the men would go that way again. He wondered if he would. Such thinking was a recent thing for him, and, in a way, had gripped him. Before their last "trip" in the line there had been Simon Teale, his cousin, to talk to, to ask advice, but now he was alone save for young Telfer, and there were so many things that such a young lad could not understand. For instance, he would not know about dreams, and dreams were guides if one understood them as Simon had done.

And Simon was a home man. He had lived at Old Bear Bay just down along from Peter, and they had fished and hunted and trapped together through many lean years. Simon was clever with tools, and he could read and was versed in many "outside" matters. Peter was more of a hunter and trapper. He knew every pond and barren and drogue all the way to Old Woman Tickle; could sense his way in the winter through dense stunted spruce where the windfalls of ages made countless pitfalls hidden under light snow coverings.

He and Simon had come to France together, and their intimacy had been a great thing for Peter. They could talk of home, and the fishing and sealing, the old folks and young folks, and Simon could read their letters to him. He also wrote to Peter's wife. It was a huge help, that letter writing, for Simon could put things in words so easily and Peter could not. He had less to write about, too, for Simon had a family, three husky sons and two daughters; Peter and his wife were childless.

Strangely, it was Simon, the family man, who had first mentioned enlisting. Peter had heard vague rumours about a war over in Europe, but his meagre geography had never caused him to think that it had anything to do with Newfoundland, and he was astounded when Simon said so. His amazement increased when within the week his partner gravely informed him that it was their duty to go to St. John's and "sign up."

"But who'll do the hunting and fishing and get the firewood?" asked Peter. Simon had upset his world.

"There'll be money from the government," Simon explained. "Wages like, that the wife will get, enough to buy 'lasses and flour. It's our duty to go, man, a wonderful chanc't, and the good Book says so."

That settled it. Peter hated to leave home but he was a pious man, a believer. He had not the religion of some of the outport Newfoundlanders, who were subject to "glory fits" and loud repentances, but he had a faith of his own, partly the result of hearing Simon read the Bible on stormy days and Sundays, and partly due to his own thinking.

Out in the vast whiteness of winter, with the glitter on the trees and an awesome silence over all, he would think and think as he visited his snares and traps, and when a perfect pelt rewarded him he would stand

and gaze about him in a peculiarly reverent fashion. On summer nights, when the huskies howled and the Northern lights rustled with the changing of a million tints, he had the same sensations, and would go up on the hills and rocky crags above the little bay and sit for hours alone. Mary, his wife, did not like such moods, and so he never told her about them.

"All right, Simon," he had said. "I'll go as soon as I fix for a winter's diet, but I know I'll hate the killing. It don't seem right to me."

"There was killing in Bible times," Simon asserted, "so it must have been right, and Samson slew the Philistines. 'Tis likely these Germans be the same."

So the two men had gone down to St. John's and there had become soldiers of the English King who needed them. Peter had hated it all, the bayonet fighting and bomb throwing and especially the heartless jesting. And he hated leaving Mary.

In France a discerning sergeant had noticed their silent cat-footed ways in the dark and made them his platoon scouts, which pleased Peter as much as anything could in that war-defiled country. Out in no man's land, lying in the stealthy quiet of a listening post, he could watch the endless flares and imagine himself back on the hills behind Old Bear Bay. Such dreamings had been easy in the sector where Simon was killed. It was rough-cratered territory in a mining region and there had been a lovely crescent moon afloat, an enchanting moon that changed the lines into soft contours until reminiscence teased his memory, for even the sombre slag heaps, huge against the luminous sky, became the dark rocky spurs that guarded his home harbour. And there had been a stillness he liked, a quiet in which he could bathe his soul as in a deep, cool pool. He had said so to Simon.

A shuddering sigh had been his comrade's first response, then came a whisper, hoarse with emotion. "It's my night, Peter. I've had my dream."

Peter had almost blamed himself afterward for letting Simon sleep. He had known, by his easy breathing, that Simon was dozing, and had not roused him, and so the death vision had come. But would it not have come anyway, or would he not have been killed without warning? Peter knew that no man could live beyond his time.

"What was it like?" he had asked, crushing back a first urge toward pity, for it could never help a man. "What were the signs?"

"I saw my door, wonderful clear," whispered Simon, "and Maggie were in it waving good-bye. It were like daylight, all the bay, and the boys were down by the fish wharf. It were my dream."

And then, because he knew nothing else to do, Peter had held out his hand and gripped Simon's with his warmest pressure and assured him that he had one consolation—he had lived clean and honest and God-fearing, and that was a comfort to anyone.

When their hour was up they had crawled back toward the trench, and Peter had noticed how the wet weeds that brushed his face were like dead fingers. Then the Germans sent up coloured lights, and he saw that the red ones made the water holes pools of blood, and the green ones gave all the area a ghastly corpselike sheen. It did not surprise him the least when a sniper's bullet came with the hiss of an evil thing and killed Simon instantly.

Peter had helped carry the dead man far back to a little cemetery, where all the graves had white crosses, bearing names and numbers. To one of his faith and nature, respectful burial was a mighty thing. When, before they marched to the Somme, he had visited the graves and seen skylarks springing up from them, flooding the earth with melody and soaring to enormous heights before dropping back to earth, he was certain that Simon was "Resting in Peace," according to the legend above him.

He was thinking of how obligingly young Telfer had written a decent letter to Simon's wife, one that she would feel was a personal message, and how the lad had clung with him since, when the sergeant returned and stared across the dugout, blinking wearily.

"That you, Peter? There was no letter. The mail's slow these times."

"It is," said Peter. "I'm a month without hearing from my woman, and the last one was long coming. I been wonderin' about my Mary."

"She'll be all right," grunted the sergeant drowsily. "The folks back home have lots to do while we're away. You'd better get to sleep. We'll be in the front trench tomorrow night and we might be unlucky."

He had not stopped speaking, it seemed, before he was snoring, and Peter blew out the candle that had been burning beside him, waxed on the top of his steel helmet. Then he lay down and stared into the murk of his corner and listened to rats in the dugout walls while he tried to visualize Mary, his wife, in the tiny garden he had made of good earth scraped from hollows in the hills and carried down in baskets, and fed each spring with decaying small fish, after which he faced again the stern fact that Mary had not written him.

Had she tried the salmon netting herself? He stirred uneasily. He had told her not to try it, for it was a man's work, and there was no need while the government sent her money. Mary! He wanted to speak the name aloud, softly, caressingly, to hear the music of it, and as he stared into the dark he saw her face, smiling, wistful, alluring, daring, gay, whimsical— she could change like spring weather—and he gazed spellbound until a thudding overhead explosion shook the dugout, and faces vanished like reflections in the still water of the bay when a ripple crossed it.

There was another jarring crash, dulled by the heavy gas blankets hung across the stairway but audible enough to rouse several sleepers. "That's big stuff," said one, and another growled assent. They listened and heard the next shells land farther away, and went to sleep again. Peter, his mind diverted, also slept.

It was afternoon and the shelling was heavy, but Peter stayed in the trench. He wanted to think and he could not do so in the foul, fetid air of the dugout. The men were boiling tea, and frying bully in mess-tin tops, and the odours of their cookers mingled with the stale, saline smell of perspiration. He wanted to inhale fresh air.

The trench was but one in a zigzag warren and had lately been German ground. A coal-scuttle helmet, daubed with camouflage paint, had been tramped into the earth, and stick bombs were piled on what had been the enemy fire-step. He moved around a bay and saw a sand-bagged hollow that had been a machine gun post. A dead gunner was sprawled over his wrecked weapon and big blue flies buzzed about him. Old boots, bottles, a gas mask, were littered about, and the German's pockets had been turned inside out by some hasty souvenir hunter. Letters, postcards and a photo had been flung down. Peter's face set grimly. He judged it an ungodly thing to rob the dead.

He looked around. There were successive explosions in the area to his right, just where a house had been, and he saw a stretcher party hurrying away with a burden. He mused, sadly. Everyone had said that July, 1916, would be the turning point of the war. It had come but nothing great had happened. There certainly was no rout. Soon the line would move on and the ruin would be but another rubbish heap; then a plot of little white crosses would be formed in what had been the garden and a signboard by the filled-in craters would say "Dangerous Corner." That was the routine of war.

He hated war, abhorred it. Over on the low ground he could see fresh graves in the swampy mud. The cross of the nearest one had been struck by a shell splinter, so that only the name remained. One name. "Karl ..." And the inscription *Ruht in Gott*. Peter looked at the letters a long time, wondering what they meant, and when a corporal passed by he got him to decipher them and explain.

"Them Heinies is all Karls and Ottos," said the non-com. as he hurried on. "Nobody'll ever know who's planted there."

The thought struck Peter forcibly. That was the worst part of war, the desecration of graves, of the dead. He had never dreaded death nearly as much as he had dreaded being left as a discard on a battlefield, to be rat-eaten and fly-blown, blackened and shrivelled, and at last hastily covered in a shell hole by a careless burial party. He moved down the trench to the dugout. The company was not to go forward until dark, and he would talk with Telfer, try to encourage the lad, and in the doing ease his own mind.

"What's it like up front?" asked Telfer. He was lying on his bunk and his face was pale and drawn.

"Not so bad," said Peter. "They're shelling all over but no place gets much. It's open ground in front and all trenches and wire and shell holes, same as we came through."

"We're to go up at nine," said Telfer. "The sergeant was here and told us. We stay in Pineapple Trench until five and then go over." Then, as if for something to say, the boy looked up with a feeble grin. "Did you know it'll be Sunday," he said, "and the first day of August?"

Peter felt as if someone had prodded him. He stared at Telfer.

"The first of August," he repeated. "It's my wedding day, ten years ago. Man, there'll be a letter, sure."

Then he moved over and sat beside Telfer and talked as if he were making explanations.

"It were a Sunday, too, when we married, though Mary didn't want it. She were a great one for jolly times and there wasn't much for to do that day, but her father had his boats to see and couldn't come before. I didn't like it because she didn't, but any day would have suited me, lad, for I knew I were the luckiest man in Old Bear Bay in catching Mary. You'd never think, to see her, that she'd have the likes of me."

Peter paused and gazed at his rough hands and wrists, disfigured by sea boils. Then he shook his head in a solemn fashion.

"I don't know what she be doing now for to keep her spirits. There won't be much going on with the men away, and Simon and two others killed, and"—he glanced at Telfer—"there were no children to make her busy. It'll be hard on her, the waiting and bad news, for Mary's not like the others. She were always a gay one, bright and joking with everybody, and there isn't her match in looks on the coast. I hope she isn't trying the nets." Peter's voice was lower. "She's not got the strength for it and there isn't the need to do it."

Telfer turned uneasily. "There's not much shelling now," he said. "Let's go and have a look. The sergeant said if it rained we wouldn't go over this time."

But there was no hope. The air was windless and cool and the sun had set with every promise of fine weather. The early dusk revealed a desolation that appalled. The trenches and dugout entrances and tree stubs were all touched with a drab greyness that seemed phantom-laden, and a faint smell, indescribable, from the unburied dead, made Telfer shiver.

"I hate it," he said nervously. "Why don't they bury them Heinies?"

"There's not the time," said Peter, "but there should be. The dead should be respected wherever they are. I hope I have a grave when my time comes."

"Don't talk that way," said Telfer sharply. "You sound as if—if you expected to be killed."

Peter's rugged features remained sombre. "I have a bad feeling," he said moodily. "In Old Bear Bay there's many has a gift of seeing ahead, and always they tell that a man's luck begins on his tenth wedding day. It's in me here"—Peter tapped his broad bony chest—"that something's gone wrong with my Mary. She were a warm-loving woman, and there's been a sickness or bad luck at the Bay. Simon told her how I keep her letters, and that I had them all." Peter unbuttoned a tunic pocket and drew forth a closely-tied bundle, rather thumbed and dirty but readable. "Them'as been a help when we're in a bad billet and there's not much to do. I know 'em, what's in 'em, every one." Then he clenched a big fist and looked over the dim snaky line of trenches. "Them transport chaps needs lookin' after," he growled. "They be careless with the mail bags at times."

"Let's go into the dugout," said Telfer. "I hate this place."

The sergeant-major met them. "I suppose you're thinking of your leave, Peter," he said. "I tried to get you off this trip, but we're short of good men. You'll be away as soon as we're out again."

"Oh, my gosh," gasped Telfer in an undertone, and when the sergeant-major had gone he was vehement. "Beat them out," he cried. "It's a dirty trick, sending a man into a scrap when his leave's due. Go sick or something. Don't let them fool you that way."

But Peter shook his head. "I don't do them tricks," he said, "and I won't start now. Besides I wouldn't want to go afore I got my letter."

"They're putting it all over you," insisted Telfer. "You've earned two leaves. Go ahead and take a chance. The doc won't think you're playing sick. And never mind your mail. Lots of chaps haven't got any since we started to move. Your wife's all right or somebody would have wired you. That's the way they send anything that's important."

Peter smiled in his slow way. "If my time's come, it's come," he said, "and being on leave wouldn't make any change. There's a chance a letter will come tonight, and if it's good news my luck will be all right for the rest of my life. If Simon were here he could tell you about it."

Pineapple Trench was swathed in darkness and the lines were fairly quiet. Now and then flares lobbed up and filled the night with an eerie whiteness, and when the machine guns were not shooting the very atmosphere seemed charged with expectancy. Peter was in a small trench shelter and Telfer was huddled beside him. The lad dozed occasionally and cowered in his sleep, whimpering with the poignant fears of anticipation.

Peter wished that he could sleep—he needed it, was heavy with it—but his restless memory made sleep something to be resisted. Dark thoughts tormented him, hovered over him like haunting winged creatures. What had happened to Mary? Had she been drowned, her dory swamped as she went out to look at the salmon nets? Had she slipped on the rocks on a wet windy day as she went to their little garden on the sunny side of the hill? Had some fever come into the village?

Then he remembered Telfer's urgings about getting away on leave, and pondered. Never before had he had such a dread of going into battle. What had happened to him? He was not a coward. Any native of Old Bear Bay knew that life was a precarious thing, and Peter believed that every man had his time limit set when he began living. But he dreaded being left in the wilderness beyond Pineapple Trench, an unsightly body suddenly emptied of life, at which those passing would glance with furtive curiosity. He fingered his chin and was glad he had shaved before he left the dugout.

Telfer pressed closer to him, as if for warmth, and Peter's heart filled with pity. It seemed a crime to send such a boy into battle. Then he wondered, with dismay, who would read his letters and write them if anything happened to the lad. Telfer was a find. He had been so apt in comprehending all Peter's affairs.

An hour before the barrage was to begin, Peter awoke from a short sleep and sat up straight. Telfer was aroused by a tug at his shoulder.

"I've had a dream," said Peter in a tense, excited way, "and it were something wonderful. The sun were coming up on the bald rock back of the Bay and there were a dory going ashore. A sunrise is wonderful good luck. I wish Simon were here. He'd know the signs."

"Signs!" repeated Telfer sleepily. "What signs?"

"He'd know," explained Peter, "whether it were good or bad luck."

"Dreams don't mean nothing," said Telfer, listening to shelling on their flank. "I never think of them again."

"Them as knows says dreams are signs," said Peter determinedly and with a renewal of his excitement. "Sunrise must mean something wonderful. There'll be a letter, sure."

Peter knew considerable about "signs." Simon and he would never risk a stormy passage across the Bay without giving their caps the "fishermen's toss," and the more he pondered it the more he felt certain that his dream was a good omen, so that when the barrage rocked the earth and sky he was almost cheerful. Telfer, white-faced, hugged the shelter of the sandbags. Smashing, pounding, rending explosions almost burst the eardrums, and gradually the reek of high explosives drifted to their trench.

The sergeant came along the trench, assisting an officer to issue a rum ration, and when he reached Peter he gave him a letter, saying it had come up in the night.

Peter was wild with thanks. He clutched the letter and thrust himself into the shelter beside Telfer.

"It's my lucky day," he shouted into Telfer's ear. "Read it quick. We've not long now."

He lighted a candle and held the stub in his fingers.

Telfer's pallor was enhanced by the flickering glow. He tore the envelope open and his fingers were trembling. Peter placed his broad back in the entrance to the shelter to keep the draught from the candle flame, and waited eagerly. "Mary would know it's our tenth wedding." His voice was strong above the tumult outside. "She have planned the letter neat to time."

Telfer nodded. He stared at the missive, his hands shaking, then glanced at Peter with the affrighted look of a cornered animal. Peter put a hand on his shoulder soothingly.

"Never mind the shelling," he said in a voice for a windy sea. "I'll stay by youse when we go. What's Mary saying this time?"

Telfer's voice was so weak that Peter could not distinguish a word, and he shouted again. "Speak up, man."

He was pushed roughly and the sergeant squeezed in beside them.

"You two come with me," he bawled. "The captain wants me to be one flank. You bring bombs, Peter. I'll use you, Telfer, for a runner."

"That'll be all right," responded Peter. "Hurry, man, and read my letter."

Telfer did not look up. He moistened his lips with his tongue, then read in a high-pitched tremolo:

"My dear Peter: You must remember our wedding day and think of me. The garden has been fine. I have not gone to the salmon nets for there is no need at all. Simon's boys have a net for me. There is plenty of grass for the goat back of the hills, and I have got berries preserved for when you come home. The boats are not running so often now and my letters will be later. Write to me as soon as you can. Simon's wife is getting a pension. I love you, Peter, the same as I did ten years ago. Your loving wife. Mary."

For a full moment Peter did not move or speak and then his rugged face broke into a smile startlingly alien to their surroundings. He puffed out the candle.

"Man," he shouted, "that's wonderful writing. It's the best letter I've ever had. Don't youse be feared today. Good luck's with me, sure."

The sergeant did not say anything. He stared at them both as they backed into the trench and made ready for "over the top." As the signal whistle blew, Peter patted the letter in his pocket and smiled again.

"Sunrise is a wonderful sign," he cried cheerfully.

An hour later Peter worked desperately, helping the sergeant establish a trench block. "D" Company had taken its objective, after heavy losses, but the enemy fought doggedly to hold a post on the extreme right. Noon found the situation unchanged and three of the flanking garrison added to the inert dead. Peter's bombs were exhausted and he was depending on his rifle. The sergeant, fighting beside him, slightly wounded, decided to send for help. Twenty yards away, across a bit of open ground, a platoon was entrenched. If Telfer could reach them …

He explained matters to the lad who crouched beside them.

"One quick rush and you're across. They'll never get a shot at you. Go on. We can't hold out here."

Peter saw Telfer gaze at dried pools of blood on the trench floor, at stained and sodden bandages beside a dead man, and knew that fear was holding him.

"Go on," yelled the sergeant. "We can't stick it here. We've got to have help."

Telfer gave him a dog-like glance of entreaty, then tried to climb to the open, slipping twice on mud-greased bags so that the sergeant swore again. Peter, watching, made sudden resolve. Telfer had helped him with his letters; he must help Telfer. Why not attack the enemy? Only a few of them remained and they might be routed. Through all the mad fighting, the plunging, stumbling, headlong charge, the shooting and bombing and clubbing, he had had only one phrase singing in his mind, carrying him, buoying him over every obstacle. "My dear Peter." Never before had Mary begun a letter so affectionately. "I love you, Peter, the same as I did ten years ago." Battered, bruised, bleeding from a dozen minor hurts, he was exuberant, exhilarated. Mary, his Mary, loved him. What else mattered!

"Wait," he shouted as the sergeant turned to enforce his order. "Youse follow me." Before they could stop him he had leaped the trench barrier and was over at the German garrison like an avenging fury.

In five minutes the German post was a welter of blood and its owners were the sergeant and Telfer, but the cost was dear. Peter lay on the fire-step with a terrible wound in his side, a wound they could not staunch.

He was conscious but he could not keep his thoughts clear. There were so many things he could not understand. How had the Germans been able to strike him down, at the very last moment of fighting, when this was his lucky day? Didn't a sunrise always mean luck, and hadn't his letter proved it?

The noise that beat on his ears troubled him. Where was he? It reminded him of the storms, the tearing, slamming northeasters at Old Bear Bay. He was tired, too, as he usually was when he had had a rough time in a dory or had just got back from his trap lines. He kept his eyes shut. When they were open he could see mud walls and broken sandbags, but when they were closed he could vision a tiny harbour with a tossing sea confronting it, and hills overhanging dark water, hills that sheltered little cottages snug on their windward side.

"Telfer!" Peter's cheeks were grey and he breathed with labour. "Read—that letter."

Telfer fumbled at Peter's pocket and then his voice rose shrill and tremulous. "My dear Peter."

Around the traverse a new parapet had been constructed and a Lewis gun mounted so the sergeant lingered and listened and wondered. Telfer's gaze was not on the writing. When he stopped reciting Peter breathed once more, a long restful sigh, and lay still. Telfer's white face strained to new lines. He made to fold the letter but the sergeant took it and read.

"Dear Peter"—the scrawled writing seemed pitifully weak—"Mary died last night. Come three weeks Sunday she were up on the rocks where you used to sit, and fell. Her wouldn't let uns write before. Her been going up there since Simon were killed. The boys will tend the goat and your nets. Last thing her thought of your wedding day. Please God you don't be hurt. I had to send this word. Your cousin, Ann Teale."

He read it a second time and stared at Telfer, who was covering Peter's face. The Lewis gun barked savagely for a moment, then stilled, and the sergeant spoke.

"You did him a grand turn," he spoke gruffly to steady his voice, "but how did you know what to say?"

"I knew what he wanted, sarge." Telfer's fear had left his voice, temporarily at least. "And if you'll let me use some of them prisoners we'll carry him back and bury him decent, like he wanted."

"Go ahead," said the sergeant. "He deserves it, and there's nothing he'd like better. But listen. What if he hadn't—what if he found out?" He glanced at the grim covered figure.

"I daren't tell him the truth," Telfer said slowly. "He's been so mighty good to me." He turned, too, and looked at the still body. "Poor old Peter," he muttered. "He thought this was his lucky day."

There was a long silence. The sergeant was reading again the letter in his hand. He stirred at last.

"I believe it was," he said softly.

Peregrine Acland

PEREGRINE ACLAND (1891-1963) served as a major with the First Contingent of the Canadian Expeditionary Force and won the Military Cross. While crossing the Atlantic on board H.M. Troopship Megantic in October 1914, he wrote "The Reveillé of Romance," a poem of thirteen stanzas. In it he hails the war as an opportunity for heroic action that enables a soldier to be "Godlike for but a day" rather than pacing "the sluggard's slavish round/In lifelong, mean decay."

All Else is Folly (1929), the novel from which "Zero Hour" is taken, is subtitled *A Tale of War and Passion*. The epigraph from Nietzsche's *Thus Spake Zarathustra* explains the title: "Man shall be trained for war, and woman for the recreation of the warrior; all else is folly." The hero, whose name, Falcon, suggests that he is the author's alter ego, is working as a cowboy on a southern Alberta ranch when the Great War breaks out. Having joined the MacIntyre Highlanders (a fictitious regiment), he soon finds himself on the Western Front. Scenes of horrific warfare alternate with romantic encounters in English country houses.

The attack described here was part of the disastrous battle of the Somme in the area of the Western Front where the German defences were strongest. The Allied commanders under General Haig decreed that waves of soldiers, loaded with 66-pound packs (weapons, ammunition, pick and shovel, food, drink and other equipment) were to go over the top in broad daylight and make their way, despite shell fire, barbed wire, bombs, bayonets and mud, to the enemy trenches. The tanks, which remind Falcon of Hannibal's dead elephants in an ancient battle between the Romans and Carthaginians, were first used here in September 1916.

The "Behemoths" appeared so ridiculous that some of their first viewers literally died laughing amid enemy gunfire.

In a prefatory note Ford Madox Ford, himself the author of a classic British war novel, describes *All Else is Folly* as "the convincing, mournful and unrelieved account of a simple soul's sufferings ... In it you see, really wonderfully rendered, the admirable Canadians going through their jobs, with stoicism, without apparent enthusiasm, with orderliness, discipline—and with what endurance!"

Zero Hour

FALCON HAD ALWAYS LOVED THE OUT-OF-DOORS at night ... the thudding of hoofs on the soft turf of the prairie ... the sound of swift waters swirling around rocks.

Here there was no prairie to gallop over, no river to ford. Just a waste of shell-plowed earth to trudge through, on the way up the line. Nevertheless, as he breathed in the cool calm of the air, he loved the out-of-doors at night.

The only objects to break the flat monotony of that dimly visible landscape were tanks ... overturned tanks ... like dead elephants on the battlefield of Cannae.

It was not easy to guide the long file of men across the open. When at last the communication trench was reached, the guiding became easier, but the going became worse. They were now under shell-fire—heavy shell-fire. Shells smashed constantly to right and left of the trench. Fragments of shell zipped frequently into it.

The front-line trench was reached, however, without casualties. That trench was already well-manned ... with the battalion that had been holding the trench, that would continue to hold it during the attack. Now, the trench was jammed.

Rivers said to Falcon:

"If the Hun shelling was good, we'd have an awful lot of casualties before the attack started."

The shelling on the front line was constant, an incessant pounding on the parapet, a steady swishing overhead of shells that went long, exploding behind the parados. Only occasionally a shell burst in the trench, to be followed by gasps, sobs, moans and cries of "Stretcher-bearers! Stretcher-bearers on the double."

Falcon left Rivers posting his platoon, went down a long flight of dark, narrow steps into a dugout illumined by flickering candles, carpeted by the grey greatcoats of dead Germans. It was the headquarters of the company holding that section of the trench.

He found in it a haggard-eyed company commander and a long-unshaven subaltern. He exchanged greetings with them.

"It's been a rough tour of duty," said the company commander.

Falcon expressed sympathy. Inwardly, he envied the other man who wouldn't have to attack. Life in that trench might seem hell, but it would be paradise compared to the attack.

"When do you go over?" asked the hollow-eyed company commander. He spoke very low. There were orders to speak low on all such matters. German detectophones might be listening in on the conversation.

"I don't know," Falcon answered in the same low tone. "The rumour is that we attack at dawn, and that can't be more than an hour away. But we have no definite order yet."

Falcon was busy sending orders and receiving messages. Number twelve platoon, commanded—since MacGregor, the subaltern in charge of it, had been taken ill—by Sergeant Sanderson, had safely reached its destination, a sort of redoubt on the left flank of the company's front. Cheplin, commanding eleven platoon, reported his men in position. A similar message about ten platoon came from Craps. And as Falcon had come in with Rivers and nine platoon, he knew that the whole company was ready.

There was still, however, another platoon to hear from. A fifth platoon, from another Highland battalion, was attached to each company.

Company commanders, of course, could know little of the general plan of the attack. They knew only that, after a heavy bombardment, the attack would be delivered on a front many miles wide, that scores of thousands of men would go over the parapet at the same moment, and that, supporting the infantry, there would be an immense array of artillery, machine guns, aeroplanes, tanks.

Falcon's company was to advance in a series of waves, a platoon in each wave. Falcon himself, as company commander, would go with the last wave.

"Ees eet Major Falcon?'

Falcon looked up from the field message-book on which he was scribbling a report to see a tall, red-haired subaltern in a kilt saluting him. The subaltern reported that he had brought the additional platoon. Where did Falcon wish the men stationed?

Falcon knew this man. A French Canadian with a Scotch name—McLagan or McLaren, was it?—who could speak English only with a strong French accent. A descendant, no doubt, of one of the officers in Wolfe's regiments that were disbanded after the taking of Quebec, and that had settled down near by, intermarrying with the French. This officer, McLagan, he had talked with several times. McLagan was extraordinarily proud of his heredity, more delighted than any other officer in his battalion to be wearing the kilt.

Falcon gave him directions. No. No word of the zero hour yet. It was very nearly dawn now.

"Sir."

Rivers, taut-faced, had descended the steps into the candle-lit gloom of the dugout. He touched his tin helmet. He said,

"We've just had two men killed and five wounded by a shell-burst. All in number three section of nine platoon. Can we afford to send the wounded out on stretchers?"

Falcon tensed his jaw, said:

"Not if they can possibly walk."

"That's what I thought," said Rivers. He went back up the steps that led to the trench, the sky, and the shell-bursts.

Falcon returned to his report ... finished it. He added a final touch to his letter to Adair. It was always well to write, before an attack, a letter that could serve, if need be, as your last. He would send back this letter, and the letters to his father and his mother, by the runner who would take his report to headquarters.

A jubilant voice shouted down the steps:

"I say, Major, they've got me."

Craps limped down to show a big gash above his knee, from which blood flowed freely, and another gash on his arm. His face was pale. He was biting his lips. The wounds must hurt. But whatever the pain, his eyes were joyful. Those wounds meant a good blighty. He wouldn't have to go through the attack. He would get back to England. He might, even, work a trip to Canada.

Falcon, seeing him, thought all this, too. Far from sympathizing with Craps for his wounds, he was filled with rage that this platoon commander should get wounded just before the attack. Damned inconvenient! It would mean a rearrangement at the last moment.

Falcon asked:

"How's Sergeant McIlhinney?"

"He's all right. I left him in charge of the platoon, " answered Craps. "With these wounds, of course, I can't ..."

"McIlhinney's a pretty green sergeant to be left in charge of a platoon. Especially your platoon ... all those Saskatchewan Russians who can't speak decent English, or understand it. However ... I suppose that's the best we can do."

"This is a pretty nasty leg-wound, Major." Craps again pointed to his leg, which was now being bandaged by a busy-fingered little stretcher-bearer. "How about it? Hadn't I better go out on a stretcher?"

Falcon was gruff.

"Just a flesh-wound, isn't it? You'll *have to* walk."

"Walk?" expostulated Craps. "It'll take half an hour to get to the dressing-station, floundering around in the dark. And this leg hurts ..."

The firmness in Falcon's tone was final as he said:

"We can't spare men to carry you. You'll have to walk."

Craps looked at Falcon as if he could have killed him with a curse. Then turned with his bandaged leg and arm, and limped up the steps.

Nine hours later, the attack had not yet started. Falcon and Rivers stood side by side in the front-line trench, chatting to forget the thunder of the German shells. In the sunlight, both were grey-faced.

Falcon looked at his watch. Yes, he would have time for one more cigarette. Though he mightn't quite finish it.

He scratched a match. Lit a cigarette, rather badly. Took a puff or two. Let the cigarette go out. Lit it again.

All up and down the trench where he was standing in the sunlight men were doing that. Lighting cigarettes, letting them go out, lighting them again.

"Just three more minutes, " said Rivers.

Falcon nodded.

At last the zero hour approached. Not at dawn, but at noon. Through hour after hour Falcon had waited, expecting the order. A whole night and half a day waiting. A busy enough time, of course. There had been an abundance of things to attend to, what with casualties, the necessity for rearrangements, and the like ....

He had been desperately sleepy all night, but had fought off that feeling. Now, with all his weariness, he was wide awake, tense, alert.

All these men up and down the trench, with pale faces, unshaven jaws, and muddied, crumpled uniforms, must be as weary as he, though some of them, in spite of all the shelling, might have snatched a few minutes' sleep on the firing-step. Twenty-four hours without sleep before an attack—that was almost always the preliminary. You went into it so weary you hardly knew what you were doing ... if it weren't for the immense stimulus of danger.

Falcon again struck a match. Relit his cigarette with fingers that were not quite steady. Looked at his watch.

Rivers exultantly exclaimed:

"By God, look at the planes!"

High in the blue above them rose the British planes, a vast fleet.

A moment of silence. Not quite two minutes of silence. Why, you could hear the scratching of matches all up and down the trench!

Then ....

From far, far back came a ripple of sound ... a wave ... a long wave ... a tidal wave of sound .... It swept up ... swept up ... swept over ... and crashed on the German trenches.

Falcon looked over the parapet, disregarding snipers. A vast cloud of smoke and flame and flying earth, a cloud that reached for mile after mile up and down the line, all but obscured the enemy trenches from view.

Falcon, with his eye fixed on his wrist watch, raised his whistle to his lips. Blew a long, shrill note.

The first row of tin-hatted warriors, in their dirty khaki kilts, scrambled over the sand-bags. Pack on back, rifle in hand, they started forward, as they had been trained, two paces interval between man and man, all advancing at a walk. They mustn't run, or they would get tangled up in the Canadian barrage, and be killed by their own artillery. But when that barrage lifted they must be in a position to leap down into the German trenches, use the bayonet vigorously and fast ....

Again Falcon blew. A second platoon went over.

With each blast, another platoon.

At the fourth blast the French-Scotch-Canadian McLagan jumped up on the parapet. It was the job of his men to do the dirty work of remaking the trench supposed by now to be captured. Each of his men carried, in addition to rifle and pack, a pick or a shovel. McLagan himself went shovel in hand.

His Gallic nature wasn't content with a farewell shake of the hand, a sober walk into action. As he leaped on the parapet he uttered a loud cheer to his men and waved around his head, as if it had been a glittering sword, his square-bladed ditch-digger's shovel.

Falcon smiled, turned to Rivers. As he blew the whistle for the fifth wave, he gripped Rivers' hand hard.

"Good luck, Hugh."

"Hope to see you later, sir," said Rivers.

With Hugh Rivers and his platoon gone, it was now the turn of Falcon and the last wave ... if you could call it a wave. A group of signalers with a telephone and telephone wires, runners to take back messages ... odds and ends. Really, his company headquarters. It wasn't expected that they would have to do much fighting at this first trench. The early waves would attend to that in this so well-ordered attack. Of course, there would be casualties, and by the time the attackers reached the German second line Falcon would no doubt be in the fight as fully as any junior subaltern.

But supposing all hadn't gone as planned at that front-line trench ....

No use thinking of that.

For the sixth time, Falcon raised the whistle to his lips.

Anonymous

Letters from the Little Blue Room By an Elder Sister to her Brother who came over with the first Canadian Contingent to serve in The War to end War was published anonymously in London in 1917. It is an epistolary novel consisting of letters which "Pauline" writes to her brother "Boy," a young Scot who has emigrated to the Canadian prairies. The family consists of a mother, who dies in 1916, two soldier sons, their older sister Pauline, and a younger sister, Sidney, a university student who works in a munitions factory between terms. The Little Blue Room of the title refers to a den with blue walls, chintz-covered armchairs, a blue-tiled hearth and a red-shaded lamp on the round table where the letters are written. As the addresses to which the letters are sent change from Portage La Prairie, Manitoba to Valcartier Camp, Quebec, Salisbury Plain, England and after July 3, 1915 to the Western Front, we learn not only about the wartime experiences of the family members and their friends but also about the attitudes which Pauline, in particular, holds. This novel records a woman's perception, a stance not common in fiction about the Great War. Responding in the spring of 1916 to the "Big Advance," misleadingly so described in the press for propaganda purposes, Pauline writes of her "very intense regret at the cost of the struggle, and a very certain belief that it ought not to have been. But just as surely I feel that all the youthful chivalry, all the generous impulses, all the heroic sacrifice of the boys who have gone out cannot be lost or in vain."

"Hard Lines!" is an ironic attack on men who "Thank God for the War" while remaining comfortably and profitably at home. The novel ends tragically. In May

1916, while carrying the wounded Boy from the front line, his Canadian friend Harry is killed. Boy's wounded shoulder eventually heals but the operation to remove a bullet from his head causes irreversible brain damage. He is doomed to the life of a violently disturbed child and his sister to the restricting role of permanent care-giver.

Hard Lines!

January 30th, 1916.

I'M SENDING THIS MONTH'S "ROYAL" among your papers. Really I got it for the "pretty girl" cover, remembering what you have said about the joy it is to a soldier out in the mud and grime of the trenches to get a brand new, clean magazine, with a pretty-girl cover, and how the owner of such can exchange it for a dozen old, coverless magazines, and even for cigarettes. You babies! You see, we're following the wisdom of your American magazine ways by making a feature of covers now-a-days. For a long time our magazine-makers didn't realize the importance of the cover, putting out the magazines with the same dingy, stodgy old cover every month. I don't know how the public endured it so long. Why, many and many a magazine I've bought just for its either pretty or striking cover alone. But this magazine has an article. At first, on reading it, I decided not to send the magazine to you; then changed my mind and bought half-a-dozen copies to send to the boys. And in answer to that article, "Thank God for the War," I'm expecting half-a-dozen enthusiastic "Hear! Hears!" from you, and Angus in hospital, and Donald in Gallipoli, and the rest of the fortunate recipients of the magazine.

When mother, one evening when I was sitting sewing beside her, read aloud the title, "Thank God for the War," I wondered was it the anonymous confessions and published bank-balance of an Army contractor, or of one of the new literary-military experts; then when she read those extracts, that war is the only medicine for ailing nations and that God will always see to it that war occurs when we're being naughty children, I thought it must be one of the dear Bishops again with an I-told-you-so and a Serves-you-right sermon; but when she came to that bit, "Pray for a long and bloody war," I was quite sure it was Nietzsche, or Treitschke, or some other of those Hun-folk with a name like an influenza sneeze. And I was just wondering how the Editor had dared let such gentry into a perfectly good magazine under the very nose of the Defence of the Realm Act, when mother said no, my guess was wrong. Then I wondered if the writer who could publicly thank God for this war, and pray for a long and bloody one, was by any chance one of the Gallipoli boys who fevered for water in summer and froze to their guns in winter, or one of the many young widows left to rear her numerous assets to the State, or any of the mothers who wait at home for news of sons reported missing. But mother said no. So I guessed it could only be one of the many little busy bees of Pressdom flitting from flower to flower, industriously gathering the golden honey while the sun shines. And there, with your Thrashing-from-God Bishop, we may leave him.

Of course, this article was written long before this new restriction put out by the Government, the Military Service Bill. Harkee, then, Boy, while I a tale unfold. You know how, from the beginning of the war, its two staunchest supporters have been the Press and the Pulpit—you have often remarked their efforts and, you cynical old thing, not always appreciated them—and how the most enthusiastic, ardent, zealous recruiters have been all men above forty. You know how well the Clergy have worked. They have told us that the only road to Heaven for men these days is *viâ* Aldershot and Verdun; they have even, forsaking home and Presbytery, gone *right* to the very bases, to assure us worrying home-people what a picnic life waist-deep in trench water is; in a hundred magazines and periodicals they have allured and tempted us with descriptions of how beautiful and picturesque it is to rest under a mound in the shadow of the old *château* (they seem to guarantee the *château*—*it's* always there, anyway); they have even told us, and they should know, that "killing Germans is a divine service."

So, too, the journalists. They asked us right at the beginning what'd we lack when the boys—those that are left, of course—come home, and we're not there to get any of the bouquets and the glad eyes the girls will be throwing; they've wrung our heart over the piteous plight and petrifying predicament of the Man-who-stayed-at-home when the Innocent Child with the Little-Willie expression and the Fontleroy suit asks sweetly what he did in the Great War; they have worn down the types of their sibilants in a generous use of such stirring words as "shirkers" and "slackers" to spur on the sluggish spirit of the stay-at-home skulkers. Together, these two devoted henchmen, with their colleague the too-old-at-forty man have, in season and out, told the world that the only possible place for MEN just now is the Front—at least one of the Fronts. And now, oh! Boy, go think of it in silence and alone, now the Government ups and exempts them! Says to them, in effect, "Li'l boys, you're not to go; you must stay at home and help mother carry up the coals to keep the home-fires burning!" Surely the most unkindest cut of all; yet just the nasty sort of trick Governments can play those who serve them best. For if it's horrid to be a conscientious objector to war and yet have to go out to fight in it, it must be a hundred times worse to be a conscientious supporter of war as a necessity and yet to be refused to go and fight. Mustn't it?

But, give the exempteds credit for this (Sid writes of them as the "contempteds," but that's Sid applying her cast-iron common-sense criterion again). Well, this new Bill is to conscript men who don't believe in fighting, and immediately No-Conscription Leagues and various bodies of that kidney have sprung up all over the country. And the same Bill deliberately shuts out men who do believe in fighting and have consistently and publicly declared their belief in it, yet I haven't heard of a single No-Exemption League being formed. No, these disappointed patriots have no wish to harass the Government with petty, personal grievances; they have taken their blow like lambs led from the slaughter. Although, I do hope the Government won't insist on Father Bernard Vaughan and Canon Wilberforce being exempted from divine service at a shilling a day. I expect both of them are out your way somewhere, though you haven't mentioned meeting them; if you do run across them in one of the neighbouring trenches, you tell them they've got to come home at once—all forgiven. Now, I hate to see good material wasted. So I would suggest that all these ultra-patriotic patriots be allowed to form a battalion of themselves. Bet my hat, Boy, they wouldn't be content to sit, like you, in a silly old trench for six months doing nothing; for their keen enthusiasm, daring spirit, and reckless courage would sweep them right across Germany up to the front door of the Imperial Palace in Potsdam.

But, seriously, I think you're rather hard on the men whose "bit" lies at home here, on the journalists, "those chaps who can arrange and carry to a triumphant close colossal campaigns, with a few scrapes of the pen"; "the professional followers of the Lowly Nazarene, at £15,000 a year" (you're wrong—they don't all have that; some have only £12,000, and some even less), and "all the rest of the bunch of bandicoots." But, dear Boy, here again I see the cloven hoof of Intolerance that I warned you of before. You wanted to come and help in the great fight, and by just saying Open Sesame, you found yourself in the firing line. You didn't want to talk; you wanted to do, and do it yourself, too. And you got your chance. But the best way to be able to judge another's line of action is to imagine yourself in that other's place. And if you can do that here you will find "all that glisters is not gold."

How would you like to go into a widow lady's home, inquire exhaustively into her household arrangements, her intimate family affairs, and re-arrange all these so she could do without the luxury of an only son? Yet men have done this. How would you like to sit on a Tribunal and send other men out to danger and death, and then have to meet every day the mothers of the lads (and women, dear Heart, have so often a painfully limited, narrowly logical way of looking at things)? Yet men are doing this. How would you like to believe very intensely, very sincerely, in the righteousness of a cause, and then be condemned, for some reason or another, to stay behind, after you had, with tongue and pen, consistently helped to work up public feeling against the stay-at-home? Yet this has been the lot of very many men.

Honestly, now, would you rather be out there, young and keen and doing your bit in danger and dirt and din, or middle-aged and fat and doing it in your own little old town? How would you like to have to be patriotic by proxy? At least, no one ever questions your sincerity or turns the silently elevated eyebrow to your courage; while—well, there are nasty sceptical people here, you know. Tell me, would you rather be the man who can say, "Come and fight with me," or he who has to say, "Go and fight for me"? Though, now I think of it, I've never known one of our boys on any of the Fronts write, "Come and fight." I guess you've all become so absorbed in your trench work out there that you've forgotten there is any other. But you know the stock phrase, "Somebody's got to do the dirty work." And if these men have volunteered to do it in this case, what right have you to condemn? Yours is a part of the battle that will go down in the chronicles of the future; but theirs is such as no historian will care to write down for succeeding generations to read and remember.

Doubtless, dear, you Canadians thought it was very fine of you to give up your good positions, your good times in the Land of the Free, all your youth's chances and privileges, to risk your health and life on the fields of Flanders. And so it was fine of you. But I dare suggest neither your patriotism, nor that of any one of you out there, could have risen to the fineness of the men who have given and are giving the kind of service you so intolerantly sneer at. For you young things have a quaint and rather egotistical conception of honour and of "keeping your hands clean," forgetting that there is a higher form of patriotism that can subordinate self-respect, loyalty to one's fellows, aye, even honour itself as it is popularly conceived, to the interests of the military necessity of the hour.

Where is your broadmindedness, your chivalry towards lesser, poorer things? Be generous towards those men, Boy, you can jolly well afford to!

Always your best sister,
Pauline

Thomas H. Raddall

THOMAS H. RADDALL (1903–1992) was born in Hythe, England, moving to Halifax, Nova Scotia in 1913 when his father, a career soldier, was loaned to the Canadian army as a small arms instructor. Subsequently having joined the Winnipeg Rifles, he was killed near Amiens in 1918. Towards the end of the war Thomas took wireless training and worked as a ship's radio operator. After business college he became an accountant for small Nova Scotia pulp mills. During the 1930s he began to publish stories in *Maclean's* magazine, in an American pulp magazine, *Sea Stories*, and the more prestigious Scottish periodical *Blackwood's*, stories which attracted the favourable attention of Rudyard Kipling, John Buchan and Theodore Roosevelt. By 1939 he was able to earn a living from writing novels, short stories, history and historical romance predominantly Canadian in content. In his foreword to *The Pied Piper of Dipper Creek and Other Stories*, first published in Britain in 1939, John Buchan, Lord Tweedsmuir, then the Canadian Governor-General, praised the author's "rare gift of swift, spare, clean-limbed narrative."

"Winter's Tale" from that collection takes as its setting the Halifax explosion that occurred at 9:05 A.M. on December 6, 1917. During the First World War Halifax was the third most important harbour in the British Empire. Built on a peninsula facing the Atlantic and surrounded by water on three sides—the northwest arm, the Stream and the Bedford Basin—it was crucial to the trans-Atlantic shipping of men and supplies. On the fateful morning a French freighter, the *Mont Blanc*, which had been loaded with munitions in New York, was sailing towards Bedford Basin to join a convoy when it was rammed by a Norwegian ship, the *Imo*, carrying Belgian relief. The resulting explosion killed 2,000 people, injured 9,000 and destroyed the northern parts of Halifax and Dartmouth. A Toronto newspaper compared the devastated city where houses "were blown to atoms" to "a small section of Flanders."

In his autobiography, *In My Time: A Memoir* (1976), Raddall described his reaction as a fourteen-year-old boy sitting in his Grade Nine classroom at Chebacto School:

> We had just finished singing the morning hymn, "Awake, my soul,
> and with the sun / Thy daily stage of duty run," and were in the act
> of sitting down when we felt two distinct shocks. The first came
> from the deep slate bedrock on which the city stood, a sort of
> earthquake in which the floor seemed to rise and drop in several
> rapid oscillations. A few seconds later the air blast smote us. In the
> same order there were two tremendous noises, first a deep
> grumble from the ground and then an ear-splitting bang … It was
> like being shaken by a maniac giant with one fist and then slammed
> on your head with the other.

Raddall's experiences detailed in the memoir are closely linked to those of the boy in "Winter's Tale." Another Canadian writer, Hugh MacLennan, made the Halifax explosion the central event in his first novel, *Barometer Rising* (1941), which analyzes, step by step, the occurrences of that fateful Thursday morning between 7:30 and 9:10.

Winter's Tale

THE AIR IN THE CLASSROOM WAS WARM AND rather stuffy, because it had snowed a little the night before, and Stevens the janitor had stoked up his great furnace fiercely. Grade Nine, coming in rosy-cheeked from the snow outside, found it oppressive, but nobody dared to open a window. Old Mr. Burtle, who conducted the educational fortunes of Grade Nine, was Principal of the school and a martyr to asthma.

The rest of the big brick school was empty and silent. The lower grades were not required to answer roll-call until half-past nine. It was just one minute past nine by the clock on the classroom wall when James hung his school-bag on the back of his seat and flung an arithmetic manual on the desk. He also produced two pencils and sharpened them with his jack-knife, dropping the shavings on the floor and keeping a wary eye on Old Gander Burtle, who disapproved of that procedure. All about him was a bustle of preparation. Fifty boys and girls were busy with books, pencils, and erasers.

"Attention!" demanded Old Gander, with his asthmatic cough. Everybody sat up very straight. "We shall sing the morning hymn." The class arose with a clatter, shuffled a little, and then burst raucously into "Awake my soul and with the sun" as Old Gander raised his bony fore-finger. James had a point of vantage when they stood up to sing; for his desk was near the windows and he could look down into the street, two storeys below. It was certainly too nice a morning to spend indoors. The sky was blue, without a speck of cloud anywhere, sun very bright on the snow, and wisps of smoke rising straight into the air from a forest of chim-neys that stretched away southward. The snow was not deep enough for sleighing. There were a few wheel-tracks in the street, and the sidewalks were a mess of brown slush already, and when the several hundred kids of the lower grades had scampered in, there would be nothing but thin black puddles. Grade Nine intoned a long "Ahhh-men!" and sat down. It was five minutes past nine by the clock on the wall.

The act of sitting down in unison always produced a clatter, but this morning the effect was astounding. The hardwood floor began to move up and down very rapidly, like a gigantic piston of some sort; the walls swayed drunkenly to and fro, so that the blackboards came down and were followed by plaster, crumbling away from the walls in lumps and whole sheets. The great clock dropped from its fastening high on the wall, missed Old Gander's head by an inch, and spewed a tangle of springs and cogs over the heaving floor. The opaque glass in the door of the boys' coat-room sprang across the classroom, sailing over James' head, and went to pieces in a mighty splatter on the wall in front of him. The windows vanished, sashes and all. Not only the inner everyday windows, but the big storm-windows that were screwed on outside every fall and taken off in the spring. The room, the big echoing school, the whole world, were filled with tremendous sound that came in waves, each visible in breakers of plaster dust.

Then the sound was gone, as suddenly as it had come, and in its place there was a strange and awful hush that was emphasized, somehow, by distant noises of falling plaster and tinkling glass. Grade Nine was on its feet, staring at Old Gander through a fog of plaster dust, and Old Gander stared back at them, with his scanty grey hair all on end, and his long seamed face the colour of snow when rain is turning it to slush. A waft of cold air came in from the street, where the windows should have been, and the fog cleared before it. A girl broke the silence, screaming shrilly. James perceived that her cheek was laid open from ear to mouth, with a great red river pouring down her chin, and that others were putting fingers to cut faces and heads, and staring strangely at the stains. Grade Nine was covered with plaster dust, and looked like a company of startled ghosts, and when James saw the thin red trickles running out of those white masks he knew he was dreaming, because things like that did not really happen. The girl with the red mask screamed again, and there was a chorus of screams, and then with one impulse the class turned and fled, as if it were Friday afternoon fire practice. James heard them clattering down the stairs into the street, with glass grinding and tinkling under their shoes. For a moment James was poised for similar flight, but in that moment he remembered the time he was frightened by a signboard groaning in the wind at night, and Dad's deep steady voice saying, "Never run from anything, son, till you've had a good look at it. Most times it's not worth running from."

Old Gander was standing beside his desk like a statue, staring at the lone survivor of his class. His watery blue eyes seemed awfully large. They looked like Mum's breakfast saucers. James moved jerkily towards him, licking plaster-dust from his lips. "What is it, Mister Burtle?" His own voice seemed queer and very far away, the way it sounded when you talked in your sleep and woke yourself up. Old Gander gazed at James in enormous surprise, as though he had never seen James before, as if James were speaking some foreign language not authorized by the School Board. Then he said in his old asthmatic voice, "James! Is that you, James?" and without waiting for a reply he added, as though it were the most ordinary thing in the world, "Some of the little boys have been playing with dynamite in the basement." James nodded slowly. Old Gander knew everything. The kids in the lower grades said he had eyes in the back of his head. He was a very wise old man.

They stood, silent, in the wrecked classroom for a space of minutes. Another gust of chill air stirred the thin hairs that stood out like a halo from the schoolmaster's head.

"You are a good boy, James," murmured Old Gander in a dazed voice. James squared his shoulders instinctively. After all, he was a sergeant in the school cadet corps. It was all right for the others to go if they wanted to. Old Gander passed a shaking hand back over his head, smoothing down the straggled hairs. Bits of plaster fell upon his dusty shoulders in a small shower, like a brittle sort of dandruff. "I think," he said vaguely, "we'd better see if there is any fire."

"Yes, sir," James said. It occurred to him that Mr. Burtle ought to look in the basement where the little boys had played with the dynamite. "I'll go through the upstairs classrooms, sir."

"Very good," murmured Old Gander, as if James were a superior officer. "I will search the lower floor and then the basement." And he added, "Don't stay up here very long, James." They separated.

James passed from room to room on the second floor. Each was like the one he had left, with blackboards tumbled off walls, heaps of plaster, doors hanging splintered in the jambs. Along the south side of the school the windows had disappeared into the street, but on the north side the shattered sashes were festooned over desks, and shards of glass in the tumbled plaster gave it the glitter of snow. The big assembly hall occupied most of the north side. Miraculously, the doors were still in place, but they refused to open. One was split badly in the panel, and James peeped through at a tangle of wood, piled against the doors on the inside. He thrust an arm through the hole and pushed some of the rubbish aside. The hall was a strange sight. The tall windows which occupied almost the entire north wall had come inwards, had swept across the hall, carrying chairs with them, and the shattered sashes had wedged against the south wall and the side doors in a complete barricade. There was no trace of fire.

James walked down the stairs, along the lower hall, and out through the main entrance into the snow. The stained glass that formerly cast a prism of colours from the transom over the great main door had gone outwards, and was littered over the snow in a jig-saw puzzle of many hues. Old Gander stood there in the snow amid the coloured fragments, staring up at the mute ruins of his school. James gave him a glance, no more. Something else had caught his eye. To the north-east, over the roofs of silent houses, a mighty mushroom was growing in the sky. The stalk of the mushroom was pure white, and it extended an enormous distance upward from invisible roots in the harbour; and at the top it was unfolding, spreading out rapidly in greasy curls, brown and black, that caught the December sun and gleamed with a strange effect of varnish. An evil mushroom that writhed slightly on its stalk, and spread its eddying top until it overshadowed the whole North End, strange and terrible and beautiful. James could not take his eyes from it.

Behind him a voice was speaking, a woman's voice that penetrated the mighty singing in his ears from a great distance. Miss M'Clintock, the Grade Seven teacher, arriving early for the day's work. She was a tall woman, masterful to the point of severity. There was a wild look on her face that astonished James; for he had spent a term under her much-libelled rule and had never seen her anything but calm and dignified. "… all along the street. I can't tell you what I've seen this morning. Are you listening to me, Mr. Burtle?" Old Gander removed his wide gaze from the ravaged building. "My first really modern school," he murmured in that quaint asthmatic falsetto. "Dear, dear. What will the School Board say?"

James was watching that poisonous fungus in the sky again, but something Miss M'Clintock was saying made him look towards the houses about the school. They were like the school, void of window-glass, and in some cases of doors as well. There was a great silence everywhere, a dead quiet in which nothing moved except Old Gander and Miss M'Clintock and James and the mysterious mushroom that grew in the sky. But now over the whole city there came a great sigh, an odd breathless sound that was like a gasp and like a moan, and yet was neither. James saluted Old Gander awkwardly. "I—I guess I'd better go home now, sir." If Mr. Burtle heard him, he gave no sign. Miss M'Clintock said, "What a blessing the lower grades don't go in till half-past nine. All those big windows. Your hand is bleeding, James." James nodded and left them, walking out through the school gate and into the street.

Now there was a flurry of movement and a chorus of wild human sounds about the shattered houses. An oil wagon stood at the kerb, with a pair of great Percheron horses lying inert under the broken shaft. The teamster squatted beside them in the slush with his hands on their heads, addressing blood-stained people who scurried past without attention.

"Dead!" he said to James in a queer surprised voice. "An' not a mark on 'em. Would you think a man could stand a Thing that killed a horse?" James began to run.

Home was not far up the street. The old brown house stood two hundred yards from the school. (Dad had said, "It'll be handy for the kids going to school. When I get back we'll look for something better.") Just now it was silent, without doors or windows. Ragged wisps of curtain dangled in the gaping window-frames fluttering with every stir of the December breeze like signals of distress. James went up the front steps shouting, "Mum! Mum!" The house was cold and still. Like a tomb. James ran, frantic, through that ominous quiet. Margery's room was empty, the bed littered with broken glass. Mum's room. His own room. Broken glass, crumbled plaster, shattered doors. Slivers of glass thrust like arrows through the panels of Margery's door. Bare laths where the plaster should have been, like the naked ribs of a skeleton. In the lower hall the long stove-pipe from the big anthracite heater lay in crumpled lengths, with soot mingled in the littered plaster, and the painting of Fujiyama that Dad brought home from a trip to the East was half-buried in the rubble, broken and forlorn. Confusion reigned, too, in the living-room; a window-sash, void of glass, was wedged against the piano, and the dusty mahogany was scored deep by invisible claws. In the wrecked kitchen he heard voices at last. Mum's voice, outside, in the garden. The rear door and the storm porch were lying, splintered, in the tiny scullery, amid a welter of broken chinaware and tumbled pots.

Mum's voice again, "James! Is that you, James?" James scrambled through the wreckage of the back door and ran into her arms, and they stood in the snow for several minutes, Mum and Margery and James, holding each other in silence. There was a bloody handkerchief about Mum's forehead, and little rivulets of blackish-red drying on her cheeks. Margery wore a coat over her nightdress.

Mum said, "I was looking out of the kitchen window, and suddenly across the way all the windows glowed red, as if they'd caught a gleam of sunset. Then our windows seemed to jump inwards." James said quickly, "Are you hurt, Mum?" but she shook her head. "Just cut a little about the forehead, I think, James. The window in Margery's room came right in on her bed, and she walked downstairs in her bare feet without a scratch. Over all that broken glass! It's a miracle, really."

"Why are you standing out here?" James demanded. It was cold, there in the snow without a coat. Mum waved her hand vaguely towards the street. "Somebody shouted, 'They're shelling the city—get behind your house!' So we came out here."

"I don't see how that could be," James considered gravely. "All the houses along the street are just like ours—doors and windows blown to pieces, and all the plaster down. The school, too. They couldn't do that. Not all at once, I mean."

There were sounds from next door. Old Mrs. Cameron appeared, embracing her husband in a strange hysterical way. He was breathing very heavily, for he was a fleshy man. Sweat made little clean streaks in the grime of his face. Mr. Cameron was something in the railway.

"Station roof came down!" he shouted across to them. "All that steel and glass! Crawled out somehow! Ran all the way!" They came slowly to the garden fence, arms about each other, and Mum walked to meet them flanked by Margery and James.

"You hurt, Mrs. Gordon?" Mum shook her bandaged head again. "Nothing serious. Mr. Cameron, what does it all mean?" Mr. Cameron took an arm from his wife's waist and wiped his streaming face with a sleeve. "There was a terrible explosion in the harbour, down by the Richmond wharves. A munitions boat, they say. A French boat with two thousand tons of T.N.T. on board. She came up the harbour flying the red flag—the powder flag—and ran into another ship in the Narrows. She caught fire and blew up. It was like an earthquake. The whole North End of the city is smashed flat. Houses like bundles of toothpicks. And the boat went to pieces about the size of a plum—that big ship! When I ran up North Street the sky was raining bits of iron. I don't think many got out of the station alive."

Mum shivered. "No use standing here," James said. They went into the house and tramped silently through the shattered rooms. A motor-truck went past, soldiers leaning from the cab, shouting something urgent and incoherent. The street emerged from its dream-like silence for a second time that morning. Feet were suddenly splattering in the slush along the sidewalks, voices calling, shouting, screaming. Another truck went by, one of the olive-green army ambulances, going slowly. Soldiers hung from the doors, from the rear step, shouting up at the yawning windows. "What are they saying?" Mum said.

James said, "Sounds like, 'Get out of your houses.'" Mr. Cameron appeared on the sidewalk outside, shouting in to them through cupped hands. "... out! Magazine's on fire! Big magazine at the Dockyard! On fire!"

"Put on your coats and overshoes first," Mum said, her mouth in a thin white line. "Where's your coat, James?"

"In school," he mumbled, embarrassed. It was hanging in the coat-room, covered with plaster dust, like all the others, and he had run away forgetting everything, like the other kids after all. "Put on your old one," Mum said. Margery went upstairs, and after a few minutes came down again, dressed in a woollen suit. They went down the street steps together, and beheld a strange and tragic procession approaching from the direction of the city. Men, women, and children in all sorts of attire, pouring along the sidewalks, choking the street itself. Some carried suitcases and bundles. Others trundled hand-carts and perambulators laden with household treasures. Two out of three were bandaged and bloody, and all were daubed with soot and plaster. Their eyes glistened with an odd quality of fear and excitement, and they cried out to Mum as they stumbled past, "Get out! Out in the fields! There's another one coming! Dockyard's afire!"

Margery said, awed, "It's like pictures of the Belgian refugees." James looked at Mum's firm mouth and held his own chin high. They joined the exodus without words or cries. The human stream flowed westward. Every side-street was a tributary pouring its quota into the sad river. Open spaces began to appear between the houses, with little signboards offering "Lots for Sale." Then the open fields. The nearest fields were black with people already, standing in the snow with rapt white faces turned to the north-east, as in some exotic worship. The vanguard of the rabble halted uncertainly, like sheep confronted by a fence, and under the increasing pressure of those behind a great confusion arose. Their backs were to the stricken city. Before them lay the little valley of the Dutch Village Road, and beyond it the timbered ridges that cupped the city's water supply. Cries arose. "Here! Stop here!" And counter cries, "Too near! Move on!" At last someone shouted, "The woods! Take to the woods!" It was taken up, passed back from lip to lip. The stream moved on with a new pace, but Mum turned off the road into a field. They halted in a group of those strange expectant faces.

At the roadside was a pile of lumber. James went to the pile and pulled down some boards, made a small platform for Mum and Margery. Some of the people turned from their fearful gazing and said, "That's good. Better than standing in the snow." The lumber pile disappeared in a space of minutes. The great retreat poured past the field towards the Dutch Village Road for half an hour. Then it thinned, disintegrated into scattered groups, and was gone. The street was empty. The field was a human mass. Many of the women were in flimsy house-dresses, hatless and coatless. Two were clutching brooms in blue fingers. A blonde girl, with rouge-spots flaming like red lamps in her white cheeks, said, "Standing room only," with a catch in her voice. Nobody laughed. Most of the men were old. North-eastward rose fountains of smoke, black, white, and brown, merging in a great pall over the North End. The weird mushroom of those first tremendous minutes had shrivelled and disappeared in the new cloud. People watched the biggest of the black fountains. "That's the Dockyard," they said.

Two hours went by; long hours, cold hours. Still the people faced that black pillar of doom, braced for a mighty upheaval that did not come. There were more smoke fountains now, gaining in volume, creeping to right and left. A tall old man joined the crowd breathlessly, cried in a cracked voice, "The fire engines are smashed. The city is doomed." A murmur arose over the field, a long bitter sigh, like the stir of wind among trees. Someone said, "Nineteen days to Christmas," and laughed harshly. Three hours, and no blast from the burning Dockyard. Only the smoke poured up into the December sky. Old Mrs. Cameron came to them. She had become separated from her husband in the crowd and was weeping. "Joey! Joey!" she moaned, very softly. James thought this very strange. Joe Cameron had been killed at the Somme last year, and her other son's name was George. He was in France, too, in another regiment. But Mrs. Cameron kept moaning "Joey! Joey!" and wiping her eyes. She had no coat.

James said, "Looks as if we might be here a long time. I'll go back to the house and get some blankets, and something to eat." Mum caught him to her swiftly. "No," she said, through her teeth. Surprisingly, old Mrs. Cameron said, "That's right, James. I'll go with you. Mrs. Gordon, you stay here with Margery." Margery was not well. James looked at Mum. "Anywhere outdoors we'll be just as safe here. I won't be in the house very long." Mum stared at him queerly. "You sound like your father, James." They set off at a brisk pace, old Mrs. Cameron clutching his arm. The snow in the field had been packed to a hard crust under a thousand feet. Farther on, where the houses stood silent rows, it was like a city of the dead. Blinds and curtains flapped lazily in gaping window-frames. Clothing, silverware, all sorts of odds and ends were littered over hallways and doorsteps, dropped in the sudden flight. There were bloody hand-prints on splintered doors, red splashes on floors and entries. The slush on the sidewalks was tinged a dirty pink in many places, where the hegira had passed.

Home at last. Smoke curled, a thin wisp, from the kitchen chimney. It was absurd, that faithful flicker in the stove, when all the doors and windows were gone and the winter breeze wandered at will through the empty rooms. They paused outside for a moment. Old Mrs. Cameron said, "We must rush in and snatch up what we want. Don't stay longer than it takes to count a hundred. Remember, James." She moved towards her doorstep, drawing a deep breath. James nodded dumbly. He clattered up the steps, making a noise that seemed tremendous in the stark silence, then along the lower hall and upstairs, where his steps were muffled in fallen plaster. All the way he counted aloud. Numbers had a sudden and enormous significance. Margery's bed was full of broken glass, cumbered with wreckage of the window-sash. He stripped a blanket from his own bed and passed into Mum's room. Mum's big eiderdown was there on the bed. Her room faced south, and the window-glass had all blown out into the street. A gust of chill air came through the empty frame, and the bedroom door slammed shockingly. The interior doors had been open at the time of the great blast, and had suffered little injury. The slam gave James a sudden feeling of suffocation and made his heart beat terribly. He went to the door quickly and twisted the handle. It came away in his hand, and the handle on the other side fell with a sharp thud, taking the shaft with it. "Hundred-'n-ten, hundred-'n-'leven." James dropped his burden and tried to force back the catch with bits of wood. They splintered and broke, without accomplishment. Outside, old Mrs. Cameron was calling, "James! James!" her voice very loud in the awful silence. Fear came to James in a rush. He fancied that sidelong earthquake again, and the big brown house tumbling into the street, a bundle of toothpicks, as Mr. Cameron had said about the houses up

Richmond way. He went to the window, and debated throwing the blankets into the street and jumping after them. It looked a terrible distance down there. Mrs. Cameron caught sight of him staring down at her, and waved her arms awkwardly and shouted. She had a blanket under each arm, a loaf of bread in one hand and a pot of jam in the other. Inspiration came to James at last. Dad's rifle kit. In the bottom drawer in Mum's big chiffonier. He snatched out the drawer, brought forth a tiny screwdriver, prised back the catch with it. Freedom! He came down the stairs in four leaps, dragging blanket and eiderdown, and was out in the street, sucking in an enormous breath. Old Mrs. Cameron scolded. "I thought you were never coming, James. You should have counted."

"I couldn't get out," James said. The breeze felt very cold on his brow. He put up a hand and wiped big drops of perspiration. As they approached the field again James stopped suddenly. "I forgot to get something to eat." He was very close to tears. Old Mrs. Cameron pulled at his arm. "I have bread and jam," she said. Mum and Margery were standing on the little wooden raft in the snow. Mum clutched James against her, and held him there a long time. It was two o'clock in the afternoon.

At half-past three an olive-green truck appeared from the city, stopped in the road by the field. Soldiers came. "Any badly injured here?" There were none. All the people in the field had walked there unaided. Most of them were bandaged roughly, but nobody wanted to go to the hospital. The hospital was in the city, too near that ominous pillar of smoke. Somebody said so. A soldier said, "It's all right now. You'd better go back to your homes. You'll freeze here. The magazine's all right. Some sailors went in and turned the cocks and flooded it." The truck roared away towards the city again. People stood looking at each other, with many side-glances at the smoke over burning Richmond. The old white-haired man wandered among them, shaking his bony fists at the smoke, a fierce exultation in his long face. "Woe unto ye, Sodom and Gomorrah! Alas, alas for Babylon, that mighty city! she shall be a heap." Old Mrs. Cameron muttered, "God have mercy." The girl with the rouge spots said, "You're getting your cities mixed, old man." A man cried, "Better to burn than freeze," and shouldering his bundle, walked off in the direction of the city, whistling "Tipperary." A few bold ones followed him. Then people began to move out of the field into the road in groups, walking slowly, cautiously, towards the city. The old man went with them, crying out in his wild voice. Nobody paid any attention.

Mum, James, and Margery got home at half-past four in the afternoon. Mr. Cameron was standing outside his house, staring up at the sky. The sunshine had vanished. The sky had turned grey, like steel. "It's going to snow," he said.

Mum said, "We'll have to spend the night in the kitchen." James looked at the kitchen stove-pipe. It was all right. He put coal on the faithful fire, and got the coal shovel out of the cellar and began to scoop plaster and broken glass from the kitchen floor, throwing it out into the snow. He counted the shovelfuls. There were seventy-five. "There's an awful lot of plaster in a room," Margery observed. Mum took a broom and swept up the fine stuff that escaped James' big shovel. They looked at the yawning window-frames. "That old storm-window," James said suddenly. "It's still in the cellar." They carried it up to the kitchen, and Mum and Margery steadied it while James mounted a table and drove nails to hold it in place of the vanished west window. It was meant to go on outside, of course, but there was no ladder, and it was terribly heavy. "We must have something to cover the other window," Mum said. They stared at each other. The people in the field had said you could not get glass or tarpaper in the city for love or money. James said, "The lumber—back in the field." Mum thought for a moment. "That lumber's gone by now, James. Besides, you couldn't carry a board all that way." They gathered up the living-room carpet, tugging it from under the tumbled furniture and shaking it clean of plaster. They folded it double and nailed it over the north window-frame on the inside, and James stuffed the gaps between nails with dish-cloths and towels. There were two doors to the kitchen. The one opening into the lower hall had been open at the time of the explosion, and was unhurt. The other, opening into the shattered scullery, had been blown bodily off its lock and hinges. Mum and James pushed it back into place and wedged it there tightly with pieces of wood. "The snow will drift into the house everywhere," Mum said. "But we can't help that." James nodded soberly. "The water-pipes are going to freeze and burst." They debated nailing a carpet over the bathroom window. Finally Mum said, "The hall stove is out and the stove-pipe is down. The pipes will freeze whether we cover the windows or not. We must let the taps run and hope for the best. We can get help in the morning, I hope. Tonight it's everyone for himself."

Through the makeshift storm-window they could see snow falling rapidly in the winter dusk. Mum made tea, and they ate bread and butter hungrily by the light of a candle. The stove created a halo of warmth about itself, but the rising wind began to whistle through the impromptu window coverings. Margery said, "Couldn't we go somewhere for the night?" Mum shook her head. "Everybody's in the same mess," James said. "Lots of the houses looked worse than ours." Mum looked at the fingers of fine snow that were growing along the kitchen floor under the windows. "We must keep the stove going, James." James carried chairs from the living-room, grouped them close about the stove, and stuffed a towel into the crack under the hall door. The candle on the kitchen table guttered blue in the cross draught from the windows. "Thirteen hours before we see daylight again," Mum whispered, as if to herself.

There was a knocking. James opened the hall door carefully, and saw the dim figure of a soldier framed in the front doorway, rapping knuckles against the splintered jamb. "Does James Gordon live here?" Mum stepped into the hall, shielding the candle with her hand. "Colonel James Gordon lives here. But he's—away, just now." The dim figure lifted a hand in a perfunctory salute. "I mean young James Gordon that goes to the big brick school down the street." James stepped forward, but Mum caught his shoulder firmly. "What do you want with James?" The soldier made as if to salute again, but took off his fur hat and ducked his head instead. He was a young man with a uniform far too big for him, and a long solemn face, rather sheep-like in the candle-light. "We—the sergeant, I mean—has been sent up to this here school for a— well, a special kinda job, ma'am. The awf'cer telephoned to the head schoolmaster's house. He lives 'way down in the city somewheres, but he said there was a boy named James Gordon lived handy the school an' would show us how to get in the basement, an' all like that."

James moved quickly, and Mum's hand slipped from his shoulder and fell to her side. "I won't be long, Mum." The soldier mumbled, "It's only a coupla hundred yards." Mum said, "Put on your coat and overshoes, James."

It was pitch dark, and the night was thick with snow. James led the way. The soldier plodded silently behind him. It was strange to be going to school at night, and the great silent building seemed very grim and awful with its long rows of black window-holes. A dark blur in the main doorway disintegrated, came towards them. Four men in fur hats and long flapping overcoats. Soldiers. "You find the kid, Mac?" James' soldier said, "Yeah. This is him. Where's the sergeant?" One man waved a vague arm at the dim bulk of the school. "Scoutin' around in there some-wheres, lightin' matches. Tryin' to find the basement door." James said, "Which door do you want? You can get in the basement from the street if you like."

"Ah," grunted the second soldier; "that's the ticket, son."

A tiny point of light appeared within the school, flickered down the stairs. James wondered why the sergeant looked upstairs for a basement door. A stout figure, muffled in a khaki greatcoat, was revealed behind the feeble flame of the match. The sergeant came out into the snow, swearing into a turned-up collar. With the shapeless fur hat on his head he looked strangely like a bear roused out of a winter den. "Here's the kid, Sarge." The sergeant regarded him. "Hello, son." James pointed. "The basement door is around there." He showed them. The door had been blown off its hinges and wedged, a bundle of twisted wood, in the frame. They pulled at the splintered wood stoutly, and the doorway was clear. On the basement steps the sergeant lit another match. Their voices echoed strangely in that murky cavern.

James knew them now for soldiers of the Composite Battalion, made up of detachments from various home-guard units. They wore the clumsy brown fur hats and hideous red rubber galoshes that were issued to the home guard for winter wear. Some people called them 'The Safety Firsts'; and it was common for cheeky boys to hurl snowballs after their patrols from the shadow of alleyways, chanting—

"Com-Po-Zite!

They won't fight!"

Mum had cautioned James against such pleasantry. Somebody had to stay at home, and these men were mostly physical unfits, rejected by the overseas regiments.

"Big as all Hell," declared the sergeant, after a tour of the echoing basement. "Hold a thousand, easy." The soldiers said, "Yeah." The sergeant fumbled in the big pocket of his greatcoat and brought forth a dark bottle. He took a long swig, wiped his moustache with a sweep of mittened hand, and passed the bottle around. "Gonna be a cold job," he rumbled. "All the windows gone, an' snow blowin' in everywheres.

Concrete floor, too." The sheep-faced soldier said, "What-say we tear up some floorboards upstairs an' cover some of these cellar winders?" The sergeant spat, with noise. "They gotta send up a workin' party from the Engineers if they want that done. We got dirty work enough." The soldiers nodded their hats again, and said "Yeah" and "Betcha life."

Wind swirled through the gloomy basement in icy gusts. The men leaned against the wall, huddled in their greatcoats, cigarettes glowing in the darkness. James walked up the concrete steps to street level and stood inside the doorway, staring into the snowy dark. He wondered how long he was supposed to stay. A glow-worm appeared down the street, a feeble thing that swam slowly through the whirl of snow towards the school. James experienced a sudden twinge of fright. There was a great white shape behind it. Then a voice from the darkness above that ghostly shape: "Hulloa!" James cleared his throat. "Hulloa!" A man rode up to the doorway on a white horse. A lantern dangled from the horse's neck, like a luminous bell. The rider leaned over, and a face became visible in the pale glow. He was a detective of the city police, and James recognized his mount as one of the pair that used to pull the Black Maria in the days before the war. He was riding bare-back, feet hanging down, and the big policeman looked very odd, perched up there. "Anyone else around, son?" James jerked his head towards the black hole of the basement entrance. "Some soldiers. Down there, sir. Do you want them?" The policeman turned his horse awkwardly. "Just tell 'em the first wagon will be right along." He kicked the glistening side of his mount and disappeared as silently as he had come, lantern a-swing. James shouted the message down into the darkness. "Okay!" There was a lull in the wind, and the bottle gurgled in the sudden stillness.

Another glow-worm came, as silent as the first. But as it turned in towards the school James caught a faint rattle of wheels, and a hoarse voice bellowed, "Whoa-hoa!" The soldiers came stumbling up the steps in the darkness, and James went with them towards the light. It was a wagon, one of the low drays that clattered along Water Street from morn to night. A man climbed stiffly from the seat. He was crusted with snow, even to his moustache and eyebrows. "Let's have the lantern, fella," demanded the sergeant. They walked to the back of the wagon, and the sheep-faced soldier held the lantern high while the sergeant whipped a long tarpaulin from the mysterious freight.

"Niggers!" rumbled the sergeant loudly. James, peering between the soldiers in astonishment, beheld six figures lying side by side on the dray: three men, two women, and a young girl. They were stiff and impassive, like the dummies you saw in shop windows. The women had dirty rags of cotton dress. One of the men wore a pair of trousers. The rest were naked. Ebony flesh gleamed in the lantern light. The snowflakes drifted lightly on the calm up-turned faces. Their eyes were closed, hands lay easily at their sides, as if they were content to sleep there, naked to the storm. "Looka!" called the sheep-faced soldier. "They bin hit, Sarge. But there's no blood!" The sergeant stooped over for a better look. Two of the dark faces were scored deeply, as if some vandal had gouged wax from the dummies with a chisel. "Concussion," announced the sergeant with immense assurance. "That's what. Drives the blood inwards. They was dead before they got hit. That boat went to pieces like shrapnel." He called it "sharpnel."

The teamster was complaining. "... get a move on, you guys. This snow gets much deeper I gotta go back to the barn an' shift to sleds. There's work to do." Two of the soldiers picked up a dummy by head and feet, carried it awkwardly down the basement steps, and dropped it. There was a dull 'flap' when it struck the concrete. They came up the steps quickly. "Froze?" asked Sarge. "Stiff as a board," they said. The wagon was cleared of its silent passengers and went away into the night. The sergeant struck matches while the men arranged the bodies in a neat row. "Once," a soldier said, "I worked in a meat packin' plant. In T'ronta, that was."

"Well," Sarge rumbled, "you're keeping your hand in."

Another lantern swam up the street. Another dray. More silent figures under the tarpaulin. White people this time. A man and four young women, nude, flesh gleaming like marble in the lantern light. There was blood, a lot of it, dried black like old paint. "Musta bin farther away," observed the sergeant. "Them niggers was from Africville, right by the place she went off." T'ronta said curiously, "Funny, them bein' stripped this way. Was their clo'es blowed off, would you say?" The teamster shook his head. "Nuh. These was all pulled outa the wreckage by the troops this afternoon. Clo'es caught an' tore off, I guess. Besides, lotsa people sleeps late winter mornin's. Prob'ly didn't have much on, anyway." More wagons. The intervals diminished. The sheep-faced soldier said, "The awf'cer's forgot us. We oughta bin relieved by now." "Quit beefin'," said Sarge. "All troops is up Richmond way, pullin' stiffs outa the wreckage, huntin' for livin' ones. If it's okay for them it's okay for us." A teamster gave them a spare lantern which they stood on the basement floor, and in the fitful glow of that lonely thing the dummies lay in orderly rows, toes up, faces towards the dim ceiling. The shadows of the soldiers performed a grotesque dance on the walls as they went about their work. Sarge pulled something from his greatcoat pocket, and James gave it a sidewise glance, expecting to see the bottle. Sarge thrust it back into the pocket again, but James had seen the silver figure of a baseball pitcher, and knew it had been wrenched from the big cup his school had won last summer. He said nothing. Sarge said, "You still here, son? We don't need you no more. Better go home."

Mum greeted James anxiously in the candle-lit kitchen. "How pale you are, James! What did they want? You've been gone three hours." James looked at the stove. "Nothing. Nothing much, Mum. I guess they—just wanted to fix up the school a bit." They sat in the cushioned chairs, huddling over the stove. Margery had her feet in the oven. James went upstairs and brought down blankets, and they muffled themselves up in the chairs. Mum said, "Don't you want something to eat, James? There's tea on the stove, and there's bread and butter." "Not hungry," James said in a low voice.

It was a long night. James had never known a night could be so long. Sometimes you would doze a little, and you would see the faces of the dead people on the drays as plain as anything. Then you would wake up with a start and find yourself sliding off the chair, and feeling terribly cold. Several times he took the hod and the candle down into the cellar and brought up more coal. When the candles burned down to the table he lit new ones and stuck them in the hot grease. After a while there was a pool of grease on the table, hard and wrinkled and dirty-white, like frozen slush in the street. Draughts came through the window-covers and under both doors, like invisible fingers of ice, and you had to keep your feet hooked in the rung of your chair, off the floor. The candles gave a thin blue light and made a continual fluttering sound, like the wings of a caged bird. Sometimes the house shook in the gusts, and twice James had to climb on the table and hammer more nails to keep the carpet in place. Snow drifted in between the carpet and the window-frame, and formed thin white dunes along the floor next the wall. The heat thrown off by the kitchen stove was lost between the bare laths of the walls and ceiling.

"There must be a lot of dead, poor souls," Mum said.

"Yes," James said.

"In the morning, James, you must go to the telegraph office and send a cable to your father. He'll be frantic."

"Yes," James said.

Mum had washed the blood from her face and tied a clean rag of bedsheet over the cuts on her forehead. James thought she looked very white and hollow, somehow. But when he looked in her eyes there was something warm and strong in them that made him feel better. When you looked in Mum's eyes you felt that everything was all right. Margery had drawn a blanket over her head, like a hood, and her head was bent, hidden in the shadow. Mum said, "Are you awake, Margery?"

"Yes," Margery said quickly.

"Are you all right?"

"Yes."

"It will be morning soon," Mum said.

But it was a long time. They sat, stiff and cramped, over the stove, and listened to the snow sweeping into the rooms upstairs, and the flap-flap of broken laths, and blinds blowing to rags in the empty window-frames; and the night seemed to go on for ever, as though the world had come to a dark end and the sun would never come back again. James thought of Sarge, and the sheep-faced man, and T'ronta, carrying frozen dummies into the school basement, and wondered if the awf'cer had remembered them. Daylight crept through the storm-window at last, a poor grey thing that gave a bleak look to everything in the kitchen. Stove, blankets—nothing could ward off the cold then. The grey light seemed to freeze everything it touched. Outside, the snow still swept fiercely against the carpet and the glass. James found potatoes in the cellar, and rescued bacon and eggs from the wreck of the pantry. Mum brushed the snow and bits of plaster from the bacon and put it in a frying-pan. It smelt good.

The telegraph office was full of people waving bits of scribbled paper. The ruins of plate-glass windows had been shovelled out into the street, and the frames boarded up. Outside, a newsboy was selling papers turned out by some miracle on battered presses in the night. They consisted of a single sheet, with "HALIFAX IN RUINS" in four-inch letters at the top. Within the telegraph office, lamps cast a yellow glow. There was a great buzz of voices and the busy clack-clack of instruments. James had to wait a long time in the line that shuffled past the counter. A broad cheerful face greeted him at last.

"What's yours, son?"

"I want to send a cable to Colonel James Gordon, in France."

The man leaned over the counter and took a better look at him. "Hello! Are you Jim Gordon's son? So you are. I'd know that chin anywhere. How old are you, son?"

"Four—going on fifteen," James said.

"Soon be old enough to fight, eh? What's your Dad's regiment?"

James paused. "That'll cost extra, won't it?" he suggested shrewdly. "Everybody in the army knows my father."

The man smiled. "Sure," he agreed reasonably. "But France is a big place, son. It's their misfortune, of course, but there's probably a lot of people in France don't know your Dad."

James said, "It's the Ninetieth."

"Ah, of course. Jim Gordon of the Ninetieth. There's an outfit will keep old Hindenburg awake nights, son, and don't you forget it. What'd you want to say?"

James placed both hands on the counter. "Just this: 'All's well. James Gordon.' That's all."

The man wrote it down, and looked up quickly. "All's well? That counts three words, son, at twenty-five cents a word. Why not just, "All well?"

James put his chin up. "No. 'All's well.' Send it like that."

J.G. Sime

JESSIE GEORGINA SIME (1863–1958), novelist, essayist, and lecturer, was born in Scotland and educated in England and Germany. She visited Canada as a tourist in 1907. Although she continued to travel extensively, Montreal became her permanent home. A feminist with an independent income, she devoted herself to commenting on the lives of Canadian women, particularly in comparison with those of men. Her pamphlet *The Mistress of All Work* (1916) was a pioneer discussion of the strategies that women must employ in order to combine domesticity and a career. "Munitions!" appeared in her short story collection, *Sister Woman* (1919).

The story contrasts the imprisoning routine existence of a society woman and her female servants in an "Upstairs, Downstairs" establishment in Montreal with the free, exuberant life of factory women who, because of the war, are admitted into a man's domain. Munitions factories were uncomfortable and dangerous workplaces where women risked explosions, fires, disease and accidents with machinery. As well, the powder used in making explosives caused pernicious anemia, signalled by yellow skin. Canadian production concentrated on artillery ammunition, totalling 66 million shells by the end of the war.

Suffragettes supported the idea of getting women into factories, demanding that they be paid at the same rate as men. The male-dominated labour movement opposed the employment of women, fearing (wrongly) that, because their wages were lower, they would continue to replace men when the war ended. A positive effect of women's war work was the granting of votes to women. In 1916 women in

Manitoba, Saskatchewan and Alberta won the right to vote and hold office provincially; British Columbia and Ontario followed in 1917. On May 24, 1918, all female citizens aged twenty-one and over were enfranchised federally.

Munitions!

BERTHA MARTIN SAT IN THE STREET CAR IN THE early morning going to her work. Her work was munitions. She had been at it exactly five weeks.

She sat squeezed up into a corner, just holding on to her seat and no more, and all round her were women and girls also working at munitions—loud, noisy, for ever talking—extraordinarily happy. They sat there filling the car with their two compact rows, pressed together, almost in one another's laps, joking, chewing tobacco—flinging the chewed stuff about.

It wasn't in the least that they were what is technically known as "bad women." Oh no—no! If you thought that, you would mistake them utterly. They were decent women, good, self-respecting girls, for the most part "straight girls"—with a black sheep here and there, to be sure, but where aren't there black sheep here and there? And the reason they made a row and shrieked with laughter and cracked an unseemly jest or two was simply that they were turned loose. They had spent their lives caged, most of them, in shop or house, and now they were drunk with the open air and the greater freedom and the sudden liberty to do as the liked and damn whoever stopped them.

Bertha Martin looked round at her companions. She saw the all sorts that make the world. Here and there was a pretty, young, flushed face, talking—talking—trying to express something it felt inside and couldn't get out. And here and there Bertha Martin saw an older face, a face with a knowledge of the world in it and that something that comes into a woman's eyes if certain things happen to her, and never goes out of them again. And then Bertha Martin saw quite elderly women, or so they seemed to her—women of forty or so, decent bodies, working for some-one besides themselves—they had it written on their faces; and she saw old women—old as working women go—fifty and more, sitting there with their long working lives behind them and their short ones in front. And now and then some woman would draw her snuff-box from her shirt-waist and it would pass up and down the line and they would all take great pinches of the brown, pungent powder and stuff it up their noses—and laugh and laugh .... Bertha Martin looked round the car and she couldn't believe it was she who was sitting in it.

It was the very early spring. The white March sunshine came streaming into the car, and when Bertha, squeezed sideways in her corner, looked through the window, she saw the melting snow everywhere— piles and piles of it uncleared because the men whose job it was to clear it were at the war. She saw walls of snow by the sides of the streets—they went stretching out into infinity. And the car went swinging and lurching between them, out through the city and into the country where the factory was. There were puddles and little lakes of water everywhere; winter was melting away before the birth of another spring.

Bertha looked. She looked up into the clear—into the crystal clearness of the morning sky. It was the time of the spring skies of Canada—wonderful, delicate, diaphanous skies that come every spring to the Northern Land—skies the colour of bluebells and primroses—transparent, translucent, marvellously beautiful. Bertha looked up into the haze of colour—and she smiled. And then she wondered why she smiled.

It was the very early springtime.

Just five weeks before and Bertha had been a well-trained servant in a well-kept, intensely self-respecting house—a house where no footfall was heard on the soft, long-piled rugs; where the lights were shaded and the curtains were all drawn at night; where the mistress lay late in bed and "ordered" things; where life was put to bed every night with hot bottles to its feet; where no one ever spoke of anything that mattered; where meals were paramount. There had Bertha Martin lived five long, comfortable years.

She had gone about her business capably. She had worn her uniform like any soldier—a white frock in the mornings and a cap upon her head, and her hair had been orderly, her apron accurately tied. She had been clean. There were no spring skies in sight—or else she had not looked to see them. She had got up—not too unreasonably early—had had her early morning cup of tea with the other servants, had set the dining-room breakfast, waited on it—quiet—respectful—as self-respecting as the house. And in the afternoons there she had been in her neat black gown with her cap and apron immaculate—her hair still orderly and unobtrusive—everything about her, inside and out, still self-respecting and respectful. She had "waited on table," cleaned silver, served tea, carried things everlastingly in and out, set them on tables, taken them off again, washed them, put them away, taken them out again, reset tables with them—it was a circular game with never any end to it. And she had done it well. "Martin is an excellent servant," she had heard the lady of the house say once. "I can trust her thoroughly."

One afternoon in the week she went out. At a certain hour she left the house; at another certain hour she came back again. If she was half-an-hour late she was liable to be questioned: "Why?" And when she had given her explanation then she would hear the inevitable "Don't let it occur again." And Sunday—every other Sunday—there was the half day, also at certain hours. Of course—how otherwise could a well-run house *be* well run? And down in the kitchen the maids would dispute as to whether you got out half-an-hour sooner last time and so must go half-an-hour later this—they would quarrel and squabble over the silliest little things. Their horizon was so infinitesimally small, and they were so much too comfortable—they ate so much too much and they did so far too little—what could they do but squabble? They were never all on speaking-terms at one time together. Either the old cook was taking the housemaid's part or she and the housemaid were at daggers drawn; and they all said the same things over and over and over again—to desperation.

Bertha Martin looked up at the exquisite sky—and she smiled. The sun came streaming in, and the girls and women talked and jabbered and snuffed and chewed their tobacco and spat it out. And sometimes when the car conductor put his head in at the door they greeted him with a storm of chaff—a hail of witticisms—a tornado of personalities. And the little French-Canadian, overpowered by numbers, would never even try to break a lance with them. He would smile and shrug and put his hand up to his ears and run the door back between himself and them. And the women would laugh and clap their hands and stamp with their feet and call things to him—shout ….

Bertha turned to the girl next her—nearly atop of her—and looked her over. She was a fragile-looking, indoors creature—saleslady was written all over her—with soft rings of fair curled hair on her temples, and a weak, smiling mouth, and little useless feet in her cheap, high-heeled pumps. She was looking intently at a great strap of a girl opposite, with a great mouth on her, out of which was reeling a broad story.

"My, ain't she the girl?" said Bertha's little neighbour; and with the woman's inevitable gesture, she put her two hands up to her hair behind, and felt, and took a hairpin out here and there and put it in again.

She turned to Bertha.

"Say, ain't she the girl alright? Did you hear?"

Bertha nodded.

The little indoors thing turned and glanced at Bertha—took her in from head to foot with one feminine look.

"You gittin' on?" she said.

"Fine!" said Bertha.

The eyes of the women met. They smiled at one another. Fellow-workers—out in the world together. That's what their eyes said: Free! And then the little creature turned away from Bertha—bent forward eagerly. Another of the stories was coming streaming out.

"Ssh! ... ssh!" cried some of the older women. But their voices were drowned in the sea of laughter as the climax took possession of the car. The women rocked and swayed—they clutched each other—they shrieked.

"Where's the harm?" the big strap cried.

Five weeks ago and Bertha had never heard a joke like that. Five weeks ago she would hardly have taken in the utter meaning of that climax. Now! Something in her ticked—something went beating. She smiled—not at the indecency, not at the humour. What Bertha smiled at was the sense of liberty it gave her. She could hear stories if she liked. She could *act* stories if she liked. She was earning money—good money—she was capable and strong. Yes, she was strong, not fragile like the little thing beside her, but a big, strong girl—twenty-four—a woman grown—alive.

It seemed a long, dim time ago when all of them sat round that kitchen table to their stated meals at stated hours. Good, ample, comfortable meals. Plenty of time to eat them. No trouble getting them—that was the cook's affair—just far too much to eat and too much time too eat it in. Nothing to think about. Inertia. A comfortable place. What an age ago it seemed! And yet she had expected to spend her life like that—till she married someone! She never would have thought of "giving in her notice" if it hadn't been for Nellie Ford. How well Bertha remembered it—that Sunday she met Nellie—and Nellie flushed, with shining eyes.

"I'm leaving," Nellie had said to her. "I'm leaving—for the factory!"

And Bertha had stopped, bereft of words.

"*The factory* …!" she had said. That day the factory had sounded like the bottomless pit. "The factory …!"

"Come on," Nellie had said, "come on—it's fine out there. You make good money. Give in your notice—it's the life."

And Bertha had listened helplessly, feeling the ground slipping.

"But, Nellie—" she kept saying.

"It's the life," Nellie had kept reiterating; "it's the life, I tell you. Come on, Bert, *sure* it's the life. Come on—it's great out there. We'll room together if you'll come."

Then Nellie had told her hurriedly, brokenly, as they walked along that Sunday afternoon, all that she knew about the factory. What Agnes Dewie, that was maid to Lady Something once—what *she* said. "It was great!" That's what she said. "Liberty," said Agnes Dewie, "a room you paid for, good money, disrespect to everything, nothing above you—freedom …."

Nellie had panted this out to Bertha. "Come on, come *on*, Bert," she had said; "it's time we lived."

And slowly the infection had seized on Bertha. The fever touched her blood—ran through it. Her mental temperature flew up. She was a big girl, a slow-grower, young for her years, with a girl's feelings in her woman's body. But Nellie Ford had touched the spring of life in her. After that Sunday when Bertha looked round the quiet, self-respecting house—she hated it. She hated the softness of it—the quietness—hated the very comfort. What did all these things matter? Nellie Ford had said: "It's time we *lived* …."

Bertha gazed upward through the window of the car—twisted and turned so that she could look right into the morning blue. The car was clear of city life. It sped along a country road. Fields were on either side, and only now and then a solitary house. Great trees stretched out bare branches.

Then in that far-off little life came the giving in of the notice. Bertha remembered the old cook's sour face—that old sour face past every hope of life and living. Could one grow to look like that? Can such things be? "You'll live to rue the day, my lady!" said the cook. And Bertha remembered how the lady at the head of things had said: "Do you realize that you'll *regret* leaving a good place like this?" And then, more acidly: "I wouldn't have believed it of you, Martin." And as she turned to go: "If you choose to reconsider—"

Regret! Reconsider! Never again would she hear bells and have to answer them. Never again would she hear someone say to her: "Take tea into the library, Martin." Never again need she say: "Yes, ma'am." Think of it! Bertha smiled. The sun came streaming in on her—she smiled.

Liberty! Liberty to work the whole day long—ten hours at five and twenty cents an hour—in noise and grime and wet. Damp floors to walk on. Noise—distracting noise all round one. No room to turn or breathe. No time to stop. And then at lunch-time no ample comfortable meal— some little hurried lunch of something you brought with you. Hard work. Long hours. Discomfort. Strain. That was about the sum of it, of all that she had gained ... but then, the sense of freedom! The joy of being done with cap and apron. The feeling that you could draw your breath—speak as you liked—wear overalls like men—curse if you wanted to.

Oh, the relief of it! The going home at night, dead-tired, to where you had your room. Your own! The poor, ill-cooked suppers—what a taste to them! The deep, dreamless sleep. And Sunday—if you ever got a Sunday off—when you could lie abed, no one to hunt you up, no one to call you names and quarrel with you. Just Nellie there.

What did it matter if you had no time to stop or think or be? What did anything matter if life went pulsing through you amidst dirt and noise and grime? The old life—that treading round with brush and dust-pan— that making yourself noiseless with a duster: "Martin, see you dust well *beneath* the bed." "Yes, ma'am." And now the factory! A new life with other women working round you—bare-armed—grimy—roughened— unrestrained. What a change! What a sense of broadening out! What ...!

Bertha Martin smiled. She smiled so that a woman opposite smiled back at her; and then she realized that she was smiling. She felt life streaming to her very finger-tips. She felt the spring pass through her being—insistent and creative. She felt her blood speak to her—say things it never said when she was walking softly in the well-ordered house she helped to keep for five long, comfortable years. "Selfish to leave me." That was what the lady of the house had said to her. "Selfish—you're all selfish. You think of nothing but yourselves."

Well—why not? What if that were true? Let it go anyway. That half-dead life was there behind … and Bertha Martin looked out at present. The car went scudding in the country road. There was the Factory—the Factory, with its coarse, strong, beckoning life—its noise—its dirt—its men.

Its men! And Suddenly into Bertha Martin's cheek a wave of colour surged. Yesterday—was it yesterday?—that man had caught her strong, round arm as she was passing him—and held it.

Her breath came short. She felt a throbbing. She stopped smiling—and her eyes grew large.

It was the very early spring.

Then suddenly the flock of women rose—felt in the bosoms of their shirt-waists for their cigarettes and matches—surged to the door—talking—laughing—pushing one another—the older ones expostulating.

And, massed together in the slushy road, they stood, lighting up, passing their matches round—happy—noisy—fluttered—not knowing what to do with all the life that kept on surging up and breaking in them—waves of it—wave on wave. Willingly would they have fought their way to the Munitions Factory. If they had known the *Carmagnole* they would have danced it in the melting snow ….

It was the spring.

George Reid Clifford

ACCORDING TO I.F.H., the unknown writer of the
Foreword to *My Experiences as an Aviator in the World War*, George Reid Clifford
was born in Scotland where at the age of fifteen he began his apprenticeship as a
marine engineer. After emigrating to Canada, he worked in engineering firms and
an automobile factory. He also took flying lessons in Toronto, qualifying as an
aviator by passing examinations in telegraphy, photography, codes, bombing, map
reading and drawing, and by completing fifty hours of solo flying. This training
qualified him to enlist in the Royal Flying Corps where his first job was ferrying new
planes to France at an altitude of one thousand feet and bringing back damaged
ones. Then he became a Captain in the Independent Air Squadron of the Royal Air
Force, joining the Canadian fighter pilots described as "aces" because they had
shot down thirty or more enemy planes. Clifford brought down forty-two, winning a
total of eight medals including the DSO, MC and DFC. Canada's top ace, Major
W.A. Bishop, was credited with seventy-two, the highest total in the Royal Air Force.
The war's supreme ace, and Clifford's chief enemy, was Baron Manfred
Von Richthofen—the Red Baron—who was credited with eighty planes before being
killed during a dogfight on April 21, 1918 by a Canadian, Captain A.R. Brown.

Only five years before the outbreak of the Great War, on February 23, 1909 near
Baddeck, Cape Breton, John A.D. McCurdy had made the first flight by a British
subject to be recorded in the British Empire in a heavier-than-air engine-propelled
machine. His plane, the Silver Dart, consisted of two fabric-covered wings with a
flap, a gasoline engine, a propeller that had to be started up by an assistant, a chair,

a rudder and three wire wheels inside bicycle tires. The planes that were being used for aerial combat by 1916 had wooden frames (largely handmade from spruce), hand-sewn fabric on the wings, a rotary or stationary engine cooled by liquid or air and a fixed machine gun that fired through the propeller. Easily damaged by fire, wind, bullets, excessive speed and rough landings, the life of the plane—not to mention the pilot—was usually short. According to Leslie Roberts in *There Shall Be Wings* (1959), "more Canadians were expert in the art of flight, in proportion to the national census, than were the citizens of any country among the Allies." This was one reason for choosing Canada as the site for the British Commonwealth Air Training Plan which began in 1941. Distance from the war zones, the nature of the landscape and nearness to American airplane factories were important factors as well.

The Foreword writer describes the ace as "daring almost to a point of recklessness, unselfish as shown many times when wearied almost to a point of exhaustion by taking the place of another incapacitated; generous, often doing without himself in order to give to others less fortunate. Modest, objecting always to having his remarkable exploits made public." Clifford is not mentioned in accounts of Great War aerial warfare. The library of the Imperial War Museum, London classifies *My Experiences as an Aviator in the World War* (1928) as Canadian fiction. Erroneous details in this account range from the number of kills required to qualify as an ace to the disposal of damaged planes. Still, the selection reveals the strategies of early aerial warfare and the enthusiasm with which Canadian pilots confronted the legendary Red Baron.

George and the Red Baron

THE ALLIES WERE NOW PREPARING FOR THE BIG offensive. Every class of fighting machines was massed around the Arras and Vimy sectors. The bombing Squadrons were out day and night. They would fly over the lines and drop tons of high explosives wherever it was considered that the resulting damage would have a crippling effect upon the defensive power of the German army. Our photographers were kept busy every hour of the sunlight, taking photographs of the German positions.

Every chance we had we went out in search of a fight. Strange to say, on those occasions the Germans always kept away from us. One morning bright and early, we went out; the sun was just rising and the sky was glorious to behold. We started about five o'clock, eight of us. I was in command and we were flying in perfect formation. I was leading the Squadron about one hundred yards ahead, always keeping an eye on it so as not to get too far ahead, for as Flight Commander I had the fastest machine. We had been in the air for about two hours, and I was about to give the signal to turn for home, when I saw straight ahead of me twelve machines painted a brilliant scarlet. My heart almost sank, for I had orders not to engage this particular Squadron if I could possibly avoid it, as it was commanded by the famous German flier, Captain Baron Von Richtofen, whom I had met before in a desperate battle and escaped from him only by a miracle. His Squadron was made up of twelve Pilots of undeniable skill. They flew single-seated machines. These red machines carried two machine guns in fixed positions, firing straight ahead, both being operated by the same control and much superior to ours.

But I forgot all about orders and gave the signal to attack. In less time than it takes to tell it they were upon us. As is always the case when one Squadron attacks another, each Flight Commander separates from the others and they have it out between them. The Baron was a relentless fighter. He made at me savagely, firing both guns as he came on. I contented myself with dodging him and saving my ammunition. I also had two machine guns on my machine, capable of firing nine hundred shots to the minute. I was fighting on the defensive when I turned on him suddenly and raked him from every direction. He must have been more than surprised, for his offensive quickly turned to the defensive and before he knew where he was I had almost shot him out of control. His manoeuvres were so skillful that he completely fooled me, and headed for home.

It must have been great humiliation for him, but he did the same to me a few weeks later. On my return to gain my Squadron I found myself mixed up with another two of the Baron's Squadron. I instantly engaged them in combat, and to my great relief found one of my own Squadron by my side. Evidently they were not anxious for a fight, for after a few minutes manoeuvering both broke away and headed for their own lines. On my way home I spotted another of the Baron's Pilots and made for him. I was a little above and dived at him; however, he was a bit too smart for me, for he dived into a cloud and escaped ...

I will tell about some more of my encounters in the air with Baron Von Richtofen. There was only one thing I had against Richtofen, and that was that he and his red devils were the first to use what was known as flaming bullets, which were as bad as the dun dun bullets which the civilized world objected to. The dun dun bullets when they hit used to expand and make a wound worse than a shrapnel wound, and their flaming bullets when they struck an object used to burn the object that it struck. Anyone can imagine how they would feel if a red hot iron was thrust into a sore place on their body. I was fortunate enough to have only one of those bullets hit me once, but not severely, and I fought Richtofen until I had not a shot left in my machine gun or a shot in my revolver, and then went at him head on in a desperate effort to lock both machines, well knowing that if we ever happened to come together it would mean certain death for both of us, for we generally fought anywhere between 12,000 and 14,000 feet in the air. I never once did give way to the red devil. He always gave way to me and made for home, and I have no doubt that he was as thankful as I was to be rid of each other for the time being.

To tell the truth, I dreaded the Baron and his red devils. There are lots of the boys that are alive today that were in the trenches when those red devils broke through. One Squadron remembers the havoc they wrought not only on the Allied gunners, but on the poor fellows lying in the trenches. The Baron flew a single-seated machine with two machine guns on it, one at his right and one at his left. These guns were capable of firing 1,200 shots to the minute and he was capable of letting go those 1,200 to the minute. As a rule when the Baron came looking for trouble with our Squadron he always got it. He would have four others with him. His four machines were two-seaters, with three machine guns on each. But when he avoided us he had under his command five huge fighting planes which were called Gothas. They were three-seated machines, with seven machine guns. The odd gun was directly behind the third man and he could turn around and blaze away at anything following him. These machines were mammoths of the air. These were the machines that later made so many successful raids over London.

I'll never forget the first time I saw one of them. When I told my comrades what I had seen, they laughed at me, but it was not long before I had the laugh on them. When we were returning to our aerodrome after a successful raid on the railways at Coblenz, near Mainz, a few days after, four of those huge Gothas and led by a little scarlet machine, hove into sight. I was flying ahead of my Squadron, but my other eight comrades must have seen them as quickly as I did. Well, I knew when I got a glimpse of that little scarlet machine who was in it, my dread enemy, the Baron Von Richtofen, but the sight of those four big machines following the little one fascinated me for a few minutes. I knew that they were returning from a raid on the front line trenches. Now, when the Baron raided the allied trenches, he and his men did it thoroughly. They would swoop down as low as two hundred feet from the ground and fly straight along the trenches at terrific speed, pouring a steady stream of lead on the poor fellows in the trenches until their ammunition was gone. Don't think for one moment that there were no Allied airmen near. The Baron was protected from above by five other German machines and they used to manouevre and throw out a few smoke bombs while the Baron was raiding the trenches and the advanced guns of the Allies.

It was quite a little while before the Allies discovered the Baron's little game, and then adopted the Baron's tactics, which proved to be successful, and a little later on I will tell you about how I beat him at his own game. The first time we made a direct hit on the Chemical factories in Karlsruhe, Germany, after we had made so many unsuccessful raids on that important part of Germany and only once did Baron Von Richtofen trick me or lead me into a trap. I was out one morning all alone. I was far inside the German lines, when suddenly a scarlet machine dashed out of the clouds and opened fire on me. Well, I knew it was the Baron Von Richtofen, as he flashed by me. I did not have time to give him a burst from my machine gun. I was about to turn my machine to go after him when I saw four machines directly ahead of me. Now that was one of the Baron's favourite tricks. He would flash by at light-ning speed all alone, and keep on going, when he knew that the pilots under his command would follow him; any machine following him would meet disaster. On this occasion if he thought so he was mistaken, for as soon as I saw the four Gothas coming towards me I said to myself, "George, discretion is the better part of valour, " and whenever that thought came into my head I beat it for home as fast as my machine would take me. However, we never had much trouble from the Gothas. That particular machine was not a real fighting machine. It was big and clumsy and hard to manouevre. It was only its superiority with its additional guns that really gave it a slight advantage over the smaller machines. When it came to a real combat, the Germans were quick to see this and soon withdrew them and kept those machines for raiding purposes. Those were the machines that made the most successful raids on England. Of course quite a few paid the price for their daring.

A few days later I was leading my patrol, which consisted of seven machines, along the German lines looking for trouble. But there were no German machines in sight, so I decided to go a little farther into German territory and find what I was after. It was not long before I got more trouble than I bargained for. Coming straight toward me were four single-seated machines, all painted a bright scarlet colour. I always carried a powerful field glass with me, so I made sure it was the Baron and his red devils that were coming towards us. Knowing his little game in flying 7,000 feet and having four or five machines two or three thousand feet above him ready to swoop down from above and take us unaware, now that was what we called a layer formation, I put the glasses to my eyes and lo and behold I made out just as I expected, four machines, painted a bright scarlet, about 2,000 feet higher and about one mile behind the Baron and his three other devils. I signalled to two of my companions to follow me, and also gave the signal to my other four comrades to fly a little higher, knowing it would not be long before they saw the remainder of the Baron's Squadron. After I was certain that all understood, my two comrades and I started for the Baron.

As I said before, we always went for each other. He always left his men in his haste to get at me, and I did the same thing. The Baron came straight for me, firing both guns at me. Before I knew where I was I had the sensation of seeing flaming bullets coming in all directions around me, but I kept cool and kept my ammunition until I was about eighty feet from him, then I let go. All of a sudden the Baron stopped firing. I'll never forget the sensation I had when he stopped firing. I thought sure I had hit him, but no—his machine gun had jammed. I could see him frantically struggling with it to try and release it, but he could not do it, so he had to break off the fight. Of course, I took advantage of his predicament and followed him, blazing away at him from every angle, but he was too smart for me, and I finally gave up the chase, much to my disgust, when I ran out of ammunition. The three others with the Baron went with him and as their Albatross scouts were much faster than ours, they soon disappeared, leaving me all alone. On looking around I saw two of my comrades succeeding in bringing one of the Baron's Gothas down, and I immediately tried to rejoin them, but by the time I reached them the big Gotha was going down in flames and the other four Gothas were too far ahead of the rest of my comrades for them to catch up with them, so we broke off the engagement and made for home.

I was a very much disgusted fellow when I reached home. I had no fewer than fourteen holes in my machine, and, worse still, to think I had the Baron at my mercy and he escaped me.

Greg Clark

GREG CLARK (1892–1977) was born in Toronto, the son of the *Toronto Star*'s editor, Joseph T. Clark. Greg began his life-long career as a newspaperman in 1911, interrupting it only for wartime service. Described as a "king-sized leprechaun," the diminutive (5'2") soldier who enlisted on March 27, 1916 received a commission within a few days, supposedly because he was too small to carry the heavy Ross rifle of an infantryman. As an officer in D Company of the Fourth Canadian Mounted Rifles, he received his baptism of fire at the Battle of Vimy Ridge, the first engagement in which all four Canadian divisions fought together.

In the spring of 1917, the British campaign on the Western Front concentrated on driving the Germans north of the Somme. The Canadian Corps, now recognized as valiant and stubborn fighters, was detailed to capture Vimy Ridge where the Germans had been strongly entrenched since 1914. Previous attempts at dislodging them had cost 200,000 casualties. At 5:30 A.M. on April 9, 30,000 Canadians went over the top and at a cost of 10,602 casualties, they conquered the site where Canada's greatest war memorial now stands. For his part in the action, Clark won the Military Cross. The following year while on the Cambrai front, he was promoted to Major and posted to Canada to become a war correspondent, a role that Armistice Day delayed for twenty years. As a Second World War correspondent he won an OBE.

The Bully

Aubrey was his name. He could have been about eight or nine years of age. I was about seven.

He would lie in wait for me on my way to school. Four times every day. Being at that time a very small, measly little boy consisting largely of freckles, knuckles, knees and feet, I believed devoutly in the principle of non-resistance. Even before I started school, I had learned I could not run fast enough to escape predators among my fellow beings. Nor had I the weight, speed or courage to fight when overtaken.

Aubrey was a large, loose boy with a sallow skin, pale eyes, a nasal voice and a frustrated character. Nobody loved him. The teachers didn't like him. He was avoided in the schoolyard. In the knots and squads of children going to and coming from school, Aubrey, large and louty for his age, was always mauling, pushing, shoving the smaller kids. The groups would either hurry to leave him behind or stop and wait for him to go on. Nobody, nobody loved him.

Then he found me. I fancy he lived two blocks closer to the school than I. He would wait for me just around the corner. He would lie in wait inside alleys, lanes, behind hedges. As Aubrey was large for his age, I was small for mine. I found difficulty joining the right gangs of children heading to or from school. I, like Aubrey, found myself often walking alone.

Aubrey would throw me down and kneel on me, his knees on my biceps. He would glare down at me out of his pale eyes with a look of triumph. He would pretend he was going to spit on me. He would grind his fist on my nose, not too heavy, but revelling in the imagined joy of punching somebody on the nose. It was inexpressible pleasure to him to have somebody at his mercy.

I tried starting to school late; lingering at school after dismissal. I tried going new ways, around strange blocks. No use. Aubrey got me. I had no protectors. My father was a fighting man, who would have laughed if I had revealed to him my terror. "Why," he would have cried gaily, "punch him in the nose!"

After about two years, Aubrey vanished. I suppose his family moved away. But as the years came and went, like ever-rising waves of the tide of life and experience, my memory kept Aubrey alive. As I grew, the memory of him grew. When I was fifteen, the hateful memory was my age too. When I was twenty, there in my life still lived the large, sallow, cruel figure of Aubrey. My hatred of him matured, became adult, took on the known shape of a presence.

In the Vimy battle, by 8:30 A.M., I was the only officer left in my company, I had started, three hours earlier, the baby lieutenant. Now I was alone with 200 men.

Orders came, now that we had reached the crest and the last final wonderful objective, that the R.C.R. having been held up at a semi-final objective, there was a gap on our left between us and the Princess Pats.

"You will take the necessary party," orders said, "and bomb across to meet a party from the Patricias, which will start from their flank at 9 A.M. You should attempt to meet their party half-way across."

"Who," I said to my sergeant, Charlie Windsor, "will I take with me?"

It was a pretty dreadful time. It was sleeting. The air shook with shell fire, whistled and spat with machine-gun fire; and without shape or form, random monsters fell around us, belching up grey earth, grey smoke, grey men.

"Me," answered Sgt. Windsor, "and five others."

We got the canvas buckets, and filled them with bombs. Sgt. Windsor got a Lewis gun and five pans for it. At 9 A.M., peering across the grisly expanse toward where the Patricias should be, we saw, sure enough, a glimpse of furtive forms, half a dozen of them, bobbing, dodging, vanishing, reappearing. They were coming toward us.

"They've already started!" said Sgt. Windsor, hoisting the Lewis.

"Let's go," I croaked.

So, bobbing, dodging, vanishing, reappearing ourselves, we seven headed out to meet the Pats half-way. Down into shell craters, up over crater lips; down into the next craters, pools, mud; fresh hot holes, charred and new-burned, big holes, little holes, we slithered and slid and crouched. Two or three times, we had to cringe while German stick bombs whanged close; we lobbed ours back until we got silence. Two or three times, Sgt. Windsor had to slide the nozzle of the Lewis over the lip of craters and spray half a pan of fire into brush clumps. And once into a tree, half-way up, out of which a grey sack fell, heavily.

But each time up, we saw the Pats coming to us. And their bombs rang nearer, and ours rang nearer to them. We now could hear each other's shouts of encouragement and greeting.

"One more spurt!" I assured my crew.

The Pats squad was led by a long-geared, rangy man for whom I felt sorry each time I glimpsed him coming toward us. A pity all men can't be half-pints in war!

Our next plunge would be the last. We could hear the Pats only a few yards away.

Out over the lip I crouched and hurled, feet first. Feet first, I slid into a big crater; and over its lip skidded, feet first, the rangy, long-geared Pat.

You're right. It was Aubrey.

His pale eyes stared incredulous and triumphant down into mine. His sallow face split in a muddy grin.

"Don't I know you, sir?" he puffed.

"You sure should," I sighed struggling erect as possible and holding out my hand.

Hate dies funny.

Louis Caron

LOUIS CARON (1942–), who was born in Sorel, Quebec, a port on the south shore of the St. Lawrence River, has roots in the village of Nicolet. He worked as a journalist for Radio Canada from 1960 to 1976. Since then, he has devoted himself to writing poetry, essays, radio scripts and, in particular, novels with historical associations. His main characters are not the famous and powerful; rather, he centres on a *"citoyen obscur"* who suffers hunger, thirst, cold and sleeplessness and who has only a vague idea of the larger events in which he is embroiled. Caron's most ambitious work is a series of novels under the general title *Fils de la Liberté* (1981–) dealing with the Rebellions of 1837–38 in Lower and Upper Canada. *L'Emmitouflé (The Draft Dodger)* was originally published in Paris in 1977; David Toby Homel's English translation, from which the following story is excerpted, appeared in 1980.

The novel deals peripherally with an American of French-Canadian descent who becomes a draft dodger to avoid serving in the Vietnam War. The heart of the novel, a tale within a tale, is his father's account of how Uncle Nazaire avoided being conscripted in 1917. Nazaire represents the view of rural Québécois that "a man has a right to live life like he wants to." As for fighting in the Great War to defend England and France, the internal narrator explains:

> That was somebody else's war, we had nothing to do with it. We'd been fighting our own war for two hundred years against the rocks, the mosquitoes and the winter. Six months in the fields, six months

in the lumber camps. Don't you think that's enough? We weren't cowards, we had plenty of guts. Our land was there to prove it.

Ironically, Nazaire's hiding place is as constricted, dark, comfortless and foul-smelling as were the front line trenches that he refused to occupy.

The Draft Dodger

TRANSLATED BY DAVID TOBY HOMEL

WHEN YOU LEAVE NICOLET FOR SOREL OR Montreal, you take a little winding road along the Saint Lawrence that follows the river, though you don't see it. The road has been laid out to run from house to house, and they were built away from the river to shelter them from the terrible spring floods.

Between Nicolet and Sorel, you cross three rivers and you know their water will swell the Saint Lawrence, but you still can't see it. Just before Pierreville, the road curves twice and wanders farther from the water. At the first curve, a little path continues straight ahead. You take that one. If you follow it to the end, you reach the Saint-François River. And if you turn right and go alongside it, right away it's another world.

It's the realm of water. The village was built on both sides of the river. You see nothing but willows, unpainted board houses and wooden docks lashed to long poles. Boats too, with old brown sails and short stumpy masts.

A lot of people say it's the most picturesque village they're ever seen. You can see round nets stretched out between poles. There used to be children in blood-stained white smocks, busy "fixing" live perch on the docks. They'd stick their left hand in the bucket, grab a big fish, then clack! cut off the head, rip! gut it, two strokes and the skin is gone, clack! the tail and the job's done. They'd throw the head, the skin and the guts, still wriggling, into the water. Dozens of tame ducks swoop down on the remains. It goes on all afternoon.

A man who'd been through the village wouldn't soon forget it, but he'd leave without seeing the most important part if he didn't keep walking along the river another hour or so. There, in the vast marshes, he'd see plots of farmland and big mowers at anchor right in the middle of the meadows. On one side is the river, on the other the marshy fields; you're never sure where the water begins and the earth ends.

And if you take a few more steps along the river, right away you come to hardened clay. The spring floods have stripped the willows as high as a man stands. Huge ferns grow there. Then there are rushes, water weeds and the ground gets softer and softer. It's harder and harder to walk on it. In the best places, you can see duck blinds made from cedar branches that have mildewed since the last season.

Then suddenly there's water! Not the river, the sea! Lake Saint-Pierre, an inland sea, so wide you can't see the other shore. It's a widening of the Saint Lawrence, and the banks are so swampy that no one goes there but hunters in the fall.

That's where Nazaire and his brother Eugène found themselves early in the winter of 1917. Eugène had fled too, after he'd gotten his notice for the medical. He went directly to the house in Port Saint-François, arriving the very day Nazaire was going to leave. The two brothers decided to hide together.

It was done at night. A farmer named Levasseur from La Baie du Febvre agreed to take them in his wagon. Two armed deserters are enough to convince anybody. They were dropped off at the big curve before Pierreville. They must have walked almost two hours to get around the village of Notre Dame de Pierreville. The first lights of dawn were glowing in the houses. They got lost in the swamp but they finally found the river. The Saint-François was frozen; it was December and the river had started freezing in mid-October.

Nazaire and Eugène finally reached a spot where some land had been cleared during the summer. Branches, stumps and heaps of earth, clay and sand were thrown up on the river bank. The mound made a little rise twice the height of a man. They dug a hiding-place in it by pushing aside the stumps and reinforcing the ceiling with branches. It worked perfectly. By pulling more branches over the doorway, the hide-out looked like nothing more than heaped-up trash from the land clearing.

It was safer than any of the deserters' usual hiding-places. Nazaire and Eugène had found the spot where they could hide till the end of time if they needed to: in the earth itself.

Then the great black misery of winter began, no light, no fire, clinging to each other to keep warm. They had stretched out a blanket on the ground, on the rough floor of branches and frozen earth. On the side opposite the entrance, they had each set their pack that served as a pillow at night and a cushion during the day. From the ceiling they had hung two pots, a little mirror and a picture of the Holy Virgin.

Their hiding-place wasn't high enough to let them stand up, but it was quite deep, so they moved around on all fours. On one of the side walls they had fastened different useful little objects, utensils, a knife, two tin cups and several little bags where they put the potatoes, turnips, cabbages and the big piece of salt pork they had brought. On the side of the opening, they had hung another blanket that took the place of a door and was good for keeping the smells, smoke and light inside. They had tallow candles, but they lit them as rarely as possible because they gave off an intolerable smell when they burned.

They spent most of their time clinging to one another to keep warm. It didn't take long for them to hate each other as much as they loved each other. They cried together. They wiped each other's noses gently, then they hit each other in the face with their fists. They hugged each other like madmen, and the next minute they were about to strangle each other. They were like a couple of young pups.

It was even more unbearable because they could hardly ever go outside. They would have left footprints in the snow, and during the day somebody might have seen them. They were condemned to going out only on stormy nights. And then they didn't dare stray far because they were afraid of getting lost in the blizzards that blurred the line between the frozen river and the marshes. When the storms raged, they walked circles around their hiding-place like condemned men. They waved their arms in the air and stamped their feet on the hardened snow to warm up. They were like characters in a fiendish tale or ghosts that return only in the dead of winter.

They could spend three or four days without going out. But they still had their needs. They had desires, like all men. They wanted to do what makes a man a man. The more time passed, the stronger it grew. They put their hands in their pants, each on his own. They never touched each other.

But to tell the truth, they must not have been that miserable. They had enough to eat, they weren't too cold and there were two of them. But for them winter was like a night, a long, cold, black night that would never end.

That's why they began prowling around their hiding-place more often than they should have. A sudden icy rain had fallen, forming a thick crust on the snow, and that made it easier. The two brothers could walk on it without leaving footprints. They made forays closer and closer to the village. They wanted to steal a chicken but all the henhouses were locked and guarded; it was the middle of the war and winter too.

Then they tried to enter a lonely little house. It was the end of day, just at dusk. All they had to do was push in a windowpane whose glass had been replaced by a piece of cardboard. They went into the summer kitchen. That's usually a big room at the back of the house where people in the country spent a lot of time during the summer. They cook there because it's cooler, and also because otherwise the men would get the whole house dirty when they come back from the fields wearing their big boots. During the winter, the summer kitchen was usually used to store supplies. There wasn't any heat, of course. The room was frozen from mid-October to mid-April with no let-up. It was perfect for keeping meat.

Nazaire and Eugène slipped into the summer kitchen in a lonely little house. They found a burlap bag and were about to search the cupboards. But a voice rooted them to the spot.

"If you need something, you'd be better off asking for it!"

The voice really didn't have much nastiness in it. There was a woman, watching them from the kitchen window. Nazaire and Eugène backed toward the wall, their hands behind them to feel for the window where they'd come in. The woman opened the door. She was wearing a flowered dress and a scarf on her head. Just opening the door sent a blast of good warm air into the summer kitchen. Nazaire and Eugène didn't move; they took in the warmth one last time. And deep inside both of them wanted to talk to somebody, to be with somebody for a few precious moments.

As it turned out, the woman said, "Come in and warm yourselves. Don't be afraid, come in!"

The brothers followed her to the threshold but they didn't go any further. They stayed there—it was already too good. They didn't dare sit down by the big two-tiered stove. They looked like two *coureurs des bois* who'd forgotten what the inside of a house was like.

The woman has already settled in by the stove. She turned her grey head toward them. "Come and sit down," she said. "Come along! Don't be afraid! There's nothing to fear, I'm all alone in here. You haven't a thing to fear, I've seen my share of deserters. If you'd like to know, I've nothing against them. Come and sit down!"

And the two brothers' resistance melted like the snow from their boots on the floor. They edged closer like frightened dogs, and it took them quite a while before they sank all the way into the two rockers the woman had pulled next to hers in front of the stove. They listened to her talk without paying much attention to what she said, busy as they were getting reacquainted with the fire. They only listened with one ear, but they still managed to understand that this grey-haired woman in her fifties was the widow Landry, that she'd lost her husband one misty dawn on Lake Saint-Pierre and that she'd raised her sixteen children by herself. She'd just found a job for her youngest as a house-keeper for Father Nadeau in Saint-Elphège. Now she was alone in her little house on the outskirts of the village, with nothing but a sick old elm to watch over her.

"So you see," she said, "I'm all alone as well."

And the two brothers felt their trust growing as the heat thawed their blood. They began by taking off their fur caps, then they untied their *ceintures fléchées* and opened their grey coats. Finally, they pulled off their boots and put their feet, wrapped in brightly coloured heavy wool socks, on the open oven door.

They felt so trusting and had such a need to confide in somebody that Nazaire was about to say who they were and where they came from. But the widow interrupted them sharply.

"No offense intended," she said, "but I'd just as soon not know any-thing about you. You don't have to have a crystal ball to guess that you're a couple of good *Canadiens* and that you're not from around here. That's good enough for me. The less you know, the better it is! I don't need to know your names to practice Christian charity, like Our Lord Jesus Christ teaches us. You just wait there, I'll be back!"

She went to the corner of the kitchen where a cupboard was built into the wall. She pulled out a large, chipped white plate on which there was a generous piece of roast pork. Then she took a little brown pan in which there could be nothing else than the drippings from the roast, the good dark kind with white jelly on top. Some bread too: a big loaf, not even started. She put all of it on the corner of the table nearest the stove. It was like a feast on the old oilcloth.

Nazaire and Eugène ate greedily, forgetting the rules of politeness. All that was heard were the little noises they made as they gobbled down the food. Then the widow cleared the table and set a big basin of water in front of them, along with an old razor with a mother-of-pearl handle, some soap and a shaving brush with a few sparse hairs. The two brothers washed and shaved obediently.

"Now you look like real Christians!"

She wanted to have them sleep in the downstairs room. Eugène refused firmly.

"Don't be afraid," the widow insisted, "I stay up all night by the stove. At my age you don't sleep much any more. If ever I hear something I'll wake you up, but there's nothing to fear. Nobody ever comes by and everybody knows I live all alone."

But Eugène explained that if they slept one single night in a good bed, they would never have the strength to go back where they came from. The widow said she understood and offered, in the course of a rambling conversation like you might have around the stove on a winter afternoon, to go from time to time to bring them a little coffee and hot food.

"No need to tell me exactly where you are. All we have to do is agree on a place, anywhere, where you can see me coming. And you can come pick up my basket once I've left."

But there was no formal agreement at the start. Nothing but yesses and heads nodding. Finally, all in one breath, the widow declared that Christmas was coming and that they couldn't go through the Holidays without the aid of religion.

"You're not animals," she said in a shocked voice. "I'll send you Father Nadeau. Whatever else, you can't doubt a priest's word! He has his share of deserters, Father Nadeau has! This is more or less his parish here, and from time to time he comes to bring my daughter. Trust him, he's a man of great kindness.

Finally, around nine o'clock at night, Nazaire explained where their hide-out was to widow Landry, and the two brothers set out in the squall, their caps pulled down to their eyes. But once they were back in their hole, they began to quarrel.

"You should never have told her where we were," Eugène grumbled. "We should never take risks. She might squeal on us!"

Nazaire took offense. There was nothing to fear from widow Landry. And he was right. Widow Landry had such a good heart that the idea of denouncing a deserter would have never occurred to her. In her mind, these boys were simply children who were a little more difficult than the rest. And difficult children, she knew a thing or two about them!

It was eleven o'clock one morning. The sun was glistening on the snow. One of those mornings when suddenly you hear the river ice cracking sharply in the cold, like a rifle shot. It was a little before Christmas.

Nazaire and Eugène were curled up in a ball at the bottom of their black hole. They were dozing but one of them was always responsible for lifting up the entryway blanket from time to time and taking a look through the gridwork of branches that formed the opening. Eugène crawled over to it, pushed aside the branches, then he turned to Nazaire, shook him violently and whispered harshly in his ear, "Somebody's coming! A man by himself wearing a wildcat coat!"

There was an uproar in the hide-out, a quick scuffling to put the battle preparations into action: push back the blankets, clear the space to manoeuvre more easily. Nazaire was responsible for taking up position by the opening. Eugène was to hide at the back and be ready in case Nazaire was hit.

Nazaire was ready to fire, his 12-gauge in his hand, his cap pushed up on his forehead. The man was coming closer, lifting his feet high in the snow; he looked as if he was searching for something. He halted a few steps from the entrance to the hide-out. He inspected the surroundings and bent over the ground—he was looking for footprints, for sure. The man straightened up, took three steps and put his hand on the branches that hid the opening to the hide-out. Just as he was about to push them aside, the mean-looking barrel of a hunting rifle came out slowly and pressed against his chest.

"Friend," said the man, "don't shoot! I am Father Nadeau from Saint-Elphège."

"Stay where you are," Nazaire replied. "Don't move!"

He kept his eye on him through the branches. But the man began untying his *ceinture fléchée* that was wound around his wildcat coat three times. He opened it up.

"See my cassock!"

"That doesn't prove anything," Nazaire answered. "Show me your hands!"

The man took off his big leather mittens. His hands were white, true enough, even if they were big and short. He might have been a priest, but his father was a farmer.

"No offense intended, Father," said Nazaire, "I'm going to ask you to say something in Latin."

The man smiled and began reciting some Vobiscums, Te Deums, Absolvo Tes and all sorts of Latin phrases that the most Christian of French Canadians wouldn't understand, though he'd heard them a thousand times at church. No doubt about it, nobody but a priest could talk like that!

Then Nazaire let Father Nadeau from Saint-Elphège crawl into the hide-out next to him. He introduced his brother Eugène to him, but Eugène was in a very bad mood and answered the visitor's questions with a grunt.

So Nazaire and Father Nadeau talked to each other, squatting face to face. The priest had blessed the place when he came in and Nazaire had been eager to point out his picture of the Holy Virgin. But first the conversation had been about the everyday concerns of life. Father Nadeau wanted to know if the two brothers had enough to eat, if they weren't too cold and unhappy too often. Then his comments skillfully turned to spiritual matters: he wanted to know if, every morning, the two unfortunate young men weren't forgetting to consecrate their day to the Lord.

"How do you expect us to?" Eugène retorted. "In here there's no difference between day and night! It's all the same."

Father Nadeau pretended not to hear the disobliging remark. He moved onto the approaching Nativity, emphasizing the sacred character of the holiday and reminding them that, to redeem all those who were suffering, the Saviour had wanted to be born in a stable. He pointed out that the manger in Bethlehem was very similar to the two men's hide-out, and Eugène muttered that it was a lot worse here because it was a cold country and there wasn't even any straw. But the priest didn't hear. He announced he was going to hear their confessions. Nazaire and Eugène each went out while the other entrusted his sins to the priest, then Father Nadeau celebrated mass right there in their hiding-place, on a little white cloth he had brought on which he precariously balanced his portable crucifix for last rites and a little altar stone containing precious relics. The two brothers and Father Nadeau were squatting together. All three of them were murmuring the Latin words, and at the moment of the elevation, the big wildcat coat slipped from the priest's shoulders. He went on with his ceremony as if nothing had happened. And every time Nazaire and Eugène opened their mouths to pronounce the responses of the Mass, a little white cloud rose up like incense.

After the ceremony, the priest conversed with them for a good hour. They spoke of Nicolet, where he'd gone to the *Grand Séminaire*. Nazaire and Eugène remembered their lives before the events, and so they came to recall their acts. Father Nadeau said that the Good Lord could not turn his wrath against people who disobeyed unjust commandments to escape killing their fellow men.

"Thou shalt not kill!" he pronounced solemnly, "is the greatest of all the commandments."

Then Father Nadeau felt obliged to explain his position. He might have put it differently than the other priests, that was true, but several of them, so he said, all thought the same way. Personally, he felt no shame exercising his ministry to deserters. In fact, he considered it his duty, and his conscience drove him to watch over their physical well-being as well as the salvation of their souls.

"A human being can't remain hidden away for months without seeing anybody," he said. "He must fraternize with his fellow men to retain his sense of values and his respect for society. Otherwise, he'll be like an animal by the time he comes out. That's why I'm offering to take you to Saint-Elphège, one at a time, to spend the evening with some people I know who are completely trustworthy.

The two brothers stared at each other in astonishment. That was certainly the last offer they would have expected. They'd gotten used to the idea that they'd have to stay hidden until the end of the war, and even a little longer, and here somebody was inviting them into their homes!

"We can't accept," Eugène answered quickly. "It's too dangerous."

"No, it's not!" replied Father Nadeau. "I know what I'm doing; you can trust me. If it was too dangerous I wouldn't offer to do it. I'll take you to a farmer's house on the sixth concession in Saint-Elphège. He's a fine man even if he does have a coarse tongue. He's not rich but he has a good heart. He has six children and his wife is an excellent house-keeper."

The two brothers faced each other, each with his own opinion. Eugène seemed locked into his determination to refuse the offer but Nazaire was tempted.

"Are you sure it's not too dangerous?" he asked.

"There's nothing to fear. I'll take one of you with me in my wagon at dusk. If ever anybody questions us, I'll say I'm on my way to bring the Holy Sacrament to an elderly person, and that wouldn't even be a lie because as it turns out I plan to stop at old lady Brochu's house on the way back. And if anybody asks me who's sitting next to me, I'll say he's my altarboy. There's nothing untrue about that either. Don't worry! I've done this plenty of times and I know the Good Lord will be with us.

A few moments later, the two brothers were quarrelling in front of the priest. Eugène wouldn't hear of it. He grabbed Nazaire by the collar. On all fours, facing each other, they'd knocked over the little bottle of holy water the priest had left on the cloth that he'd used as an altar.

"Are you crazy?" Eugène repeated. "You know it makes no sense! We said we'd stick together until the end! I'm warning you, if you go, you won't find me here when you get back."

Father Nadeau tried to make Eugène listen to reason.

"But don't you see, it's for your own good! Look, you're already behaving like savages!"

"You let us settle this ourselves!"

But Nazaire had turned a deaf ear to him. He didn't want to hurt his brother Eugène, but he couldn't help wanting to spend a warm evening in the kitchen of a real house, especially before the Holidays. Already he pictured the children around the table, their hands folded behind their backs. He heard them singing the only hymn you're permitted to sing during Advent:

Venez, Divin Messie,
Sauver nos jours infortunés!
Vous êtes notre vie!
Venez, venez, venez!

They might only eat boiled potatoes, certainly no meat, let alone a dessert! It was Advent, people were preparing for the celebration. Nazaire couldn't bear it any more. Hastily he gathered his knife, his rosary—mostly to please Father Nadeau—his big clean handkerchief and the little coil of rope he used to take everywhere he went.

Eugène repeated, "I'm warning you, you won't find me here when you get back!"

But Nazaire didn't hear him. He kissed him tenderly and followed Father Nadeau out into the blue air. The two men headed toward the village of Notre-Dame. At widow Landry's house they met up with Françoise, the young house-keeper visiting her mother. Hastily the priest hitched up the sleigh and the three of them sat down side by side on the bench, the runners whistling on the icy road, by the glow of a low twilight that foretold snow for the night.

The two men had seated Françoise between them and covered their legs with a big brown caribou skin that smelled of horses. Nazaire swung his hefty arm around the back of the bench and when they took a curve, he hung on with all his might, which made him lean against the girl's shoulder. The clouds raced above them. Nazaire was touched and between his clenched teeth he sang, *Venez, Divin Messie!*

The horse seemed to know the way. Nazaire couldn't have said how long they'd glided over the icy road before they spotted the lights of a village. It was the first one they'd ridden through after they'd dropped off Françoise at the presbytery: fifty houses around a meager looking wooden church.

They slipped through the night a while longer, then Father Nadeau pulled on the reins.

"Whoa! We're here! Whoa, grey mare!"

The sleigh came to a halt in the yard of a lonely farm. There was more light from the stable than from the windows of the house. A little man came out, wearing a red and black checked shirt, his hands bare and his head covered with a brightly coloured cap.

In the cold air, he shouted, "Christ on a crutch! It must be the devil himself coming to roust us out this time of night. Who could the damned old trickster have sent us this time, for the bloody love of Jesus?"

He came closer, waving his hands in the air. As soon as he recognized Father Nadeau, he respectfully removed his cap.

"My deepest apologies, Father. I didn't recognize you."

"No harm done, Auguste, no harm done to me, but you could at least let the Good Lord's name alone during Advent."

"It's bigger than me, Father. I inherited it from my late father."

"I know, Auguste, I know! But look who I brought with me."

And with his big mitten he pointed to Nazaire who was wrapped up in the caribou skin.

"A poor young man," the priest went on, "a good fellow who's fallen on hard times lately."

"You'll get over it!" the man said in his frightening voice. "You're not going to spend the evening freezing yourselves out here in the yard, are you? I bet you haven't eaten anything!"

And he turned toward the stable; two figures were standing in the low doorway. "Hey, in there! Baptiste! Arthur! Come and unhitch Father Nadeau's horse!"

And he led them promptly into the overheated kitchen where a blast of icy air swept in at the same time they did. The mother and two of her daughters were standing by the big wood stove. A bony dog came up to sniff them with a growl, then went back to lie under the stove. The chairs were already pulled out.

"Come and get warm, Christ on a bike!"

Nazaire tried not to stick out too much. He sat down as far away as possible, in the darkest corner of the kitchen.

"This young man has had a hard life just lately," the priest explained, pointing to Nazaire. "You can be sure that where he's living, he doesn't see many people. That's why I decided to bring him to spend the evening. He's a fine fellow, I guarantee it."

Nazaire smiled. "Good evening, everybody," he said.

And turning to the priest, he said, "The Good Lord is certainly merciful to have allowed me to meet you."

"You'll get over it!" the man thundered.

A moment of silence. The mother and her daughters busied themselves around the stove. The door opened and the two from the stables
came in, two boys of fifteen or sixteen with thin mustaches and pipes in
their mouths.

They ate in silence after having recited the Benedicite standing up,
with big signs of the cross. From time to time the father thundered,
"Arthur, bread! More potatoes, Elise!"

After supper everybody filled his pipe, including the priest, and
Nazaire lay low in his corner. The lamp lit the deserted table.

Finally, Nazaire said, "We'd better start thinking of going. It's late
already."

But the priest motioned him to stay put. So Nazaire sunk down a
little further into his chair and from under his thick eyebrows, he
watched the people passing the evening. The father and his two sons
were smoking. The mother and her daughters were around the table,
darning multi-coloured socks and lumberjack shirts. And the priest
talked in his droning voice. He talked about how Christmas was coming
up and about the uncertain times they were living in. Around nine-
thirty, Auguste went out to have a look in the stable, and he came back
with the news that big snowflakes had started to fall.

"Would you like to stay the night?" the mother asked. "It would be
such an honour for us!"

"I have to be going," the priest answered, "but without abusing your
kindness, I'd like to ask you to keep my young friend for the night. He'll
be better off here than in the village and besides, it will do him good to
be with a family for a night."

Nazaire tried to protest but he was drowned out in a flood of gestures
and words. Then Father Nadeau left, saying he'd return to pick up
Nazaire the next morning. A half hour later, Nazaire was stretched out
on the beggar's bench next to the stove. Everything around him was dark
and the reflection of the fire that slipped through the chinks in the stove
door made will-o-the-wisps on his blanket.

He lay on his back, unable to sleep. And he couldn't help wondering
how he would escape if somebody came knocking on the door. To calm
himself, he began reviewing the faces of the evening. Without realizing
it, his mind came to rest on the face of the oldest daughter, Elise.

Now that he was back all along in his hole again, Nazaire shivered like a drowned rat. Sitting hunched over, he rocked back and forth all day. The last days of December were turning out to be colder than usual. And Nazaire had only his frozen breath to keep him company.

He dozed on and off all day, like a puppy, an hour or two at a time, never more. He would have easily lost track of time if he hadn't been especially careful to keep the big pocket watch running that Father Nadeau had given him. With his knife he made cuts on a branch that served as a calendar, and so he made his way, hour by hour, toward the miraculous moment of Christmas when, it seemed to him, a great miracle might come to pass.

At night, he pushed aside the opening of his hiding-place to examine the stars, trying to reckon which of these points of light might have guided the Three Wise Men to Bethlehem. That had happened long ago; perhaps the star had gone out in the meantime. Besides, those things had taken place in such distant lands!

The most pessimistic thoughts began to assail him. Perhaps this Christmas would mark the passage of the exterminating angel. Perhaps the end of the world would find him huddled in his hiding-place, frozen to death. Nazaire remembered having heard of those missionaries of the Far North, white fathers with prophet's beards, who had lain down by their wolf dogs on the frozen tundra, never to wake again. Shivers ran down his spine.

That's why, in spite of all caution, he began to sing the exhalting hymns of Christmas at the top of his lungs, day and night.

"Glo-ooooo-ooooo-ooooo-ria! In excelsis Deo!"

Night and day merged. The wind buffeted the frozen Saint-François River; the stars, paralyzed by the cold, hovered on the horizon an extra measure longer. Then the snow brought milder weather. For hours, flakes as big as a fist fell. The silence thickened. Then the cold took hold of the air with a single blast. Snow began to fall in dense little pellets. Day and night.

And with his pocket knife, Nazaire began whittling the little branches that pushed through the walls of his hiding-place. First a little Baby Jesus, as big as a finger, with a little round head, lying on some wisps of straw. A Holy Virgin carved into a curved branch, better to bend over the infant. A St. Joseph with a bark beard. Three or four shepherds rising from the edges and sheep everywhere, barely sketched into the ends of the branches.

Sometimes Nazaire lit his candle to guide the Wise Men. Not too long because of the smell, but just enough to show the way. For he had not the slightest doubt that the Three Wise Men had set out on their journey, somewhere across Lake Saint-Pierre, frozen and snow-covered like a desert. They were heading toward the humble manger and Nazaire was sure there couldn't be a manger anywhere as humble as his.

And on the evening of the twenty-fourth of December, just at midnight, on his knees before his sculpted branches, the deserter intoned *Minuit, chrétiens*:

> *Minuit, chrétiens, c'est l'heure solennelle*
> *Où l'homme-Dieu descendit jusqu'à nous*
> *Pour effacer la tache originelle*
> *Et de son Père apaiser le courroux.*

Warmth filled him at the same time as the smell of the steaming *tourtières* and the plump turkey. His father was standing in the centre of the room, hands crossed before him. He was saying, "The Baby Jesus was born this night to save mankind. He was born for the poor and the unfortunate, for those who are hungry and cold. For Nazaire and for Eugène, our children whom we haven't heard from. For all the boys of Nicolet too who went to war and who are shivering this night at the bottom of their trenches."

Then he blessed the family kneeling at the foot of the tree. Nazaire fell into a deep sleep.

Hugh Garner

HUGH GARNER (1913–1979) was born in Batley, West Yorkshire, England. In 1919 he moved with his mother to Toronto to join his demobilized father, who soon deserted them. A poverty-stricken childhood and peripatetic youth during the Great Depression, when it was difficult to find even labouring jobs, made him sympathetic to socialism, represented in Canada by the Co-operative Commonwealth Federation (CCF) and the Communist parties. The outbreak of the Spanish Civil War in 1936, he later commented, "affected me more than anything else in my life, up to or since that time." In 1937 he enlisted in the Abraham Lincoln Brigade to fight on the Loyalist side.

Spain had become a republic in 1931 and in 1936 the Popular Front, a party of the left, was elected. The army, under General Franco, backed by landowners, Fascists and the Roman Catholic Church, rebelled against the legitimate government. While the inexperienced Loyalist forces, assisted by factory workers, the intelligentsia and the International Brigades (which the Communists in Britain, France and America organized), lacked even basic equipment and food supplies, the Fascists had the support of Hitler's new war machine, including crack army units and planes that carried out the most extensive bombing of civilians to that time, except for the Germans' use of dirigibles in the Great War to drop bombs on London. Between 1936 and 1938 (when the Loyalists dismissed the International Brigades), 12,000 Canadians volunteered for Spain out of political conviction, desire for adventure or lack of employment. Only half returned. Their story has been told in a National Film Board documentary, *Los Canadienses: The Mackenzie-Papineau Battalion 1937–1939* (1975).

In July 1937 Hugh Garner participated as a machine gunner in a Loyalist attempt to relieve the siege of Madrid. During a lull in the firing, he made his way to the rear, where he was assigned as a stretcher-bearer. That experience inspired the following story. Two other short stories, "The Expatriates" and "How I Became an Englishman," provide other views of his civil war service, as does his autobiography *One Damn Thing After Another* and a series of articles in *Liberty Magazine* (1960–61). In the Second World War Garner served with the Royal Canadian Navy, chiefly on corvettes doing convoy duty in the North Atlantic. *Storm Below* (1949) is a novel about naval life.

The Stretcher-Bearers

THE WOUNDED MAN LEFT THE FIELD DRESSING station as a walking casualty. He was not yet groggy from the antitetanus injection, and except for the line of dried blood running down his shirt into his back pocket you would not have known he was wounded. On top of his left shoulder was a small gauze pad held to the skin with adhesive tape, as if covering an aching carbuncle.

It was July, 1937 and the International Brigades were attacking south from the hills towards the town of Brunete on the plain. It was the biggest offensive our side had made since the Spanish Civil War had begun.

By the time we met the automatic-rifle ammunition party the wounded man was getting drunk from shock. He was afraid to stand up for long, for the bullets were still coming over a bank to our right, and you get very careful after you're wounded once. One of the ammunition carriers, a new kid in our outfit, came with the Jew and I to help the wounded man along. We borrowed a stretcher from a Spanish battalion and began carrying him, taking turns on the handles every few minutes. We filled a tunic full of grass and made him a pillow, and he told us he felt pretty comfortable now. Once in a while we rolled him cigarettes, which he smoked until the paper came loose and the tobacco spilled on his chest.

I was envious of the wounded man. There seems to come a time after you've been in the line a few months when the wounded men are the lucky ones. They *know* what kind of wound they are going to get, but you don't. You never know, and you have to keep on going back into it until it happens to you, and all you hope is that it won't be in the head or the groin.

For the first two kilometres we had to follow the bed of the dried-up stream, and the sand was soft and fell over the tops of our boots, making our socks gritty. We took turns on the stretcher at fifty metre intervals, and for the first few metres the stretcher felt light, but after that the slings bit into your shoulders, and he was the heaviest man in the war.

The wounded were being evacuated from the advance dressing stations by relays of stretcher-bearers, who carried them eight kilometres to the ambulances that waited on the paved highway at the top of the hills.

We met a fellow called Harper lying under a clump of willow trees without his rifle, and he joined us, glad to have a legitimate excuse for not being up there with the battalion. We made better time after that, but the wounded man sometimes complained of the bumping. Once in a while we sat down to rest, and the Jew gave the wounded man drinks of tepid water from his canteen.

When we reached the stretcher relay station, where we were to hand over the wounded man to another group, a Spaniard told us that all their men were busy, and we would have to take our man to the next relay station where they had some mules to transport them up the hills. We grumbled a bit, but realized that the longer we were back of the line the longer we would be in one piece, so we hoisted the stretcher out of the gully and set across the wheat stubble in the direction of the hills.

A big Swede from the English Battalion passed us on a stretcher, smoking a cigarette. One of his legs was bent at the knee, and a bandage was wrapped around the thigh. There was a steady drip of blood from beneath the bandage.

"Hello, Swede. Much pain?" I asked him.

"No, no pain. My leg is stiff though. Maybe I'll be a bloody cripple."

"You'll be able to carry a cane. All wounded heroes have stiff legs and carry canes."

"To hell with that."

"Where's your outfit?"

"Around the other side of the village. Did you see us go over?"

"Yeh."

"The Frenchmen are in there now. They went in with the bayonet; I'm glad we didn't have to do that."

"Yeh!"

"They should have sent us up the gully. We had no cover at all."

"It's the artillery's fault."

"F ... the artillery!"

We sat down to rest, and the Swede and his bearers disappeared over the fields. When we set out again the wounded man cursed us for being so slow. I was beginning to think of him as merely a hundred-and-seventy pounds of dead weight rather than a man. He was a Canadian from my home town, although I had never seen him until a few days before. He had been in the group of replacements sent up to the Lincoln Battalion when the offensive began.

As we crossed the fields we passed a peasant driving his sheep towards the rear. His shaggy dog came and nosed the stretcher. "Hey, Comrade, do you live in the village?" I asked him in Spanish. He shrugged his shoulders but didn't answer.

"He's a fascist," said the kid.

"Not now he's not. He's come over to our lines."

"If the fascists advance he'll go the other way. These guys are fascists or republicans depending on which side happens to be in front of them."

"His sheep won't last long over here."

"See!" the kid said. "He must be a fascist or else his sheep would have been eaten long ago."

"Did you hear about them eating the animals out of the Madrid zoo?" asked Harper.

"Hear about it; I think I ate them," the Jew said.

Nobody laughed.

"Please, Comrades, hurry up! I'm beginning to pain here in the chest," the wounded man said, his mouth dribbling with pink spit as he spoke.

We kept going, but slower now.

The temperature had been 120° in the sun all day long, but it grew cooler towards evening. The water in our canteens was the same that we had dug for in the sand of the stream bed before attacking in the morning. It was tepid, and you kept the grass and twigs out of your mouth by clenching your teeth when you drank it. We were tired, for we had marched all the night before, and several nights before that, and had advanced down the hills with the dawn. When it began to get dark we realized that we had taken the wrong path into the hills, and we saw no other wounded men being carried along.

There was a bushy hill to our left below a cemetery, and it was on fire, the flames making patterns in the grass. One of our tanks was lying on its side in the trees. Another one was scuttling back and forth in front of a trench at the top of the hill, and its gun was banging like a loose fence board as it blew up the earthworks at point-blank range. The enemy machine-guns were drumming, and we knew that the Campesino Brigade was making another attack against the Moors in the cemetery.

There had been no aeroplanes in the sky for hours, but our artillery was sending salvos into the village of Villanueva. The shells tore long strips of paper overhead, and sent up explosions of smoke and flames from the village houses. The church tower was burning, but the noise of the enemy machine-guns was as heavy as ever.

There were field telephone lines running alongside the mule track, and halfway up the first hill was a dug-out in which was a telephone operator wearing a head set and eating a sandwich. We asked him for food, and he gave us a loaf of bread. Harper began to complain about his varicose veins.

None of us liked Harper. He had come up to us as a replacement too, and had got drunk the last night before we moved out of billets for this attack. He was a very big man, and he had challenged anybody in the battalion to a fight.

"We'll be at the top in an hour or so," I said. "We can't stop here."

"How do you know? Maybe this path will take us right into the other guys' lines."

"We'll have to chance that. I think it'll get us up to the highway all right."

The wounded man had been unconscious for some time now, but it was impossible to realize that he was badly hurt.

"This poor bastard's dying," said the Jew.

"You're crazy!" Harper said.

"Look at his back, all covered with black spots! The bullet is down in his lung."

"I can't help it," said Harper. "I can't carry him any farther. My legs are aching like hell."

"So are mine," said the kid.

"I can't carry him any more."

"This is his first day in the line," said the Jew, sarcastically. His name was Katz and he had been with the battalion since we were formed at Jarama.

Harper said, "Comrades, I can't carry him any farther. My legs have given out."

"You're a son-of-a-bitch!" I said to him.

"I'd kill you if my legs weren't so sore."

"You're only brave in billets," I said. "In the line you're a cowardly son-of-a-bitch."

"So are you."

"We're all cowards," said the Jew, "or we'd have stayed near the village. We all wanted to get away, that's why we carried this man up here."

"I've got a weak heart," the kid said. "When the bullets cracked near my head, I couldn't stand it."

"Let's go!"

"Not me," Harper said. "I've got pains all the way up my legs."

"You're a dirty son-of-a-bitch," said the Jew. "We'll report you to the battalion, and you'll be shot."

Harper sat down on the path and rubbed his legs. The kid, the Jew and I picked up the stretcher and stumbled past him up the path. After we had climbed out of sight we had to rest again, and that's the way we went on for the next few hundred yards. The kid fell asleep one time, and we woke him by kicking him in the shins. The wounded man was delirious, and he mumbled things about a dog, and coughed up small amounts of blood.

"We haven't slept for forty-eight hours," said the Jew.

"Let's stop here and rest for a while," the kid pleaded.

"No, not yet."

After it got dark I began to cry with exhaustion. I couldn't see how we were ever going to get the wounded man up to the highway.

"Don't cry," said the kid. "It scares me to see a man cry."

The Jew said, "I'll go up and get help. You two wait for me here."

The kid fell asleep on the path. He was a good-looking kid, but his cheeks twitched in his sleep and his nose was running. I fell asleep too, and when I woke up I knew that it was very late. I woke up the kid and we struggled another few yards with the stretcher. A file of soldiers passed us going the other way; each carrying a long tank shell under either arm. They were laughing and joking and they greeted us in Spanish as they passed.

"Is he dead yet?" asked the kid, pointing to the stretcher.

I felt the wounded man's chest. "No, not yet," I answered.

"Do you think Katz will come back?"

"No."

"Neither do I."

"We can't let this poor bugger die when we've carried him this far," I said.

"I wish we hadn't lost the right path."

"What's this guy's name anyway?" I asked.

"I don't know; he wasn't in my group."

"He told me earlier that he was from my home town," I said. "I wish I knew his name."

"Why?"

"When I go home maybe somebody will ask me if I know what happened to him."

"Do you think any of us are ever going home?" the kid asked.

For the next hour or more we struggled up the path, which got steeper the higher we went. We would stumble forward a step or two at a time and collapse on the ground with the stretcher slings loose over our shoulders. The next time the kid fell asleep I could not wake him up. Then I heard the noise of *camions* running along a road a short distance ahead, and I went forward alone.

I felt as light as a feather without the weight of the stretcher pulling at my shoulders, and after a couple of minutes I passed some dug-outs at the side of the path and beyond them was a paved highway with some ambulances drawn up under some trees.

A doctor wearing a leather jacket was sitting on a box at the edge of a clearing, and around him on the ground lay about thirty stretchers filled with wounded men. The doctor had a carbide lamp set up on a table, and beside it was a cracked wash-bowl holding ligatures and needles, and a card board shoe-box filled with rolls of bandage.

I walked over to him. "Comrade Doctor, we have a wounded man down the path," I said, pointing behind me.

"*Que?*"

"*Yo tengo herido-mucho metres,*" I said in my poor Spanish.

"*Una momento,*" he said, and called over a nurse from one of the ambulances. He spoke to her in German.

"Are you English?" she asked. "What would you wish of us?"

"We have a badly wounded man down the path. We would like some help to bring him in."

She translated to the doctor, then she turned and said, "We have no able men here. You will have to carry him alone."

"But surely—"

"Excuse us, please," she said as she walked away.

By the time I reached the stretcher again the kid was awake and crying, but the wounded man was dead. I had to plead with the kid to help me; he didn't want to be bothered carrying a dead man any farther, but I warned him that if we left him now they'd blame us for letting him die.

After what seemed like another hour we reached the clearing by the highway, and placed the stretcher on the ground beside the doctor. Then we stumbled across the grass and lay down to sleep under a broken truck.

Max Braithwaite

MAX BRAITHWAITE (1911-1994) was born in Nokomis, Saskatchewan and grew up in Prince Albert and Saskatoon. After graduating from university, he taught from 1933 to 1940 in rural schools, an experience related to his novel *Why Shoot the Teacher* (1965). During the Second World War, he served with the Royal Canadian Naval Volunteer Reserve in Toronto, being discharged in 1945 as a Lieutenant Commander. After the war he became a full-time writer, his stated object being to depict people, times, places and events as accurately and entertainingly as possible. "Writing is a great way to make a living and a great way to live," he said.

In 1938 the governments of Britain and France, unprepared for war, tried to appease Hitler by signing the Munich agreement which allowed Germany to march into Czechoslovakia on condition that the Nazis made no further territorial demands. But when Poland was threatened in the following year, Neville Chamberlain, the British Prime Minister, made this "sad declaration" on September 3:

> This morning, the British ambassador in Berlin handed the German government a final note stating that unless we heard from them by eleven o'clock that they were prepared at once to withdraw their troops from Poland, a state of war would exist between us. I have to tell you now, that no such undertaking has been received and that consequently, this country is at war with Germany.

Canada's declaration of war followed on September 10.

"The Porpoise that Couldn't Swim," from *The Commodore's Barge is Alongside* (1979), takes place at a time when the Royal Canadian Navy had only four destroyers fit to go to sea. Most volunteers were members of the RCNVR, the Royal Canadian Naval Volunteer Reserve or "Wavy Navy."

The Porpoise That Couldn't Swim

To say that the War—that's the big war of 1939–45, not the numerous little ones they've had since—changed the lives of an entire generation is a cliché, but like a good many other clichés it happens to be true.

Now, looking back on it some forty years later, I realize that it changed my life beyond recall. On that fateful Sunday morning of September 3, 1939, when I crawled out of bed at four o'clock in the morning to listen on the radio to that sad declaration of Neville Chamberlain, I was living in the small city of Wabagoon in the middle of the Canadian prairies. I had been out of high school for two years and, except for my paper route, had never had a steady job in my life. I was a member of that "great army of unemployed," a useless appendage on the body economic, a bum.

The worst kind of bum, really, because I was bumming off my parents who, with Dad unemployed for two years, could barely afford to support themselves and my brother and sister. Lord knows I'd tried hard enough to get a job. I'd even travelled by freight as far as Vancouver looking for work on the boats and to Flin Flon looking for work in the mines. No dice. From all that, I and the rest of my generation were rescued by that madman Adolf Hitler.

I remember vividly how Dad got the whole family up in the middle of the night so that we could hear the actual words of the British Prime Minister, a great thrill in those early days of radio. We huddled around the old gothic-shaped Philco in the livingroom of our house on Duke Street: Dad in his pyjamas with the ragged string hanging down over his pot belly, Ma in her scruffy dressing gown curled up in the old black leather chair, Doug and Mary lying on the rug.

When Chamberlain finished with the words "and consequently this country is at war with Germany," Dad viciously turned the knob of the radio to Off.

"I knew it!" and then he swore, which was unusual for him, and Ma didn't protest, which was unusual for her. "The bloody fools have done it again!"

Mary uncurled her gangly legs and said, "I think war is nuts!" and went back to bed.

Ma said nothing, but her tired face was a little more creased than usual as she got up and walked wearily towards the stairs.

Doug leaped to his feet. "Are you going to go, Dink?" he shouted.

"Not on your life."

And I meant it. All through high school our pacifist-minded teachers had convinced us that war was evil and that if nobody went there would be no more wars. The world was finished with war, we were told over and over again. In our debating clubs we proved that "The Treaty of Versailles was the most unjust document ever signed by nations of the first rank," that wars were arranged for profit by "robber barons," and that total disarmament was the way of the future. All the time ignoring the fact that Nazi Germany was building the mightiest war machine in modern history. Was ever a generation so naïve?

The day following Chamberlain's speech, no less a voice than that of King George VI was heard direct from Buckingham Palace warning us that "The task will be hard," and "There may be dark days ahead," thereby putting the official stamp on the war to come. We were for it.

But no dark days came. In fact, for quite a while, apart from the sinking of some ships, nothing happened. We talked of the phony war and were somewhat disappointed that all the flag-waving seemed to be for naught. Then in the spring of 1940 all hell broke loose, and within a few short weeks France and Belgium and Norway had been occupied and Britain stood alone, facing her greatest danger since 1066.

By that time we'd all become gung-ho for war. The flag-waving and the speech-making had been too much for us. Besides, enlistment for many meant the first good overcoat in years, not to mention dental work and a release from the terrible boredom of the Depression.

So it happened that on the second day of July, a hot, dusty day, which is to say a typical summer day on the prairies, I put on my blue serge suit, applied elbow grease and polish to my shabby black oxfords, vase-lined my unruly blond hair into a gooey pompadour and, with as much bravado as I could muster, marched down Ridgeway Street, across the bridge over the wide Wabagoon River, down Regal Avenue to the corner of Queen Street, where His Majesty's Canadian Ship *Porpoise* lay at anchor in a patch of weeds, and went aboard.

HMCS *Porpoise*! Was there ever in the history of naval warfare a more scruffy ship?

The war had caught everybody unprepared, and Canada's fledgling navy most of all. Suddenly the service was required to recruit and train men for the hundreds of corvettes and other small fighting craft feverishly being built. This meant dragging youngsters from the city streets, farms, and small towns, and in a matter of weeks making sailors of them. Most of us on the prairies had never seen a body of water larger than a slough or been aboard a floating craft larger than a raft. To accomplish its task, the navy established training divisions in all of the major cities and called them "ships." They ranged in size from HMCS *York*, the automotive building in Toronto's CNE grounds, to HMCS *Porpoise*.

The only available building in Wabagoon was a one-storey brick garage, long abandoned and falling apart. Suddenly, like the men who were to man her, she was given a new lease on life and elevated to the eminence of junior partner in the world's mightiest and proudest service, The Royal Navy.

She wasn't even close to the Wabagoon River, which wound like a great muddy snake through the centre of the city. Rather she was across the street from a spur of the Canadian National Railway, with the usual things found along such a track: a grocery warehouse, a farm implement company headquarters, some coal shacks, and a lot of weeds.

The front—oops—*bow* of the ship extended about one hundred and fifty feet along Regal Avenue and the starboard side about three hundred feet along Queen Street. On the port side was a vacant lot full of pigweed through which peeked rusty bits of fender, old engine blocks, tires and other junk that accumulates around old garages. The stern faced on a back alley.

The port side of the ship, extending from the big garage doors in the bow to the c.p.o.'s office in the stern, was the parade deck. The starboard side of the bow consisted of offices and officers' wardroom. This latter had been the garage's showroom in other days and boasted a hardwood floor and huge draped windows that faced both Regal Avenue and Queen Street. The remainder of the garage, with its floor of bumpy concrete and its grease-splattered brick walls, had been scrubbed and polished to give it some semblance of nautical grandeur.

So here I was, joining the navy.

As I walked through that front door (pardon me, went aboard), my thoughts were a jumble of things nautical. All the nice girls love a sailor; a girl in every port; sailing sailing, over the bounding main. From years of reading about pirate ships and First World War stories and seeing dozens of movies, I knew what sailors were all right, and what was expected of them. I also knew that I would rather enlist in the navy than be drafted into the army where, it was well understood, people got shot.

I found myself in a large room filled with desks and filing cabinets, with three small offices partitioned off along the sides which, I later learned, were inhabited by the captain, the paymaster, and the recruiting officer. The main room was full of officious-looking young men dressed in natty blue uniforms and wearing peaked caps, either sitting at desks or rushing about with papers in their hands. Naturally, since I knew that ordinary seamen wore jumpers, bell bottom trousers, and flat peakless caps, I took these to be officers.

I approached the nearest one and made my first of many snafus by saluting him smartly. He looked at me blankly.

"What the hell is that for?" he asked.

"I want to enlist, sir."

"I'm not a sir. I'm a writer. You want Donner. That desk over there."

I went over and stood in front of a desk where another writer was banging away on an ancient Remington upright. He stopped, ripped the page out of the machine, ran another in, and without looking at me barked, "Yeah?"

"I want to enlist."

"Last name?"

"Diespecker."

He glanced up at me as though to say, what in hell kind of name is that? and I went on the defensive. But worse was to come.

"First name, or names?"

"Robin."

"As in redbreast?"

I nodded.

"Other names?"

Well, I might as well. "Evelyn Francis."

He didn't look up this time, but kept on typing without batting an eye.

Those damned names of mine. I think that, allowing for the awfulness of the others, Diespecker was the worst. There are so many things that dirty-minded kids can do with a name like that. Bruce Sharnon called me Leastpecker until I punched him out, but that was one of the least opprobrious derivations.

A name like that can do terrible things to a kid. Imagine standing up beside your seat on the first day of school and announcing to the world that your name is Robin Evelyn Francis Diespecker. The only thing I could do about the laughter that swelled from every side of the room was join it. Which may account for the clownish twist to my nature which I'm sure was at least partly responsible for the trouble I got into aboard *Porpoise*.

My name affected my personality in another way. You can't back away from such a handle. Like a hockey player who is speared or elbowed or high-sticked, when taunted with your name you must retaliate or be forever branded as a poltroon. So I became a scrapper. The smallest hint of a gibe on my name and I'd pile in and either beat up the offender or get beaten up. This proclivity to fisticuffs also helped foul up my naval career. Clowning and pugnaciousness are two qualities not greatly appreciated by the hard-headed leading seamen and petty officers who were to become masters of my fate.

I didn't tell Donner that my nickname was Dink. This had been donated to me early on by the kids in school. I didn't care much for it, but it sure beat the three my mother had inflicted on me, and so, to everyone but my parents, my teachers, and certain girl friends, I'd become Dink Diespecker.

Donner's next questions were routine.

"Age?"

"Twenty."

"Education?"

"Senior matric."

"Got your diploma?"

"Yes. Here it is."

"Hmm … nineteen thirty-eight … honours. Okay. Nationality?"

"Canadian."

"No such thing. What was your father?"

"Canadian."

"Where did your folks come from originally?"

"From their folks, I guess."

"Never mind that. What's your racial origin?"

"I'm not sure. Quite a mixture. Why not just put down Anglo Saxon?"

And so it went. He found out I'd been born in Wabagoon and lived there all my life, that my parents were both living, that I had two siblings, both living, that I went to the United Church and that if I got into the navy I could live at home since there were no messing facilities aboard *Porpoise*.

He ripped the form out of the typewriter, handed it to me and said, "Over there," indicating a worn bench along a way beside a door, where two other civilians sat in worried silence.

I sat down beside a big fellow of about my age with a ragged haircut and a faded work shirt, baggy pants and boots with brown stains around the soles. Cow manure if I'd ever smelled it. He shifted over the bench to make room, and muttered, "Hello."

"Hi. Nice day for it anyway."

On the prairies a sure conversation opener is always the weather, for the weather is always uncertain and determines absolutely the economic status of all those who live off the land and of those who live off the people who live off the land.

"Could use rain, though," he said, confirming, along with the smell of the boots and big rough hands, my first impression that he was a farm boy.

"Where you from?" I asked.

"Wannego. Ever been there?"

"No."

"What you going in for?"

"What?"

"I mean what branch?"

"Haven't thought of it. Just want to be a sailor and get to sea."

"Stoker's the best," the man sitting next to him stated flatly. He was smaller, better dressed, and looked as though he'd been around some.

We both looked at him, me leaning forward to see past my neighbour.

"Why do you say that?" I asked.

"Friend of mine, he told me. Been in the reserves. Stokers got it made. Used to shovel coal but now they just turn taps and watch gauges. Got it made."

"But don't you have to spend your time, like, down in the—" farm boy began.

"Down below?" town boy prompted. "Yeah, sure, but that's the best place to be when the bullets start to fly. Up on deck you're a sitting duck."

Farm boy shook his head with a frown. "I don't know. Hate like hell to be closed in like that. What if the ship gets hit or something? How would you get out?"

Town boy laughed. "If she takes a fish amidships, you're a gonner wherever you are. No, it's the boiler room for me."

"My name's Sam," farm boy said. "Sam Waldress. What's yours?"

"Mike," town boy replied. "Mike Jones."

Gawd, it must be nice to have names like Sam and Mike. They were both looking at me and I knew I was in for it.

"Dink," I said. "My first name's so awful ..."

"Dink? Jees, what a handle." And then noticing the belligerent look on my face. "But not bad. Yeah, Dink. Glad to know you, Dink."

We shook hands all around awkwardly. From somewhere beyond the flimsy partitions came the hollow sound of heavy boots on cement floor, many heavy boots. And then a high voice. "Halt." The footsteps stopped abruptly. Then the voice again. "Jee-sus kee-ryst. I mean gawd-amighty! Youse guys. You march like a bunch of farmers!"

Sam winced.

"I told ya. Pick em up and put em down smartly, and swing yer arms high. Elbows straight, hands loosely clenched." It was a singsong now. "Keeping in step with the man next to you at all times." Then the disgust again. "Some of youse guys honest-to-gawd don't know yer right foot from yer left! This is yer right. This is yer left. Memorize that." Then tiredly, "Okay, stan at ease. Stan easy!"

This was followed by a rush of feet and a cheery jabber of voices.

"Sounds like a real tough killick," Mike whispered happily.

Sam's forehead wrinkled in the frown I was soon to know so well. "What's a killick?" he asked.

Mike regarded him with the scorn of the enlightened. "Jees! Leading seaman. Do most of the drilling and teaching of the new entries. Friend in the reserves, he told me all about it. Boy, the navy." Mike's square face beamed. "That's the service!"

A harried civilian emerged from the recruiting office and a bored voice from within shouted, "Okay, Donner, next man."

"Yes, sir!" Donner looked at us. "Jones, you're next. Right in there." Mike disappeared through the door and the murmur of voices began again. We went on waiting. Fighting the Hun, I was to learn in the months ahead, consisted mostly in waiting somewhere to hear your name called.

Sam squirmed uneasily, knowing he'd be called soon. "I never done anything like this before," he said. "Ain't been in the city more'n a couple a times."

"Nothing to it," I said uncertainly. "Just like any interview in high school."

"Never been to high school. Quit in Grade Six when they closed the school because nobody could pay no taxes."

"What have you been doing since?"

"Working at home on the farm. Gosh all crop to take off these last years, though."

We sat in silence. Then Mike came out with a big grin on his face. "I'm in."

"Great."

"Over here, Jones," Donner barked, and with a broad, happy smile Mike left us.

Sam went in through the door like a kid going into the principal's office. I watched Donner type and answer the phone and wondered what it would be like to be a "writer." No, I didn't want that.

Sam finally came out, looking completely bewildered, shaking his head and muttering the word "cook." Donner directed him towards the next step of the process.

Now it was my turn. A pudgy man of about fifty was sitting at a desk. He wore a blue uniform with two gold wavy stripes with a circle above on each sleeve. His shirt was white, his collar stiffly starched and his tie black. He looked up at me and said, "Sit down ... Dies ... Dies ... Diespecker? Is that your name?"

"Yes, sir. I'm afraid it is."

"Robin Evelyn Francis Diespecker?"

"Yes, sir. I'm usually called Dink."

"Well, as the bard said, what's in a name? A dink by any other name would still stink." He chuckled to himself, obviously making a mental note to repeat this rouser in the wardroom.

He gave me what I'm sure he considered to be his sharp, penetrating look. "Why do you want to join the navy, Diespecker?"

"Well ..." I'm always floored by damned fool questions.

"Consider it safer than the army, eh?"

"Is it?"

He looked up sharply and I'd swear he was going to say, as in a cops and robbers movie, "I ask the questions here, wise guy!" But he refrained and just grunted.

"So, Diespecker. I see you passed your senior matric in June of 1938. What have you been doing in the two years since then?"

"Nothing. Unemployed."

"You mean you couldn't get a job? The Depression was over by then, surely?"

"Maybe down east, but not out here. It was worse than ever."

"How did you put in your time?"

"Well, for one thing I tried to get into the naval reserves. You see I've always been fascinated by the sea. Read all the stories I could get my hands on. And the poems we had in high school. Like those of John Masefield."

"Oh yes, 'Give me a tall ship and a star to steer her by.' Why couldn't you get into the reserves?"

"I was on the list, but they weren't taking any more guys. I hung around the barracks some."

"What else did you do?"

"Well, I went harvesting. But there wasn't much crop to harvest. Delivered leaflets. Tried selling encyclopaedias door to door, but couldn't do it. Nobody had any money. Stuff like that."

"But you didn't try to join the army?"

"No, I guess I was kind of hooked on the navy. I was waiting for this place to open."

"All right. Tell me what you can do that might be of some use to the navy."

"I don't know. But I could be trained to do something."

"Can you sail a boat?"

"No."

"Ever have any military training?"

"Just in cadets in school."

"Officer, sergeant, corporal?"

"Private."

"I see."

I thought it might be time for a little levity. "The drill teacher tried to make me a corporal once, but I turned the platoon right instead of left and marched them down a twenty-foot embankment."

He just looked at me.

"Don't suppose you've ever been in a boat, out here on these godforsaken, drought-ridden prairies."

"Just a rowboat once at camp."

He brightened. "Scout camp?"

"No. Trail Rangers."

"Never heard of them. Can you cook?"

"No."

"How do you know? We could teach you. We have openings for cooks."

"I don't think I could ever learn to cook, sir. I'd rather be a seaman."

He sighed heavily and shoved some papers around on his desk. "You're in luck, Diespecker. Just so happens we've had a signal from headquarters to take on twenty seamen. Although I don't know how they're going to make seamen out of you plough jockeys."

"Where are you from, sir?" I ventured to ask.

"Me? Nova Scotia. Been around boats and ships all my life. Why in the last war … but no matter, no matter." He became all business. "Okay, Diespecker. We'll try to make a seaman out of you. Cannon fodder, cannon fodder. That is, if you pass the medical."

So I went where Donner directed me, down a corridor and into the sick bay. Mike and Sam were already there, sitting on a bench stark naked, clutching pieces of paper and shivering. Mike jerked his eyes towards the closed door of the inner office and whispered huskily, "Know what that joker tried to make me? A cook! No chance!"

"What did you tell him?" I whispered back.

"Up yours! That's what I'd like to of told him."

"Are you going to be a stoker?"

"Damned right, or it's aye-woll for me."

"What?"

"Aye-woll. Over the hill. Split. Take it on the lam."

"Oh sure."

We were interrupted by a sick bay tiffy in a white coat and glasses who stuck his head out the door, pointed a bony finger at me and snarled, "You. Get those clothes off."

I did.

Sam was still looking bewildered, and terribly embarrassed. I don't think he'd ever bared himself in front of another before, not having the advantage of a YMCA swimming pool. I looked the other way and was careful not to let my eyes go in his direction throughout our conversation.

"How about you?" Mike asked Sam.

"I don't know. Gosh, I never cooked anything in my life. How can he say I'd make a perfect cook?"

Mike whispered a snicker. "You've been diddled, Sammy me boy."

The tiffy stuck his head out again. "Okay, you're next." Mike winked at us and swaggered through the door, pendulum swinging jauntily.

"So you're going to be a cook," I said to Sam.

"Gosh help the guys who got to eat it." "Gosh," I was gradually to discover, was the strongest expletive in Sam's vocabulary. He sat there on the cold bench, hunched over his nakedness, one big paw covering his genitals, and brooded over his fate. Then he brightened. "Ever hear the joke about the three hunters and them cooking?"

If I'd known Sam then as I later got to know him, I'd have quickly said I knew the story, for Sam, like many another prairie farm boy, was an irrepressible story-teller. Frowning seriously, he began his recitation, never stopping for breath.

"Well, there was these three guys went hunting, see, on a week's trip it was and they decided that they'd draw straws to see who'd be cook see and then that guy would cook until somebody complained about the cooking and then he'd have to take over the job. Well, the guy who drew the cook job made a couple of good meals and then he saw that he was going to be the cook for the whole week if he didn't get somebody to complain, so he made some awful meals. Man, they were terrible, but still nobody complained. Well, finally he got desperate and went out and got a cow flap and heated it up in the oven, you know a cow flap, and served it with salt and pepper and ketchup and everything for dinner that night. Well, the guys were hungry after being out all day and the first guy took a big bite of it and started to chew and then his face went white. 'Gosh almighty,' he said, 'that tastes like cow manure!' And then real quick he added, 'But good!'"

I guffawed lustily, but the hollowness of it in those sterile surroundings stopped me and I grinned my appreciation.

Mike came out and hurried off to his next assignment. Sam had his turn, and then the tiffy stuck his head out again. "Okay." He consulted his sheet and actually grinned. "Diespecker. Yer next."

I followed him through the door into an anteroom just wide enough for his small desk and a straight-backed chair.

The tiffy ran a long sheet of paper into his typewriter and started barking questions at me. After the usual name, address, place of birth, age, education, he rattled off some new ones. "Ever have measles, mumps, chickenpox, tuberculosis, jaundice, VD, kidney trouble, fainting spells?" I tried to tell him about the fainting spell I had in Grade Six when I was standing at the blackboard in ninety-five-degree heat trying to figure out the complexities of decimals, but he didn't listen. On went the list and to some I answered yes and some no. Then he ripped out the sheet, handed it to me and barked, "In there."

Inside the next door was the doctor's office, with all the usual paraphernalia and a nice man. He was tall, well over six feet, and held himself with a slightly bent position as though to compensate for his height. His head was big and slightly bald, and he had a wide, friendly face that smiled a lot. He was in his shirt sleeves and sweating slightly. He looked like, and in fact had been, a family doctor from one of the prairie towns, used to dealing with farmers and small-town people.

"Hi," he said. "Sit down." He looked at my form. "Diespecker. Robin Evelyn Francis Diespecker." Pursed his lip. "Bet you've licked a few guys over that one!" His tone was friendly and I didn't bristle. "Wait until I tell you my name. Coffin. Imagine a doctor named Coffin. Should have either changed my name or my profession years ago." I grinned my appreciation. "That's not the worst of it, either. My first name is Hyram and so I get Hy. Hy Coffin. Everybody here just calls me Doc."

Doc was "okay." I was soon to learn that everybody who came into contact with him designated him so. From a rating's standpoint there are two kinds of officers, and only two—"prick" and "okay." Doc was okay.

Doc prodded, poked, and listened, peered into my various orifices, told me to come around some time and a tiffy would syringe the wax out of my left ear, said, "Wish to hell I were in as good shape as you," and said he'd be seeing me around.

That afternoon I went back to the recruiting officer and was sworn in. I was in the navy. My Gawd, in the navy! Wowee!

Edward Meade

EDWARD MEADE (1912–) was born in Winnipeg and
moved to the West Coast of British Columbia in 1930. Like the hero of his war
novel, *Remember Me*, he enlisted in the Canadian army at the outbreak of the
Second World War, serving as a platoon commander in a transport unit. Since
unauthorized writing by members of the armed forces was forbidden, he worked
on his manuscript surreptitiously, sometimes while lying in a ditch or sprawled over
the hood of a jeep. Then to avoid the censors, he concealed the pages a few at a
time in magazines and newspapers which he mailed to his wife in Vancouver.
While on leave in London in 1944, he had left a partial manuscript with a literary
agent. He was amazed to receive a letter from the English publisher Faber and
Faber summoning him from Belgium to London to arrange censorship clearance.
"How the devil was I going to get clearance?" he recalled. "I didn't have permission
in the first place to even write the book." A chance encounter with General
Montgomery on an evening walk facilitated the clearance and the timely death of
another author freed a paper quota so that the English edition of *Remember Me*
could appear in 1946.

After the war Meade settled in Campbell River, Vancouver Island. A public
accountant by profession, he became an authority on West Coast aboriginal art and
helped to found the Campbell River Museum. His pioneering work on petroglyph
sites culminated in a definitive study, *Indian Rock Carvings of the Pacific Northwest*
(1971). Bob O'Rourke, the central character of *Remember Me*, is a recently married
man whose war takes him from the small town of Yellow Prairie to the battlefields

of Normandy. A documentary attention to details of time and place is combined with emotional responses—pity, disgust, homesickness, anger—that are both typical and individual. "A Moonless Night" is set during the "Blitz" of 1940–41 when Hitler's *Luftwaffe* systematically pounded British cities and towns with explosives and incendiary bombs. During the Great War, the Germans initiated aerial attacks on civilians when they dropped bombs from zeppelins on England, killing 1,413 people. The Spanish Civil War (1936–1939) gave the Nazis the opportunity of testing saturation bombing of civilian targets, using airplanes instead of airships. Pablo Picasso's painting *Guernica* immortalized the resulting horror. The "Blitz," the most extensive terror bombing in history up to that time, killed or seriously injured 100,000 people in Britain and made close to a million people homeless.

A Moonless Night

IT WAS A MOONLESS NIGHT, THE STARS BRILLIANT in the black immensity. He stood for a while outside the pub door and looked up, seeking the known stars, Polaris, the Dipper, Cassiopeia. As he looked he heard the soft, far-off drone of planes rising and falling and rising again. Instinctively he raised his arm skywards, with his thumb upthrust. "Here's to you, boys," he said aloud. "Give the bastards hell for me."

The pub was warm and filled with the smells of beer, tobacco and damp clothes. O'Rourke took his pint of bitter to a table in the corner. He sat watching the men playing their games, and listened to their voices, trying to catch the way they spoke, to discover how they pronounced their soft "r's," the way they ended a sentence on a rising inflection that was almost nasal and sharp. He found himself repeating certain words he heard to himself, trying to get the same sounds from them.

Over beyond the fireplace a group played darts. It was apparently a close game. There were moments when the teams stood silent and intent while a player poised a dart in front of him, then, with a sharp thrust sent it flying. A florid-faced man in a tweed jacket sat with a slate and kept score in a way that was undecipherable to O'Rourke.

The atmosphere was one of warm and homely fellowship. Here were the men of the village—the labourers, the clerks, the small shopkeepers—calling each other Tom and Harry and Ted and Jack—all friends from boyhood. They sat there every Saturday night, leaving their "missus" at home with the ironing and the kids. There was fat John Bull, with pouchy cheeks, and Harry, the stonemason; there, Ted the clerk, and Horace the butcher, and Walter, who used to pitch well as a boy, and old Mason "the bloody gripe," and Jimmy the carpenter, a little tipsy, and Bill, whose "missus" was in the family way again (and at her age)—all there, with the brand of beer they liked, the quiet bartender, the smells, the homeliness, the warm familiarity. As O'Rourke watched them, he could not help envying England's "little man," who went off to the pub of a Saturday night, with the missus busy at home. He fancied, somehow, that she did not mind being left out of it.

When he went out of the pub, finally, he passed a woman, the only one there, who was sitting with folded hands waiting for her man to go home. He thought again of Gerda, with a pang of sudden remorse, for it occurred to him that she waited, even as this woman did, for her man to finish with the foolish business of "man's play," waited for him to come home—to the known door, the familiar step. He felt like speaking to the woman. He wanted to be kind and gentle a moment, to explain the foolish ways of men. But then he saw that she was quietly happy, sitting there, and he did not speak but went out into the night where searchlights knifed the sky and great motors throbbed in the dark immensity.

As he walked along the street the sound of planes grew louder. One swept low overhead, then another and another. Their whistle and scream filled the night until there was nothing else.

"Ours," he thought to himself. "They're going up to meet Jerry."

Instinctively he moved a little faster. He walked closer to the high brick wall that ran along the sidewalk. He felt the quickening of his blood-beat. The sense of danger tensed his nerves. He was in the middle of a raid. He had not heard the sirens.

He passed a soldier and a girl. The girl tripped quickly along beside the soldier, her arm in his, her face upturned to the sky. He heard her laugh, a gay, rich little laugh. And she said, casually, lightly: "I'm never nervous in a raid, until I hear the bombs whistling. And then, of course, it's too late to be nervous ... I remember ..." Her voice trailed away.

The pause of hushed expectancy deepened. The planes droned and screamed in the sky amid the sweeping shafts of the searchlights, but on the earth, in the streets, all was suddenly silent, tensed, waiting.

Everything told O'Rourke to take cover, to hide, yet he moved along gingerly, step by step. He passed the opening of a lane and saw a small group of people huddled in the shadows, their faces upturned to the sky. They seemed to sway and waver, like something caught in the path of a whirlwind. He walked on, rounded a corner and came suddenly upon the town square. Here he was halted by an incredible sight. Out of nowhere, yet from everywhere, every doorway, alleyway and street, people streamed into the square. They were like columns of ants running for the safety of the anthill. Now and then a body broke from the moving columns, but it was quickly drawn back again. The shuffle of feet, the low nervous murmur of a multitude rushed like a wind through the square. In the spectral light from the sweeping searchlights amid the phantasmal shadows, these columns of people converged upon the centre of the square and disappeared into the mounds that were shelters. Suddenly the square was empty, still and desolate in the eerie light.

Now O'Rourke felt a terrific compulsion to hurry. He almost ran past the still and shuttered buildings. He cast a glance into the dark yawning doorways of the shelters, but no power on earth could have turned him into one of them. Beyond the square, in a narrow street, he came upon a small queue of people at a bus stop. The buses had apparently ceased running, for O'Rourke had seen none since leaving the pub, but these few people were hopeful that they could still get out of town before the raid.

It had taken him only a few minutes to arrive at this point from the pub. In that brief time the searchlight batteries had been synchronized, interceptors had taken to the air to turn back the raiders, and the entire population of the town had gone to the shelters. Ack-ack guns began to fire. A battery on the southern edge of the town opened up: Bofors, he thought, by the sound of them. Two other batteries opened up immediately after, as if in answer. Then he could not tell how many were firing, for the bark and crack of them filled the streets and rocked the buildings.

Strangely, it was not the whistle of bombs that first warned him of immediate danger, but the sound of splintering glass. It came so unexpectedly, without any apparent cause. He heard the glass break and tinkle as the pieces fell to the pavement. It was immediately after that that the rising whistle of the bombs came to him. For a moment he stopped and turned about in the street, searching for shelter. Then he dropped upon the pavement, beside a high brick wall, with his legs together, his face pressed against the stone. For a second more he heard the whistling and whir of a bomb falling.

"Jees," he said to himself, and heard his voice a long way off. A thought flashed across his mind then. "If this is it, I may as well see it." He raised his head a little and looked across the street.

The people who had been standing in the queue were crouched together in a mass, their bodies bent and their heads downthrust to ward off the terror. In the next instant there came a terrific explosion, and then another which felt right beside him. He clawed at the pavement for support. He was thrown prone along the side of the wall and found himself spread-eagled across the sidewalk. The earth rocked, and broken brick and rubble rained upon him. He buried his head deeper in his shoulders and held his breath.

He waited a minute while the falling debris settled. Then he raised his head cautiously and looked about him. The wall beside him had a gaping, half-moon crescent blown out of it. In the centre of the roadway a shell crater smoked. Across it a great length of iron pipe had been hurled from nowhere. On the other side of the crater, he saw the huddle of people who had been waiting for the bus. They were flattened now, one upon the other, and lay motionless. Above them, the brick building was pock-marked by a dozen holes, and the windows were blasted and the wooden frames hung out over the street.

At that moment he heard the soft whine and plop of a missile in the street, further down. He ducked his head again. But in a moment he knew it was not a bomb, for the world, even though his closed eyelids, became startlingly bright. He looked up again and saw an incendiary bomb burning intense and white in the centre of the roadway. He saw men running out to it. The light was so bright their bodies were without shadows.

He lay as he was and did not move, but slowly he began to think of escape. His eyes probed the length of the street, lighted brightly now by the incendiary and the searchlights overhead.

He saw a stir of movement in the huddled group across the street. A woman lifted herself from the others, and stood a moment wavering back and forth unsteadily with her arms outstretched for support. Then she took a step, suddenly grasped her belly low down, and holding herself thus, she bent doubled with pain. O'Rourke heard her scream. All at once he saw that she was far pregnant. Still screaming, she moved, blindly out into the roadway. She wavered on the edge of the bomb crater, and then staggered away from it. Finally she could go no farther. She stopped in the road, bent over. Her screams died. Slowly she sank to the pavement, still clutching the weight of her belly.

O'Rourke ran out into the road, and bent over the woman. He turned her upon her back and felt for the pulse in her throat. It beat strongly under his fingers. She raised a hand and, groping, caught hold of his wrist. Her grip was astonishingly fierce. She moaned and writhed, "Dick! Dick! Help me now! Dick! Help me, please ... Oh ... please!" She cried pitifully, yet there were no tears.

He had to twist his wrist to break her grip. He picked her up and started down the street in search of a first-aid post. When he came to an intersection he had to stop and rest, leaning against a concrete tank block beside the kerb. He could see no F.A.P. sign. When he had caught his breath he went on, past a pub whose sign had been knocked into the gutter, past a draper's shop, past a building of flats. When he had passed this building, he suddenly realized that he had seen an F.A.P. sign over a basement stairway. Gingerly, feeling for each step, he descended. At the bottom, in the pitch black, he bumped against a door. He kicked at it with his foot. He was about to kick it again when it opened wide and he stepped into a hallway lit with a dim bulb. A nurse led him into a room opening off the hall, and he laid his burden upon the floor between two other wounded women who lay with blankets over them.

The room was filled with injured people. There were several children, two very old women sitting on the floor against the wall sipping something from mugs, some men, old, too. It was a small room. At one end a doctor sat by a table on which lay heaps of bottles, instruments, dressings of all kinds, and case cards.

The nurse who had let him in came back from the table with a case card in her hand.

"Do you know her?" she asked him, nodding toward the pregnant woman.

O'Rourke shook his head.

"I picked her up in the street near the bus stop," he replied, and started to indicate with his arm the direction he had come from. It was quite useless. What did it matter?

The nurse bent over the woman, and made a swift, cursory examination.

"Doctor," she called.

"Yes," the man at the table answered. He did not look up from what he was doing.

"Will you please look at this woman?"

"Right," he replied, but there was a weariness and strain in his voice.

He picked up his stethoscope and came over and knelt to the woman. O'Rourke could not see what he was doing, but he heard the doctor breathing hard in the still room and saw the look of intenseness on the nurse's face as she watched him. Presently the doctor straightened up and took off his spectacles and wiped them on his handkerchief.

"Miss Niser, phone for the ambulance. This woman will have to go to hospital right away. A rather bad case. The child is already half born. It is dead."

He put his glasses in his breast pocket and went back to the table. The nurse picked up the phone and began to speak.

"Tell them it is an urgent case," the doctor said.

"I'll be getting along now," O'Rourke told the nurse. "Good night."

"Good night," she said, turning from the phone. "Good night, Canada."

He climbed the steps to the street and leaning against the railing, lit a cigarette. As he put the packet back in his pocket he felt a wetness against his hand. He raised it to the glow of his cigarette and examined it. It was blood. The front of his tunic and trousers were wet with it. Why, he wondered, would a pregnant woman, so far gone, be out on the street in a raid? Maybe she had been on her way to the hospital, or to a friend for help .... Husband away on the night shift, or fire fighting, or out in the Middle East, or God knows where. Well!

He threw the cigarette away and started back for camp. The sky over the far edge of town was bright yellow from a burning fire and smoke clouds. But the earth was still now: no sound came from the skies: only, faint and far away, the crackle of burning wood and the smell of smoke and brick dust, and another smell, acrid and suggestive of fire, that he could not identify.

Many were late into barracks, for everyone had taken shelter during the raid. Nothing was said when O'Rourke showed his paybook and passed into the camp. The hut was in darkness but no one was asleep. The men lay in the dark, smoking and talking about the raid, and how Jerry had tried to get the camp and missed.

O'Rourke listened to the talk while he undressed. It was the old barrack-room argument and opinion, with every man clamouring to be heard. It was good stuff for morale, usually; let every man have his say and get the steam off his chest. But tonight it galled him.

He was dead tired, but he could not sleep. His mind turned back to the pregnant woman in the middle of the road, clutching at the weight of her womb with both hands and screaming like a doomed animal into the night. And over and through this ran the chatter of voices in argument and exposition. Finally he could bear it no longer. He sat bolt upright on his cot.

"Listen," he snapped into the dark. "Listen, you goddam bedtime warriors. If Jerry wanted to get this camp he'd have got it and you'd be food for the daisies now. He wanted to get the town, and he got it. This is his innings, right now. Ours is next. But one of these days you're going to meet up with him, and if the whole bloody lot of you don't shut up and get some sleep you aren't going to be quite as good as he is when that day arrives. Now shut up and go to sleep."

The noise subsided. There were some faint whisperings, but no one spoke aloud. He was, after all, the hut corporal. He was in a bad mood, no doubt about it. He was also tough.

Joy Kogawa

JOY KOGAWA (1935–) was born in Vancouver; she
was a Nisei, the third generation of her family to live in Canada. When Japan entered
the war by bombing the American fleet at Pearl Harbor, Hawaii on December 7,
1941, Canada had 23,000 people of Japanese origin. Most of them had settled on
the west coast where they made a living as fishermen, boat builders, market
gardeners, loggers, and workers in sawmills and pulp and paper mills. Prompted
by the public's fear of spying and terrorist activities and by discriminatory attitudes
against Asians, on February 26, 1942 the government ordered all Japanese to be
deported from the west coast, including those who were Canadian citizens.
Among those relocated in the deserted mining towns of the East Kootenays was
Joy Kogawa's family.

Obasan (1981), the source of the following story, is fiction but Naomi (Nomi),
who provides a child's-eye view of the events, is to a considerable extent the
author's alter ego. The character of Obasan (aunt) is based on Kogawa's mother
while the Anglican minister Natayama-Sensei resembles her father. As an adult
Kogawa has written in support of appeals to the federal government for apologies
and compensation for lost property. She believes that one must deal with past
history, both personal and public, before one can trust and be trusted. In 1982
Obasan won both the Books in Canada First Novel Award and the Canadian
Authors' Association Book of the Year Award. Kogawa has also published a
children's version, Naomi's Road (1986). Itsuka (1992) is a historical sequel to
Obasan. As an adult, Naomi Nakane becomes involved in the Japanese Canadians'

struggle to obtain redress for their wartime treatment. In 1988 the Government of Canada offered an apology and expressed appreciation for the loyalty of their Japanese citizens. It committed $350,000,000 to compensate for lost property and to fund ethnic organizations.

Obasan

TWENTY YEARS LATER, IN 1962, AUNT EMILY wanted to take a trip through the interior of British Columbia. Off we went—Uncle, Aunt Emily, Obasan, and I—through Banff, down the Rogers Pass, through Golden, and Revelstoke, Uncle pointing out a small side road which he said was the place his work camp had been. I drove through what was left of some of the ghost towns, filled and emptied once by prospectors, filled and emptied a second time by the Japanese Canadians. The first ghosts were still there, the miners, people of the woods, their white bones deep beneath the pine-needle floor, their flesh turned to earth, turned to air. Their buildings—hotels, abandoned mines, log cabins—still stood marking their stay. But what of the second wave? What remains of our time there?

We looked for the evidence of our having been in Bayfarm, in Lemon Creek, in Popoff. Bayfarm and Popoff were farmlands in Slocan before the tar-paper huts sprang up. Lemon Creek was a camp seven miles away carved out of the wilderness. Tashme—formed from the names of Taylor, Shirras, and Mead, men on the B.C. Security Commission—also rose overnight, fourteen miles from Hope, and as quickly disappeared. Where on the map or on the road was there any sign? Not a mark was left. All our huts had been removed long before and the forest had returned to take over the clearings. What remained the same was the smell of pine and cedar. The mountains too were unchanged except for the evidence of new roads and a larger logging industry. While we stood there in Slocan, we could hear the wavering hoot of a train whistle as we used to years before. But the Slocan that we knew in the forties was no longer there, except for the small white community which had existed before we arrived and which watched us come with a mixture of curiosity and fear. Now, down on the shore of the Slocan lake, on the most beautiful part of the sandy beach, where we used to swim, there was a large new sawmill owned by someone who lived in New York.

We left Slocan and drove towards Sandon. The steep one-vehicle road dropped at such a perilous and tortuous slope, I turned around the first chance I could get. What a hole!

"It was an evacuation all right," Aunt Emily said. "Just plopped here in the wilderness. Flushed out of Vancouver. Like dung drops. Maggot bait."

None of us, she said, escaped the naming. We were defined and identified by the way we were seen. A newspaper in B.C. headlined, "They are a stench in the nostrils of the people of Canada." We were therefore relegated to the cesspools. In Sandon, Tashme, Kaslo, Greenwood, Slocan, Bayfarm, Popoff, Lemon Creek, New Denver, we lived in tents, in bunks, in skating rinks, in abandoned hotels. Most of us lived in row upon row of two-family, three-room huts, controlled and orderly as wooden blocks. There was a tidy mind somewhere.

Some families who had gone ahead or independently had been able to find empty farmhouses to rent. In Slocan, several families lived in an abandoned bunk-house at an old silver mine. Our own house was just a two-roomed log hut at the base of the mountain. It was shabby and sagging and overgrown with weeds when we first saw it on that spring day in 1942.

"Thank you, thank you," Obasan says to a man, an ojisan in a grey cap who reaches up and puts an arm around Stephen hesitating at the top of the train steps. I pick up Stephen's crutches and follow him as he is carried through the slow crowd of boxes and bodies. People are bustling about on the wooden platform in groups, carrying luggage here and there. Even in all this crowd, there is a stillness here. The sudden fresh air, touched with the familiar smell of sawdust, is crisp and private. Yet there is a feeling of open space. Through a break in the crowd, I can see a lake with a sandy beach and drift logs. All around its edge are mountains covered in trees, climbing skyward. The highest farthest mountains are blue and purple and topped with white snow.

I am holding Obasan's hand and looking around when I hear Stephen say "Hello, Sensei." Sensei is the word for teacher. I look up and recognize

Nakayama-sensei, the round-faced minister with round eyes and round glasses from the Anglican church in Vancouver. He is talking to Obasan and to the man who helped Stephen. The boy carrying the kitten is holding the hand of a woman in a blue dress who is waiting to speak to Nakayama-sensei.

"It is not so far," Sensei says to Obasan. "I will show you the way." He turns to the woman in blue and nods gravely, says a few words to the ojisan and to a missionary, then disappears into the crowd.

Except for Stephen on his crutches, we all carry bags, furoshiki, suitcases, boxes and follow Ojisan down the middle of the road, past the gaunt hotels swarming with people, like ants in an overturned ant-hill. Ojisan puts down his heavy box and we wait till he returns with a homemade wheelbarrow.

"Ah, joto, joto," Nakayama-sensei says rejoining us, "excellent, excellent."

We arrange our luggage and follow Nakayama-sensei and Ojisan down the street again, turning to the left past a building with the sign "Graham's General Store," and we walk up the flat gravel road through the valley to the mountain's foot. There are no streetcars here, no sidewalks or large buildings. On either side of the road are a few houses, smaller than the ones in Vancouver.

As we pass a wooden bridge over a creek, I think of the curved bridge over the goldfish pond at Obasan's house, and the bridges Stephen and I made in the sand to the desolate sound of the sea, and the huge Lions' Gate Bridge in Stanley Park, and the terrifying Capilano swinging bridge that trembled as we crossed it high up in the dangerous air.

Perhaps it is because I first missed my doll while standing on this bridge that often in the evenings, when I cross it, I feel a certain sadness.

Obasan, carrying a large furoshiki, waits for me as I linger looking down at the water burbling over the stones and a crow hopping on the bank.

"Where is my doll?" I ask, calling to her. I am not carrying anything since putting the bag of food and the furoshiki I was given onto Ojisan's pile.

Obasan looks startled and utters that short sharp word of alarm.

"Ara!"

She puts down her furoshiki and opens it, then calls to Ojisan.

He and Obasan examine the boxes on the wheelbarrow, lifting them off one by one.

"Ojisan will find your doll," he says heartily as I reach them. He squats down and faces me.

"The others are in the bin in the kitchen," I tell him.

His round face, crinkly with laugh lines, bounces like a ball. I do not doubt that he will bring them all. He slaps his knees as if the deed is already accomplished.

Stephen, on his crutches, has disappeared ahead of the rest of us. The mountain, immediate and immense as night, swallows us as we turn onto a path into a clump of trees.

"Stephen! Wait!" I call, running to catch up with him.

I find him and Sensei peering into the woods. There is nothing to be seen except trees, trees, and trees. The ground under our feet is soft and bumpy with needles, moss, pine cones, and small acorn hats. On either side of the path, green fronds of ferns are everywhere, open and extravagant as peacocks.

"See that, Nomi?" Stephen says, pointing. I can see nothing and everything, a forest of shadows and green shapes. "Over there," he says impatiently.

We walk a few steps farther down the path, and there, almost hidden from sight off the path, is a small grey hut with a broken porch camouflaged by shrubbery and trees. The colour of the house is that of sand and earth. It seems more like a giant toadstool than a building. The mortar between the logs is crumbling and the porch roof dives down in the middle. A "V" for victory. From the road, the house is invisible, and the path to it is overgrown with weeds.

"That's our house," Stephen says. "Sensei told me."

We wade through the weeds to the few grey fenceposts still standing beside a gate flat on the ground, anchored to the earth by a web of vines. Behind the house, the mountain lurches skyward above a vertical rock wall. When I look up the side of the mountain, above the grey rock, to the left, there is a thin stream of water falling straight down a grey rock wall.

Stephen clumps up the porch steps and pushes his way in the front door. It scrapes along the floor. I stand at the broken gate waiting, then follow him, crossing the rickety porch step. The pine-green outside air changes suddenly to the odour of attic grey. Everything is grey—the newspapered walls, the raw grey planks on the floors, the two windows meshed by twigs and stems and stalks of tall grasses seeking a way in. A rough plank bed is in the middle of the room. Greyness seeps through the walls and surrounds us. "See that?" Stephen says, pointing to the ceiling which is an uneven matted mass of fibres. "That's grass and manure up there."

"What?"

"Sure. Cow manure."

"Says who?"

He shrugs his shoulders.

The ceiling is so low it reminds me of the house of the seven dwarves. The newspapers lining the walls bend and curl showing rough wood beneath. Rusted nails protrude from the walls. A hornet crawls along the ledge of a window. Although it is not dark or cool, it feels underground.

There is no expression on Obasan's face as she comes in following Nakayama-sensei and Ojisan. The room is crowded with the three adults, the suitcases, boxes, Stephen, and me. Obasan takes a handkerchief from her sleeve and offers it to Ojisan. "Such heavy things," she says. "You must be weary."

"Ah," Ojisan says, "when one is almost fifty."

"Chairs just to fit," Sensei says pulling up the wooden boxes. "A small house for small people."

Ojisan reaches up to touch the ceiling. "Short people lived here, the same as we are."

"So it seems," Sensei sighs.

Obasan sits beside me on the edge of the bed.

"Together," Sensei says, "by helping each other ...." It sounds half like a rallying call, half like an apology as if he is somehow responsible.

"As long as we have life and breath," Ojisan says.

"That is indeed so," Sensei repeats, "while we breathe, we have gratitude." It is comforting to hear them talking calmly.

"For our life and that we are together again, thank you. For protection thus far, thank you ...." Nakayama-sensei is praying with his eyes open.

I follow Stephen into the other room. A rusty wood stove is against one wall. Stephen is poking at a bolt on the back door and pushes it back finally with the edge of his crutch. The rusty screen door opens with a scrape and shuts with a dusty clap as Stephen and I go outside.

Ah! The green air once more.

As we stand here looking over an overgrown tangle of weeds and vines, the air is suddenly swarming with butterflies. Up and down like drunken dancers, the gold and brown winged things come down the side of the mountain fluttering awkwardly. There are dozens of them. Some park like tiny helicopters on grass stalks, flexing their wings as if for take-off. Others hover near the ground before spilling back up into the air, ungainly as baby ballerinas. They are all dressed in the same velvet brown.

Stephen whacks his crutch into the grasses, scattering the butterflies. Each wing bears two round circles of gold and when the pairs are spread, they are infant eyes, staring up at us bodiless and unblinking. I stare back as Stephen tramples and slashes, hopping deeper and deeper into the tall grasses, swinging his crutch like a scythe. Within moments, the ground and grasses are quivering with maimed and dismembered butterflies. The ones that are safe are airborne and a few have reached the heights of trees.

"They're bad," Stephen says as he wades through the weeds. "They eat holes in your clothes."

His crutch clears a wide path through the middle of the backyard as he continues his crusade. When he reaches the end of the yard, he turns around. Some brambles and vines are clinging to his pant leg and one butterfly he cannot see is hovering above his head.

Agnes Newton Keith

AGNES NEWTON KEITH (1901–1975) was born in Oak Park, Illinois and grew up in California. In 1934 she married an Englishman, Harry Keith, who was Conservator of Forests and Director of Agriculture in the British colony of North Borneo. *Land Below the Wind*, Agnes Keith's account of her life in Borneo, was an international best-seller. When the Second World War broke out, the Keiths were on leave and living in Victoria, BC, where Harry owned a home. Forbidden to enlist, Harry was ordered back to Sandakan to continue in government service. On January 19, 1942 Japanese invaders conquered Borneo and within four months the Keiths, including their two-year-old son George, and other enemy aliens were incarcerated in an abandoned quarantine station on Berhala Island. On January 20, 1943 they were moved to Kuching on the Sarawak River, two degrees from the equator. Here there were eight segregated camps for 3,000 prisoners of war and internees: Australian officers and NCOs, British soldiers, Indonesians, civilian men, Roman Catholic and Anglican priests, and women and children, including 140 Dutch and English nuns.

In spite of international agreements concerning the treatment of internees and prisoners-of-war, all were systematically abused, starved and forced to provide slave labour in fields, forests, Japanese quarters and the roads. In the women's camp the food ration was five tablespoons of cooked rice per day (frequently reduced as punishment), supplemented with flowers, grass, weeds, dogs, cats, snakes, grasshoppers, snails and sometimes eggs, sugar and coffee which the women obtained by bartering their few personal belongings. Colonel Suga, Commander of all Prisoners of War and Internees, who had a degree from the University of

Washington and wore Allied World War I military decorations, ordered Agnes Keith to write an account of her captivity which would present her captors in a favourable light. But the real basis for *Three Came Home* (1947) was acquired as she describes in her Foreword:

> I wrote in the smallest possible handwriting, on the backs of labels, on old Chinese papers that our tobacco came in, on the margins of old newspapers given us by the Japanese ... I stuffed George's toys with these notes, I sewed a layer of them in his sleeping mat, I stuffed his pillows, and I put them in tins which I buried under the barrack.

The guards frequently searched her things, removing everything with writing on it: documents, passport, marriage license and so on. Had they found her story, the offence would have been punishable by death.

Agnes Keith wrote *Three Came Home* in Victoria, concluding it in November 1946 with these words:

> When we work as hard in peacetime to make this world decent to live in, as in wartime we work to kill, the world will be decent, and the causes for which men fight will be gone.

The Keiths returned to North Borneo after the war, remaining until 1952, as recounted in *White Man Returns* (1951).

Getting Rid of Proudery and Arrogance

THE NEW CAMP SITE WAS TO BE OVER THE excrement pits of the soldiers' camps, where the ground was full of hookworm, and the air was full of mosquitoes. It was the third time we had moved in fourteen months, and with each change we lost strength, and gained new diseases. This time we were exchanging our newly planted vegetable garden for an offal pit.

We begged Colonel Suga not to move us, pleading that the children would die of hookworm, as they had no shoes; the adults would die of malaria, as they had no medicines; we would both die of starvation if we had no garden; we would all die of the move anyway, as we were over-worked and underfed.

Colonel Suga answered that it was too bad and he was very sorry because he liked us to be happy, but we must be removed from the sight of our husbands.

He could not move our husbands to the new camp, he said, because it was half a mile further down the road and he did not trust them so far from the Japanese officers. Thus isolated, husbands might smuggle—might even escape! But not so ladies ... ladies he trusted!

So we trusted ladies were to move camp at nine o'clock in the morning. George and I had been ill in our barrack for three days and nights with malaria, which was always with us. George had a high temperature, and I had had no sleep, fearing convulsions for him again—and I was dopey with fever and fatigue.

Now moving day came, muster was called, and I was not there. Had I been executed for it, I could not have been ready at nine that day.

I arrived at camp square ten minutes late, dragging two suitcases, and George; he feverish, but uncomplaining, with an unchildlike submission now to pain—which hurt me more that his tears. In the square there were eight other women and five children standing at attention, under arrest for being late. The rest of the camp personnel had already left for the new camp.

The Nipponese officer was furious with us. We ladies had no sense of discipline! (Bang! Bang!) We were not standing at attention even now! (Bang, bang.) If the Japanese were not so kind they would beat us! (Three bangs.) For kindness was wasted on us! (Bang, bang.)

We had insulted him, and the entire Japanese Army, by being late! Therefore we would spend the day standing in the public square, and the night in the guardhouse, and not proceed to the new camp until tomorrow, in order to wipe out the insult we had paid the Japanese Army by being late! (Bang! Bang! And a Bronx cheer!)

The way I felt about the Japanese Army at that moment, the insult could not have been wiped out by a lifetime spent in a brothel.

So we stood at attention in the sun, while our husbands, who had arrived at the old camp in a group, to help with the moving, were allowed inside with the guards. I saw Harry, but couldn't wave; when he saw me he looked worried. It was an unusual concession on the part of the Japanese to let the husbands help us move.

Fourteen months before we had been imprisoned with one suitcase each. Since then we had acquired furniture. Inside the barrack our homemade acquisitions of stolen timber had been comparatively inconspicuous, lost under the seething mass of women, children, dirty clothes, falling mosquito nets, and reclaimed garbage. But when our husbands came to remove the furnishings from the old barracks, one wall of the place fell in, and when they carried the furniture down the road to the new camp the Japanese officers were confronted with the fact that 50 per cent of the old housing system had been converted into furniture.

Faced with the evidence of our wholesale disobedience, they were put to it what to do. The ladies had been naughty again! But what could one do? One could not shoot them all, one could not beat them all, one could not shame them, for they had no shame. One could not even successfully ignore them.

Meanwhile Lieutenant Nekata rested in the shade of the trees near by, watching the movers at work. His polished army boots were off, his stocking-clad feet propped upon a tree trunk, his trousers undone and open, with cotton underpants visible underneath. If the Britons had built their Empire in dress suits, the Japs were equally determined to tear it to pieces in their underpants.

The movers themselves matched the goods that they handled: they, like our material belongings, were broken-down, ragged, pathetic; they, like our beds, chairs, stools, and tables, were inelegant, but invaluable. Shirtless, shoeless, stockingless, hatless, each one bandaged, with a septic leg or arm, a cough, a limp, a droop—in the past these men had suffered with excess punctilio; today they scarcely had pants. Yet when one looked from them to Nekata, one could appreciate the fact that even so one distinguished them from apes.

Our husbands soon finished their moving work, and I saw Harry look anxiously over at me in the punishment party, before he disappeared into his own camp. We had been told to stand at attention for punishment: soon we just stood, and then we sat.

It was twelve o'clock now and very hot, and we were in the sun, and George became sick at his stomach. I carried him over to the side of the road and placed him in the shade of a tree, and stayed with him. Soon we all moved under the trees, opened our baskets, and took out the bottles of boiled water and tea without which we never left camp. Lieutenant Nekata watched us without comment from his seat near by. All I could think of as I looked at him was, "The little army-adjective so-and-so!"—which was a quote from Harry that used to comfort me greatly.

After a while Teresa, another one of the late mothers, who was always 101 per cent Mother Love, came to me and said, "You should tell Nekata that George is ill. Tell him we are all very sorry we were late, and ask him to let us go on to the new camp now. Perhaps he'd do it."

"No, I'm not going to. He's just sitting there waiting for us to plead with him. Look at him, with his pants half off! I'm sick of these Nips! No. We were late, and they can punish us."

"For George's sake, you ought to," she urged. I knew that I ought to, but I wasn't going to.

"You go over yourself and tell him about Alastair's sore toes!" I said rudely.

However, I did go over to Nekata and say, "It is lunchtime, and we have no food. Will you send rations for the children?"

He nodded "Yes," and I returned to tell the others. We made a little fire with twigs, and started boiling water for tea. Then Teresa could stand it no longer, she had the courage of a hundred convictions where the kids were concerned. She went to Nekata and spoke as always—volubly, dramatically, hysterically, as if demonstrating complete, utter, abject misery. In answer to her story of pain, Nekata's face remained as blank as a piece of paper. She returned, and we drooped in the heat.

Then "Wilfred," the Japanese civilian who interpreted for the military, came over to me. Wilfred was almost invisible owing to negative personality plus anemia, but the Japanese had awarded him a position of contentious importance, which perpetually involved him in breaking bad news to people, conveying insults and epithets, telling people unpleasant things about each other, witnessing violent scenes. All this had made poor Wilfred into a nervous wreck.

He came over to me, sent by Nekata, and asked if George was ill. I said yes, he had malaria; yes, that was why I was late to muster. Several voices around me spoke up and said the children were not well, it was too hot for them, we all felt ill, and could we go on to the new camp now?

Wilfred returned to Nekata and reported. Then after some time he came back and ordered us to go over to the lieutenant. We did so, and stood at attention before Nekata, who still lolled at ease with trousers agape. Nekata spoke, and Wilfred interpreted:

"The lieutenant says you are very bad ladies because you were late, and you have thus offended the Japanese officers. This is a great crime. If you were soldiers he would put you in the guardhouse for five days, without food, or beat you, or shoot you.

"But you are ladies—and the guardhouse is not big enough for you all. Also Nekata is very kind, like all Japanese, and very kind to ladies and children, like all Japanese. So he will forgive you this time, and you may now pick up your luggage and proceed to the new camp."

So then like good ladies we proceeded down the road to our new camp, swinging three and four suitcases on long poles between every two women, and dragging our children behind us, while the Japanese, like very kind Japanese, permitted us to do so.

At the new camp I found that my "flat" was a good one, near a doorway, which meant opportunity for air and expansion: here in my allotted space I found our beds already delivered by Harry. The locating of a claim in a new camp was done by alphabetical arrangement, gambling, or fighting, and as I was late in arriving I would have been out of luck had not Shihping Cho staked my claim for me, by her side.

In this camp I found we had five long palm-leaf barracks, but only four were to be used for sleeping in, as the Japanese had ordered one kept free. This one, they said proudly, was to be our chapel.

This meant that we were painfully overcrowded still, and again George and I had only four feet by six feet in which to exist. Again there were no partitions or privacy. The mothers and children settled together in one end of the first barrack.

George continued to be ill all afternoon with a high temperature and vomiting. I washed our flat and unpacked the belongings, and stole some nails out of the beams for shelves, prying them up with a table knife, and knocking them cockeyed with a stone, and extracting them by wiggling. There was little to eat all day as the new kitchen fires wouldn't burn, the chimneys wouldn't draw, the water wouldn't boil; no wonder, as the firewood consisted of the branches of green rubber trees we had cut down that day.

I was awake all night with George, but towards morning his fever broke, and he slept. I got up at six o'clock, as I liked to arise early and dress quietly before the pandemonium of the children broke loose, to be ready for my morning job. Although I was writing for Suga I was doing camp work also. It was six by arbitrary prison time, but 4:30 by sun time, and pitch black outside the barrack and in. The stars scarce showed, the dawn still hung far in the distance, and the only other people awake in camp were the Sisters, who got up early to say their prayers.

I sat on my doorstep in slacks, for I was chilly with the aftermath of fever, and brushed my hair, and thought. Thinking was sometimes the way to wisdom, when bitter realities could be left behind in the fore-tasting of dreams and ambitions; but sometimes it was the way to destruction, when one was overwhelmed in an agony of despair. This morning, with me, it was despair.

Daily I saw myself becoming hard, bitter, and mean, disgracing the picture I had painted for myself in happier days. My disposition and nerves were becoming unbearable. I was speaking to George with a hysterical violence which I hated, but could not control. I did not have the food to give him when he asked for it; if I did I was so hungry I could not sit with him when he ate it; for this he was not to blame—and yet he must suffer.

I wept in despair for what I could not give to him. Not for material things alone, food, playthings, comforts, but for the gentle, loving mother that I could not be to him. I was the only living thing that stood between George and destruction. I was not a mother, I was the whole force of circumstances in his world. My body was worn, my nerves torn, my energies flagging; because of this I could only show him a stern woman struggling grimly to get his food.

As I sat grinding the teeth of despair I became conscious that some-body was watching me. Glancing over my shoulder I saw the dim outline of a Japanese soldier in the doorway on the other side of the barrack.

He shuffled across, stepped through my doorway, descended two steps, and stood very close to me, while I continued to brush my hair. He mumbled to me in a combination of Japanese, Malay, and English, and offered me cigarettes. I shook my head, wanting nothing from them that day. Some days, yes, but this day, damn it, no! He continued to proffer the cigarettes, pressing against me on the steps. I shook my head, but when he persisted, I morosely jerked my head backward, meaning that he could toss the cigarettes on the floor behind me, if he were fool enough to give them. He leaned his rifle against the door, fumbled with the cigarette pack, bent over me, and put them on the table.

The thought came to me, I should say Thank you. I should get up and bow. Or I should say Get away, you're too close! Or I should move away myself. What is he? A jailer, or a Sweetie-Pie?

The guard hesitated, giggled, and shuffled his feet—and then bent quickly over me, ran his two hands roughly down my breasts, over my thighs, and forced them violently up between my legs. The gesture so astounded me that I was paralyzed. I could think of nothing but, Well, it's fortunate I have on slacks.

What followed then was unpleasant, a kind of unpleasantness that a woman resents more than any other, and which hurts her as much psychologically as physically. The soldier was strong and rough and crude and nasty, and he enjoyed humiliating me; his ideas of pleasure were new ones to me; had they been familiar I still could not have liked them. I hated everything that he represented; but that was superfluous, for that was endowing him with human faculties, when all that he represented at the moment was an animal.

I was not strong enough to combat him, and did not have the power to escape him, but circumstances were with me. To debauch a captive thoroughly even the jailer needs time and quiet; he should have chosen the latrine or the bathhouse for his assault. The scuffling, the pawing and groveling, that we made, plus shouting on my part, began to arouse my neighbours. They were worn-out and sleep-sodden, and they had long ago learned to mind their own business where soldiers were concerned; still, the noise and struggle aroused them, and they began to stir and call out. The soldier relaxed his embraces for a moment, and I swung on him, taking advantage of his distraction and an unprotected stomach area, and almost knocked him down. He stumbled backwards down the stairs, and there he hesitated as to what to do: whether to kiss, or to kill, or to pull up his pants and go.

I was on my feet and shouting, "Get out! Get the hell out!" and a lamp was approaching us from the Sisters' barrack across the way, and our barrack was awakening, and I guess he'd lost the primary urge. He picked up his fallen rifle, and went sourly down the path.

I stood wearily in the doorway in the darkness: the stars were still dim, the dawn not yet come, the Sisters still praying; I had not even seen my assailant's face.

My neighbours slowly aroused themselves. Shihping Cho crawled out of her mosquito net and asked me what the trouble was, Maureen called across to me and said "What's up?"—and Mary said sleepily, "I thought I heard a noise." I told them that a guard had been unpleasant to me, and they accepted my reply without discussion. We had learned in camp to ask no questions, and give no answers; each person's trouble was her own affair; she must bear it, or otherwise, as best she could.

We were captives, we were helpless, our life was unbearable, and we had to bear it. We cried out "I can't stand it!"—and we stood it.

A captive has no rights: I knew that one. I felt now that there was no further way for me to demonstrate it. But I was wrong.

I got my morning mug of tea, and even took some sugar in it: I needed something to stimulate me, and sugar, when one is unaccustomed to it, will do almost as much as whiskey.

As I drank tea, and thought about the happening of the morning, I became apprehensive. Only yesterday we had been moved to the new camp, last night the guards had sat on women's beds, laughing and talking until late, today I had been attacked. Would the new camp, because of its isolation from the Japanese officers' supervision, repeat the same conditions of unwelcome intimacy under which we had suffered on Berhala Island? I felt that, at this stage of fatigue and strain, it would be unbearable to put up again with the intimate antics and unwelcome familiarities of guards. The thought made me desperate.

Since we had been moved to Kuching we were under constant supervision, and regulations were numerous, but the life had been one of reason and consistency compared to Berhala. Within the boundary of our camp we had comparative security, and persecution was official, rather than personal. The contrast in our treatment in the two camps convinced me that it was not the intention of the Japanese Command that women prisoners as a sex should be subjected to indignities by the guards.

While still drinking my tea, and worrying about the future in our new camp, I heard a commotion near by, the order "*Kutski!*" was shouted, and the people about me struggled to their feet. The toy-soldier figure of Colonel Suga, very immaculate, fresh-shaven, clean-shirted, appeared down our aisle between children and pots. He was alone, had come apparently to inspect the new camp quarters, and as usual had come to the children's barrack first. It was easy, I thought to myself, to smile benignly upon us, with a stomach well-filled, and a body well-soaped, and the odour of Shanghai perfume seeping out of every pore.

I bowed as he came to my place, and on the impulse of anger and worry I said, "Colonel Suga, I wish to complain."

He stopped in surprise, and said politely, "Yes, Mrs. Keith?"

I told him then that a soldier had behaved indecently to me. I described the incident in unequivocal terms, and ended by saying, "Although I am a prisoner, I believe I have the right to live decently, even in prison. I believe that you intend us to do so. For this reason I report this occurrence to you, and as a prisoner I ask you for protection. This barrack is the only place we women have to live. I request you to forbid the guards to enter our quarters."

His reaction to my words was unmistakable: he was shocked. He looked at me in blank amazement, and said, "Perhaps I do not understand you. Please repeat."

I repeated my words, while he listened carefully, and then answered, "If another person had told me this, I would not believe it. But I know you, and I believe that you are an honest woman. Come to my office at ten o'clock, and I will talk with you. I am sorry that this has happened."

Since we had been moved to Kuching, Colonel Suga and I had had many conversations. He had recently ordered me to write for him, and had read the first chapters of "Captivity." I believe that each of us had become convinced of the desire in the other for sincerity—but each knew also that he was dealing with the enemy, and must by wary in order to save himself. Still, we wished that it might have been otherwise. It was this effort for mutual respect which had made him say, "I believe you are an honest woman."

I went up the hill to his office at ten o'clock, and repeated my story, telling him that I feared a repetition of Berhala Island conditions, from which so far we had been free in Kuching. He requested me to describe these conditions. I did so, and ended by saying, "The Japanese accuse European women of immodesty, but such conditions do not allow us to live with modesty, decency, or honour."

He then surprised me by saying, "My soldiers have orders never to enter the women's barracks, unless there is a disturbance inside. I am shocked! Japanese soldiers are honourable …. If I did not know you myself, and believe you to be an honest woman—I would not believe what you tell me."

I answered, "I am not a girl, I am not flirtatious, I have done nothing to attract this soldier—in fact he could not see me in the dark. If he could, I am sure he would not have chosen me. He came to me because he wanted a woman, and I was helpless and a prisoner. I know that Japanese men are not attracted by Western women—but they enjoy humiliating us."

He looked at me silently for some minutes, pressing his clean delicate finger tips carefully against each other; then he said again, "I believe what you tell me, Mrs. Keith. I am very sorry that this has happened. I apologize to you on behalf of a Japanese soldier."

He asked me then to identify my assailant, but I said that I could not do so because of the darkness. He called for Lieutenant Nekata, and asked me to repeat my story to him. Nekata listened, obviously did not believe me, became obviously very angry with me. He said that if the soldier had embraced me as I described I must know who it was. Then he said, how did I know that it was a Japanese soldier? Said it might have been a Chinese loiterer from outside, or a POW.

I replied that in all Kuching only a Japanese soldier had a rifle, boots, and a uniform, and all these my assailant had.

I remembered then that Nekata was always jealous of Suga's power, and jealous of his own position in the Kuching camps, and that they never liked the same people. In appealing to Suga I had made the mistake of passing over Nekata. But had I appealed to Nekata first I believed he would not have allowed the appeal. Because Suga liked me, Nekata disliked me, and disbelieved me. In telling Nekata of the affair it became not only an unpleasant episode but a nasty, dirty, grubby piece of lechery—on my part.

The interview ended with Suga repeating his apology to me for the incident. At that, I could feel Nekata squirm.

The next morning at ten, Nekata sent for me to come to his office, some distance from Colonel Suga's. At my request, Dorie Adams accompanied me, and Wilfred was present.

Nekata first told me to repeat my story, which Wilfred wrote down. He then said, "You are lying."

"I am telling the truth."

"I say that you are lying! I say that you accuse this Japanese soldier of attacking you, in order to revenge yourself upon the Japanese for the humiliation which I inflicted upon you three days ago."

I looked at him with surprise, and asked, "What humiliation did you inflict on me?"

"I punished you for being late, on the day that you moved to the new camp. I made you stand in the square in the sun, where your husband and others could see. You were angry with me that day, I could see that. Now you tell me a lie about a Japanese soldier in order to revenge yourself on the Japanese!"

As Nekata raged, I recalled my mood of exhaustion and perversity that day in the square, and I saw that coincidence was against me. From his point of view Nekata had a case against me, perhaps even believed himself that I was lying, especially as I could not identify my assailant.

I answered him, "You punished me because I was late; that was your duty as a soldier. But my duty was to my child, who was ill, and whose illness made me late. Therefore your punishment did not humiliate me: it was just, it gave me no cause to revenge myself on you."

Nekata listened, unconvinced. He ordered Wilfred to type out a copy of my statement, and have me sign it, saying, "If this story proves to be false, it is serious. It is a death offence to conspire against a Nipponese soldier." We then went through it all again, he demanding that I identify my assailant, and saying that I was lying, and I reiterating that I was telling the truth. He demanded that I produce witnesses to my story, and I assured him that the women in the barrack near by heard my shouts and the struggle, and I gave him their names. He dismissed me, and Dorie and I returned to camp.

That evening, Poker Face, the sergeant major, brought in the soldiers of the guard, one after the other, demanding that I should identify some-one as my assailant. There were approximately twenty who had been on duty amongst the camps, and it might have been any one of them. They had all been beaten by their officers for slackness now, and they were determined to make me name a culprit. Time and again I repeated my statement that it was impossible for me to identify the soldier because of the dark. In fact, even in the daylight and after several years of association, most Nipponese soldiers still looked a good deal alike to me.

Meanwhile, I learned from an Indonesian prisoner that Colonel Suga had departed suddenly from Kuching that evening, to be absent for an unknown period. My only hope was gone.

The next day at ten o'clock Wilfred comes for me again, and orders me to the office, telling me to come alone, without the camp master. At the office, I find Sergeant Major Poker Face, a guard, and Nekata. Wilfred is dismissed, and I am seated in a chair in front of Nekata's desk, and a type-written document is placed before me, which I am ordered to sign. I read this through and find that it purports to be a statement made by me, in which I admit that I have falsely accused a Japanese soldier of attacking me, in order to revenge myself upon Lieutenant Nekata and the Japanese for the humiliation which recent punishment by them has caused me. I "confess" to having lied about the whole matter, and say that I am sorry.

Nekata orders me to sign this. I reply that it is impossible for me to sign it because it is not true, reminding him that I have given him the names of several women who can witness to the truth of what I say. Nekata says never mind about witnesses, sign that. Again I refuse.

He turns to the sergeant major, and speaks rapidly in Japanese; and then he, Nekata, leaves the room. I think to myself, "Can it be over this easily?"

The sergeant major looks at me with the coldest eyes that I have ever seen, and his tight lips fold over like a creased brown paper. I feel there hatred, contempt, dislike; behind that cold face I see subconscious memory of the years when we and our race have shown contempt for him and his race, when our power and strength have humiliated him. I see years of resentment resolving themselves now in his complete power over me. If he hates me as much as he seems to do, I admire his self-control in not murdering me.

He speaks to the guard in Japanese, and walks to the furthest doorway in the room, and he turns his back on me. The guard comes close to me as I sit before Nekata's desk, and I look up at him in surprise. He takes hold of my left arm, and twists it backwards so violently that I cry out with pain. He pulls it back further, and twists it time and again, letting it relax and then jerking it again, and the pain becomes sickening.

I call out to the sergeant major, I cry out again and again; but he remains standing at the door with his back to me. Subconsciously I know that he will not help, that this is going to happen to me, that I can do nothing—but I cannot stop calling to someone for help. The guard proceeds with his treatment.

Many times in my mind, since imprisonment, I have lived through such scenes vicariously; I have almost expected something like this to happen today—still, the surprise and the shock are great, now that it happens. It is the sort of thing which occurs to other people, but not to oneself.

Bearing pain before people who hate you is not like bearing it before those who admire you and expect you to be brave; there is no stimulus here, no standard for you to live up to. When the enemy hates you and hurts you and you cry out, it is what he wishes you to do, and he likes it; and if you don't, he just hurts you more. Nothing is any avail then. You become too weak to be shamed by your weakness, or to attempt to be bold. It takes great courage, or much phlegm, to stand torture, and I have neither. I can behave like a heroine for a moment, but I can't just sit and take it.

The guard continues his work on me, and I think that I must be making too much noise, for the sergeant major says something suddenly in Japanese, and the guard lets go of my arm. When he releases me I am so faint that I slide forward out of the chair onto my knees. He shouts at me in English to get up, and as I try to do so he pushes me back on my knees again, then kicks my knees, and I fall flat on the floor, and lie there.

Now another surprise comes, although I have seen this happen often enough to soldiers. The guard kicks me heavily with his boot in the left side in the ribs a number of times, and then in my shoulder several times, and very hard. I cover my breasts with my hands to protect them, and roll onto my stomach. He kicks me then again and again, muttering to himself while I cower under him. Then he stops kicking, and just stands and mutters. I cannot tell if the scene is just beginning, or ending, but I am too frightened to move.

Then the guard walks away from me, and nothing else happens. I turn over and look cautiously up. The sergeant major has disappeared completely, and the guard is looking out of the window as if none of this were any concern of his.

I lie still for a few minutes, there is an acute pain in my ribs, my left arm and shoulder ache badly, and I am sore all over, and worse than the pain is the shock.

In time, as nothing else happens, I pick myself slowly up from the floor, and sit in the chair again. I try to straighten my clothing and hair, but am trembling too much to do so. The guard pays no attention. The thought in my mind is, Just a minute, wait a minute, before you do anything more!

The sergeant major comes into the room again, and he looks at me. If he wanted revenge for old humiliations, he has it now; he should be satisfied now, but he shows nothing on his face, and says something to the guard which might equally well be "That's enough!" or "Give her the works!"

Then Nekata comes back and sits down, pretending to be busy, and not looking at me. The thought goes through my mind that I should protest to him at the guard's beating, followed by the thought that I have done too much protesting. Well, perhaps in time I will learn about these people, but not soon enough.

Nekata leans over and pushes his version of the "confession" towards me on the desk, and for the first time looks at me, and says, "It is a very serious matter to accuse a Japanese soldier. It is better for you to confess the truth."

My instinctive reaction is to agree to anything in order to escape. I understand now why people confess to crimes they are guiltless of, and I know that I can never again criticize anyone who does anything under physical stress. But I have thought this matter out beforehand, and, distraught though my body is, my mind still tells me, How can it help you to say that you have lied? Be careful. Keep your wits. The truth may still save.

I reply to Nekata, "I cannot sign this. It is not true. I have told you the truth." But my voice trembles, and I do not present a convincing picture. Nekata busies himself again at his desk. I have the feeling that the situation has gotten the best of all of us. I imagine Nekata thinking to himself, "Damn the woman, why couldn't she let herself get raped, and keep still about it!" I mentally agree with him.

But the feeling that Nekata is also at a loss what to do gives me courage. I reach out and push the confession away from me, and say, steadily this time: "I have told you the truth. I am a decent and self-respecting woman, and it is very bad that I should be insulted by your soldier. You are a Japanese officer and a gentleman, and you know yourself that this action is very bad. I tell you this story in order to ask for your protection. This is all I can say."

Nekata shows a definite reaction to this, breaking into a rash of embarrassment at my appeal to his chivalry as an officer and a gentleman: it seems to me that I have broken the impasse. He speaks to the sergeant major, then turns back to me and says, "You may return to your camp. You are not to speak of this to anyone, do you understand? That is my command. To disobey is very bad. Do not speak to anyone."

I pull myself together and leave the room with more relief than I have ever left any place in my life. Oh God, just let me get back safely again to the boredom, drudgery, and dirt of that which I have hated, I pray, and I won't complain. Miserable though prison life is, I know that I don't yet want to die.

The air braces me, but I still feel so ill that if anyone had been around to help or sympathize, I would have collapsed. As it is, I walk home the half-mile to our camp as if nothing had happened.

Arrived at camp I had a bath, and put on the remnants of my make-up which I had saved for the special occasions of meeting my husband. Today was a special occasion of another sort—and I needed make-up.

There was little temptation to tell my story in camp; probably half of the people there had been suppressing the desire to kick me. And I could not risk going to Dr. Gibson for medical aid in my present condition, for that would have meant being questioned, and I dared not confide. Nekata meant business when he said "Keep quiet."

I was particularly anxious that the truth should reach Harry. Rumours could not be avoided, but we no longer believed rumours. He need not know the truth if I refused to give factual evidence of it. He could be of no help to me now, and in anger or indignation at my trouble he might endanger himself.

I went to Violet, however. I told her that I was being questioned in the office, and that I did not think I would get out of camp alive, and I asked her to take care of George if anything happened to me. I told her also where my diaries were hidden, and asked her to try to save them when the end came. She promised me she would do what I asked. I gave her no details of my trouble, not wishing to involve her more than was necessary.

At last night came, and George and I went to bed, and I thanked God for the dark. Nothing in this war, I thought, could be so hideous as having to do everything before people—having to eat, sleep, bathe, dress, function physically and emotionally in public; having one's private sentiments washed in the public bathhouse, and hung up to dry on latrine walls. If I ever get out of this camp, I thought, dear God, just give me privacy—take everybody away, and let me die alone. I wept then secretly, painfully, in the dark.

George was very good to me that night. For his sake I usually didn't cry; I was his world, and the world collapsed, if I did. But he knew that tonight was something different; he was only three and a half then, but he had maturity in matters of suffering. So George said to me, as we lay together on our beds, that he was going to do my camp work for me tomorrow, if I was ill. I thanked him. He said then he would stroke my head until I went to sleep, for we both loved being stroked. So he sat by me cross-legged, stroking gently with one soft hand, sucking the other thumb, until his eyes were glassy with slumber, and he fell over asleep on my breast. He lay there then with his fair, hard head on my stomach, his lips just open, snoring and sucking.

But I could not sleep. The pain in my ribs was acute, my left shoulder was swollen and aching, I could scarcely move my arm, and I was bruised and sore. I felt my breasts anxiously, for like most women I feared bruises there, and in addition to physical discomforts, I was sick with the dread of what might happen tomorrow.

I saw that I had been incredibly stupid not to foresee the course of these events. There was an almost routine procedure in such cases. A prisoner comes accidentally into Japanese notice, either because he is accused of something, or he asks for something, or he is unwilling witness to something. He is taken to the office and questioned, and if they cannot force a confession, he is freed. Shortly after, he is taken, and requestioned, and freed. Shortly after that, he is removed from Kuching, for further questioning. In time his removal is followed by the report to Kuching that he has died of dysentery or malaria, these being the equivalent diseases to knowing too much.

I had become a thorn in Nipponese flesh. They knew that I was a writer, they constantly searched my belongings for notes, they believed that if I got out of camp I was going to write what had happened there. The threat was not strong enough to alter conditions, but it was strong enough to be an annoyance to them. My presence reminded them that the things they were doing would not look well in print, and they did like to be thought nice people! And now I had committed the crime of becoming myself the victim of assault and brutality.

I believed that Colonel Suga had left Kuching in order to avoid an unpleasant situation, for to interfere between Nekata and myself, Suga would have had to run the risk of being labelled "Pro-British." And why should he risk himself to save me?

Next morning came. At ten o'clock Wilfred again ordered me to Nekata's office, alone. I sent George to Violet, and told myself that this was the finish. I put on my neatest dress and make-up, to meet the end.

At the office there are Nekata, the sergeant major, and a guard. Nekata's typed "confession" is again offered to me to sign, and I refuse. My own statement is then read through to me, and I affirm that it is the truth.

Then we proceed as we did the day before: Nekata speaks to the sergeant major and the guard in Japanese, and Nekata leaves the room. The sergeant major speaks to the guard, and the sergeant major leaves the room. The guard lounges over to the window, and leans against it. I sit and wait: nothing to come can be more terrifying than this sitting and waiting for something to come. Dressed for slaughter, hair carefully combed and braided, lipstick on colourless lips, rouge on malaria-yellowed cheeks, in neatest white dress, good shark skin, once very smart—this is how the Well-Dressed Internee will dress to be beaten up, I tell myself.

Through the window I see Nekata walking slowly up the hill towards the Japanese officers' quarters. He disappears. Nothing happens. After ten minutes he comes into sight again, descends the hill road, and re-enters the office. He has in his hands a newspaper-wrapped bundle, which he places on the desk.

About that bundle my mind jumps instantly to a conclusion: it contains some of the articles which I have traded to the Japanese guards in exchange for contraband food, articles which, now that the heat is on, have been identified and brought in to make more trouble for me. Oh, for a clean conscience! That white hand-knit wool sweater that somebody made for Harry—they can't prove that's mine, can they? Still, I wish they didn't have it. And Harry's wool socks, and his grey flannel trousers with Wm. Powell's Hong Kong label in them! And my gold thimble with "Agnes Newton on her sixteenth birthday from Mom and Dad." Oh, what a fool I've been.

Nekata dismisses the guard, and we are alone. He motions towards the newspaper-wrapped package and says to me, "You do not look well. You are very thin. Here are six eggs for you. Take these eggs and eat them. This affair is finished. But remember, I order you not to speak of this. Also remember, if your statement is not true, that is a death offence. You may return to your camp now."

With difficulty, I arise, bow and say "Thank you," pick up the eggs, and leave.

What an incredible people, I think. An omelet for my honour! Six eggs for broken ribs! Well, an egg is still an egg! This time I intend to eat some myself. Three for George, and three for me. I really do need something ....

I walk down the road towards home in a state of semi-hysteria; the eggs have brought the situation down to earth; surely Nekata can't swing it back to the high tragedy level after this!

Andrew Campbell Ballantine

ANDREW CAMPBELL BALLANTINE (1889–1962) was
born in London, England and received training as an organist and choir master
before emigrating with his family to Regina in 1910. From 1914 to 1919 he served in
the Canadian army overseas. Subsequently, he worked as a newspaper reporter
for the *Regina Leader*, the *Winnipeg Free Press*, the *Calgary Albertan* and the
Edmonton Bulletin. As a member of the Veterans Guard, he was called on to guard
prisoner-of-war camps in Canada during the Second World War. A government job
with Alberta's Department of Cultural Affairs in Edmonton left him time for organ
and choral work as well.

"Lion-taming for Beginners" takes place at an Air Force station in North Africa.
Between June 1940 and May 1943, powerful military forces confronted one another
in the deserts of North Africa as Italy, supported by Germany, defended its empire
while Britain fought to keep open its sea route to India through the Suez Canal.
At first German armoured regiments under General Erwin Rommel outclassed
the British in numbers and equipment. After General Bernard Montgomery took
command of the Eighth Army, reinforced by British and American units that had
landed in North Africa, Rommel's German and Italian army surrendered. The Battle
of El Alamein was the turning point.

RAF stations in North Africa served British squadrons that included Canadian
support units. Their bombing operations against enemy supply ships and tankers
were so dangerous that 95 percent of air crews had to be replaced every three
months. At post-war reunions veterans recalled that the comradeship of the desert
was greater than any achieved in other theatres of war.

Lion-Taming for Beginners

"LUMME!" SAID LEADING AIRCRAFTMAN Smithers J.C. "Look who's 'ere, wouldja."

He stooped, half squatting, and tenderly patted the little sand-coloured kitten's head. He was rewarded by a feline smile and a parting of the lips that might have meant, "Good morning, chum," or perhaps, "Boy, am I ever in trouble!"

"Wotsa matter?" Smithers inquired. "'Ungry?" He took the tiny ball of tawny fluff into his arms: "We'll introduce y' to the cook."

LAC Smithers had a permanent duty at this Air Force station in North Africa; he served with the devotion of an artist and the diligence of a scientist. Punctuality in arriving at his place of employment, which was the septic tank, was a point of probity with him, but this morning he had even a few more minutes than usual to spare—time enough to call at the cookhouse on his way.

As a rule Smithers was not welcome in the cookhouse. Not infrequently his appearance had been the cause of some mass panic and cries of, "Git outa here!" It was not that he was in himself an undesirable character but simply that because of his occupation it was thought that his working clothes exuded the effluvia of his calling. But just now he glowed with the reflected warmth of the attention bestowed on his little pet as cooks, dishwashers, hewers of wood, drawers of water and peelers of potatoes gathered around.

"Blimey!" observed Higgins, the sergeant cook. "A young lion, wot! Where'd you get 'im?"

"Guess 'e's lorst 'is muvver," Smithers conjectured, beaming with almost paternal love upon his treasure.

"More like 'is mother lorst 'im," Higgins suggested.

It did appear likely. Terrified by the roar of a low-flying plane, the mother lioness might have fled from the strange winged monster with the intention of returning later for her cub. But when the youngster became hungry he went foraging for himself and wandered into the RAF station, almost on the edge of the inhospitable Sahara.

Homeward at evening, like Gray's ploughman, plodding his weary way, LAC Smithers had almost forgotten his little protégé until he found the cub trying to scale the six-inch step of Hut K, where he and eleven other airmen spent most of their off-duty hours. The name Buster was immediately attached to him. Smithers fed him with milk from the kitchen and shielded him from the sins of the flesh—to which he was exposed by unscrupulous airmen who offered him beer.

Although he soon became the station mascot, Buster was universally recognized as Smithers' kitten. Buster himself, though not unfriendly to the rest of the troops, attached himself with touching affection to Smithers, whom he welcomed boisterously whenever they were reunited. Morning and night he was taken for short strolls, and at less regular hours during the daytime. In the beginning he was escorted by his master, but as he grew bolder an open door seemed to invite him into the outside world unattended.

At first he left the hut very cautiously, after tumbling two or three times down the precipitous height from the doorstep to the ground, but he quickly gained confidence. Besides, such heights became less formidable for the cub was growing—in wisdom and in stature and in favour with the troops. But not with the commanding officer, although the c.o. continued to tolerate the lion's unauthorized presence, even at the expense of the troops' rations. After all, if they didn't mind going short by, say, a quarter of an ounce of meat per man per day, why should *he* complain?

But the c.o. was less indulgent by the time the cub had grown to full lionhood and occupied as much cubic footage as the sanitary regulations allowed for two airmen. Furthermore, with no training in such duties, the lion had become an efficient watchdog, growling whenever anyone entered who was not one of the regular tenants of Hut K. If he failed to frighten off the intruder by such hostile gestures Buster would rise and roar at the top of his lungs.

It was not until the mascot had thus assumed the offensive against the c.o. at a Saturday morning inspection that the latter suggested the lion ought to be destroyed, turned loose on the desert or otherwise liquidated without further delay.

Smithers simply said, "Very good, sir." But he saw to it, with the connivance of the rest of the troops, that at any given moment thereafter the lion was always somewhere the c.o. was not. These efforts at concealment, however, were not completely successful.

"I thought I told you," said the c.o. to Smithers one day, "that your lion had to be got rid of."

"Yes, sir," Smithers said.

"Well?"

"Well, sir. I 'ave took 'im out on the desert, sir. We've even took 'im out on a jeep and ditched 'im. But 'e always came back."

"Then suppose," the c.o. suggested, "we take him up in a kite and drop him."

Smithers felt a catch in his throat.

"Oh, no, sir. Not that."

"Well, if you can think of any more humane way of getting rid of the damn thing—"

"Very good sir," Smithers said.

It was long after midnight but the station was alert and awaiting the arrival of a giant plane that was to bring the air marshal from London on a hurried inspection trip of African stations. The white beams of many floodlights illuminated the runway. Control had just reported the approach of a plane and the monotonous droning of four motors was already vibrating the air when the terrible thing happened.

At leisurely pace an enormous lion walked out into the centre of the spotlight, lay down, stretched its limbs luxuriously and seemed to be preparing for sleep. After the initial gasp of astonishment some of the troops dared to laugh. But the c.o. was fuming with rage. The hum of the approaching motors had risen to a roar and navigation lights were circling the sky, like the gleaming eyes of a bird of prey.

"Where the hell's Smithers?" the c.o. shouted. But the amateur lion-tamer was not to be found.

"Somebody," thundered the c.o., "boot that animal off the runway. *And* out of the camp."

No one moved and the c.o.'s voice rose, choked with indignation.

"Tell control to delay landing. And someone kick the beast off."

The plane could be seen withdrawing as requested. The lion seemed to decide against his first idea of sleep. Instead, he rose, settled on his haunches and proceeded to wash his face in the manner familiar to every cat.

The c.o. was jumping mad, waving his arms to express the murderous thoughts for which he had no words. At last he stepped boldly into the lighted area, walked up to the lion and delivered it a kick in the hindquarters that must have been heard even in the cockpit of the returning plane.

"Ooooo!" the troops gasped in mixed astonishment and admiration. No less astonished, the lion rose, looked offended at the c.o., and walked slowly into one of Africa's darkest nights.

The c.o., obviously conscious that his prowess had not been unnoticed by the troops, walked out of the arena like a victorious gladiator. "Runner!" he called.

"Here, sir," a voice answered from the sidelines.

"Tell control to give 'em the green light now."

"Very good, sir."

Meanwhile the v.i.p. plane had been hovering over the scene, its navigating lights describing circles against the blackness, its engines droning languidly, impatiently awaiting permission to land. Suddenly the drone broke into a roar, the lights retreated, circled in a descending pattern toward the landing field, and the huge bomber came angrily down the strip. While a landing ramp was being brought into position the commanding officer and his adjutant advanced to greet the distinguished visitor.

They saluted smartly. The air marshal raised a forefinger to the peak of his cap in frigid acknowledgment.

"Good evening, sir," said the c.o.

The air marshal grunted witheringly.

"Good—er, morning. Are you the commanding officer?"

"Yes, sir."

"Your name?"

"Johnstone, sir."

"Johnstone, eh? Why the devil did you have to keep us hanging in mid air? You knew I was coming, didn't you?"

"Terribly sorry, sir. We were having a spot of trouble with the lights."

"Hadn't you checked them? Oh, never mind. We'll discuss that in the morning. Now show me to my quarters. I hope you haven't forgotten *that*."

At nine o'clock the next morning, while the air marshal was still sleeping peacefully, LAC Smithers J.C. was up before the commanding officer. Having pounded his desk savagely three times, the C.O. said:

"Haven't I told you, Smithers, to get rid of your lion?"

"Yes, sir," Smithers admitted.

"Why didn't you?"

"I don't know, sir. 'E wouldn't go."

"Well, after last night's frightful incident I'm not telling you any more. The air marshal is *terribly* annoyed."

"I'm sorry, sir."

"As luck has it," the C.O. went on, "the beastly creature has gone—forever, let's pray. But Smithers I'm warning you—if it ever comes back it'll be shot at sight. *Shot*, Smithers. You understand?"

"Yes, sir. But—"

"There are no *buts* about it, Smithers. I won't tell you again."

"No, sir. But, sir—weren't my lion. Mine was locked up in me 'ut."

D.A. MacMillan

WHILE SERVING AS A FLIGHT LIEUTENANT in the Royal
Canadian Air Force, D.A. MacMillan (1891–1963) wrote a series of stories about the
bomber squadrons stationed in England. The title of the collection, *Only the Stars
Know* (1944), was suggested by the RCAF motto—*per ardua ad astra* ("through
adversity to the stars"). When war broke out in September 1939, Britain's Bomber
Command had five operational groups and a sixth that was non-operational. In
1943 when Allied strategy demanded intensive bombing of Germany's industrial
and military resources, the Canadians, who formed twenty percent of the RAF,
were given a separate identity, Number Six Group RCAF. Although Sir Arthur Harris,
Air Officer Commander-in-Chief Bomber Command, expressed his disapproval—
"I fail to see why we should give these people who are determined to huddle into
a corner by themselves on purely political grounds, the best of our equipment at
the expense of British and other Dominion crews"—the Canadian squadrons proved
their worth by flying more than 40,000 operations, although at a terrible cost.
Out of 1,312 aircraft, 814 failed to return and of 5,700 airmen aboard, almost three-
quarters lost their lives.

After the war, from 1945–49, MacMillan was a newspaperman on the staff
of the *Regina Leader-Post*, fulfilling in real life the role of his narrator in "The
Newspaper Writer."

The Newspaper Writer

THE NEWSPAPER WRITER GOT THE PHONE CALL late in the evening.

The papers at home wanted a first-person story by one of the aircrew in the Group on how it felt to raid Berlin.

They had to have it that night.

He thought:

Now how in hell can I get one of these guys to give me that? They'll call it a line-shoot and laugh at me.

He looked in the mess. It was empty.

He checked the living quarters. There wasn't a soul around. There was no one in the sergeant's quarters either.

It was a stand-down.

Everybody had gone to town.

Cursing the fat heads at home who sat behind a desk and asked for things, he caught a bus.

There were a lot of aircrew at the pub where he called first, but none that he knew well enough to spring a job like this on.

He wished, now, that he'd gone out himself instead of staying in to do some writing. Then they wouldn't have been able to find him.

After two more tries, he found the one he wanted.

"Hi," he said, "what are you doing here?"

The young man looked up.

He was a bright-looking kid and very neat. His hair was black and very wavy and carefully parted on one side. He looked about nineteen.

The writer came right to the point.

"I'm on the spot; I've got to get a story."

The kid grinned at him.

"What is this? A line-shoot?"

The writer was honest. He found it paid. If you ever double-crossed these kids you had it. They'd shut up like clams and never tell you a thing.

"Yeah, in a way. But just think; it will save you the trouble of writing home."

"Okay, what's the gen?"

"I want a first-person story, quoting you, on just how it feels to go on a raid over Berlin."

The young man winced.

"Oh, dammit, no. Not that. I'd never live it down."

"I know it's grim, but there it is. I've gotta have it, or I'll get my neck in a sling. Now be a good boy and give out. I won't misquote you or anything like that."

"Sure, sure … but why pick on me?"

"You're the only guy I can find. The mess is empty."

The youngster sighed.

"Okay, then. What do you want?"

"Just tell me what it's like; before you go; while you're going; when you're coming back."

"This is getting worse and worse. Will the guys on the station see it?"

"Maybe, eventually. But not for a long time. This is for the Canadian papers."

"Okay. Well, as soon as you know you're going, and what the target is, you're kind of mixed up. You want to go, and yet you don't. If you go, and get back, it'll count as another Op, and you know you gotta get your tour in. You're scared—scared as hell—but you know you've got to do a tour and you want to get it over as quickly as possible.

"You feel kinda cold and tight inside. Funny, though, you're usually pretty hungry and you eat a big operational meal because you know how hungry you get in the kite.

"If it's an early takeoff, you haven't got much time. You usually go back to your room and sort of take a last look around and tidy things up a bit.

"I've got a letter written and lying on my dresser. It's to be mailed home if I don't come back from an Op some night. I usually check to see that it's around where they'll be sure to find it."

He paused.

"How'm I doing?" he asked.

The writer nodded.

"Fine. You ought to be in this business yourself. You tell a better story than I do."

"Well," the young man continued, "it's funny how you take a last look around at the sun and the trees. Ordinarily you don't notice these things. But, just before an Op, you take a last look.

"And you think quite a bit. It's hard to explain, but you don't think so much about yourself as about the folks at home and how they're going to feel if you go missing.

"You think of a lot of childish things, too; like your first day at school, and the first time you went skating.

"Then it's time to go out to the kite and you're too busy to think much. You take off and head for the enemy coast. It's dark, of course, but that's the way I like it. But, soon after you leave, you can see the channel. Then, pretty soon, the enemy coast looms up. About that time, you get a "G" fix to check that you're on track. That's your last chance because, after that, you get in range of the enemy stations and they jam it.

"You look down and likely see lights on the ground. If you're smart, you go right between them; never right over.

"Then you keep right on going and, every once in a while, you see more lights down there. They're likely to be fighter airdromes or else a path marked out by the Jerries to show what direction you're taking.

"By this time, you're probably entirely on your own and you keep right on plugging along. You know the target is 'so many minutes ahead.'

"Then you get in range.

"If you're in the first wave, you've got to be careful. Usually, the target isn't lit up. But, if you go stooging around in there, it's liable to light up all of a sudden and you'll find yourself coned in a sky full of flak. At least, that's what it used to be like. Now we wait for the P.F.F. flares.

"What some guys do, if they're a bit late, is wait around outside until somebody else gets coned. Then they sneak in well to one side. It's kind of a hardboiled way of looking at it, but what can you do? There's no point in both of you getting coned. They're shooting up predicted flak these days, too; it seems to ride along the searchlight beams.

"Anyway, after you get over the target, the bomb aimer takes over. He says 'Left, Left, or Right, Right' until he's ready. Then he says 'Bombs gone.' Then all you gotta do is get out of there and get home.

"If you look around while you're over the target, you're likely to see bombers on all sides. Maybe you'll see one that has been shot down by a fighter.

"I saw one one night. They swooped in on it from both sides and above firing cannons. You could see the tracers and the bomber shooting back. It just blew up and burst into flames. It was grim.

"The worst nights are when there is a lot of moon above the clouds and the clouds, themselves, are lit up by searchlights from below. You can look over and see bombers silhouetted against the clouds. It's just like the pictures you see in aircraft recognition classes.

"You can see them above you, too. I usually fly just a little lower. Some fellows always try for all the height they can get. Personally, I figure that is where the fighters are. They usually ride along on top and swoop down. Then it's the guy on top who's going to get it. At least, that's the way I feel about it.

"Coming home, the biggest problem is to keep awake. I sometimes pity the gunners. They've got to be right on their toes from the time we leave until we get back.

"It drives you nuts just looking out into the darkness and never knowing when, or if, a fighter is going to jump you."

"Then you see the coast again and your navigator gets a couple of fixes. You land and, when you get out, you almost want to bend over and kiss the ground. I've seen some of the guys do it after finishing the last trip of a tour."

"Then you're interrogated and get your operational breakfast and get to bed."

"Sometimes you can't sleep. You're tired, but your nerves are on edge. Sometimes when you do get asleep you dream of fighters."

He paused.

"Well," he said, "that's the story. If the guys at the station ever see it I'll get the chop."

The writer smiled.

This was the most honest and straightforward story he had ever heard.

He said:

"Don't worry. I'll see the papers get the story just the way you told it. You won't be misquoted or anything."

"Remember," the kid said, "if I don't like that story when I see it printed, you've had it."

The writer smiled again.

"You'll be all right. When I get through with this story, you'll probably be a hero. They'll have the brass band out to welcome you when you go home."

★★★

As it happened, the kid did finish his tour and was posted home for a rest.

And there *was* a reception held in his honour at home.

He was glad it worked out that way, but he thought of all those boys who did not get home.

What had the world lost because so many of these kids were killed at a time before they were old enough to even start making their real contributions to life?

He liked writing these stories. It was little enough, but he could imagine some mother or father at home clipping them from the paper and saving them through the years.

Colir) McDougall

COLIN MCDOUGALL (1917–1984) was born in
Montreal. Immediately after graduating from McGill University he joined the
Princess Patricia's Canadian Light Infantry, ending the war as a major. For his
service as a company commander in the Allies' Italian campaign he received the
DSO. After the war his career centred on McGill where he was, in turn, a student
advisor, director of placement services, registrar and secretary-general. "The Firing-
Squad," originally published in *Maclean's* magazine in 1953, was expanded into a
novel, *Execution*, which won the Governor General's Fiction Award for 1958.

In 1943 the Allies invaded the Italian mainland through Sicily to draw Hitler's
forces away from the eastern front where Germany was at war with Russia and to
engage in active combat their troops stationed in North Africa and England. As a
result Italy, Germany's ally, withdrew from the war and powerful German divisions
that should have been used to repulse the Normandy invasion were held up
defending the Adolf Hitler Line south of Rome and the Gothic Line across
Northern Italy. The Canadian units that assaulted the virtually impregnable Hitler Line
on May 23, 1944 included the Princess Patricia's Canadian Light Infantry, the Seaforth
Highlanders and the Loyal Edmonton Regiment. This attack provides the background
of the following story. Death by firing squad was the usual penalty for desertion. In
the novel one of the characters, Major Bazin, describes execution as "the ultimate
injustice, the ultimate degradation of man … Perhaps it is man's plight to acquiesce.
On the other hand, even recognizing execution as the evil may be a victory of sorts.
Struggling against it may be the closest man ever comes to victory."

The Firing-Squad

HE WAS THE FIRST CANADIAN SOLDIER sentenced to death, and rear headquarters in Italy seethed with the prospect of carrying it out. At his marble-topped desk in Rome Major-General Paul Vincent read the instructions from London with distaste. The findings of the court martial had been confirmed by Ottawa—that meant by a special session of the cabinet, the General supposed—and it was now the direct responsibility of the Area Commander that the execution of Private Sydney Jones should be proceeded with "as expeditiously as possible."

The hum of voices and the quick beat of teletypes in the outer office marked the measure of Rome's agitation. No one had expected this confirmation of sentence. Not even the officers who had sentenced Private Jones to death. For them, indeed, there had been little choice: Jones had even wanted to plead guilty, but the court had automatically changed his plea, and gone on to record its inevitable finding and sentence.

The salient facts of the case filed quickly through the neat corridors of General Vincent's mind. This Jones, a young soldier of twenty-two, had deserted his unit, had joined with a group of deserter-gangsters who operated in Rome and Naples, and had been present when his companions shot and killed a U.S. military policeman. All this Jones admitted, and the court could pass no other sentence. The execution of a Canadian soldier, however, was more than a military matter: it touched on public policy; and higher authorities had never before confirmed a sentence of death.

General Vincent sighed. He preferred to think of himself as the business executive he happened to be rather than a general officer whose duty it was to order a man's death. An execution was something alien and infinitely distasteful. Well, if this thing had to be done under his command, at least it need not take place under his personal orders. From the beginning he had known just the man for the job. Already the teletype had clicked off its command to Volpone, the reinforcement base where Private Jones was imprisoned, and a staff car would now be rushing the commander of that base, Brigadier Benny Hatfield, to Rome. The General sighed again and turned to some more congenial correspondence on his desk.

A dirt track spiralled out of Volpone and mounted in white gashes upon the forested mountainside. Fifty infantry reinforcements, fresh from Canada, were spaced along the first two miles of zigzag road. They carried all the paraphernalia of their fledging trade: rifles, machine-guns, and light mortars. Some were trying to run, lurching ahead with painful steps; others stopped to stand panting in their own small lakes of sweat. One or two lay at the roadside, faces turned from the sun, awaiting the stabbing scorn of their sergeant with spent indifference. But they all spat out the clogging dust, and cursed the officer who led them.

Farther up the hillside this man ran with the gait of an athlete pushing himself to the limit of endurance. Head down he ran doggedly through the dust and the heat; he ran as though trying to outdistance some merciless pursuer. Captain John Adam was going to run up that mountainside until he could run no more. He was running from last night, and all the nights which still lay ahead. He was running from his own sick self. Almost at the halfway mark, he aimed himself at a patch of bush underneath the cliff and smashed into it headlong. He lay quite still; he had achieved exhaustion: the closest condition to forgetfulness he could ever find.

For Captain John Adam found it unbearable to live with himself and with his future. He had lost his manhood. As an infantry company commander, he had drawn daily strength and sustenance from the respect of his fellow fighting men. They knew him as a brave leader, a compassionate man. He had been granted the trust and friendship of men when it was all they had left to give, and this he knew to be the ultimate gift, the highest good. And then, one sun-filled morning, he had forfeited these things forever. He had cracked wide open; he had cried his fear and panic to the world; he had run screaming from the battle, through the ranks of his white-faced men. He had been sent back here to Volpone in unexpressed disgrace while the authorities decided what to do with him.

Now Captain John Adam rolled over and then stood up, a tall young man, looking brisk and competent. His sun-browned face, his blue eyes, the power of his easy movements, even the cigarette dangling negligently from his lips, all seemed to proclaim that here was the ideal young infantry officer.

"Sergeant Konzuk," Captain Adam called now. "Get these men the hell back to barracks, and leave me alone here!"

The sergeant did not look surprised. He was used to such things by now, and this was no officer to argue with. Sure, he'd take them back to barracks, and let Adam do his own explaining. "All right, you guys—on your feet!" said Konzuk. It was no skin to him.

It was late afternoon by the time he had smoked the last of his cigarettes and Adam came down from the mountain. Striding through the camp he frowned with displeasure when he saw the hulking form of Padre Dixon planted squarely in his path. Normally, he knew, he would have liked this chaplain, but he made a point of refusing the friendliness which this big man was trying to offer.

"Mind if I walk along with you, son?" Adam was forced to stop while the Padre knocked his pipe against his boot.

The two men walked on together through the dusk, picking their way between the huts and the barrack blocks. As they neared the officers' mess the Padre stopped and his fingers gripped Adam's arm. He pointed to a small grey hut just within the barbed wire of the camp entrance. "That's where poor Jones is waiting out his time," the Padre said.

"Well?"

The Padre shrugged and seemed busy with his pipe. "No matter what he's done he's a brave boy, and he's in a dreadful position now."

"He won't be shot." Adam repeated the general feeling of the camp without real interest. "They'll never confirm the sentence."

The Padre looked him directly in the face. "Adam," he said. "It has been confirmed. He is going to be executed!"

"No!" Adam breathed his disbelief aloud. He was truly shocked, and for this instant his own sick plight was forgotten. This other thing seemed so—improper. That a group of Canadians could come together in this alien land for the purpose of destroying one of their own kind .... And every day, up at the battle, every effort was being made to save life; there were so few of them in Italy, and so pitifully many were being killed every day. This thing was simply—not right.

His eyes sought for the Padre's. "But why?" he asked, with a kind of hurt in his voice. "Tell me—why?"

"The boy's guilty, after all."

"Technically—he was only a witness. And even if he is guilty, do you think this thing is right?"

The Padre could not ignore the urgency in Adam's voice. He spoke at last with unaccustomed sharpness. "No," he said. "It may be something that has to be done—but it will never be right."

The two men looked at one another in the gathering Italian night. For a moment their thoughts seemed to merge and flow together down the same pulsing stream. But then a new idea came to Adam. "Padre," he said, "why are you telling me about this?"

Then they both saw the figure running toward them from the officers' mess. It was Ramsay, the ever-flurried, ever-flustered Camp Adjutant. He panted to a stop in front of them. "Adam," he gasped out. "The Brigadier wants you at once!"

Brigadier Benny Hatfield waited patiently in his office. He liked to feed any new or disturbing thoughts through the mill of his mind until the gloss of familiarity made them less troublesome. Early in his career he had discovered that the calibre of his mind was not sufficiently large for the rank he aspired to, and so deliberately he had cultivated other qualities which would achieve the same end.

He emphasized an air of outspoken bluntness, his physical toughness, a presumed knowledge of the way the "troops" thought, and his ability to work like a horse. Indeed the impression he sometimes conveyed was that of a grizzled war horse, fanatic about good soldiering, but with it all intensely loyal, and a very good fellow. Now he sat and considered his interview with General Vincent. He understood his superior's unexpressed motives perfectly well: it was a straight question of passing the buck. This execution was a simple matter of military discipline, after all, and he would ensure that it was carried out in such a way that no possible discredit could reflect on himself. The General, he believed, had made an intelligent choice, and he had an equally good selection of his own in mind. Ramsay was ushering Captain Adam into his presence.

The Brigadier looked up at last. "Well," he stated, "Captain John Adam." His eyes bored steadily at Adam's face and he waited in silence. He knew that in a moment his unwavering stare would force some betrayal of guilt or inferiority. He waited, and at last he was rewarded:

the sweat swelled on Adam's forehead, and the man before him felt it essential to break the intolerable silence. "Yes, sir," Adam had to say.

The Brigadier stood up then. "Well," he said again. "It can't be as bad as all that, can it, boy?" His mouth lifted the straggling moustache in a grimace of affability, and despite himself Adam felt a small rush of gratitude.

But then the smile died. "It does not please me," the Brigadier said coldly, "to receive the worst possible reports about you." He consulted the papers on his desk. "You have read this report from Colonel Dodd?" It was a needless question. Adam knew the report by memory. It was an "adverse" report: it was the reason why he was back here at Volpone. That piece of paper was his doom. "Not fit to command men in action," it read; "not suitable material for the field."

With ungoverned ease Adam's mind slipped back to that sun-filled morning on the Hitler Line. They were walking through a meadow—slowly, for there were Schu mines in the grass—and they moved toward a hidden place of horror: a line of dug-in tank turrets, and a mine-strewn belts of wire. And then the earth suddenly erupted with shell and mortar bursts; they floundered in a beaten zone of observed machine-gun fire. A few men got as far as the wire, but none of them lived. There was a regrouping close to the start line, and Adam was ordered to attack again.

The first symptom he noticed was that his body responded to his mind's orders several seconds too late. He became worried at this time-lag, the fact that his mind and body seemed about to divide, to assume their own separate identities. Then the air bursts shook the world; no hole in the ground was shelter from the rain of deafening black explosions in the sky above them. Then he remembered the terrible instant that the separation became complete, that he got up and shouted his shame to the world. He got up from his ditch, and he ran blubbering like a baby through his white-faced men. And some of his men followed him, back into the arms of Colonel Dodd.

"Yes," Adam said now, his face white. "I've read the report."

Brigadier Hatfield spoke softly. "If that report goes forward from here you'll be in a bad way—at least returned to Canada for Adjutant General's disposal, some second-rate kind of discharge, the reputation always clinging to you ...." The Brigadier shook his head. "That would be a pity."

If the report goes forward …. A pulse of excitement beat in Adam's throat. What did he mean—was there any possibility that the report could be stopped here?

"Adam!" The Brigadier pounded a fist upon his desk. "I have confidence in you. Of all the officers under my command I have selected you for a mission of the highest importance."

Adam blinked his disbelief, but the hope swelled strong inside him.

"Yes," the Brigadier said steadily. "You are to command the firing-squad for the execution of Private Jones!"

Adam blinked again and he turned his head away. For a moment he was weak with nausea, the flood of shame was so sour inside him. "No," he heard his voice saying. "I can't do it."

The Brigadier's smile grew broader, and he spoke with soft assurance. "But you can, my boy. But you can." And the Brigadier told him how.

It was all very neat. Adam had his choice, of course. On the one hand, he could choose routine disposal of his case by higher authorities. Colonel Dodd's report, together with Brigadier Hatfield's own state-ment, would ensure an outcome which, as the Brigadier described it, would cause "deep shame to his family and friends," and Adam was sure of that. On the other hand, if he performed this necessary act of duty, this simple military function, then Colonel Dodd's report would be destroyed. He could return to Canada as soon as he desired, bearing Brigadier Hatfield's highest recommendations.

The Brigadier went on to say that the man Jones was a convicted murderer—that Adam should have no scruples on that score … Adam listened and each soft word seemed to add to his degradation. This was the inevitable consequence of his lost manhood.

The Brigadier's voice was kindly; his words flowed endlessly like a soft stream of liquid. Then the voice paused. "Of course," the Brigadier said, "it is a task for a determined and courageous man." His glance darted over Adam's bent head and flickered around the room.

Adam broke the silence at last. He spoke without looking up. "All right," he said. "I'll do it."

The Brigadier's response was quick and warm. "Good," he said. "Good fellow!" His smile was almost caressing. "Your sergeant must be a first-rate man, and—it is most desirable that he be a volunteer. Do you understand?"

Adam forced himself to nod.

The Brigadier stared directly in Adam's face. His voice now rang with steel of command. "All right," he said. "Bring me the sergeant's name and a draft of your parade orders by 1100 hours tomorrow." He leaned back and allowed the smile to possess his face. He had selected exactly the right man for this delicate job.

By next morning the news had raced to every Canadian in Italy. At the battle up north men heard about this execution with a dull kind of wonder. Advancing into the attack it was brought to them like bad news in a letter from home; they looked at each other uneasily, or they laughed and turned away. It was not the death of one man back in a place called Volpone that mattered. It was simply that up here they measured and counted their own existence so dear that an unnecessary death, a planned death of one of their own fellows, seemed somehow shameful. It made them sour and restless as they checked their weapons and ammunition loads.

In the camp at Volpone it was the sole topic of conversation. It was soon known that the news had reached the prisoner also, although, to be sure, it did not seem to have changed his routine in the least. All his waking hours were busied with an intense display of military activity. The guard sergeant reported that he made and remade his bed several times a day, working earnestly to achieve the neatest possible tuck of his blanket. The floor was swept five times a day and scrubbed at least once. His battle-dress was ironed to knife-edge exactness, and his regimental flashes resewn to his tunic as though the smartest possible fit at the shoulder was always just eluding him. At times he would glance at the stack of magazines the Padre brought him, but these were thrown aside as soon as a visitor entered his room. Private Jones would spring to a quiveringly erect position of attention; he would respond to questions with a quick, cheerful smile. He was the embodiment of the keen, alert, and well-turned-out private soldier.

The truth was, of course, that Private Jones was a somewhat pliable young man who was desperately anxious to please. He was intent on proving himself such a good soldier that the generals would take note and approve, and never do anything very bad to him. The idea that some of his fellow soldiers might take him out and shoot him was a terrible abstraction, quite beyond his imagination. Consequently, Private Jones did not believe in the possibility of his own execution. Even when the Padre came and tried to prepare him, Private Jones simply jumped eagerly to attention, polished boots glittering, and rattled off, head high: "Yes, sir. Very good, sir."

A surprising amount of administrative detail is required to arrange an execution. The Brigadier was drawing up an elaborate operation order, with each phase to be checked and double-checked. There were the official witness, the medical officers, the chaplain, the guards, the firing-squad, of course; and the conveyance and placing of all these to the proper spot at the right time.

Captain Adam's first problem was more serious than any of this: his first attempts to recruit the sergeant for his firing-squad met with utter failure. After conferring with the Brigadier he decided upon a new approach, and he went in search of Sergeant Konzuk.

The sergeant was lying at ease on his bed reading a magazine. When Adam came in, Konzuk scowled. He swung his boots over the side of the bed and he crossed his thick arms over his chest. Adam wasted no time. "Konzuk," he said, "I want you as sergeant of the firing-squad." The sergeant laughed rudely.

"Never mind that," Adam said. "Wait till you hear about this deal."

"Look," Sergeant Konzuk said. He stood up and his eyes were angry on Adam's face. "I done my share of killing. Those that like it can do this job."

Adam's tone did not change. "You're married, Konzuk. You've a wife and two kids. Well, you can be back in Winnipeg within the month."

Konzuk's mouth opened; his eyes were wide. His face showed all the wild thoughts thronging through his mind. The sergeant had left Canada in 1940; his wife wrote him one laborious letter a month. But his frown returned and his fists were clenched.

"Look," Konzuk said, fumbling with his words. "This kid's one of us—see. It ain't right!"

"Winnipeg—within the month."

Konzuk's eyes shifted and at last his glance settled on the floor. "All right," he said, after a moment. "All right, I'll do it."

"Good." Adam sought for and held the sergeant's eyes. "And remember this, Konzuk—that 'kid' is a murderer!"

"Yes, sir."

The ten members of the firing-squad were detailed the same day. Adam and Konzuk prepared the list of names and brought the group to be interviewed by Brigadier Hatfield in his office. And after that Sergeant Konzuk had a quiet talk with each man. Adam did not ask what the sergeant said; he was satisfied that none of the men came to him to protest.

Adam found his time fully occupied. He had installed his ten men in a separate hut of their own; there were some drill movements to be practised; and Sergeant Konzuk was drawing new uniforms from the quartermaster's stores. Ten new rifles had also been issued.

Crossing the parade square that night he encountered Padre Dixon, and he realized that this man had been avoiding him during the past two days. "Padre," he called out. "I want to talk to you." The Padre waited. His face showed no expression.

"Padre—will you give me your advice?"

The Padre's glance was cold. "Why?" he asked. "It won't change anything."

And looking into that set face Adam saw that the Padre was regarding him with a dislike he made no attempt to conceal. He flushed, and his anger slipped forward. "What's the matter, Padre—you feeling sorry for the boy-murderer?"

Adam regretted his words at once; indeed he was shocked that he could have said them. The Padre turned his back and started away.

Adam caught at his arm. "Ah, no," he said. "I didn't mean that. Padre—is what I'm doing so awful, after all?"

"You've made your choice. Let it go at that."

"But—my duty ...." Adam felt shame as he used the word.

The Padre stood with folded arms. "Listen," he said. "I told you before: no matter how necessary this thing is it will never be right."

Adam was silent. Then he reached out his hand again. "Padre," he said in a low voice. "Is there no way it can be stopped?"

The Padre sighed. "The train has been set in motion," he said. "Once it could have been stopped—in Ottawa—but now ..." He shrugged. He looked at Adam searchingly and he seemed to reflect. "There might be one way—" After a moment he blinked and looked away. "But no—that will never come to pass. I suppose I should wish you good luck," he said. "Good night, Adam."

That meeting made Adam wonder how his fellow officers regarded him. In the officers' mess that night he looked about him and found out. Silence descended when he approached a group and slowly its members would drift away; there was a cleared circle around whichever chair he sat in. Even the barman seemed to avoid his glance.

All right, Adam decided then, and from the bar he looked murderously around the room. All right, he would stick by Benny Hatfield—the two of them, at least, knew what duty and soldiering was! Why, what was he doing that was so awful? He was simply commanding a firing-squad to execute a soldier who had committed a murder. That's all—he was commanding a firing-squad; he was, he was—an executioner!

His glass crashed to the floor. Through all the soft words exchanged with Brigadier Hatfield, all the concealing echelons of military speech, the pitiless truth now leaped out at him. He was an executioner. Captain John Adam made a noise in his throat, and the faces of the other men in the room went white.

When he left the mess some instinct led him toward the small grey hut standing at the camp entrance. Through the board walls of that hut he could see his victim, Jones, living out his allotted time, while he, Adam, the executioner, walked implacably close by. The new concept of victim and executioner seized and threatened to suffocate him.

Brigadier Hatfield had the most brilliant inspiration of his career: the place of execution would be changed to Rome! There was ample justification, of course, since the effect on the troops' morale at Volpone would be bad to say the least. No one could dispute this, and all the while the Brigadier relished in imagination the face of General Vincent when he found the affair brought back to his own doorstep.

The Brigadier was in high good humour as he presided at the conference to discuss this change. All the participants were present, including one newcomer, an officer from the Provost Corps, introduced as Colonel McGuire. This colonel said nothing, but nodded his head in agreement with the Brigadier's points. His eyes roamed restlessly from face to face and his cold glance seemed to strip bare the abilities of every person in the room.

Colonel McGuire, the Brigadier announced, had been instrumental in finding the ideal place for the affair. It was a former Fascist barracks on the outskirts of Rome, and all the—ah, facilities—were readily available. Everyone taking part, and he trusted that each officer was now thoroughly familiar with his duties, would move by convoy to Rome that very after-noon. The execution—here he paused for a solemn moment—the excu-tion would take place at 0800 hours tomorrow morning. Any questions? No? Thank you, gentlemen.

Adam was moving away when the Brigadier stopped him. "John," he called. He had slipped into the habit of using his first name now. "I want you to meet Colonel McGuire."

They shook hands, and Adam flushed under the chill exposure of those probing eyes. After a moment the Colonel's glance dropped; he had seen sufficient. As Adam moved off to warn his men for the move he felt those cold eyes following him to the door, and beyond.

Adam kept his eyes closed while Sergeant Konzuk drove. In the back of the jeep Padre Dixon had not spoken since the convoy was marshalled; it was clear that these were not the travelling-companions of his choice. Although Adam would not look, all his awareness was centered on a closed three-ton truck which lumbered along in the middle of the convoy. The condemned man and his guards rode inside that vehicle.

The concept of victim and executioner filled Adam's mind to the exclusion of all else. He had tried throwing the blame back to the com-fortable politicians sitting at their polished table in Ottawa, but it was no use. He knew that it was his voice that would issue the last command. He was the executioner .... Then another thought came to torment him without mercy: How did his victim, Jones, feel now?

They stopped for ten minutes outside a hill-top town, where pink villas glinted among the green of olive trees. Adam followed Padre Dixon to the place where he sat in an orchard. The Padre looked up at him wearily. "How is he taking it?" Adam demanded at once.

The Padre scrambled to his feet. His eyes flashed with anger. "Who? The boy-murderer?"

"Please, Padre—I've got to know!"

The Padre stared at Adam's drawn face. Then he passed a hand across his eyes. "Adam—forgive me. I know it's a terrible thing for you. If it makes it any easier … well, Jones is brave; he's smiling and polite, and that's all. But Adam—the boy still doesn't understand. He doesn't believe that it's really going to happen!" The Padre's voice shook with his agitation.

Adam nodded his head. "That other time, Padre—you said there might be a way of stopping it ..."

"No, forget that—it's too late." The spluttering cough of motorcycles roared between them. "Come. It is time to go." And the Padre laid his hand on Adam's arm.

Adam and Konzuk stood on the hard tarmac and surveyed the site gloomily. The place they had come to inspect was a U-shaped space cut out of the forest. The base of the U was a red-brick wall, and down each side marched a precise green line of cypresses. The wall was bullet-pocked because this place had been used as a firing range, although imagination balked at what some of the targets must have been. On the right wing of the U a small wooden grandstand was set in front of the cypresses. Adam looked around at all this, and then his gaze moved over the trees and up to the pitilessly blue sky above. "All right, Konzuk," he said. "You check things over." And he went away to be alone.

At midnight Adam was lying on his bed in the darkness. His eyes were wide open, but he made no move when he saw the Padre's big form stumble into his room. The Padre stood over his bed, eyes groping for him. He was breathing loudly. "Adam—he wants to see you!"

"No!"

"You must!"

"I couldn't!" Now Adam sat up in bed. His battle-dress tunic was crumpled. His face was protected by the dark, but his voice was naked. "No, Padre," he pleaded. "I couldn't."

"Look, son—it's your job. You've no choice. Do you understand?"

There was silence. Adam made a noise in the darkness which seemed to take all the breath from his body. "Yes, I understand." He was fumbling for his belt and cap in the dark.

The provost sergeant came to attention and saluted. His face was stiff, but he could not keep the flicker of curiosity from his eyes. Adam saw that this was a real prison: concrete flooring, steel doors, and iron bars. They stood in what seemed to be a large, brightly lit guardroom. A card game had been taking place, and there were coffee mugs, but the guards stood now at respectful attention.

"Where is he?" Adam turned to the sergeant.

A dark-haired young man stepped from among the group of guards. A smartly dressed soldier, clean and good-looking in his freshly pressed battle-dress. "Here I am, sir," the young man said.

Adam took a step back; he flashed a glance at the door.

The sergeant spoke then, apologetically. "He wanted company, sir. I thought it would be all right."

"It was good of you to come, sir." This was Private Jones speaking for his attention.

Adam forced himself to return the glance. "Yes," he said. "I mean—it's no trouble. I—I was glad to."

The two men looked one another in the face, perhaps surprised to find how close they were in years. Jones's smile was friendly. He was like a host easing the embarrassment of his guest. "Would you like to sit down, sir?"

"Yes. Oh yes."

They sat in Jones's cell, on opposite sides of a small table. Because he had to, Adam held his eyes on the prisoner's face and now he could see the thin lines of tension spreading from the eyes and at the mouth. It was certain that Jones now believed in the truth of his own death, and he carried this fact with quiet dignity.

"It was good of you to come," Private Jones said again. "I have a request."

Surely, Adam thought, it took more courage to act as Jones did now than to advance through that meadow to the Hitler Line ....

"Well, sir," Jones went on, his face set. "I'm ready to take—tomorrow morning. But one thing worries me: I don't want you and the other boys to feel bad about this. I thought it might help if I shook hands with all the boys before—before it happens."

Adam looked down at the concrete floor. Well, he had to say something. The thing was impossible, of course.

Jones read the working of his face. "Never mind, sir—maybe you'd just give them that message for me—"

"I will, Jones. I will!" Adam stood up; he could not stay here another moment.

Jones said, "Maybe—you would shake hands with me?"

Adam stood utterly still. His voice came out as a whisper in that small space. "Jones," he said, "I was going to ask you if I could."

It was a softly fragrant morning. The dew was still fresh on the grass and a light ground mist rolled away before the heat of the climbing sun. In the forest clearing the neat groups of soldiers looked clean and compact in their khaki battle-dress with the bright regimental flashes gleaming at their shoulders. The firing-squad stood "at ease," but with not the least stir or motion. Captain Adam stood several paces apart at the left. The grandstand was filled with a small group of official witnesses, and in front of it stood Brigadier Benny Hatfield. A step behind the Brigadier was Ramsay, his adjutant; then Padre Dixon, and the chief medical officer. The assembly was complete—except for one man.

Somewhere in the background a steel door clanged, a noise which no one affected to hear. Then there came the sound of rapid marching. Three military figures came into view and halted smartly in front of Brigadier Hatfield. Private Jones, hatless, stood in the centre, a provost sergeant on each side. The boy's lips were white, his cheeks lacked colour, but he held his head high, his hands were pressed tight against the seams of his battle-dress trousers. It was impossible not to notice the brilliant shine of his polished boots as they glittered in the morning sun.

Brigadier Hatfield took a paper from Ramsay's extended hand. He read some words from it but his voice came as an indistinct mumble in the morning air. The Brigadier was in a hurry. Everyone was in a hurry; every person there suffered an agony of haste. Each body strained and each mind willed: Go! Go! Have this thing over and done with!

The Brigadier handed the paper back to Ramsay with a little gesture of finality. But the three men remained standing in front of him as though locked in their attitudes of attention. Seconds of silence ticked by. The Brigadier's hand sped up to his collar and he cleared his throat with violence. "Well, sergeant?" his voice rasped. "Carry on, man!"

"Yessir. Left turn-quick march!"

The three men held the same brisk pace, marching in perfect step. The only sound was the thud of their heavy boots upon the tarmac. They passed the firing-squad and halted at the red-brick wall. Then the escorting ncos seemed to disappear and Private Jones stood alone against the wall. A nervous little smile was fixed at the corners of his mouth.

Again there was silence. Adam had not looked at the marching men, nor did he now look at the wall. Head lowered, he frowned as he seemed to study the alignment of his ten men in a row. More seconds ticked by.

"Captain Adam!"

It was a bellow from Brigadier Hatfield and it brought Adam's head up. Then his lips moving soundlessly as though rehearsing what he had to say. "Squad," Captain Adam ordered. "Load!" Ten left feet banged forward on the tarmac, ten rifles hit in the left hand, ten bolts smashed open and shut in unison. Ten rounds were positioned in their chambers.

There were just two remaining orders: "Aim!" and "Fire!" and these should be issued immediately, almost as one. But at that moment a late rooster crowed somewhere and the call came clear and sweet through the morning air, full of rich promise for the summer's day which lay ahead.

Adam took his first glance at the condemned man. Jones's mouth still held hard to its smile, but his knees looked loose. His position of attention was faltering.

"Squad!" Adam ordered in a ringing voice. "Unload! Rest!" Ten rifles obeyed in perfect unison.

Adam turned half right so that he faced Brigadier Hatfield. "Sir," he called clearly, "I refuse to carry out this order!"

Every voice in that place joined in the sound which muttered across the tarmac.

The Brigadier's face was deathly white. He peered at Private Jones, still in position against the wall, knees getting looser. He had a split second to carry the thing through. "Colonel McGuire!" he shouted.

"Yes, sir!" McGuire came running toward the firing-squad. He knew what had to be done, and quickly. The Brigadier's face turned purple now; he appeared to be choking with the force of his rage. "Colonel McGuire," he shouted. "Place that officer under close arrest!"

"Sir?" McGuire stopped where he was and his mouth dropped open. Private Jones began to fall slowly against the wall. Then a rifle clattered loudly on the tarmac. Sergeant Konzuk was racing toward the wall and in an instant he had his big arms tight around Jones's body.

"McGuire!" The Brigadier's voice was a hoarse shriek now. "March the prisoner away!"

Padre Dixon stood rooted to the ground. His lips were moving and he stared blindly at Adam's stiffly erect figure. "He found the way!" he cried then in a ringing voice, and he moved about in triumph, although no one paid him attention. At his side Ramsay was spluttering out his own ecstasy of excitement; "Jones will get a reprieve after this! It will have to be referred to London and then to Ottawa. And they'll never dare to put him through this again ...."

Ramsay looked up as he felt the Padre's fingers bite into his shoulder. He laughed nervously. "Yes," he chattered on. "Jones may get a reprieve, but Adam's the one for sentencing now." He peered across the tarmac where Adam still stood alone, his face slightly lifted to the warmth of the morning sun. He looked at Adam's lone figure with fear and admiration.

"Yes," he said, suddenly sobered. "God help Adam now."

"Don't worry about that, son," said the Padre, starting to stride across the tarmac. "He already has."

Ralph Allen

ANDREW RALPH ALLEN (1913–1966) was born in
Winnipeg and grew up in the small Saskatchewan town of Oxbow. Unable to afford
university because of the Depression, at the age of sixteen he became a sports
writer for the *Winnipeg Tribune*. In 1938 he joined the Toronto *Globe and Mail*
news staff, leaving on December 13, 1941 because, following the Japanese attack at
Pearl Harbor, he had enlisted. In 1942, as a gun-crew sergeant, he was serving
under Con Smythe (formerly of hockey's Toronto Maple Leafs) in the Thirtieth Anti-
Aircraft Battery. The following year he was discharged from the army to become the
Globe's war correspondent, filing reports from the front line. Wearing yellow
corduroy pants, a faded turtle-neck sweater, rumpled battle dress jacket, dirty shoes
and a beret, he was hardly an example of sartorial splendour, but his courage and
fairness were legendary. His reports, says Christina McCall Newman in *The Man
from Oxbow: the Best of Ralph Allen* (1967), are "undimmed in their perception
and unsettling in their poignancy ... evocative of the horror and glory of that war."

"The Landing," first published as a short story in *Maclean's* magazine and then
integrated into Allen's novel *Home Made Banners* (1946), reflects the author's
observations as he accompanies Canadian troops in the D-Day landings. The hero,
Michael Tully, is a prairie boy whose experiences growing up in Saskatchewan
parallel those of his creator. Throughout the novel he maintains the perspective of
a private, recording the Germans killing Canadian prisoners, the battles for Caen,
Falaise and the Scheldt, the attitude to Zombies, the cynicism about propaganda.
Rather implausibly, he is also able to describe prisoner-of-war camps, death camps

such as Buchenwald and the refugee migrations by the device of attaching himself to a war correspondent with a jeep.

From 1946 until 1964 Allen was a member of *Maclean's* editorial staff (including a long stint as editor-in-chief) and then was managing editor of Canada's largest newspaper, the *Toronto Daily Star*. His war-related publications include *Ordeal by Fire: 1910–1945* (1961), *The High White Forest* (1964), and a *Maclean's* editorial, June 1950, entitled "War is Hell and the Hell of it is that we forget."

The Landing

Mike wished Rinowski would stop talking. He rubbed a damp hand across his wet forehead and then carefully wiped the sweat away on the bristly nap of his tunic. The air behind the black-out curtain was hot and thick. The ship pitched a little sometimes and slipped when it changed course, but the motion was slow and steady. Stealthy.

You could imagine the ship was listening for something and did not want to make too much noise lest it fail to hear.

The men were not in bunks. They were lying close together on their blankets on the floor, unrecognizable and formless and, for the time, uncomprehending. Most of them were asleep or lying quietly in the darkness and willing sleep to come. Mike was sure he would be able to sleep if Rinowski would stop talking.

Rinowski had a monotonous voice. It was high-pitched and almost childish in tone, the voice of a boy, and although he was trying to keep it low, it carried. His attempts to keep it low merely made it flat; there was no inflection in it, and Rinowski sounded like a schoolboy reciting, droning his words by rote without fully understanding them.

"The wife and me used to bowl a lot," Rinowski said. "That was when she was working for Eaton's. The wife's a good bowler. She can still beat me as often as I beat her nearly. She's good at picking up splits. She don't get as many strikes as I do, but she spares up them splits. Well, this night we went bowling, I forget if she beats me or I beat her. It's funny I don't remember. Usually we had a bet. I used to bet two bits against her 15 cents. She beat me a lot. I'd get more strikes than her but she picked it up on spares."

Mike turned on his side and pulled his life belt into the U of his neck, allowing his head to loll back across the life belt's bloated curve.

Rinowski was saying: "This night we went to the drugstore, the one near Coxwell, and we were just sitting there talking when I told the wife she was going to marry me. I forget what we were talking about. About the bowling most likely. We'd had a couple of beers and I guess I was feeling kinda cocky, and I just said: 'You're going to marry me,' just like that. The wife said after, you could have knocked her over with a feather. She let on she didn't take me seriously, but I said I meant it, and finally she said: 'Well, if you do, ask me again tomorrow and see what I say.' I didn't know if she wanted me to ask her again or not. I nearly didn't. I kept thinking all the next day, 'I'll bet she's laughing at me,' and I nearly didn't ask her again at all. The wife comes from a real good family. One of the best families in the Beach. Her uncle was an alderman. Everybody knew him. He ran for Board of Control one year but got beat. He nearly won, but when he got beat he just dropped out of it. He had a good job, anyway."

Mike twisted his head away from the life belt. He half-raised his body and dragged the blanket across the deck under him until there was enough of it above his shoulders to roll into a little pillow. The steel deck was like bone pressing against the bone of his hips, but his head rested easier. He listened to the motors and the slapping of the sea on the bulkheads, trying to make them exclude Rinowski's voice, but it was no use.

"The wife and me had a big wedding," Rinowski was saying. "We had the reception afterward at her uncle's place. That was the alderman. Alderman Harry Aitken. The wife's got all kinds of friends. We had all kinds of little things on trays at the reception. We had six jugs of whiskey and three jugs of gin. No beer, though. The wife said a wedding was no place to serve beer. My old man pretended to be real sore about it. He said if any son of his ever got married again and there was no beer they could count him out. My old man likes his beer. He don't drink any more than he can handle, but he likes it. He don't like whiskey. I don't like it much either. I'd rather have beer."

Mike raised the upper part of his body on one hand and levered himself to his feet. He stood erect for a minute, swaying with the easy motion of the ship and peering down at the dark deck until his eyes had picked out a channel among the sleeping men. When he was sure of the channel, he walked through it to the steel companionway and up the steps past the black-out curtain into a dark corridor. He guided himself along the corridor with his hand and turned his body sideways and edged it through another black-out curtain. The air hit his face and splashed into his lungs with the sharp force of a cold douche. It was a while before he could bring himself to raise his face into the wind again.

At first all he could see was the sky, which seemed as uniform and obdurate in its blackness as the heavy canvas curtain at the end of the corridor. Then he saw that it was shot with smears of slaty grey, and with something like a thrill he saw a star hanging close to one of the smears. But the main expanse of sky was sulky and remote, as if it saw a portent and wished to withdraw itself from what was about to happen and have no part in it.

Mike moved to the side of the ship and put his hands on the wet rail to brace himself. The first ship he saw was level with the starboard bow and not far away. The ship had no shape or being of its own; it was independent of neither the sea nor the night, but was like a tumour of them both, a black formless growth that clung to the sea and the night and could go only where they willed to take it. He did not dare take his eyes off the ship for fear that he might lose it and not be able to find it again, but at last he left it and looked for others.

There was another ship directly behind the first and another farther away, abreast of the stern. And suddenly a fourth stood out bravely against the barely visible line between the sea and the sky. It stood out not as a growth or a shadow but as a ship; it had funnels, and the black triangle which moved above it along the dim backdrop of the horizon was unmistakably a gun turret. This was a warship. It might be a battle-ship, and at the least it was a cruiser. Moreover, the warship had volition and power of its own. Its course was not the same as the courses of the other ships, and it moved faster than they did; it was not a creature of the sea or the night, it could go where it chose. As though to confirm the point, the warship changed course again and was soon engulfed in the darkness.

A sentry walked up behind Mike and said: "Nobody allowed up here, mate."

Mike said: "I couldn't sleep. It's stuffy."

The sentry said: "All right. Watch out for officers."

Mike moved toward the stern of the ship and stood for a while looking at the inky sledlike bottom of an assault boat which hung from davits above the rail.

A man in a shallow woollen toque and a heavy turtle-neck sweater came and stood beside him.

"You for that one, mate?" the man asked.

"No," Mike said, "mine's on the other side."

"First time, I guess," the man said.

"First time for keeps," Mike said.

"It's never as bad as they think," the man said. "It's never been, anyway."

"You Navy?" Mike asked.

"Combined Ops. This is our fifth."

"That's a lot," Mike said.

"Torch," the man said. "That was North Africa. Sicily and Messina and then Anzio. We get in and out," he said apologetically.

Mike said: "How do they seem, going in?"

"Them things?"

"No," Mike said. "The men. The army."

"All right," the man said. "Good."

"I mean do they—" Mike said. "Do they seem—"

"Afraid?" the man said. Mike was grateful to the sailor for using the word for him. He had not wanted to use it himself. He was not afraid and did not want the sailor to think he was. But the subject interested him. He wanted to hear about it.

The sailor stood unspeaking for a moment, while they listened to the stealthy hum of the ship's motors and felt the gentle vibration of its decks under their feet.

"A lot of them, yes," the sailor said. "But it doesn't seem to make much difference. Sometimes the ones that are afraid are better than the ones that aren't. And none of them ever know they won't be afraid. Some of them know they will be, but nobody ever knows he won't be, right until the last. Some people say you can tell which way they'll be from their eyes or the way they talk. My mate says you can tell from their hands. But you can only tell if they're going to be afraid. If they're not going to get the wind up, there's no way you can tell. It's like putting a beer in front of a stranger. If he picks it up and holds it to the light, you know he's going to drink it. But if he doesn't pick it up right away, you don't know he's not going to drink it. Me, I'm always windy," the sailor said. "But I never know when it's coming on. All of a sudden there it is, and there's nothing you can do about it."

A glow of impatience came over Mike, an urge to get back to the hold, to the privacy of the floor and his blanket, to lie in solitude with his new discovery and try to winnow a meaning from it. It seemed a good discovery to him and an important one, and he wanted to examine it.

He said: "Well, I've got to try and get some sleep. Thanks."

"Good luck," the sailor said.

"Good luck."

He paused at the outer hatchway and listened while a plane muttered in and out of hearing in the distance. Then he felt his way back down the companionway to his blanket, groped for the little ball at its head and lay down again. At first he thought Rinowski had gone to sleep, but the toneless litany began blending a third monotone with the hum of the ship's throttled-down motors and the stroking wash of the sea against her plates.

"The wife always has a dog," Rinowski was saying. "I never liked dogs. But this dog she's got now is no trouble at all. It's just like a person some of the things it does. Not tricks. It don't hardly do any tricks at all. But it's smart and some of the things it does you can see it thinking just like a person. It's an Airedale. Airedales are supposed to be mean, but don't let anybody tell you that. Our dog's name is Spike. The wife named him that. She said she named him from his hair. His hair is spiky. Wherever the wife goes the dog goes, but if she don't want him to go in she just tells him to wait outside, and when she comes out, if it's an hour or five hours, he's there sitting and waiting for her. Maybe it's a store where they won't let dogs in, or the apartment of some girl that don't like dogs around. It don't matter. The dog just sits there and waits, if it's an hour or five hours."

After a long while a new man came down the companionway and stood at its foot for a few moments, looking uncertainly at the sleeping men, as though he could not make up his mind to disturb them. Then he said loudly: "All right!" He repeated it, more loudly still: "All right!"

The new man played a flashlight around the room. Now and then he would catch a soldier full in the face with the light and hold it there until the soldier blinked his eyes open, stared vacantly into the light until he remembered where he was, and then stumbled to his feet. When there was enough room for him to move about, the new man walked across the hold and turned a switch on the wall. A single electric light bulb winked to life, yellow and very dim, and as the men rose from the floor, stretching and scratching and tugging the twists out of their battledress, their shadows danced between the steel ribs of the bulkheads like deformed giants in some silent tribal rite.

Soon they were all on their feet and soon they all remembered where they were. At first no one spoke in anything but the lowest undertone. Finally a man belched. It was a firm and deliberate belch and it produced such a satisfying ring that its author belched again. This second belch was even better than the first. It was solemn without being pompous, eloquent without being flowery, rueful without being downcast and droll without being flippant. It said a great deal. It said, for instance: "Ho hum, what a way to make a living!" It said: "Come! Now let us to the task!" It said: "Our dog's name is Spike. The wife named him that." It said: "Our Father which art in Heaven, hallowed be Thy name. Thy kingdom come."

Under the familiar impetus of the belch, the fractured hush disintegrated and the hold became almost cheery, with the half-forced, half-grumbling cheeriness of any reveille. "Hey, sarge!" someone shouted, "when do we get our bloody breakfast?" The man who had come in and turned on the light shouted back, for everyone to hear: "You eat in five minutes. Everybody eat a good meal whether you're hungry or not. It may be a long time before you get hot grub again."

When they came above decks it was almost light. The clouds hung low, but they were breaking, and past their dissolving edges they could already see the first hint of blue, swallowing the last wan straggling stars. The sea was a vast sweep of grey water, covered with vast reaches of grey ships, but it was something more than that, it was something so big that it could only be grasped in the abstract. It was a mighty rush of wind, a giant beating of wings, it was the thirsty slaver of an awful God, the stirring of a universe.

Everywhere they looked there were ships. Long gaunt warships, swashbuckling through the grey swell, wheeling and turning through their own spume, flexing their leashed muscles in the dawn after their long night of vigil. Fat little minesweepers and tank carriers and clumsy

LSI's toddling up to the horizon, hanging there momentarily, and coasting out of sight down its slope. Tiny torpedo boats darting in and out among the slower craft at 30 knots and flat steel barges wallowing at three. Tugs and merchantmen of a hundred designs, recruited for a thousand different ends. A blowsy sidewheeler threshing doggedly ahead with her decks piled high with supplies.

Their coloured rows of signal pennants stood out bravely from their masts, like the teeth on papier-mâché dragons, and the signal beacons on their bridges winked companionably across the water. The ships could not be counted. They could only be measured by the acre and the township. As he looked at them and tried to guess how many they might be, Mike's heart expanded with hope and gratitude and something close to downright cockiness. In the same degree that it had seemed evil and hostile in the dark of a few hours before, the sea now seemed good and friendly. It was no longer a fetter dragging the imprisoned ships to some fearful unknown. It was a staunch ally which lent its hard grey flesh to the ends of their flesh and entwined its sinew with their sinew and heaved and rushed beside them toward their common future, sparing nothing, withholding nothing and portending nothing that was not ordained already.

"They can't stop us!" Mike whispered exultantly. "They'll never stop us."

An officer came above deck, moving stiffly in his corset of webbing, and walked slowly through their lounging ranks, asking each man the same set of questions.

"Water bottle full?"

"Rations okay?"

"Any questions about our objectives or your assignment?"

A few Spitfires sang overhead, and a man near the rail yelled, "Look!" and pointed ahead past the bows of their ship.

In the far distance, beyond the horizon, a bleary ripple of gunflash faded out of sight and a jet of tracer, brighter than the gunflash, cascaded up a bank of cloud, hung there for a moment, and then faded too. The sound was too far away to be heard. The officer looked at his watch. "The real stuff starts in 14 minutes," he said.

The ship gathered itself and stretched out in the heaving sea. The hum of its motors became a quick growl, and the ship left its place in the pattern of moving vessels and hurried through the sea with the abstract intentness of a man hurrying through a crowd when he is late. A few other ships stirred and began to hurry in the same way; and as these hurrying vessels surged by, the men aboard the vessels that had more time looked at them with a mixture of envy and compassion, and called and waved to them across the water. "Good luck, Infantry!" they called faintly. "Give 'em hell!"

The officer said: "Here goes the first team!" and the ship rushed on until the traffic thinned out a little. Abruptly it cut its motors and idled.

"Look!" the man near the rail yelled again. This time it was the land he pointed to, a low blob of purple looming through a far haze, mysterious and indistinct. The men stared at the land, not anxiously or apprehensively, but with great absorption. Thin V's appeared at the corners of their eyes, and their eyebrows came together in little paunches of flesh as they stared across the sea into the haze, searching for some link between this distant shadow and the land they knew from their maps and photographs—the land of the Normandy beaches. They saw nothing of what they were looking for, but they continued to stare.

And now, high above them, above the Spitfires and Typhoons that raced back and forth from the ships to the land, they heard and partly saw the first wave of bombers. The clouds muffled the sound of the bombers' motors and hid them from view except in brief, scuttling, microscopic dashes from one cloud to the next. But in a little while, after the first of them had gone and others were overhead, a hollow hoom-hoom-hoom rolled back across the water. They stared at the land again and saw its dingy outlines stir and quiver and finally rise in a black blend of smoke and shadow, like a genie summoned from its rest.

"The poor bastards!" Mike whispered. "The poor bastards!"

But as the first hoom-hoom-hoom rumbled into a second and then into a third, a fourth and a fifth, and as smoke above the land became a thick billow, his eyes grew bright with excitement and he was possessed by a savage exhilaration. He felt the pores opening under the rubber band of his steel helmet and he squeezed the stock of his rifle until his hand was numb.

"Give it to the bastards!" he cried hoarsely. "Pour it to the bastards! Powder them to hell!"

As the ship idled closer to the land, they saw the first buildings and soon they picked out two little towns, gleaming whitely against the black smoke, like naked corpses lying on their shrouds. Away off their bow a drifting battleship squirted a huge ball of flame toward the towns, and before the sound that went with the flame reached their ship, it was lost in the mighty retching and hammering of a thousand guns. The whole fleet erupted in one cosmic belch and threw its thunderous vomit at the beaches in cosmic bucketfuls.

Mike scarcely remembered boarding the assault boat. But the steel plates of the boat acted as a cushion against the pounding tumult of the guns, and as the boat pitched away from its mother ship he found that he was able to put aside the drugging indulgence of thinking about the bombardment and think again about the trivialities that he knew he must not forget. He settled on his haunches, wedging his life belt between his back and the plates of the boat, and carefully slid open the bolt of his rifle. There was a cartridge in the chamber. He closed the bolt, put the catch to safety and reminded himself that the last thing he must do before leaving the boat was to move the catch again. He felt for the handle of the adzelike trenching tool strapped to his back beneath his small kit bag, and wrenched at the cork of his water bottle to make sure that it was pushed down tight. He opened the two ammunition pouches above his front ribs and closed them again. He counted the grenades hanging from his belt. Then he unscrewed the valve on his life belt and blew an extra lungful of air into it. The last thing he did was open the mouth of a heavy paper bag and place it on his knees directly beneath his head.

The boat had found its course and was reaching swiftly toward the last yawning arid slipping and rolling in the swell and then shaking itself doggedly and plunging on ahead. Mike's stomach heaved as though under the massaging of a fleshy unseen hand. He dropped his head on his chest and closed his eyes. With his free hand he moved the paper bag to his mouth and tried to empty his stomach into it, but nothing came but a series of dry, aspirate coughs from deep in his chest, and a trickle of thin bodiless saliva drooling across his lips. He lifted his head again and drew a lungful of salty air out of the small rectangle of space that hung above the sides of the boat. The colour seeped back into his face and he knew he wasn't going to be sick after all.

He looked across the boat to the row of men squatting and standing inside its flat steel haunch. The men were close together, and yet each man was now alone. Some were grey with sea-sickness and some were grey with another sickness. No one talked. There was no need to talk now. There was no need to sing, or pray, or curse, or to dredge tough little wisecracks out of the toughened recesses of their tough quickening hearts. Those who were afraid had no need to hide their fear, and those who were not afraid had no need to show their fortune off. For there was enough fear in them all, or near them all, to give them the knowledge that fear, or the lack of it, was not a matter for shame or pride, but only a matter of chance.

The barrage was thinning out, preparing to lift from the beaches and grope farther inland toward the secondary defences. It was possible to hear the stuttering grumble of the adjacent landing craft driving toward the shore, and the liquid ping, like elastic breaking under tension, of an occasional enemy shell landing in the sea nearby. And in a while, from what seemed to be very far ahead, a machine gun chattered.

"*Oh, God!*" Mike formed the words in his mind without uttering them. "*Make it now. Make the boat stop and make the ramp open and let us out, on the beach. I'm all right now. But a minute from now I might not be any good at all. I might not be any good in 30 seconds. Make it now. I could do it all now, exactly as they told me to. But in 30 seconds I might not be able to do anything. I might just sit here and watch the others go. I might not be able to lift my arms or move my legs. Make it now. Make it now.*"

The boat jarred and a tremulous grating shook its hull as it came to a stop on the gravel floor off the shore line. The shivering impact threw Mike heavily into the man beside him, but when he caught his breath it was a sob of gratitude. He heard the impatient clanking of the opening ramp and stumbled toward the square of the daylight that had replaced the boat's flat bow, shoving at the man ahead of him in his haste. Above the loud scrape of his hobnailed boots on the ramp, he heard a sailor's voice call from above him: "Watch out—sand bar!" He held himself at the crest of the ramp for an instant, and in the same instant the man ahead of him on the down slope of the ramp turned and looked past him into the emptying belly of the boat. The face was as set and naked as the face of a child awakened in a nightmare. Its owner, with a kind of hopeless shrug, turned his back and slithered quietly into the sea.

Mike slithered after him, took a step on the edge of a sand bar and then found himself waist deep in water. Holding his rifle above his head, clear of the water line, he half ran and half pushed his way straight ahead until he felt the heavy warm grip of the water drop by degrees from his waist. To his hips and finally to his knees. Then, when he was able to get his feet clear of the water, he quickened his gait to a high-kneed lope.

He did not see much at first. His attention was focussed partly on the backs of the two men immediately ahead of him. As he splashed through the shallowing water, the panorama of the beach rationed itself out to the corners of his eyes in small glimpses, without much pattern or cohesion, like pieces of a jigsaw puzzle spread out at random. He saw some more soldiers spilling out of a boat that had driven straight up to the dry sand. He also saw several dead men, as well as one man, badly wounded, using his arms like flippers to drag a mash of crushed legs and shredded battle-dress back from the shore into the water. He saw any number of black mines and yellow shell cases bobbing in the water on big wooden stakes. He saw concrete blocks and iron tank traps at the water's edge in great profusion, some of them broken and twisted by the bombing and shelling or by the demolition parties, but many of them still intact. He saw much barbed wire, some of it lying in rusty whorls and spirals and some of it staked out neatly in little garden patches.

Straight ahead and very close, not much more than 100 yards away, he saw the main beach position of the enemy, a straggling settlement of tall pillboxes and squat machine gun turrets anchored to a high continuous concrete breakwater and sprawling back through a grey-brown belt of low dunes and marshes to a village. The nearest building of the village appeared to have been a water-front hotel of fawn stucco; now it was a smoking fossil, its face eaten away by shell holes, the red tile shingles of its roof lying in front of it in untidy piles and tiny waves of flame lapping against its wooden beams. There were several other fires in the village, and most of the houses he could see were shorn and broken by concussion.

The fading hammer of the shifting and diminishing barrage made the beach seem not exactly quiet but unreal, as the street outside a great and noisy factory seems unreal after you have left the factory and can only hear its dim echoes. As his feet bit the sand, Mike scarcely noticed the thwack-thwack-thwack of Bren guns merging with the quicker slurp of German Spandaus and Schmeissers from the back of the breakwater.

But then, in quick succession a rifle bullet sang hard and high above his shoulder, like a violin string plucked almost to breaking point, a heavy mortar broke nearby with a testy crump, and a German 88-mm shell fused the last split second of its warning swish and the cruel smack of its explosion in one venomous package.

He made no conscious catalogue of the things he saw and heard in those first few seconds. The real centre of his world was the two backs ahead of him, which he must follow. Suddenly the second back straightened out of its crouch, stiffened momentarily and then pitched to the sand. The other swerved and lunged to the left and then the man was running straight down the beach under the curve of the breakwater. As he reached the lee of the worn rampart, he twisted his body into a crabwise jog and lobbed a grenade over the top.

Mike involuntarily shifted his eyes to watch the flight of the grenade, and swerved to follow a second too late. Something thin and hard kicked across his shin with brutal force and he plunged headlong into the sand. As he fell a hot claw raked through his battledress into the flesh of his thigh, and wet sand jammed into his nose and mouth in a stifling jet. As he spat and blew it out, he tried to roll back to his feet, but from the hip to the ankle one leg was pinioned as in a vise. He squirmed and tried to reach his leg with his hand. But his hips lay between a tangle of wire, which sealed off the whole lower part of him in a jagged impenetrable corral. He cursed, bitterly, despairingly and supplicatingly, and then raised himself on his elbows, brought his rifle to his shoulder and waited.

He waited almost calmly. It could not be long.

He had been told enough about his battalion's plan of attack to know that there would be no frontal assault on this part of the enemy defences. Later they would take this part from the flanks. They would tidy up the barbed wire in front of it, and that would be much too late for anyone caught in the wire now. It was already too late to pretend he was dead. His first frantic attempts to free himself had committed him; if there were any Germans on the breakwater or the dunes ahead of him, they must have seen his movement.

He kept the rifle at his shoulder until his arms began to ache with the weight of his body and the back of his neck was a steady agony. In this time his instinct was conscious of many things that merely hovered at the outskirt of his senses. He was conscious of the snarling little eruption of grenades and Sten guns on his left, where those of his section who remained were trying to take out a Spandau. He was conscious of the noisy Donnybrook on his right, where the rest of his company swarmed through the fresh wet shell holes on the beach and spat their tracer off the thick hides of three connecting casemates, like glowing hornets attacking a herd of elephants. He was conscious of a submarine tank growling in from the sea, half swimming and half waddling in its square water wings, and poking its gun through the giant loophole of a pillbox straight into the protruding muzzle of a German 105. He was conscious of the continuous V of spraying sand behind him, at the rendezvous of two German machine guns sweeping the beach from opposite ends on fixed lines of fire.

At last, when it seemed he could support the rifle and his body no longer, he saw what he was waiting for. The threat he had been watching most intently was a small two-man pillbox sitting squarely on top of the breakwater a few yards farther down—a round shallow boulder with two shallow loopholes cut into its face and staring out to the beach like empty eye sockets. Now, in one of the sockets, he saw the thick short funnel of a machine gun muzzle feeling carefully along the lower rim. He fired quickly and heard his bullet splatter against the side of the pill-box. The machine gun muzzle disappeared hastily.

In a moment it poked back into view again. Mike fired once more and worked the bolt of his rifle. But this time the bolt came back sluggishly, and when he tried to shove it forward, it thwacked against the palm of his hand and would not move. Feverishly he pulled the bolt back again and clawed with his finger nails at the scarred cartridge case wedged into its grimy bore. His nails tore away on the base of the cartridge and left the ends of his fingers raw and bloody. He fumbled for the big issue clasp knife at his belt, stuck the edge of the largest blade in his teeth, and tugged it open with his hand. But the cartridge was driven home as firmly as a rivet. When he tried to pry the knife under its base, he could get no leverage.

He let the useless rifle drop into the sand and yanked the grenades out of his belt and laid them in a pile beside his right hand. He rolled over on his side, pulled a pin from a grenade, and lobbed it blindly over his shoulder, toward the pillbox. Without waiting to hear its flat metallic splash, he threw the next in the same way, and then the next, the next, and the next, and finally the last. He did not expect to hit anything with the grenades, but each of them would keep the German machine gunner's head down a few seconds longer. And, as a corollary, when the last grenade was gone, the German was free to bring his head up and keep it up until he had done his work.

Mike rolled back on his face, tugged one last time at his imprisoned leg and lay still. With his hands he slid his steel helmet forward to cover the top of his head, and then he cradled his face in his hands, smelling the wet sand close to his nostrils as he filtered the air into them between his fingers.

I should be crying, he told himself. *I should be praying. At the very least, I should be saying something brave and corny. "This is it," maybe. Or, "What's the holdup?" I should be lighting a cigarette and lifting my head up into the sun and blowing smoke right into that bastard's face. I used to dream about this sometimes, in my crazy, bigshot dreams. Me lying somewhere on a beach, and taking it, and then the others standing around afterward and saying: "That was Tully. They didn't come any gamer." I wonder if the others lying here ever had dreams like that. It doesn't matter anyway. It doesn't matter how we die. The only person who will see me is that bastard up there in the pillbox, and all I'll be to him is a sack of khaki caught in a piece of wire. And pretty soon he'll be dead too.*

He was trying to keep himself relaxed, perhaps because of some subconscious pride or vanity. But slowly and inexorably, like the pull of a rack, the suspense drew him taut. And then, when all his muscles had contracted into tight, waiting knots, poised for some final convulsion, a sound as harsh and sudden as terror itself split the air beside his ear. He threw his body away from it in one writhing lunge, and above the sound he heard his own voice scream.

The new sound stopped and a voice called anxiously, very close to him: "It's me, Tully. Rinowski."

He threw his body back on its side. Beside him in the sand and level with his thigh, the muzzle of a Bren gun pointed across its stubby spraddling bipod toward the pillbox on the breakwater. Rinowski, sprawled beside it, kicked a leg across the sand toward him, briefly exhibiting a tatter of khaki cloth and bleeding flesh.

"I got caught too," Rinowski panted. "I'm all right now."

Mike looked at him stupidly and then, with a great effort, not because he thought it was the thing to say, but because he thought nothing else would be any use, he shouted above the disorder of sound from the rest of the beach: "You better get out of here, kid. There's a machine gun covering us."

"I seen him," Rinowski panted. "He'll keep his head down a while. That last burst scared the bloody hell out of him. If I could put one through that little loophole it would shut up for good."

Rinowski dragged himself forward a few feet, lifting the legs of his gun's bipod clear of the sand and inching it ahead in tiny cautious bounds. When he was even with Mike's shoulder he carefully moved the gun over to Mike. "You take it," he said. "Where's your knife?"

Mike pulled the gun into the crook of his shoulder, trained it on the closer of the two fissures in the pillbox and stretched his free hand across his back with the knife. Twice while Rinowski was hacking at his battle-dress with the knife and untangling the wire from his foot, the muzzle of the German machine gun appeared in the aperture of the pillbox and drew back again as Mike squirted the Bren.

"Try it now!" Rinowski shouted. Mike pulled the numbed leg in with the muscles of his thigh. It came easily, he was free.

Rinowski squirmed up beside him again and said: "I'll take it now."

"I'll take it," Mike said. "You hit for the breakwater."

"No," Rinowski said doggedly. "It's my gun. I can't leave it go." His voice was high and childish again, as it had been when Mike lay listening to it in the hold of their ship. It was the voice of a boy, an earnest boy claiming his place in the world of men.

"Jesus Christ!" Mike shouted. "Let's do something." He allowed Rinowski to tug the gun back. His face was pale with excitement and doubt, but in spite of himself, in spite of what he knew was implied in the transfer, he had no power to argue further.

"Go when I say," Rinowski shouted: "Get ready!"

When he heard the quick stammer of the Bren again, Mike scrambled to his feet and ran for the concave wall, running low and digging his feet into the sand like a football plunger. When he was halfway there he heard the Bren hammer again and heard the bullets biting at the concrete. He fell into the sand, lay there for a moment, and then backed into the breakwater and dropped on one knee, looking across the beach to where Rinowski was stretched out beside the gun. There were more dead on the other parts of the beach than he had thought. He spent an instant appraising the flung litter of bodies and the litter of landing craft disgorging their streams of men across the smoking shore line. But Rinowski, alone in the microscopic eddy of his one-man battlefield, reclaimed his attention at once.

Rinowski lifted the bipod free of the sand, threw it forward a few feet and then hastily hauled his body up the side of the gunstock and picked up his aim again on the pillbox. He repeated the action twice before he had to fire his next burst. Altogether he had come perhaps six yards closer to the shelter of the curving wall.

He crawled a little way farther and paused again. He was so close now that his head almost reached the pale line of shadow made by the wall in the sand. He fired a third burst. This burst was shorter than any of the others had been. And after it coughed out, Rinowski did not advance the bipod again. He glanced anxiously at his chest and began grappling with an ammunition pouch, quickly and furtively, aware that what he was about to do must be done without delay and without being observed.

"Oh, God," Mike whispered, "his magazine is empty." Mike prayed, not to God, but to the boy fumbling in the sand with his gun and ammunition. *Run for it, Rinowski*, he prayed. *Don't try to put on a new magazine. You're so close he can hear you. He'll hear you and know he's got you. Run for it, Rinowski.*

With great stealth the boy drew a flat, chopped-off crescent of black metal from his bullet pouch and held it in his right hand beside the stock of the gun. Then he lowered the other hand from the stock and stabbed swiftly at the body of the gun with a quick two-handed motion, like a boxer throwing a one-two punch in a close clinch. The first punch knocked the empty magazine forward and away from the gun into the sand, and the second brought the new magazine up to its place in a hard metallic clatter. There was no firm click as the magazine slipped into place. Instead, into a tiny vacancy in the uneven racket of the beach there crept a furtive scraping. It was a sound that Mike had heard many times on the ranges, the sound of a magazine missing its slot and being dragged across the top of a gun in hurried, probing stabs.

The German in the pillbox recognized the scraping too. Before Rinowski could jab the magazine home, the German's gun opened up in a long rippling purr, throwing a low curtain of sand around Rinowski and kicking his whole body back from the Bren as though someone were yanking at his heels with a rope.

Rinowski shook himself and slithered back to the gun, fondled it unsteadily with the magazine, and fired back. The pillbox was quiet again.

Rinowski was badly hurt. No new blood showed on him, but he was breathing in long, sucking gasps, which even the steady rivet beat of fire from the two ends of the beach could not submerge. His hold on the gun was weak and uncertain and its muzzle waved, rather than pointed, at the pillbox, like the accusing finger of a drunk.

Mike, flattened against the saucer-like face of the breakwater, rose and took a half step toward the struggling boy. But when his hips came clear of the concrete he could go no farther.

For the first time since his unit had been ordered into its marshalling area more than three weeks before, his mind was fully concentrated. His thoughts were no longer diffused and obscured by the strange complexities of watching an army prepare for this day, of preparing himself for it, nor by the mighty tremors of the day itself.

His reason ruled him now. It told him what he ought to do. It also told him brutally that he could not do it, and, more brutally still, it told him why he could not do it. He could not do what he ought to do because he was not quite the man he had hoped to be, and his reason did not add that no man ever is.

Rinowski was still pawing feebly toward him, inching forward with his hands and elbows, and clumsily driving the gun ahead of him with his shoulder. The Spandau lashed at him again. It might have hit him or it might not. Rinowski squeezed on the Bren and kept coming across the sand with the slow doggedness of a sick animal that is close to home.

When the distance between Rinowski and himself was no more than twice the boy's length, Mike was still frozen to the breakwater like a badly synchronized mechanism in which the controls are in perfect order and the working parts are in perfect order, but the circuit between the controls and the working parts simply will not function. But as Rinowski clawed the sand again and began to haul his limp body another hopeless foot or two, the circuit closed. Mike felt it happen. The sensation was physical. It stung his muscles and his flesh and filled his head with rushing blood. His throat choked out a cry of gratitude, of challenge and of anger. With his hand he threw himself away from the breakwater and hurtled across the sand to Rinowski's side. He stooped, grabbed the boy around the armpits, shook him into a rough state of balance across his hip, and lurched back across the slope with him, the gun trailing after then in the grip of Rinowski's dangling hand.

The machine gunner in the pillbox stuck his head up again, just in time to see them fall under the eave of the breakwater, and his parting tattoo chunked wildly into the furrow left by Rinowski's dragging legs.

Mike put the boy down, slid his steel helmet forward off his head and ripped a big wad of shell dressing from under the green camouflage net which covered the helmet. He jerked a black Commando dagger out of Rinowski's webbing and cut away the khaki waterproof cover on the dressing. He squeezed open the buckle at the front of the web belt and peeled the bullet pouches and their straps back over the boy's shoulders.

Rinowski's whole side was a soggy drench of blood, and set in the red drench, like black mother-of-pearl buttons on the jacket of a London coster, a row of bullet holes ran the full length of his ribs. Mike counted the holes. There were nine.

He turned Rinowski on his back again and lifted his head off the sand, cradling it across his own legs. He opened a water bottle and spilled a little water across his lips. Rinowski was breathing hard, fighting for every breath in liquid gurgles. His face was drawn and yellow and the yellow deepened with every breath. His breathing reached and passed its climax in one gasping tremor, and then became slower and more even. The yellow faded from his face and became a luminous green, the colour of decay stealing up on life. Mike felt the racked body loosening and falling away from its struggle.

He bent his head close to the boy's ear. "Rinowski!" he shouted wildly. "I'll write your wife! I'll tell her how you talked about her all night long, about getting married and your dog and where you live."

There was no sign that the boy heard and soon there was a sign that he was beyond hearing. His broken body tightened into a hard knot, quivered two or three times, and then unwound and relaxed like an uncoiling spring. Mike laid the boy's head in the sand, pried the Bren gun from his loosening fingers and stood up against the breakwater.

He snapped the magazine off the gun, stooped over Rinowski's body to remove a fresh magazine from one of the bullet pouches and slapped it into the gun's thin dorsal cavity. He stood for several minutes beside the body, debating what his next step should be.

His fear had not diminished; if anything it was more insistent than before. But his fear was only one part of him. In a way that he could not understand, the dead boy had released him from some dimly comprehended bondage and restored to him the freedom to do such things as he believed to be necessary.

He slithered a few yards down the breakwater until the flat appendage on its morning shadow told him that he was directly beneath the pillbox.

He did not hurry his calculations. When he was satisfied with them, he folded the legs of the bipod, grasped them near the top with his left hand under the barrel, curved his trigger finger around the grip, and punched the butt of the weapon into his hip with his right elbow. He filled his lungs with air, like a trained sprinter who senses the impending report of the starter's gun. Then he catapulted himself off the breakwater, with his back squarely in the line of vision of the pillbox, and ran out into the naked sand of the beach.

He squeezed the trigger while he was beginning his pivot in the soft sand, hose-piping an uneven arc along the wall until the loophole was full to his face and startlingly close. It must have been either the first ricochet or the second that hurt the German, because his head came up almost at once, unmarked but lolling stupidly, and then, when the last bullets from Mike's magazine gnawed through the steel and bone, it turned away slowly and petulantly as a man turns his cheek from a sudden gust of rain.

After the rest of him had dropped out of sight, the German's arm jerked angrily on the ledge of the pillbox and pointed the nose of the machine gun out to sea. The German fired only one shot, and that after he was dead.

Earle Birney

ᴇᴀʀʟᴇ Bɪʀɴᴇʏ (1904–1995) was born in Calgary, Alberta, the son of an English immigrant who served in the Great War with the Canadian Expeditionary Force as an ambulance driver and stretcher-bearer. By the time Earle enlisted in the Second World War, he had completed a PhD in English with a thesis on Chaucer's irony, broken with the Trotskyists who held his political allegiance in the 1930s and become known as the author of *David and Other Poems* (1942). In May 1943 the soldier-poet with the rank of captain arrived in England to serve as a personnel selection officer, working with psychologists and psychiatrists to assess recruits' intelligence, verbal and mathematical skills, mental fitness and ability to deal with "battle exhaustion" or "shell shock," as it was called in the Great War. His wartime experience inspired his first novel, *Turvey: A Military Picaresque Novel* (1949). Its combination of satire and burlesque was intended to present "the goofier side in any army." So close did some characters and incidents come to reality that Birney and his publisher feared libel suits.

The central character, Private Thomas Leadbeater Turvey, from Skookum Falls, BC, is, says Birney, "a dumb backwoods private ... an innocent born for trouble, a youth with the cheerfulness and reckless morale of a hero but with the intellectual and soldierly capacities of a farmyard duck." The adventures described in "Turvey Is Considered For Knighthood" occur in the immediate aftermath of D-Day, June 6, 1944, when the Allied invasion of Normandy began. Turvey never does come face to face with the Germans. His war is spent in holding units, training camps, hospitals, ships and trains, a victim of the army administration's red tape, incompetence, corruption and well-intentioned absurdity. *Turvey* was awarded the Stephen Leacock Memorial Award for Humour. Birney also wrote some war poems, the best being "The Road to Nijmegen."

Turvey is Considered for Knighthood

That evening hundreds of bombers moved high and steady across the sky, like letters on a teletype, and their deep throbbing, as night came down, seemed to fill the world and well out of the earth itself. From midnight on, bombardments flashed on the French coast. And in the warm dawn a whole division of troop-carrying gliders paraded slowly over the camp, two by two, some so low Turvey waved at pilots in the tow-planes. This must be it! And it was. At 0930 the radio RHQ crackled out Eisenhower's announcement. D-Day.

After supper, Turvey was summoned to the Orderly Tent by Mac. He was holding a roll-sheet at arm's length, as if it were a rattlesnake. His lean face was dark with rage. It was the first time Turvey had seen Mac really angry. "Of all the cockeyed armies, this one takes the fucking cake. Bad enough sitting here. But now—now!—on *D*-Day!—they're sending me all the way to Buckinghamshire to make me into a bloody officer." Mac paused for breath and looked wildly at Turvey; the sight of him seemed to restore the sardonic light in his black eyes. "What puts the plush-lined cork in it, Tops—*you're* coming too."

"Me?" said Turvey. "O no! I'm going over to Normandy. The corporal give me a pamphlet this mornin all about how I gotta behave myself in occupied France."

For answer Mac passed him the roll-sheet order a Despatch Rider had just brought in. It announced that Sergeant MacGillicuddy and twelve other Okanagan Rangers (including Turvey, Private Thomas Leadbeater) would proceed immediately to Number Three Canadian Testing Panel for the usual three-day appraisal. "Serves you bloody right for applying," said Mac, grabbing the paper back and hauling him out of the tent with him.

"But gosh I didnt ask to be a nofficer! I aint even a lance-corporal yet!" They were walking back to Turvey's lines, the noise of Normandy guns tantalizing their ears.

"Dope! Remember about three months ago? Unit parade. Everybody ordered to fill out forms, from the RSM down to you. No crime-sheet barred. Well, some screwball's gone and taken it seriously. And it's Top Priority. Got us by the short and curlies. To hell with a little thing like D-Day!"

In the early morning train next day, Mac gave Turvey and the rest of the compartment his reconstruction of the events leading up to the catastrophe. "The scene, fellow-victims, is London; nice airy room in CMHQ. Half a dozen purple brigadiers in confab—AAGS Three and Five, let's make it; at least one general; chest and shoulder hardware everywhere. Civvy steno, with a lush pair of charlies, taking notes. General with five-row fruit salad tells em Ottawa wont sent any more new officers. One brig figures exact number of loots to be killed between D-Day and next Christmas. Engineering Big shot whips out sliderule, shows em they'll have to promote every third corporal overseas to supply deficiencies. Admin Brasscock says unit colonels wont let their good NCOS go. Another Redflannel, full of piss and vinegar, brother-in-law of the general, has memo ready for issue to Commanding Officers all overseas units, threatening em, pain of something or other, to let every NCO and private in army fill out officer application if he wants to. General says that's just a job and they give it to the steno to straighten out the grammar. Then they knock off, Royal Auto Club, to hoist a few."

"But why did we *all* have to sign it if they only wanted one in three?" asked Randy Crane, who had been following Mac's analysis solemnly.

"Ah, that was our C.O. Took a poor view of it, and quite right. Wanted his sergeants, tried and true, for Do-and-Die Day. Keep Rangers at battle strength. So he played safe, made everybody apply; *but* he signed the recommendation line for only thirteen. But why *this* thirteen, only God and the colonel—"

"Hold your hosses," said Flighty Bagshaw, an RHQ clerk, suddenly. "*I* know which ones the Old Man recommended because I saw em before they went out. And you want to know somepn? He didnt sign for a bloody one of this crew. Not one!"

"Ah, calls for a slight revision in Situation Report," Mac went on unperturbed. "Applications go up to CMHQ, see, masses of em, every overseas unit. Pile up in hallways. Fatter brigs cant get past. Complain. Junior officer told to sort out recommended files, stack rest in basement. So makes clerk do it. Long job. Teatime, clerk bored rigid, wool-gathering, shoves rejected Okey Rangers in accepted heap, put c.o.'s recs in basement. Right? Only hole in theory is—c.o. must have passed *me* over. Improbable, I suppose, except, yes, of course—he wanted to keep best sergeants with regiment! Explains how my dear old Mucking-in Pal Turvey's with us, and I wont have a word against him."

"By God," said Crane slowly, "It could be."

Whatever the reason, by early afternoon the thirteen were detraining at a quiet Buckinghamshire way-stop. They bounced in a big sixty-hundredweight past a field with sleepy cows and a mouse-coloured donkey, under pylon wires neatly arranged with sparrows, and beside cosy gardens dripping with roses and tiger lilies. Then they crowded against a box hedge while a covey of Tiger tanks went whang-clanging by. They turned by a stone keeper's lodge into a grove of oak, and up a long elm-way to a high turreted mansion surrounded by lawns and flower beds.

"Cripes," said Mac, "this cant be for us." It wasn't. Their vehicle veered around the back to the usual tin-town, a collection of corrugated Nissen huts lying like black caterpillars among the greenery. Just beyond were lawn-tennis courts with a sign OUT OF BOUNDS TO OTHER RANKS.

After stowing their kit into the twilight of one of the caterpillars and scoffing a late lunch in another, they were paraded, along with an assort-ment of candidates who had arrived earlier, on to a clipped lawn bordered with tall spikes of lupins. Here they were harangued by a tiny cropeared lieutenant-colonel wearing a green beret, a battle tunic with a great bank of ribbons, and muddy fatigue trousers shoved into a pair of gleaming leather boots that reached his knees.

Turvey couldnt follow very clearly what the colonel was saying. He spoke with great urgency and an odd accent, sometimes waving his arms like a band conductor, but Turvey could find no beginning or end to his sentences.

"What I wan a from you, my fellows, I wan," he was shouting, "is a *goosto, goosto*, plenty of dat is better dan, you know we no try to fail you boys we wan a know how moch you got, you got a veem you got a drrrive, here is where you show, we don expect you are officer already no but you be smart on a toe and you jump, for it only tree day so you keep your nose a clean an an uniform a too and I don expect you do more dan anybody, you take all a dese test wis a *goosto* an an a drrrive an don be afraid a nobody get hurt unless a maybe he don go in dere wis a poonch on a my catwalk an an my officer when dey interview now you boys a be natural joos a speak up de troot because a we don fail you for, now ...."

His teeth shone very white and healthy in the sunlight and when he had finished the sweat gleamed on his swarthy little face from his own gusto. The candidates, as they now found themselves called, were issued with fatigue coveralls, each with a large number chalked on the back, broken up into squads of six, and doubled along cinder paths to various parts of the estate. Mac and Turvey were separated.

The latter's squad was taken in tow by a rosycheeked lieutenant who talked in a cheery vague English voice which reminded Turvey of Victoria. He led them into a hazel copse and put each in turn through a series of large-sized puzzles. "Great mistake to be all over active with these; horsesense, you know, that's all you need. Spot of agility perhaps. I mean to say, it's all under battle conditions."

Turvey, looking at Test One, thought a bit of luck would be handy too. It was a wide gate wrapped round with barbed wire and so constructed that it twirled like a murderous millwheel as soon as weight came on it. He decided the best idea was just to walk around the whole thing, since that was clearly what he would do in a battle, but the lieutenant wouldnt let him. Then he noticed a long pole lying beside the trail. While the lieutenant was entering something in his notebook, Turvey grabbed the stick and ran back up the cinders. The colonel had said he wanted them to be smart and jump to it and have something or other. He came charging down with a warning whee, plunged the slim rod in the "contaminated" sand in front of the gate and perilously, with less than an inch to spare, polevaulted the barbed monstrosity before the alarmed officer could block him.

"I say, I say, old chap," Pinkcheeks called almost apologetically across the gate, "that's not really the way to do it, you know. I mean to say, you've done it, I suppose, but that pole wasnt meant for that, you know. Not supposed to be there, in fact. Might have broken. Fact, you can consider it has." Turvey looked at the pole but he couldnt see a crack in it. "I mean to say, for purposes, of the test you know. Too risky—what?" He chuckled hollowly. "Supposing you were under fire, dont you think, old chap? However, you're across. No harm done. Carry on." And he put another mark in his Field Notebook.

After some more hocuspocus involving blindfolds and concealed ramps, Pinckkeeks turned the squad over to a middle-aged captain with an artillery badge on the side of his wedge-cap, and Mutt and Jeff medals from World War One. He took them off at the double through a break in the woods to a spidery trestle of tubular steel that rose twenty feet to a level with the middle branches of the knobbly oaks nearby. Sucking on a cold swaybacked pipe the captain ignored the ominous affair and briefed them on other, invisible dangers ahead.

Turvey was sent along a ditch which very rapidly acquired a roof of turf and withes, under which he had to crawl. Soon it shrank to a point in utter darkness where crawling became belly-wriggling through marshy slime. Then the tunnel bent, and Turvey stuck in the bend.

Only a few yards ahead he could see a gleam of light, the exit; going back was impossible; the next victim was already snorting and slithering up the tunnel. Turvey grunted and sweated, lost more breath, and began to feel a touch of the claustrophobia the designer of the tunnel had been interested in. He framed other words for it but they didnt help, and his squirming only planted him more firmly in the suprisingly cold sub-soil of England. Desperately he arched his back—and felt the roof give slightly; he put everything into another upward hoist—and poked his head up through a canopy of dirt and leaves into the blessed sunlit air. But try as he might he couldnt get his shoulder through. He swivelled his neck for a better position and saw a vaguely familiar pair of boots, brown, high, and gleaming. His eyes travelled up, over the soiled dunga-rees, the five tiers of ribbons, to the little open mouth and astonished eyes of the colonel. The sight added the needed erg to Turvey's martial power; he pressed with his boots, shot his shoulders up, and scrambled panting to his feet. Then, thinking rapidly, while the colonel's mouth was still ajar, he put everything he had into a wide magnificent salute, and spoke first:

"Please sir, we was told to hurry and I couldnt get my stomach round the corner so I come this way. Where do I go next?"

It may have been the salute, the expressed morale, or the novelty of Turvey's solution to the tunnel problem. The astonished glitter in the colonel's eyes softened. "Madre de Dios!" he said, "I wan you com a straight wis me for a my catwalk. Dis I mus see!" Following the rapid little strides of the colonel—he walked very upright but splayfooted like a pigeon—Turvey chugged safely past the Artillery Captain, who stood glaring at him near the tunnel's legitimate outlet. They bypassed several lesser instruments of torture to which the candidates in advance of Turvey were being submitted. Bagshaw perched dismally, not daring to move, midway on a greased log suspended between trees; Crane sat trapped in a set of barbed-wire hurdles; Callicutt was hurtling in a rope cradle down a high wire slung over a muddy swamp. Circling, Turvey and the colonel came to the tall spindly trestle where the course had begun. The Commandant, who had been silent since his first remark, now wheeled on him, teeth bared and sparkling, black eyes snapping with imagined battle:

"Ok-*kay*, you got *eem*portan message you save a de lives if you, *oop* a de ladder now, *ovair* my catwalk an down a catch a catch can. *Urry* now let see you got a *goosto*—but *carajo* don you bus notting no more!"

Fired by the colonel's excitement Turvey felt himself already in a world of shell and smoke, carrying a despatch of life and death, a message he must give personally, immediately, to the Commanding Officer of the Kootenay Highlanders. Up the rope ladder he swarmed to the plank. It was along its twenty swaying feet and down the trestle's steel legs to the ground that the message must go.

But as soon as he made his first step the catwalk took on a mad snaky life of its own, springing and shaking so much he couldnt, for all his will, get the next foot down. Something flicked his cheek and a twig fell on the plank.

"A-BOWWWW, PEEENG! A-BOWWWW! Dats a boollet. You under a fire!" It was the colonel, his booted leg stamping with excitement, his canines flashing. He hurled another handful of twigs. Turvey took another step and the catwalk curtsied and bounced. His feet glued, his knees swayed with the watery sway of the board and his eyes were drawn and pinned by the dizzy sight of the hard pathway and the scraggly bushes below. When had all this happened before? He was back at the Basic Training Centre; already he felt a shooting pain in his wobbling left ankle from the jump he hadnt yet taken, or had he?

Then across Turvey's rigid vision, while the shouts of the colonel continued to spurt skywards to him, appeared a new face. It belonged to an officer who walked over and was now looking up. Ordinarily it was not a face that inspired bravery in the rank and file; it was puffy and alcoholically veined, and the expression was a mixture of meekness and boredom. But above the face there gleamed something that sent the blood of courage rushing through Turvey's veins; it was the badge on his cap—the golden-feathered head of an Indian chief set in the silver cross of St. Andrew and surmounted by a limp salmon—the badge of the Kootenay Highlanders! With a yell like a stifled warcry Turvey bounded in three great leaps down the catwalk. The third bounce took him almost to the end, and its impact, coinciding by some dynamic chance with a tremendous buckle of the now thoroughly aroused planking, catapulted Turvey forwards and up so that he sailed clear of the whole mundane trestle, clear and out in a neatly turning khaki ball.

He landed mercifully in a leafy limb of the nearest oak from which, after some delay, he was able to unhook himself and descend fairly intact to the ground. Then Turvey executed for the first time a salute which, though directed by military requirements at the astounded colonel, was intended for a delivery in the presence of a lieutenant of the Kootenay Highland Regiment.

Over a supper of tinned herring, under the curved iron walls of the Nissen, where the candidates at last got together to compate notes, Mac was holding forth. His squad had tackled a set of educational tests, then spent the rest of the afternoon loafing in their hut, getting the lowdown on the Panel from available members of the sub-staff.

"Look, fellows, we got it cold. It's a nut house, a loony bin. First, this colonel. Hut Orderly says he's all the way from South America. Most of that chest fruit's from revolutions in Nicotina or somewhere. Came up with the rations. Never heard an angry shot in this man's army. Next, place is crawling with psychologists, psychiatrists, every other kind of psychic. They all have a bang at you first two days. Then they hold a powwow, a Panel, pool scores, pick the winnah. Ah well. People have more fun than anybody!"

"I heard," said Bagshaw, "some a them psycho-low-gists are snoopin around dressed as privates and pretendin to be orderlies and the like. That's how they get the real gen on you."

"Gosh, maybe that's who you were talkin to, Mac," said Turvey.

"Nonsense. Heard about that too. Latrinogram. Started by that pint-size doorman. Old soldier type. Seen him? Even smaller than the colonel. Most of him's turned under for feet. But little joker goes around pretending he's officer in disguise. Probably palms odd quid that way."

"Frig him," said Bagshaw, "I'd pay good foldin money to fail, that's if I thought it'd get me over to Normandy."

"It wont," said Mac, "might as well play it their way. Might get over sooner. All a rat-race anyhoo. Six Spos; six Flos (that's Field Liaison Officers, johnnies putting you fellows through the hoop today); one Toe (Tests of Education Officer), two Sikes; and a Major-2-i-c. If all of them cant down you, there's always Little Carioca to boot you out for being short on a goosto."

"What's this agoo—?" Turvey began but Crane spoke at the same moment and louder.

"How the hell did he get to be a colonel?"

"How do any of em?" Bagshaw put in.

"Ah, got the gen on that too. Gets chucked out of Uramania, wherever he was, before the war, counter-rev. Beetles up to Vancouver, becomes Export Bigfart, gets to know right people, joins Permanently Non-Active Militia. Need I go on?"

"Then that little shatterbust aint a psych-a-low-gist too?" asked Bradshaw.

"No bloody fear. Got one speech—you heard it—and three questions. Still, maybe he's the smart one."

"Let's have the questions," said the rest of the table at once.

"Ahh. Corporal wanted ten bob a piece for em. I'm not that crazy to pass. Besides, one of the sarges tipped me off. They dont matter a hoot. All you got to do is walk his wormy catwalk. Course the others can scupper you in the Panel. Bless em all. Friend Turvey here's a cert, from all I hear, for the colonel's fur-lined jerry. Most of em crawl across, or shamble. Nobody ever made that oak tree before, I'll bet a pretty. Tops, you kill me, daily. But I love you. You're in for one of the colonel's special diamond-studded interviews, dollars to doughnuts."

Mac was right. Turvey had scarcely settled down to a game of hearts in his hut when a runner pulled him out to the colonel's office. The converted master-bedroom of Great Buzzard Manor was an impressive chamber with an ancient beamed ceiling. As Turvey padded in and saluted he was confronted not only with the little figure half hidden at the huge desk but with two knights in full armour looming in the room's corners behind. He took a second look and was glad to see the armoured figures were empty. On the panelled wall between them were tacked two crossed flags, the Union Jack and a strange brightly striped affair Turvey had never seen before, Nicomania or somewhere, he guessed.

The colonel had his hat off; his black hair was cropped stiff as a Fuller brush, his black eyes gleamed like shoe-buttons. But his voice, though still full of urgency, was friendly. He invited Turvey to remove his headdress and take a seat. Then he seized a large leather-backed pad and picked up a massive fountain pen.

"Now my boy you don have a no fear a for me, we two a soldier we jus sit for a talking togezzer." He leant back in his big swivel chair. "An I sink you are a good soldier, *verdad*? You have fear, what it is to fear—but you trow eet off, you run, you leap, you got what I like for to see, you got, *positivamente*, you got *entusiasmo*, you got a *goosto!*"

"Yessir," said Turvey, grinning vaguely and looking first at the thick carpet and then at the crossed flags to get away from the colonel's little coalfire eyes.

"*Bueno*. An firs I ask you—" the colonel leant forward intently—"why you apply for a commiss-i-on?" He inclined back again, folding his arms over his stunning cascade of ribbons.

"Well, I didnt exactly sir, that is, they were handin out forms and I was told to fill one out like." Turvey started to scratch his stomach—he was having trouble with grass nits.

The colonel seemed to sag a little. He swung sideways in his chair and stared mournfully at one of the knights in armour. "Dis *gringo* army .... Ok-kay." He swivelled back. "Secon' I ask a what you do in de ceevil life?"

As Turvey stumbled through the labyrinths of his occupational career the colonel started big scrawls on the pad with his pen, but he soon gave up, eyes glazing. Turvey had just got to the winter of 1940 when he interrupted:

"*Bueno*. You have a know life yes. I ask a now tird question." He half-rose on his elbows over the desk, light quivering again in his eyes; he leant so close Turvey thought their noses would touch. "What makes a good officer in battle, yes?"

Turvey pondered and grinned feebly. He felt very much behind the eight-ball. "Well, I guess he oughta be in there punchin, like you said, sort of in the lead like, and puttin out—" he had an inspiration—"this here agoosto." He scratched again, lower down.

The colonel suddenly drew back as if Turvey had stabbed him. Had he said the wrong thing after all?

"*Caramba!* You mock a me! You, you *bobalicon*—take off a dat *green*! You try to be fleep? Maybe I can' help a speak a de Spanish way, what a for you make insult to your Commandant hey?"

"Gosh I didnt mean nothin, sir! I dont know what agoosto means. I just heard you sayin it."

The colonel's expression passed from anger to incredulity, to disappointment. "You don know what de word it mean? You—*imbécil*! I sink I wait for to hear what a my psychiatreest he have to say about you ... Ok-kay, you go now. You have," he sighed, "disappoint a me verry moch. *Totalmente!*"

Turvey found the rest of the candidates in the NAAFI waiting on benches for a free film title as yet unknown. He sat down beside a big pimply infantry sergeant who soon mooched a cigarette and began giving Turvey his woes in a loud mournful voice.

"If it werent for the stripes, I'd tell the whole cocksuckin issue to go plum to hell. You know when I come to England?" he asked Turvey with a glower, "December-fuckin-thirty-nine."

"Golly, you musta seen lots of action by now. Where've you been?"

"Where've I been? Listen. First I was a whole bloody winter in Aldershot. Then they put me on a train for Norway."

"Gee, I never met anybody who fought in Norway before!"

"Well, you aint now. They turned us back at Dunfermline. Next month I got another train ride—to Dover. Whole First Infantry Brigade was goin to France."

"You mean you was fightin there in 1940!"

"Who, me?" He laughed sourly. "First time we never even sailed. Then next month we got all the way to Brest. And I sat in the friggin harbour two days. Then we got the bum's rush back to Aldershot. June

1940, that was. And now it's June 1943, and I'm fightin Hitler from a Buckingham castle. What kinda shitheels runnin this army? Dont tell me they aint got a saw-off with the Krauts. Last year they didnt even send us to Dieppe—took the Second Div boys hadnt been overseas a year. You know what's wrong with those cunts back in Ottawa?"

The lights went out suddenly and the projection machine whirred. "It's these tycoons that's runnin em. The bosses only want one of these phony wars because—"

"Stop the jawin," somebody yelled, "show's on."

It was a National Film Board short on the herring industry in which a young man with an artificially lively voice assured everybody millions of cans of Canadian herring were pouring over to England's defense.

"See," the sergeant whispered, "ca-pit-alist b.s. The guy that owns the herrin industry must be cornholein King's Cabinet. Canned herrin for supper. Smoked herrin yesterday for breakfast. I'd like to tell em to work it. And now herrin for movies. Propaganda, that's all it is."

The next film was a pre-war western with a soundtrack so old the actors all seemed to have quinsy. The projector broke down at the end of a reel, in any case, and couldnt be fixed. The candidates filed out for bull sessions in their huts.

"Well, anyway, you got sent to Sicily and Italy with the First Div, didnt you?" Turvey asked the sergeant as they groped out of the NAAFI.

"O sure," he said, "and we got torpedoed on the way down. Funny how they would know we was comin, eh? And I bloody near drowned. And the boat that picked us up took us back to England. And I got pneumonia and landed in hospital—Aldershot, of course, that twathole. When I come outa there they shot me to a Third Div outfit and I trained for D-Day." The sergeant laughed dismally. "D-Day they sent me here! Aah, I tell yah there's pricks high up in this army dont want any of us to mix with the Krauts. They're savin us up."

"What for?"

"For the Russkies, of course. World War Three. You wait and see. Ca-pit-alist swine. And now I get a Blue from my wife my dog is sick. Always somethin."

The next morning Turvey's squad was taken over by a Field Liaison Officer with fat cheeks and a behind as plump as a matron's. He walked them sedately out to a small damp meadow and, after hunting through a big folder of notes, read them a long set of directions for a game called Sandbag. It was designed, he said, to test their ability both to lead and be led, under emergency conditions. The next thing Turvey knew—he had gone into a slight coma trying to memorize the directions—he was blindfolded with a sour-smelling towel and set loose with similarly hand-icapped comrades to blunder across the pocked terrain trying with out-stretched arms to capture Bagshaw, who, blindfolded also, was carrying the sandbag. At least that was how Turvey understood the game. But it turned out that Callicutt had been made Squad Leader and wasnt blind-fold; he had been shouting directions at the others to guide them in seizing the bag-toter, using the numbers chalked on the backs of their coveralls to preface his cries. "Number Eight! Halt—grab! … no, about turn," Callicutt would shout, "Number Six, two paces back—grab, GRAB!" and so on. But most of the squad had forgotten their numbers, including Turvey, so that the game quickly degenerated into a confusion of human collisions, rollicking shouts, howls of pain, and tumbles. Bagshaw, still untagged, meantime wandered off the meadow and fell into an ornamental lily-pond, sack and all. This was an accident which the plump Flo would no doubt have prevented if he had not been at the time fully engaged in picking himself and his folder of notes out of the mud into which he had been toppled when Turvey, in the belief that he had found the candidate carrying the sandbag, tackled the officer from the rear.

The next half-hour Turvey and his squad cleaned up at the stock pump by the stables and then paraded into the ex-nursery of Great Buzzard Manor, a bald room decorated with peeling white stars and pink fairies. They were sat down to benches around a barrackroom table for a Discussion Test.

The officer in charge of this experiment was a squarefaced young man with cold grey eyes and a great air of efficiency. "All right, men. We will spend the next"—he flipped his wrist watch—"fifty-three minutes dis-cussing any subject you wish. You may converse with complete frankness. I am not interested so much in your opinions as in how well you can ver-balize them within a group. Any suggestions for a topic of discussion?"

Bagshaw, who had had to change from the skin out and seemed to have decided he didnt want to be an officer anyway, muttered, with heavy irony, "We oughta discuss Discussion Tests." The squarefaced lieutenant looked as if he hadnt heard. His eyes travelled over the candidates and lighted on the one with the smile. Turvey was still wondering what "verbalize" was, and praying he wouldnt be called on directly.

"Number 22. Candidate Turvey. What do you suggest?"

There was a long tense pause. What subject would last out a whole fifty-three minutes?

"Women," he said finally.

There was a guffaw from Bagshaw, and a feeble unidentified cheer.

"Subject normal," said Trail.

The lieutenant flinched slightly but spoke with careful calm. "If the *majority* of you wish to carry through a discussion of that subject, you may. But I'm sure we could find a more *fruitful* topic—" there were several quick sniggers—"topics relating to world problems, economics, politics—" he flashed an empty smile.

In the end they accepted a topic which the lieutenant picked for them, The Problem of Civil Rehabilitation. Turvey, once he realized that no one was going to order him to talk, sat in cheerful absent-mindedness for the rest of the hour scratching his harvest-bugs.

After the ten-minute break for a smoke, they went back into the nursery for another parlour game with a new officer, a greyhaired Infantry Major with a kind apologetic air. He explained this was a Leadership Test and that each in turn was to imagine he was already a Platoon Commander; he would be given a paper with a typewritten "Situation," allowed two minutes to brood on it, and then asked to give extempore lecturette.

Turvey was unlucky enough to be the first goat. He read his slip. "Two men in your platoon have both become v.D. casualties within the past week. Give a talk to your platoon on the subject." This was fun, after all. He spent his two minutes deciding which men he would pick as casualties, finally choosing Trail and Bagshaw. He began his talk by announcing their names and was going on to an imaginary but detailed account of how each acquired his injuries when the fatherly major interrupted.

"I think it would be better, lad, if you, umm, used the situation given you to say something *generally* about the dangers of venereal infection and the soldier's responsibility to, umm, you know—" He waved vaguely.

"O yessir, I was just comin to that. Fellahs, I guess you know it aint no fun havin clap. You oughtnt to get it." The eyes facing him all had a skeptical look. Turvey paused to think of some good reasons. "None of us oughtnt. Cause why? Cause you know it's a hang of a thing to get rid of. A shot in one arm now, and the next arm three hours later, and then your behind three hours after that, and they keep on needlin you like that for four whole days and nights."

"You're bloody lucky it wasnt a packet a siph you caught, you'd been in for ten," said a large sardonic corporal whom Turvey didnt know.

"Chuch-cha," said the major, "he's supposed to be your officer. You, you wouldnt use that kind of language to your officer, now would you boys?"

"That birdbrain an officer!" the corporal muttered, subsiding.

"Anyway," Turvey struggled on, "it's a month before you feel like havin a girl again and—"

"What about the consequences to platoon morale or, umm, the family, umm, wife and children?" said the major, pursing his lips in deprecation.

"O yes, fellahs, the kids! You know what'll happen to em if you get a real dose, like siph?" He paused dramatically. "They wont be no good in the head. They'll grow up to be, to be illiterate!"

The sad face of Candidate Sorensen paled with alarm. He put up a hand slowly. "Ay tank is not right, major. A fellah he yoost need to get fixed up with the doctor." Sorensen's phrasing was impersonal but there was no mistaking the quiver in his voice.

"Well, umm, yes, I suppose," the major broke in hurriedly. "Ummm, always go to the M.O. for anything like that, son. But, umm, better not have to go at all, you know. A real family man, now, he should love his wife and children and not play around, or he should want to have umm wives, I mean a wife, and now who is next? Corporal Trail, isnt it?"

By mid-afternoon, in the former bedroom of the pantrymaid in the cramped flag-tower of Great Buzzard Manor, Private Turvey was once more rendering up his Occupational Record to a Personnel Selection Clerk. Just before lunch he had taken the O-test again, since the documents containing his previous scores had not yet arrived at Number Three Testing Panel. Lunch itself, and breakfast for that matter, had been a bit of a test, for at both meals the officers of the unit had sprinkled themselves over the tables. The dimplechinned young Spo who sat with Turvey each time, however, seemed even shyer than the candidates and concentrated rather greedily on his food.

After lunch Turvey had been exposed to a Universal Knowledge Test, a Level of Education Test (Part I: English; Part II: Arithmetic), and a set of puzzles called the Z-test Non-Verbal. Now the Preliminary Interview was over. The Personnel Sergeant had covered all the available spaces in a long sheet, added some extra foolscap notes, picked them up and disappeared up a dark passageway.

After an hour's wait on a folding chair Turvey was led down the same corridor and abandoned at an open door.

"Number 22?" asked an impersonal voice. Turvey entered, saw a captain's three pips behind another barrackroom table, and saluted. It was a Spo.

He was a young man, but no slouch, Turvey decided. He seemed to have all of Turvey's test papers spread over the desk and was embroidering calculations from them on a yellow sheet. He had large deer's eyes, moist but searching, and rounded as if always asking a question.

And never had Turvey, as hardened an inverviewee as the Canadian Army possessed, been asked such questions. First the captain wanted to know all about Turvey's health. The mere "how" of breaking an ankle and getting the wrong prophylaxis in Niagara, and bashing a toe in Aldershot, were not enough for Captain Youngjoy. Was he sure—the captain raised his head in a slow dream-like stare at Turvey—that he had *wanted* to take Basic Training? Had he really, frankly now, this interview is absolutely secret, he could take his back hair right down, hadnt he really, deep down within him, *wanted* to break his leg just a little—it was only an ankle chip, wasnt it?—so that perhaps he would be discharged into civil life again? Turvey stopped scratching the rash on his rear and indignantly repudiated the suggestion.

The captain waved his hands gently. "A natural wish, we all get fed up with the army, especially at first. Well, let that go. But tell me ...." The captain's voice went on and on, vibrating in a strange way that made his questions seem of the utmost importance—how did it happen that he didnt *see* the night orderly pour the prophylactic from the wrong bottle? ... Had he been having trouble with his girlfriend about that time? ... Was he sure now—the liquid eyes held him while the captain's right palm curled suggestively—was he sure that he hadnt wanted to *revenge* himself on his girl by making it impossible for him, just for a little while, to have intercourse with her?

When it came to Turvey's toe, Captain Youngjoy's voice mellowed with exchange of confidences. Now he himself, we're all human, had a touch of diarrhoea when he found himself in Holding Unit. And do you know how he had cured it? By facing up to the fact that he didnt like the P.T. Instructor, who had doubled the P.T. period before breakfast. "Now why do you think you got yourself in the hospital while serving in this particular unit, Turvey, and yet stayed out all the rest of the time in England? ...."

Turvey, because the captain's eyes were so overpowering, found himself saying "yes" rather sleepily all the time except when assent seemed like a betrayal of the spirit of the Kootenay Highlanders. Even that spirit was burning low in Turvey since Mac had discovered that the Kootenay officer Turvey had seen yesterday was just a junior accountant from CMHQ checking up on messing balances.

Then the captain shifted to Turvey's crime-sheet, and they settled down for the rest of the afternoon.

After supper he reported to the psychiatrist, a shaggyheaded man with an abstracted stare and a Groucho Marx moustache. He was very kindly and after he had looked over Turvey's Educational Test answers and asked him to tell what he saw in a lot of comical big ink-blots, he showed little interest in Turvey's life, sexual or otherwise, and seemed curious only about what Turvey had said to the colonel to make him so annoyed. Turvey explained that he didnt know till Mac told him later that goosto was just the colonel's way of saying pep. The psychiatrist promised he would clear it all up with the colonel before the Panel met the next morning but warned Turvey not to expect to be made an officer right away.

Next morning each candidate, as he was called, marched stiffly into the Great Hall of Great Buzzard Manor, saluted the assembled Panel, announced his name, saluted again, and marched as stiffly out. Turvey provided one or two variations. First he tripped over the suprisingly large feet of the peewee doorman just as he was marching in, smart as a CWAC. He did remember his name and number, and the first salute, but he forgot the second till he was in the door on his way out, and ran back in and gave it. This (Turvey heard later) thoroughly confused the absentminded major-2-i-c, who had been dozing and thought there were two Turveys, and wanted to pass only the second one.

Ceremonies were completed by noon when all the candidates were drawn up on the lawn and harangued by the colonel with much the same speech as two days before, except that this time he also bid them good-bye and warned them apparently (it was hard to get the drift) that some had failed but, to know which, they would have to wait for a posting of the information in their unit orders after it had flowed through the Proper Channels of Communication. Just before dismissal Turvey was startled to hear the colonel say he wanted to see him in his office.

It turned out to be a meeting of reconciliation and destiny. "Now my boy I wan you should know how happy I am you are not a de fleep kine. My psychiatreest he tell me you are a jus dumb. Das a too bad, because he say you are too dumb even to be officer but now you are very brave a soldier. No? You have a goos—, you have veem an an pep, yes, and I take a fancy for you. You like to stay here an work a for me?"

"Gosh, thanks sir, but I'd rather stick with my pal Mac, that's Sergeant MacGillicuddy, and go back to the Okie Rangers. They oughta be goin over to Normandy anytime now."

"Sergean Makeelacuttee? Ah, him I pass. He's a top-hole! Two-tree day he get his order an leave you for OCTU. And I don sink your Okie Ranger dey get action for a long a time maybe. Now how about a my nize job? I am going a fire my doorman das a fac' he is no bloody good. How you like a to be my new doorman, hey? An a maybe you bat a for me a little?"

Turvey's opinion of the colonel had gone up, a good deal, but—"But heck, then I'd *never* get to the front. No, thanks just the same sir. No hard feelins, though."

The colonel pattered around from behind his desk and reached up a fatherly hand to Turvey's shoulder. "What if I promees I get you a draft to de fron' before Okie Ranger I bet you ten poun? One, maybe two mont?" His eyes glittered and he launched an utterly fascinating smile with all his teeth. "An now I attach you here till your colonel he give a permission I take you on a strengt, yes?"

And that was how Turvey came to spend the next three months in one of the more charming country estates of Buckinghamshire.

Roch Carrier

ROCH CARRIER (1937–) was born in Sainte-Justine, Quebec, a French-Canadian village which often provides the setting for his fiction. Novelist, short story writer, dramatist, poet, professor at Collège militaire royal de Saint-Jean, director of the Canada Council and currently Canada's fourth National Librarian, he has been described as a combination of Voltaire and St. Francis. In his best-known war fiction, *La Guerre, Yes Sir!* (1968), the chaotic village is a microcosm of the world at war between 1939 and 1945. When six *anglais* soldiers under the command of a sergeant return the body of a local boy who has died unheroically overseas, the villagers' antagonisms erupt in a bitter mingling of realism and caricature.

Set in the same time and place, "Son of a Smaller Hero" appeared in a short story collection, *Les Enfants du bonhomme dans la lune* (1979), published in English as *The Hockey Sweater and Other Stories* (1979). Although the Québécois aversion to participating actively in the war is just as determined here as in *La Guerre, Yes Sir!* Carrier's irony is gentler. He jocularly exaggerates both the local "havoc" that the war causes and the magnitude of the villagers' war effort. The garage pictures convey the power of propaganda as a tool to form civilian attitudes when Quebec's defender, Monsieur Duplessis, faces down the demonic, child-abusing Nazis. Behind the naïve child's-eye-view of the narrator, who sees his father as a hero, lies an adult consciousness. The innocence of childhood is nostalgically recaptured while the delusions and deceptions of adult life are revealed. Carrier's father, too, was a salesman.

Son of a Smaller Hero

TRANSLATED BY SHEILA FISCHMAN

WAR HELD SWAY OVER THE EARTH: "THE greatest conflict in the history of mankind," it was said in *L'Action catholique*. Never had so many men done battle; never had men borne such powerful weapons; and never had men died in such great multitudes. And never had those who were not at the front been so well informed about what was happening in the war. You had only to put your ear against the big radio to hear the voice of the war as you might have heard people quarrelling on the other side of a wall.

The war sowed havoc in our village too. If you wanted to get butter at the general store—or meat or sugar—the law required you to supply a prescribed number of coupons. Onésime, behind the counter, his patience tried by this requirement, grumbled as he crammed coupons into his pocket.

"Oh! life won't be so complicated when this war's over!"

Boys from the village had been called up, as they said, and sent far away, to Europe, to the countries at war. On Sunday at mass we'd hear their mothers sniffle when the curé asked the good Lord to "protect from fires of Hell their souls, whose lives are in far greater danger than their bodies." When we came out of church my friend Lapin and I, listening to the local gossip, would sometimes hear: "Pray for them, sure, but not too hard, or they'll come back too soon and start drinking like pigs again and singing shameful songs that make your ears blush!"

The strong arms of the war had come to collect the sons of the village and its hideous face came to haunt my father's garage. Never will I forget the poster that faced the enlarged photograph of Monsieur Duplessis on the wall opposite: on it was drawn a group of uniformed officers; they stood so stiff they seemed to be dressed in steel; they wore tall caps with a swastika on them. And they wore rows of coloured medals. Their faces looked like death's heads. All carried revolvers whose barrels, tragic crowns, rested against the shaven head of an emaciated child—who wore a star. (My unshakable conviction that war is a way for adults to persecute children was, no doubt, sown there.) I wished I could help the child flee from the hands of his macabre executioners. But I was only a child myself.

From time to time a truck came to collect scrap iron. My father explained to me:

"They'll melt the scrap iron in a factory, just like your mother melts sugar when she's making jam. The iron turns liquid and clear as water. Then they pour it into moulds to make hulls for boats, and tanks and bombs."

To help the war effort, people gave the truck any old iron that was lying around in their barns and attics: pieces of pipe, old bed-springs, rusty nails, horseshoes, buckets with holes in them, nicked scythes … Lapin and I went exploring in the rock piles, those long rows of stones heaped up in the fields where the farmers would leave tools and implements they couldn't use or repair, abandoning them to rust. With all the generosity of our young strength, we wanted to help make tanks and cannons and shells to destroy the people who were torturing the little boy on the poster. If we scraped our hands on the rusty metal, or saw a drop of blood, we were filled with pride like war heroes.

And then one day our house was invaded by toothpaste. A flood! The man who carted goods between the train station and the village unloaded dozens of crates of toothpaste at our house. We piled them in the cupboards and behind the drapes, we hid them behind the sideboard and under the beds. My father had carried off another of his deals! My mother was doubtful but my father was convincing.

"That toothpaste cost me *nothing*. And I'll sell it for twice as much."

"Two times nothing," my mother retorted, "is still nothing."

She had been a schoolteacher.

It wasn't easy to sell toothpaste to the farmers.

"My horse," said one of them, "he never used that stuff in his life and he's got two rows of choppers that look better than your plate."

The women seemed interested. They knew instinctively that beauty requires loving care, but at the very moment they were about to buy, their husbands would interrupt:

"Woman! don't waste your money on soapsuds when there's a war on. After it's over, then we'll see."

My father had promised me that in a few days the house would be free of the clutter of the cases of toothpaste because he would have sold them all. But his customers hardly helped him keep his promise.

One evening the truck that collected old metal for the war stopped in front of our house.

"If your tubes of toothpaste didn't cost you anything," said my mother, "why don't you just get rid of them?"

(In those days toothpaste tubes were made of soft lead.) My father started. He thought for a moment then, smiling, almost triumphant, he said:

"When you're holding onto a fortune you don't throw it away, you help it grow."

The next day he decided I was to accompany him on one of his trips. It would be a fine day, he told me, because I'd learn something from it. He'd prepared his sales pitch in his head. I listened to him talk to the customers.

"Bonjour, lovely lady. I hope everything's all right with you, aside from the World War. It's sad when you think of it: here we are, all quiet and peaceful, and over there on the other side, in Europe, folks are killing each other off ... a sad thing it is. Doesn't matter if the enemy falls, but our side ... our own children ... mustn't let them get killed, eh lady? Gotta help them defend themselves. Can't send guns in the royal mail, but, you know, if everybody sent a little metal, just an empty tube of toothpaste say ... Lovely lady, there'd be enough lead for cannons, bombs, tanks ... Now if I'm wrong there, you tell me ..."

I listened to my father in the evening too, after supper, out on the gallery that went around the house. The men from the village came there to smoke and chat and rock in their chairs with him. He'd described the tanks he'd seen pictures of in *L'Action catholique*, he'd describe them as though he'd been born in one. (I listened, my mother sighed.)

"Now you see how deep the foundation of this house is: broad as your two arms spread wide open. Now the sides of a tank are just as thick. Our soldiers are safe inside them ... No bullet's gonna get through that. Even the good Lord, he'd have a hard time getting through. But I hear the army's short of tanks ... Oui Monsieur ... The folks on this side, at peace, aren't sending over enough lead ... Now if everybody gave a hand and sent a little lead—well, our soldiers'd be saved; it's drops that make an ocean. If everybody just sent one empty tube of toothpaste ..."

He was silent then, smoking and dreaming. The men with him smoked and dreamed as well.

A few days later there were no more cases of toothpaste in the house.

When the war was over the children from the village who hadn't been killed returned to the fold. A party was organized to celebrate the victory and their homecoming. One of the veterans invited my father to take part.

"Why sure, I'm gonna go and celebrate with the rest of you," said my father.

"You," said the former soldier, "you sacrificed yourself for us from one end of the country to the other ..."

"That's the truth," said my father. "You notice what nice white teeth the women got?"

Henry Kreisel

HENRY KREISEL (1922–1991) was born in Vienna,
Austria where the atmosphere, in his own words, "was conducive to the growth
of one's literary and artistic consciousness." His mother's parents were Polish Jews
who had moved to Vienna during the Great War to escape maltreatment by
Russian soldiers. When Nazi Germany annexed Austria in 1938 and the Gestapo
began arresting Jewish residents, the Kreisel family moved to Leeds in England
where they had relatives. As a "Refugee from Nazi oppression," Kreisel was allowed
to work in a clothing factory but in May 1940 he was interned as an "Enemy Alien"
first in England, then in Canada. Internment gave him the opportunity to learn to
write in English rather than German—poetry, fiction and an internment diary—for he
decided that, having cut his ties with his old country, he must assume the language
of his new home. Released in 1941, he enrolled in the Honours English program at
the University of Toronto and eventually became Professor of English and then of
Comparative Literature at the University of Alberta in Edmonton.

In an essay, "Vienna Remembered," Kreisel wrote, "when I was a child, and
in spite of ominous signs, the horror of the 1930s and 1940s was unimaginable.
The extended family in which we lived gave us a sense of security, a feeling of
belonging." But all the family members who had remained in Poland—uncles,
aunts, cousins—perished during the Second World War. (Of 3.3 million Jews living
in Poland before the war, only 300,000 survived.) It was this family connection
that inspired "Homecoming: A Memory of Europe After the Holocaust." Kreisel had
originally intended to write a novel about the experience of a man "who returns to

the wreck and ruin of his former home" but the subject proved unbearable. Instead, he abstracted a chapter and developed it into this story. The form allowed him, through the use of waste-land imagery, nightmarish recollections and an encounter with an anti-Semitic peasant, to recreate Mordecai Drimmer's desolation and pallid hope without a large repertoire of individual experiences. Two of his novels do explore the Jewish theme of exile, *The Rich Man* (1948) and *The Betrayal* (1964), juxtaposing Canadian and European scenes. Excerpts from Kreisel's internment diary, stories, reminiscences and personal letters are published in *Another Country: Writings by and about Henry Kreisel*, ed. Shirley Neuman (1985). "Homecoming" appeared in *The Almost Meeting and Other Stories* (1981).

Homecoming

A MEMORY OF EUROPE
AFTER THE HOLOCAUST

THE LITTLE DIRT ROAD WOUND ALONG LIKE A moving snake. It was narrow and soggy, and two deep furrows marked the way where a horse-drawn cart had passed. An austere March sun, partly hidden, burst through the slowly-moving cloud banks now and then, transforming greyish-white patches of snow into murky little puddles along the road. But spread across the fields, covering them with a hard, porous, dirty crust, there was still a lot of snow. On both sides of the road tall, bare poplar trees stretched curved branches against the low-reaching sky, and in the distance, scattered irregularly through the fields, a few peasant huts, built of unpainted split logs and covered by old, heavy, rye-thatched roofs, broke the monotonous flatness of the countryside.

A young man was walking along the road, taking slow, even steps, his eyes scanning the landscape intently. He wore an old, grey coat made of coarse cloth and high boots that had once been brown. On his head he had a turret-shaped hat of curly black sheepskin which he had pushed deep down over his ears so that it completely hid his forehead and threw sombre shadows about his eyes. Slung over his left shoulder he carried a dirty brown knapsack which seemed quite empty and sagged against his back.

Towards noon he rested. Taking the knapsack from his shoulder, he walked to the side of the road and sat down beneath a tree, on the driest rock he could find. Then he opened his knapsack and took from it half a loaf of black, hard-crusted cornbread which he began to eat slowly, cutting off small pieces with his pocketknife, as if he were whittling wood.

When he had finished eating he put what was left of the bread into the bag again and leaned back against the tree. After a few minutes, overcome by drowsiness, his head fell forward onto his chest, almost touching his drawn-up legs, and he sat there, hunched up upon himself, slumbering uneasily.

He was awakened suddenly by a sharp, rasping voice that was cursing violently. He roused himself with a start, almost toppling off the stone. Not far from where he was sitting he saw an old peasant furiously beating a horse, trying vainly to get his cart out of a mudhole. The horse was old and bony and, frightened by the curses and hurt by the lash, it strained powerfully, its hide glistening with the perspiration of its labour. But with each pull the rear wheels ground themselves deeper into the soft, muddy ground, and the peasant, growing more furious, lashed out insanely against the beast. The horse, writhing wildly, its hoofs digging deep into the earth, made one last tremendous effort, every muscle stretched taut so that it seemed as if at any moment a bone would break and pierce the hide.

The young man jumped up and ran towards the cart. "Stop it!" he shouted. "Stop it! You'll kill the horse!"

The peasant did not seem to hear him and he kept on lashing the horse until the young man was directly upon him and pulled back. Then he turned round and glowered at him with a hostile stare.

"Who are you?" he asked after a while. "Where did the devil send you from to come here interfering with my work?"

"I don't want to interfere with you. But you'll never get your cart out of the mud that way. Have you so many horses that you can afford to kill this one?" He went up to the steaming horse and patted it softly.

"Let me worry about my own horses," the peasant said crossly, his voice filling with stubbornness and anger. "It's my horse, and if I want to beat it I can beat it, and if I want to kill it I can kill it, and it's nobody's business."

The young man shrugged his shoulders. "Go on, then, and kill the horse," he said. "I won't stop you. It's your horse, as you say. But when the horse drops dead, then take the cart and lift it onto your back and carry it to your hut. And if you find that your arms are not strong enough to lift the load, and that makes you angry, go and cut them off. They're your arms, and you can do anything you want with them. Go and cut them off." He lowered his voice and spoke as if he were giving away a dark secret. "There are better ways of using the brains God gave you. And then you can save a fellow creature, and you will come home with your horse pulling your load and your hands holding the reins." He put his left hand into the deep pocket of his coat and fumbled about in it. Then he brought out a cigarette, turned it lovingly in the palm of his hand and broke it in two. "Here," he said, offering one half to the peasant, who was staring at him in utter amazement. "Sit down for a minute and rest yourself. And afterwards I will help you get the cart out of the mudhole."

The peasant pulled his ragged, home-spun coat tightly about him. He was suspicious of the stranger, and he didn't know what he should say. He reached out a reluctant hand, almost snatching the cigarette away, like an animal afraid of being caught in a trap. Then with his ferret-like eyes still resting on the young man, he shambled over to the side of the road and sat down, stretching his legs out before him. He had neither shoes nor boots. His legs were wrapped around thickly with several layers of rags held together by pieces of string, and birch-bark sandals were on his feet.

The stranger came over to him and lit his cigarette. Then they puffed away in silence, enjoying the smoke.

"This is the first cigarette I have had in such a long time that I don't remember even when it was," said the peasant. He inhaled deeply. "Real tobacco, not rolled bark. Real tobacco. I forgot how it tasted." He was becoming more jovial now. He kept the smoke inside him as long as he could. His little brown eyes did not for a moment stray from the figure of the young man. They watched him, puzzled and perplexed.

"Where do you come from?" he asked after a while.

There was no answer. Instead, a question. "How far is it to Narodnowa?" He was leaning against a tree with his back to the peasant, and his eyes were turned up towards the sky.

"If you walk and make no stop along the way, you can be there in five hours. I have often walked there in the summer, carrying loads. And then it takes me seven hours. But you are young and you carry nothing heavy. You will be there in five hours."

"It looks like rain," said the young man softly. "Five hours, you say? I'll be drenched to the skin before I get there."

The peasant finished smoking his cigarette. There was only a tiny stub left. He looked at it wistfully and then put it away carefully in a pocket of his smock. "Don't throw away what is left of your cigarette," he said to the young man in a pleading, almost whining tone of voice. "Give it to me. I can still get some tobacco out of it. But you don't need it, for you are a rich man."

The other turned and smiled. "Why do you say that I am a rich man?" he asked.

The peasant took off his cap and scratched his head. "You wear boots on your feet, made of real leather. And then—and then, you have cigarettes, and I think you must have a lot of cigarettes if you are willing to give me half of one."

The stranger laughed out loud. "Surely I am a rich man," he said. "I an rich in sorrows. If I could buy land with sorrows, peasant, then I would have enough to buy the whole world."

The peasant rose slowly to his feet. He tried not to look at the stranger. He was suspicious of him and somewhat afraid.

"Tell me," the stranger asked, "when were you in Narodnowa the last time?"

The answer came slowly, haltingly. "It is now a long time. Almost a year. I was there last on the day when the war was over."

Remembrance of the event quickened his tongue and for a moment he forgot his suspicions. "Almost the whole village walked into the town and we danced and drank and cursed the Germans. We stayed there till it was long past midnight. It was a dark night, and I don't know why we began to fight on the way back, for we were all feeling very happy." He shook his head. "And Stanislaus Kaziemiercz was killed with a knife that night and we were all very sorry because he was a good man and people liked him in the village. But otherwise nothing happened, and on the next day we buried him and he had a much better funeral than he would have had if he had died in his bed, for he was a very poor man." He stopped abruptly and suspicion crept back into his voice. "But why are you so interested in Narodnowa?" he asked, glancing sideways at the stranger.

"I knew the town well. I knew it very well. I am going there now to see some people. It was a nice little town. Tell me, did it suffer much when the Germans came here?"

The peasant spat with great contempt. "God's stinking curses upon them," he growled, and his narrow eyes contracted into a leer of hate. "They're in hell now, and the devils are cutting pieces of flesh from their arses .... They came here and took away everything we had and then they burned the houses in the villages and drove the young men off like herds of cattle. They robbed the stores in Narodnowa and broke into the houses. They carried away everything and sent it to their bitches and bastards in Germany." He spat again. Then he went on, speaking slowly, savouring his words. "They did only one thing in Narodnowa which was good and joyful to hear." A smile spread slowly over his face and his eyes brightened. "They went into the quarter where the Jews used to live, and first they took everything. Then they threw torches into the nicest houses of the Jews, and you could see the red glow in the sky from where you stand now. Then they started to drive the Jews away, first in small groups, but then more and more at a time until there was not a Jew left in Narodnowa." His voice became glowing. "And now there are not many Jews left in the country because Germans killed them and gassed them and burned them to death. And that is the only good thing they have done. Now the Germans are gone and the Russians have come, and with them the Communists. Now they sit in the great city of Warsaw, the godless, stinking, accursed bastards, and everybody says that they are going to take away all that we have left."

"You talk too much." The voice of the stranger was suddenly hard and cutting. "You should keep your mouth shut. You say things that it would be better for you not to say. I told you before to use the little brains you have, but perhaps you are too old now, and you never learned while you were young."

The peasant cringed and shied away from him. He mumbled to himself and did not dare to look up from the ground. He waited, cowering like a frightened beast, expecting the stranger to step forward and hit him across the head. He was used to this. The masters for whom he had worked had always punished him like that. But the young man only picked up his knapsack and threw it over his shoulder.

"Why are you so much afraid of the Communists?" he asked. "Why are you afraid that they will take things away from you? What have you got that anybody would want to take away? The rags you wear? That carcass of a horse or your stinking cart?"

When the peasant saw that the stranger was not going to hit him, he dared to raise his eyes from the ground and whispered, "You said for me to rest a while, and you said you would help me to get my cart out of the mud."

The young man looked down at him contemptuously. "I've wasted a lot of time with you already," he said. "I'm sorry now that I said I would help you. The horse is yours, you said. You can kill him if you like, you said. Well, then, go and kill him. Go on and kill him. And then go and dig out the cart by yourself, and if the hole is big enough, lie down in the dirt and bury yourself. And then you will have all the rest you want. You can rest then until the judgement day, if there's any rest in hell." Then he turned sharply and walked away.

The peasant straightened up and watched him go. In his slow brain he was brooding over the things the stranger had said to him. He remembered all the gossip he had heard in the village inn, and the horrible rumours that were circulating round the countryside, and there rose in his mind the lean, sharp-faced figure of Father Wojcieck, haranguing the assembled congregation wildly from the wooden pulpit of the little village church, telling fearful parables and calling up dark images whose terrors had penetrated deep into his consciousness, so that he was never able to obliterate the memory of them. Now he was suddenly sure who the stranger was. Yes, he had heard of him. He was the devil figure Father Wojcieck had talked about so often and so vividly. Now that he knew who the stranger was, he crossed himself hurriedly and he mumbled a prayer to his patron saint, for he was terribly afraid.

He stared after the stranger, who was walking quietly, taking sure, even steps, his eyes straight on the road. Suddenly, obeying an overpowering impulse within himself, the peasant began to run tremblingly after him, calling loudly to him and gesturing wildly with his hands, beckoning him to stop.

The stranger paid no heed to him, and though he turned round and saw the grotesque, rag-tattered figure of the peasant panting towards him, he continued to walk on as if he had neither heard nor seen him. It was only when the peasant came within arm's reach that he turned sharply, facing him, for he was afraid that the peasant, angered by his sudden refusal to help him dig the cart out of the mud, wanted to attack him.

But then an astonishing thing happened. The peasant, his breath coming fast, fell down on his knees before the stranger and clasped him round. For some time neither of them said anything, and the silence was only broken by the heavy panting of the peasant as he was trying to catch his breath. The young man looked down at the crouching figure, completely taken by surprise. He could feel the heaving body of the peasant against his thighs, and he didn't quite know what he should do. At last he pushed him away, more rudely than he had intended, and the peasant fell backward into the oozing sludge of the road.

"What is it? What do you want from me?" the stranger asked, feeling uncomfortable and ill at ease. "Why did you get down on your knees before me?"

The peasant got up slowly. He pulled off his cap and stood there, his straw-dry hair dishevelled, his head bent.

"I know who you are," he said slowly, his voice trembling and monotonous. He did not look up from the ground, but spoke as if he were addressing an impersonal, powerful force.

"Who am I?"

"I know who you are," the peasant repeated. "And now you will go and tell them all I have said, and soon men will come to my hut in the night and take me away. Come with me now to my hut, and I will let you take everything you want to take if you will not tell them what I have said."

"You are a fool," the stranger said softly. "You are a fool .... Who do you think I am?"

The peasant remained silent, and the other repeated his question. "Who do you think I am?"

"You are sent to spy on us," the peasant answered, and his voice was so low that the young man had to strain forward to hear the words. "I have heard many things about the spies."

The stranger laughed. He took his knapsack from his shoulder, stood it up on the ground, and leaned forward, closer to the peasant. "What have you got in your hut that would make me want to come with you?" he asked.

The peasant hesitated. He seemed to be turning something over in his mind. At last he spoke. "I have a few chickens, and a cow, and there is still a loaf of bread left from the last baking. I would let you have the chickens and the bread."

There was a pause. Then the stranger said, "I am not a spy. But—let us say I am a spy. Do you think you could bribe me with a chicken or two and a loaf of bread?"

The peasant disregarded him. "Come with me to my hut," he insisted stubbornly.

The stranger stepped forward quickly and grabbed him by the shoulder. "Look at me," he said sharply, but the peasant did not raise his eyes to him. He stood there silently, slightly trembling under his grip. The young man began to feel a kind of pity for the ragged, tattered figure who stood before him like a beast, ignorant and afraid. "Listen to me," he said, and a bit of softness mingled with the hard, metallic tone of his voice. "I am not a spy, and I am not going to send anybody to fetch you in the night. What you said about the Communists is nothing to me. I have nothing to do with them. But what could they take away from you? What have you got that they would want? Chickens and bread? Maybe they might even do something for you. Who has ever done anything for you? As far as I am concerned, you can hate them or you can love them. It is unimportant to me. I have nothing to do with the party or with the government. So it is all the same to me how you feel. But I tell you again that I am not a spy. I am a Jew and I am going back to Narodnowa where I was born. I am going back to see if I can find my mother and my father."

The peasant looked up quickly, peering closely at the stranger, scanning his face. For a moment their eyes met coldly, the little brown ferret-eyes of the peasant, and the tired, brooding eyes of the stranger.

The peasant said slowly, "You don't much look like a Jew." But yet— there was relief in his voice, and his tension relaxed a little.

"I am a Jew. I had to control my temper when you spoke to me about the Jews. I wanted to hit you, but I thought better of it. You are older than I and I didn't want to beat you. And now go about your business and let me go about mine."

The eyes of the peasant filled slowly with a fierce hatred. "If you are really a Jew," he hissed, "I am not afraid of you. Only I am sorry that you are still alive. But if you go to find your mother and your father, you will not find them because they are not there. Their bodies are now rotting away in the earth and the worms have eaten them, or they are burned and their ashes are thrown to the winds." The corners of his mouth widened into a grimace and his whole frame seemed filled with a silent, mocking laughter.

The young man could no longer contain himself. He threw his knapsack down on the ground, out of his way, and stepped quickly up to the peasant. With his left hand he got hold of his smock and pulled him towards himself, and with the flat of his right hand he slapped him twice across the face. Then he slowly relaxed his grip and let him go. He picked up his knapsack and went away quickly, without saying a word. Behind him the voice of the peasant rose to a high pitch and the air was suddenly filled with foul and horrible curses.

The young man never looked back, but he doubled his pace as if he wanted to escape from the curses that were hurled against him. Suddenly he became filled with a strange excitement. He reproached himself for having succumbed to a sudden impulse. He began to walk more quickly, and then he ran, as if someone were pursuing him.

Now he will go and fetch people from the village and they will come after me, he thought.

He broke into a cold sweat and kept on running. Then the feeling of excitement gave slowly way to fear. That was not new to him, for in the past few years he had experienced it often. He had known that sensation when he was hiding from the Germans in a cellar in Warsaw; when he fled the city by night, making his way cautiously through dark alleys and smelly backstreets, through woods and forests, into Russian territory; later, when he fought with a small band of guerillas behind the German lines. It was always the same. First, tense excitement, and then panicky fear, giving way slowly to a period of cool detachment and a kind of nerveless existence.

He could no longer hear the peasant's voice, and he turned round, but the road was empty and only the bare branches of the trees were moving restlessly in the wind.

Nevertheless he decided to approach Narodnowa in a round-about way, and he swerved from the road, cutting across the still snow-covered fields towards the wood.

Once there, he stopped for a moment, feeling shielded and more secure. His mouth was dry and parched. He bent down and picked up a handful of hard-crusted snow and put it to his lips. Strangely enough, he was not hungry, though he'd had nothing hot to eat for two days. But all he wanted was water. Just water.

After half an hour's walk he came upon a brook, still thinly covered by a crust of ice. He knelt down, broke the icy crust, and with a great gasp of relief drank the water from cupped hands. He splashed water over his face, feeling unbelievably revived. The softly gurgling water of the brook calmed him, and he sat there listening to the sound for a few minutes.

The sun had now completely disappeared and a solemn grey was spread across the countryside. He got up from the ground, picked up his knapsack again and began to walk rapidly, trying to make up for the time he had lost by his detour.

Towards five o'clock it began to drizzle, a cold rain mixed with snow. He put his collar up and pushed his hat even deeper into his face. The rain pricked him lightly, like thin needles. And yet he could hardly feel it.

II

Through the haze of the misty twilight the spire of the church rose in the distance, tapering off to a thin point, crowned by the cross. When he first became aware of it, the young man stopped and for several minutes stood gazing, shielding his eyes with his right hand. The thin strings of the falling rain and the monotonous greyness of the oncoming dusk made him think what he saw was a mirage, for the picture blurred before his eyes, receded tremblingly into a vast expanse of space, then suddenly came back into sharp focus. He walked on, feeling restless and disturbed. There was a force within him that seemed to want to pull him away from the town, and a weak, dull voice made itself heard and whispered to him, Why do you want to go there? What do you expect to find? And it answered its own question in the same dull, soft, slightly mocking tone, and said to him, Until now you had some hope. But you might find only ruins, and haunting memories of frightful things. Why do you want to find these things?

He had to silence the voice because it threatened to turn him back from his purpose. It is better to know the worst than live forever in doubt, he said to the voice.

Once you know, said the voice, you lose all hope.

I have lost all hope long ago, he said, and there is nothing more to lose. You heard what the peasant said. I must find out, once and for all. There has to be an end if there is to be a new beginning.

After that the voice was quiet and did not bother him any more.

The road was broader now and somewhat less muddy. As he came closer to the town the number of vehicles increased, and he passed several women, wearily trudging along, their backs stooped with bundles of firewood which they had gathered in the forest beyond the town. Now the spire of the church stood out clear and distinct against the sky, so that the gold of the cross could plainly be seen. But suddenly, as he looked at it, it quivered and seemed to vanish into nothingness. And then everything around him, the horse-drawn carts, the dirty, tired stragglers, the road itself, receded and dissolved, shaking off time and space. It was if he were walking through a dream, seeing things, feeling things, but perceiving them as through a gently-swaying screen of gauze, now very clear, now hazily shimmering, and never quite real.

He entered the town from the south side. The road stretched up-hill, flanked by trees on both sides, and he knew that he would soon pass the big cemetery. He remembered it well because when he was a child of about six he had once passed this way with his mother and he had wanted to go into the cemetery, but his mother would not allow it. Then he had begun to cry, tugging violently at her arm, and his mother had said sternly, Do you see the big iron fence and the tall spikes all around? Do you know what happens to little boys who want to go in? Do you know what happens to them? Little devils come swooping down and pick them up by the bottom of their trousers and nail them on the tall, sharp spikes.

He shuddered, remembering. It seemed strange now. Why had she said those things? Why would she want to frighten him? Why was she so afraid? Of what? She was not a superstitious person. And yet. Deep fears must have lurked within her.

His mother now entered his waking dream, and he thought he saw her walking beside him, a tall and stately matron, keeping pace with him without apparent effort, briskly and easily. She seemed to observe him critically, her eyes full of concern and worry, yet she never came quite close to him. She walked near the side of the road, and there was an air of coolness and detachment about her. It was a strange picture, not at all like her. But yet she was very real.

He saw her sitting in a tall chair, talking to his father in her soft, firm voice. He couldn't hear what she was talking about, but she seemed very agitated, sometimes making emphatic gestures with her fine hands, and he could see her ring shooting off little sparks when the light caught in it. His father sat quietly, now and again nodding his head, and stroking his pointed little beard. He held a long yellow cigarette-holder in his right hand, turning it lightly between middle and index finger, from time to time lifting it to his lips. The cigarette came to life, glowing a warm red. He exhaled. The blue smoke seemed to shoot out of his mouth, spread slowly, floated in thin waves through the room, filling it, then vanished.

Blow smoke through your nose, Papa. I want to see you blow smoke through your nose.

His father laughed. He inhaled and extended his nostrils slightly, then drove the smoke through them.

The boy clapped his hands in delight. His mother motioned him away impatiently. She went on talking. His father rarely threw in a word. She dominated the conversation. After a while his father rose and left the room. He was now alone with his mother. She talked to him. He shook his head. Her voice rose. She was usually gentle, but she could be hard and stern when she wanted to. He stamped his foot defiantly on the floor in an obstinate gesture of refusal. She commanded. He slunk from the room, still defiant, still stubborn.

Curious, he thought, walking along the road in a half dream, how real the gestures were, how real the figures. But what did his mother say to him? He could not hear the words. But sometimes he could hear them. Only not now.

Where did his sister come from? She entered suddenly. He had not seen her come in. The door was closed. Had she come through the window? She talked to him. And now he could hear the words. His and hers. He wore long trousers and smoked a cigarette. So he was grown up. How had he grown up so quickly?

I know why you've come, he said. You've come to talk to me about Mother. I regret the scene. It was ridiculous of me to become so excited. It won't happen again. I won't let it happen again. I promise you.

You said that before. And I thought we had an understanding. Didn't we? And yet you broke that understanding.

I know, he said. But does it really matter? What games are we playing? Mother knows that her ideas are no longer my ideas. I don't want to argue with her. But sometimes I cannot keep quiet.

You must, when you are at home. That was our understanding. She's tolerant enough in her own way. She doesn't care what you do when you are away at University. But at home it's different. All those strange and heretical ideas of yours. You seem to taunt her with them. Why do you do it?

I'll reform, he said, and laughed.

His mother kept walking beside him, tripping lightly, as if she were dancing, her feet hardly touching the ground. She did not say anything, and that was strange. It wasn't at all like her. There was much about him that she could not possibly like—his unkempt appearance, the sweaty, three days' growth of stubble that covered his face, his dirty, mudcaked boots. But she said nothing. Not a word. Silently she floated at his side. Then she vanished suddenly, without a stir, without a rustle, like a ghost.

He stopped and stared at the empty space. He shook himself, rubbed his eyes, laughed uneasily.

He was now on top of the hill and the cemetery stretched on his left, row upon long row of wooden crosses and gravestones, and tall trees standing guard over the graves. The big iron fence, however, was no longer there. The cemetery seemed to jut out into the road, becoming a part of it.

No barrier divided the dead from the living.

It took a while for him to become fully aware that the fence was no longer there. The tall, sharp spikes were gone. Melted down, he thought, and long since shot off. How many people had been killed?

A sad smile spread over his face. Now I could walk into the cemetery and I would be safe from the little devils, he thought. Or would I? Perhaps they are now everywhere. No longer just in the cemetery. Everything he saw and felt had about it a curious texture of abstraction and unreality. It merely grazed his consciousness, and then evaporated, like steam escaping from a boiling kettle, leaving no trace of its substance.

One part of him said, I have passed here before and my mother told me stories about little devils and I was afraid, and the other asked, When? Where? How?

Yet he clearly recognized the streets that would lead him into the centre of the town. Everything seemed unchanged, as if he had only left yesterday and was returning today, as if there had not been an interval of almost seven nightmarish years.

It seemed as if Narodnowa had not been touched. The war had passed it by. There were no signs of devastation. No vast heaps of rubble, no hollow, burned-out buildings, no bomb-craters in the middle of the streets. Perhaps nothing was changed here. Perhaps his parents were still living in their old apartment. Narodnowa was such a small town, so insignificant, so unimportant.

But the peasant had said that the Germans had driven all the Jews from the town. What did he know? He was ignorant. He had said they had burned the nicest houses of the Jews. But why only those houses? Why had they not burned other houses? Why did the houses stand here along the streets he was passing now? In other towns the invaders had not been so merciful. They had burned and destroyed and killed without provocation.

In Narodnowa, the peasant had said, they had only robbed. A kind of miracle, then. Then the Jews were perhaps also spared by the miracle. His parents certainly. After all, his father was a doctor, and doctors had always been badly needed.

His parents were alive! Of course, they were alive, hoping for him to be alive, too, waiting for him to come home, praying for him to come home!

Yes, he was alive, he was well, he had survived! He was coming, he was coming home! This was the homecoming! Another half hour. After all the years, now only one half hour, and he would be home!

It was still drizzling, and not many people were in the streets. The church was only minutes away, almost within reach of his arms it seemed, and the spire was no longer so dominating and imposing as it had been from the far distance.

He turned into the market-place and looked up at the church. From a niche in the tower two gargoyles stared down at him, their eyes screwed up curiously, their lips pursed into a scoffing pout, their bodies twisted and warped like a misshapen root.

He was fascinated. They seemed to draw him towards them as if by a powerful magnet, beckoning to him to come closer, and mocking him even as they beckoned.

He walked slowly nearer. They drew him inexorably closer, and yet he hated them. He hated their deformity, their monstrousness, the insolence of their grimacing faces, and yet there was also something attractive in their very ugliness. He kept his head turned up towards the tower.

When I was a boy, I was afraid of you, he thought. I never dared even to look at you. I thought you would come down from your tower and do me harm. But I am no longer afraid. Ugliness no longer repels me. I have seen ugliness so revolting that you seem beautiful. And your ugliness is remote, it cannot touch me, you cannot come down from your niche.

The gargoyles laughed derisively, threw back their heads in a convulsive fit, screwed their eyes deeper into their sockets.

He walked up the steps of the church, keeping his eyes fixed on the carved figures in the tower, as if he meant to challenge them.

Suddenly the gargoyles freed themselves from their pedestal and stepped forward, out of the niche. For a moment they hung suspended in mid-air, twisting and squirming, contorting their ugly bodies into fantastic shapes. But they did not swoop down on him. They seemed nailed to the air. He kept his eyes unwaveringly on the two figures, more fascinated than ever, not at all afraid, waiting for them to swoop down on him, prepared to encounter them.

Suddenly a hand was thrust forward, gnarled, hooked fingers almost touching his mouth. He reeled backwards, staggered down a few steps, then caught himself on the balustrade. Raising his head, he saw a beggar crouching on the topmost step where the protruding portico shielded him from the rain. His hand was still stretched out.

"Alms for the poor, master," the beggar whispered.

"I need alms myself," he answered, breathing heavily, his hand clutching the balustrade. "I have nothing to give."

The beggar withdrew his hand, crouched deeper into his corner, and let his head fall forward onto his chest.

The young man lifted his eyes slowly to the tower. The gargoyles were back in their niche. Nothing was changed. He was amazed at the absurdities his brain could foist upon him, and he began to laugh, a stertorous, fitful, nervous laughter.

The beggar craned his scraggy neck forward, screwing it out in short thrusts, like a turtle. "Why do you laugh in the presence of God?" he cried out. "This is a place of God. Only the devil laughs when he is in a holy place."

The young man stopped laughing and pointed his finger up towards the gargoyles. "You know the two figures in the tower," he said. "Did you ever see them coming out from their places and hanging in the air?"

The beggar began to tremble. He pressed closer into his corner into his corner and with his gnarled left hand he crossed himself three times. "Jesus Christ and Virgin Mary and holy Joseph and all good angels preserve me," he mumbled. "Leave me lying here in peace. When the two figures come down it's a sign that the great judgement day is near. It's a sure sign and they'll come down to search out all sinners. God preserve me from such a sight."

"So I was told, too, when I was a boy," said the young man. "Our teachers told us that in school. And now I tell you that the great judgement day is very near. For when I walked up the steps I saw the figures come out of their niche and they twisted and squirmed and hung in the empty air. But now they are back again, just as they were before. Look up and see."

The beggar trembled. He rose slowly, gathering up the rags that clothed him. Grabbing hold of the railing, he slid down the steps more than he walked, stopping for a moment as he came parallel with the young man, mumbling incantations and charms, and casting spells upon him. Then he averted his eyes and hurried past him. At the foot of the stairs he turned once more, traced a large, trembling cross in the air, and shuffled off like one possessed.

The young man looked after him. He felt sorry that he had frightened him. Once more he looked up at the tower. The gargoyles were safely back in the niche. So the judgement day was not yet at hand, he thought. Then he turned and went slowly down the steps.

It was quite dark now, and only a dimly-glowing lamp in the centre of the market-place threw a pale circle of light onto the wet-glistening cobblestones. He crossed over to the other side. He saw things very clearly now, no longer as through a screen of dreamlike unreality. He wanted to walk quickly, but his feet, suddenly heavy as lead, seemed to drag him down. He felt them, tender and swollen, rubbing against the hard, unyielding leather of his boots. And then he suddenly felt the knapsack on his back pressing hard against his shoulders, weighing him down, as if all the heaviness of his heart and all the sorrows if his young life had accumulated in it. He shifted it onto the right shoulder, but the relief was only momentary. Everything in him cried out for rest. He longed to immerse his body in warm water, ever renewed, flowing over him gently, filling his whole being, soothing and relaxing.

People passed him and he overheard snatches of talk. He envied them. They are going home, he thought. They will sit by the fire and warm themselves in front of it. And then they will go to bed, stretching out on a soft, deep mattress. The thought of this moment of ease and comfort overwhelmed him. On the bed now, on the mattress, there were two bodies, a man and a woman, touching in the dark, caressing, embracing. It was so marvellous that it was almost unbearable.

Now I am going home, he thought suddenly. I , too, am going home! The thought brought forth a feeling of great elation and optimism, and made him walk faster, hurrying to rush home, out of the darkness into the light, out of the cold into the warmth, to end all sorrow and to have rest.

Rest rest peace in peace rest warm water laving my tired body.

And then, coming on slowly, worming its way into his consciousness, the figure if the peasant was before him, small, crouching.

The coarse voice whispered, They are not there, they are not there. Burned, burned, and ashes thrown to the winds. Joyful to hear, joyful to hear, joyful to hear.

He had to stop, and he pressed his hand against his stomach, as if to strangle the apparition and silence its terrible murmurings.

But now his joy was all gone, and he walked very slowly, wishing for something to happen that would make it impossible for him to go where he knew he had to go and was now afraid of going.

A dog came running up behind him and circled round him, barking hoarsely. He tried to kick the mongrel, but missed him. The dog shied away from him and kept on barking, and after a while drew close again. He sniffed at the young man's trousers, yapping lightly, his tongue hanging out of his mouth, his flanks heaving. He lowered his head and began to lick the muddy left boot. He opened his mouth, trying to sink his teeth into the leather, but before he could do it the other boot caught him deep in his side and he dashed off wildly across the street, yelping.

The young man watched him warily. He saw him trotting slowly towards him again, and bent down to pick up a stone. When the dog was quite close, he took aim and hit him straight between the eyes. For a moment the dog stopped barking and stood quite still, and a thin trickle of blood oozed from his mouth. Then suddenly he let out a long, sorrowful wail, almost like the cry of a child, but still he did not move. The young man felt pity for him, and he was sorry that he had hit him. He went up to the dog and squatted down by him, and the dog did not run away. When he stretched out his hand the dog, whimpering softly, licked it with his tongue, and when he got up to walk on, the dog trailed after him.

He was glad now that he had hit the dog because it had relieved some of the tension in him, and his head was clear. His excitement grew again, hope and fear mingled, and he was afraid that his conflicting emotions would tear him apart. He tried hard to keep control over himself, to steel himself against himself, and he kept thinking, Whatever I find, it will at last be the end of uncertainty. To know even the worst is better than not knowing at all.

Through the rain and through the dusk he glimpsed the corner of the street where he had once lived, and from the distance he could plainly see that the house there on the corner was still standing.

A wild feeling of joy surged up in him. He ran. He would soon be able to touch the house.

But when he came close, he saw that there was no house to touch. There was only a mangled, gutted structure. There was no street, only heaps of rubble and bits of rugged slabs of wall set over the rubble heaps, marking them, like rough-hewn gravestones.

And then for a moment everything was blotted out and he could see nothing. A cold hand gripped his heart and pressed it and pushed upward, choking him, and his cry remained stifled in his throat. He felt something rubbing itself against his leg and opened his eyes and saw that it was the dog. An insane fury overcame him, and he turned viciously against the dog and chased him off. He wanted no witnesses, not even a dog.

For a long time he stood there, unable to move, as if he were rooted to the ground. His eyes did not want to see, and yet he could not prevent them from seeing; his brain did not want to know, and yet he could not prevent it from knowing.

This is how it ends. This is how it ends. This is how it ends. Endlessly the words revolved round his mind. All my dreams and all my hopes. This is how it ends. No light, no outstretched hand of greeting, no kiss of welcome. A gutted block of buildings, a pile of rubble half-cleared, a bit of wall left standing, a few gaping holes for windows. This is how it ends. This is the end of my long road. This is the end the end the end … and with a terrifying hopelessness he realized that the end was not the end. It was a terrible beginning. He did not want to begin. He did not want to come to terms with what he had now discovered.

His body felt numb, as if his nerves had been anaesthetized. Only his stomach distended and contracted in short and painful spasms. He let go of his knapsack and it dropped down on the ground. He was not aware of it and for some time he kept his hand up near his shoulder-blade and his fist closed as if he were still gripping his knapsack.

Just ruins just ruins just ruins. I'm used to ruins. All Europe is in ruins. Always the same ruins. Destruction is destruction everywhere. All ruins are the same ruins. Ah! But this is special destruction and these are special ruins. My ruins, not someone else's ruins, my own destruction, and under the rubble perhaps the man who fathered me and the woman who bore me. And my sister too. I played with her and quarrelled with her and loved her and loved her. And where is she now? Where are they all?

He opened the palm of his hand and closed it. Opened it and closed it. Looked at it. The knapsack? Where was the knapsack? Why did the hand open and close and why did the knapsack not drop down on the ground? He looked about for it, found it lying behind him and picked it up. Then he walked on slowly, treading cautiously, as if he were afraid of destroying something, as if it were important that each stone be left exactly where it was, an eternal reminder of chaos and havoc.

The drizzling rain kept falling, regular, monotonous, thin.

Six years and not yet cleared. Tomorrow I'll clear it, make it clean, wipe away the memory, build the houses again.

My ruins, the ruins of my father's house.

He brushed against a piece of standing wall. His hand touched the wall, caressed it.

This is my welcome, the hand extended to grasp mine. This what if left of my home. A bit of wall, stones, pieces of brick, an odd bit of slate.

He felt the wall, damp and rough against his hand. The sharp edges cut into his flesh and made the blood come. He felt the pain, and he was glad. It was good to feel the pain, and he was glad. It was good to feel the pain. It released the tension and allowed feeling to come pouring forth. His body was no longer numb, the pain from the hand spread all through it. And then suddenly tears came welling up and he pressed his body close against the wall, his arms extended as if he meant to embrace it, his lips touching it as if he meant to kiss it. Then he slumped against the wall, crying softly, noiselessly, without a whimper, without a sob.

Two men passed by on the other side, looked briefly at the figure hazily outlined in the deep dusk, and passed by. They thought it was a beggar, starved, cold, and weakened, laying himself down to die.

He did not move. He lay perfectly still, his head touching the wall, weeping through closed eyes. There was no suffering now, no pain, no anguish. There was only the stinging sensation of hot tears coursing slowly down his cheeks, and the cool, humid dampness of the wall against his forehead.

Now there is peace, now there is rest. Now I have come home to rest and to have peace forever.

The wall was like a wet piece of linen, cool and soothing. He lifted his head and leaned his flushed and feverish cheeks against the stone, first one and then the other.

A piece of wall. A piece of stone. Now I can lie here, and yet I cannot lie here. I have come to the end of the road, but it is not really the end of the road. I am in limbo. Neither the end nor the beginning. But I cannot move. My legs will not carry me further now. I must lie here, waiting. Yes, waiting. But for what?

Surely my mother will come to me now, for she must know that I am here, waiting. There is blood on my hand.

Why is there blood on my hand? Why does she not come to me? If she does not come to me, then I must go and seek her. But I cannot move. I am cold and wet and lonely. And there is blood on my hand. I must try and get up and search for her.

He began to grope about in the moist ground with his hand, digging his fingers into the earth, picking up a dark-brown lump of wet earth and crumbling it slowly in the palm of his hand, then letting small pieces of earth fall through his slightly-spread fingers. He put his hand on the ground again, wanting to pick up more earth, but he did not bring it up immediately. He felt something slimy and mucous trying to crawl onto his hand. He wanted to see what it was, and he laid his hand down as flatly as he could, making it easier for the thing to crawl on. He felt it lift what must be its head, exploring his flesh, then wriggling onto the hand, drawing its long, slimy, legless body after it. He shivered, imagining the thing to be something unspeakably loathsome. He did not look down at his hand, but brought it slowly up to the level of his eyes where he could see the worm writhe and bend, twisting its transverse furrows, its body-rings narrowing and expanding.

Only an earthworm, he thought, and he was disappointed, only a blind, helpless, squirming earthworm, not a terribly disgusting reptile, frightful and sickening, fitting the time and the place. He grasped the worm with two fingers and let it dangle in the air, watching it twist and squirm.

Shake hands with the worm. It bids you welcome. It has come crawling out of the earth to greet you. A good worm, a blind worm, perhaps even now come from feasting on your father.

Cold shivers ran down his spine and revulsion rose in him. Furious and angry, he flung the worm aside, hurling it far from him. Then he scrambled to his feet, something within him driving him away from this place which seemed suddenly cursed and haunted, full of memories and ghosts of a past he did not want to encounter.

It was dark now and he could hardly see where he was going. His feet seemed to be on fire, and each step caused him intense pain. He walked aimlessly, not knowing where he might find people who could help him.

He was now in the oldest part of the ghetto, dragging himself forlornly through narrow, deserted, cobble-stoned alleys, passing by the dilapidated, unlighted houses whose low brick walls shut out all air and exuded a mouldy odour. From the deep, scummy gutters where streams of dirty water had turned the ground into loose black mud there rose a reeking stench, foul and stale.

Oh, for the touch of a warm human hand, he thought longingly, and for the sound of a kind, reassuring voice.

But there was no movement, no stirring, except the unvarying, interminable patter of the wearisome rain, and from afar came the howling of dogs, calling and answering each other.

He kept close to the houses, supporting himself against the walls, trying to take the full weight of his body off his legs. His feet were aflame, as if all the devils and all the inmates of hell had come to hold a merry celebration in his boots.

Then suddenly he saw the thin figure of a woman detach itself from one of the dirty court-yards and step out into the street. She came scurrying towards him, without seeing him. He hailed her in a low, friendly tone of voice. She let out a short, startled cry and stood for a moment, staring at him. Then she tore herself away, turned sharply and ran off.

He became desperate. "Don't run away from me!" he called after her. "Please don't run away from me."

She did not stop. He began to run after her. She could not keep up her pace, and he caught up with her and grabbed hold of her arm. She tried to wrench her arm away from him, her breath coming short and heavy.

"I've done nothing wrong," she whimpered. "I've done nothing. Let me go! Please let me go!"

He looked into her gaunt, line-drawn, prematurely aged face. Fear, fear, he thought, everywhere I go I meet fear and blind superstition. God, God, he wanted to cry out, when will it end? When will we be rid of our fears?

"Don't be afraid," he said softly, trying to reassure her. "I don't want to hurt you. I only want to ask you what has happened here. I don't want to hurt you."

"Let me go," she cried. "Look, I have nothing you can take away from me. What do you want from me? Let me go."

"I'll let you go," he said. "I want nothing from you. I only want somebody to talk to." He pleaded with her. "First talk to me, and then I'll let you go. I must know something, and perhaps you can tell me. Are some people still alive here? This used to be the Jewish section of the town. My family once lived in this town, not far from where we are standing. Tell me, is anybody left living among the people who lived here before the war? Is anybody left living among the Jews?"

When she heard him ask this question in a trembling voice, she grew calmer and more composed. "A few have come back," she answered slowly. "A very few. More dead than alive." Then after a short pause she asked, "Who are you?"

"I have just come back, too," he said. "But I have found only ruins where our house used to be."

"You said your family once lived here," she said.

"Yes," he said, "and I found the house I lived in burned to the ground."

"What is your family's name?" she asked.

"Drimmer," he said. "And my name is Mordecai. Mordecai Drimmer."

He took his hand from her sleeve, and for a while they stood facing each other in silence.

At last she asked, "Who was your father?"

"My father's name was Aaron," he said quietly. "He was a doctor. Many of his patients lived in these houses."

She let out a sharp cry. "Aaron Drimmer! The doctor! You are the doctor's son?" She groped for his hand and grasped it tremblingly with her own.

"You knew him?" he asked. "You knew my father?"

"Everybody knew your father," she said simply.

He nodded his head. Slowly and with painful difficulty he brought himself to ask the crucial question. "Is he alive? Is my father alive?"

She did not answer immediately.

"Is my mother alive? And my sister? Have you seen them? Have you heard anything about them?"

"Your father and your mother have not come back," she said slowly. "And I don't know your sister, but I haven't heard her name mentioned. So perhaps .... But your father and your mother have not come back to the town. I would know if they had."

His heart sank. A great chasm opened up before him and he felt himself falling into its yawning depths and there was no end to his fall.

The woman recalled him. He heard her say tenderly, "Perhaps your father will come back. He must know that people need him. Perhaps your mother will come back. Perhaps all your family will come back. Every day a few people come back, and it is always like a miracle to us who are here already. When you told me before that you had come back this evening, it was to me as if someone had risen from the dead."

He put up his hand. "I don't want you to think of me like that," he said. "It would be cruel if the dead had to rise from their graves to find what I had to find this evening."

"It would not be cruel," she snapped angrily. "I wish my husband would rise from the dead and come back to me."

He looked past her into the darkness of the street. "If I were dead," he said softly, "and someone brought me back to life, I would not thank him. I would hate him for all eternity."

She drew back against the wall of the house. "Don't talk like that," she said. "Please don't talk like that. You frighten me."

He reached out his hand and touched her lightly. "Forgive me," he said. "I didn't want to frighten you. I was talking out of my own bitterness, and I was thinking only about myself."

"My husband would not hate me if I could bring him back," she said proudly. "Even if he had to suffer new agonies, he would come back, because he would not want me to be so alone." He saw her eyes fill with silent tears, and she lifted a corner of her shawl and wiped them away. "Only a few weeks," she said softly. "We were married only a few weeks before we were torn apart."

"Perhaps he will come back," he said.

She did not respond to him.

He asked awkwardly, "Where did you come from when I first saw you?"

She stiffened and a sudden coldness crept into her voice. "Why do you ask me? What business is it of yours?"

Fear and suspicion, he thought, fear and suspicion. Trust has vanished from the earth.

"It's none of my business," he said quickly, lifting his hand in protest. "None at all. I didn't mean to be inquisitive."

"It's not a secret," she said. "I was coming from the courtyard over there. In the cellar of that house there is a bakeshop. I thought they were baking tonight and I wanted to get some bread. But it is all dark. They are not baking, because they have no flour."

"Is there enough food?"

"Too much to starve and not enough to live."

"Black market?"

"If you have money."

"How many people have come back?"

She shrugged her shoulders. "I don't know," she said. "It's hard to say. Perhaps a hundred. Perhaps two hundred. Not more. A lot leave again. They say there's more work in the bigger cities. And some people don't want to stay in Poland anymore. They want to go far away. Away from all the memories. To America. Or to Palestine. They say there is some kind of underground organization that helps people."

"How long have you been here?"

"About two months."

"And are you going to stay here?"

"I don't know. I am waiting."

"Waiting for what? For your husband to come back?"

She remained silent. Tears came again and coursed down her cheeks and she did not wipe them away.

"Has the community organized itself?" he asked. "Is there somebody who is looking after things?"

She nodded her head. "David Mantel," she said. "He has organized a community office to try to help people when they come back, and to talk to the government officials."

The name electrified him. "David Mantel!" he gasped. "David Mantel is alive! Where? Where is he? Where does he live? Come, come! Show me where he lives." He took hold of her arm and pulled her towards him.

"Do you know him?" she asked. "Do you know David Mantel?"

"Yes," he cried, full of excitement. "I know him. He—he is my uncle. My mother's brother. Where does he live? You must know where he is. Come. Show me where he is. Please show me."

"He lives on Planty Street. Number 2," she said. "I know because it is the community house now. He uses one room for himself, and I think his is the first door in the second floor of the house."

"I've forgotten where the street is," he said, "and I don't know how to find it. Come with me and show me where it is."

She shook her head. "Don't ask me to do that," she said. "In the daytime I would come with you, but not now, not at night. It's so dark and lonely in the streets. I would be afraid to walk back alone. It's not safe to walk in the streets after dark. During the past few weeks bands of young hoodlums have been roaming around the streets and they've beaten people up when they've caught them in the streets. So people don't go far from where they live after the dark comes on. That's why I was so frightened when you called to me … But Planty Street is easy to find. Go to the end of this street and then turn right and walk three more blocks. The third is Planty Street."

"Where do you live?" he asked.

"I live here on this street. Only a few houses away," she said, pointing her finger. "That's why I came out. It was worth the risk. If I had been able to get some bread …. Will you be able to find Planty Street?"

"I'll find the street," he said.

He was quiet for a few moments. Then he said, "I have a piece of black cornbread left in my knapsack. I want to give it to you, so you won't have come out for nothing."

"Bread!" she cried out incredulously. "Bread! But don't give it away. Keep it for yourself. You will be hungry and you will want it yourself."

"I'll manage," he said, groping about in his knapsack. He found the bread and brought it out of the bag. "It's less than I thought," he said, smiling apologetically. "But it's all I have left."

She took the bread and hid it in the folds of her shawl to preserve it from the rain. "God bless you," she said.

He inclined his head lightly towards her. "I don't know what I would have done if I hadn't met you here in the streets. I was lost and didn't know where to go. And then you told me that David Mantel is alive! I felt that a miracle had happened."

She smiled.

"I didn't ask you what your name was," he said.

"Rachel," she said. "Rachel Pokorny." Then, after a pause, "Perhaps I will see you again."

"Probably," he said. "Perhaps another miracle will happen. Perhaps your husband will come back."

She looked up at him. He could see her eyes shining in the darkness. "No," she said slowly. "He will not come back." Her voice was inexpressibly sad. "Only the living can come back. I found out a week ago that he is dead."

"But how can you be sure?" he cried in anguish.

"Someone came back last week. He was with him. In one of the camps. He saw him die."

"But he could be wrong," he said. "How can he be so sure it was your husband who died? It could have been someone else. There are miracles. You said so yourself. Your husband will come back. You are waiting for him. He will come back."

"No," she said, and her voice was quite firm, bereft of all illusion. "He will not come back. I know that he is dead, and the dead don't rise from their graves."

He reached out his hand and stroked her cheek gently. Then he folded his arms around her and embraced her and felt her body trembling against his.

For some minutes they stood together, so. Then she freed herself from the embrace, turned quickly and, without saying a word, hurried away.

He stood watching her until she disappeared into the courtyard of the house where she lived, and then he, too, hurried on, almost running in spite of the pain each step caused him.

The way seemed endless, the goal impossible to reach, like trying to grasp at low-hanging clouds. But David Mantel was alive! At least that was true. And what if it was not? But why should she have mentioned his name? What if it was another man by the same name? No, that couldn't be. It had to be his uncle, his mother's brother.

He will know where my mother is. At least somebody is alive who can connect the present with the past, at least one familiar face among all the strangers, one friend left amid the chaos and the desolation.

Three streets. Only three blocks. Three streets away. But that can be as far as eternity …. The devils are dancing a mad waltz in my boots, and if I don't come to Planty Street soon, I won't get there at all. I'll collapse in the street. The devils will out-dance me and bring me down. She said three blocks. Three streets …. One block I have already walked. Two blocks. Two streets …. One more street. One more block …. What will he say when he sees me?

He tried to run, but he couldn't. There was a sharp pain in his side, and his feet seemed to be on fire. He had to slow his pace. It was as if he were walking on glowing coals.

I can't go on much longer, and one block can be as long as a thousand miles. But now I must be close to the house. Only a minute longer. Count till sixty. The devils are dancing like mad.

This must be the house. Number 2. Weary and stooped, he limped up the wooden stairs, holding on tightly to the crumbling, worm-eaten banister, drawing himself up step by step.

The first door on the second floor of the house. That is what she had said. The first door on the second floor the second floor on the first door the first on the first on the second on the door the devils are dancing on the first door on the second floor.

Dimly he perceived the wooden door on the top of the stairs. He lifted his right hand and began to knock on the door, slowly, mournfully, as if he were beating out the rhythm to an unheard funeral march.

Inside all remained silent. Nothing moved, no one stirred. A feeling of blind panic began to overwhelm him. David Mantel is not living here! Has she told me a lie? But why would she do that? She had no reason. Perhaps she was mistaken. Perhaps this is not the right house or the right door.

He began to pound harder on the door. Then he began to shout, "David Mantel! David Mantel! David Mantel!"

And when there was still no answer and no one came to the door, "Mordecai is here! Mordecai! Your nephew! Uncle David! Open the door! Open the door! Open!"

Now there was an excited shuffling of footsteps behind the door, but he did not hear it. Nor did he hear a trembling voice ask, "Who is it? Who is it? Who is it?"

He kept on pounding his fist against the door mechanically, furiously, raising his voice above the din of his own insane tattoo and shouting, "I'm Mordecai! Mordecai! Open the door!"

"Mordecai?" asked the voice behind the door, loud and insistent, "Mordecai?" Now he could hear it. "Mordecai Drimmer?"

"Yes," he cried. "Mordecai Drimmer. Open the door. Let me come in."

He let his arm sink down, exhausted. His body stiffened, his nerves were stretched almost beyond endurance. Then he heard a bolt being pushed back, and the door was opened. A small, thin man stood facing him. His face was pale, his hands were trembling.

For a long moment the two men stared at each other in great consternation and disbelief, as if neither could comprehend that the other was actually standing there before him, breathing and alive.

At last David Mantel drew Mordecai into the room and closed the door. He took his knapsack from him and put it down on the floor. He helped him to take off his heavy, rain-soaked coat. They moved silently, slowly, as if they were in a dream. Then suddenly, as if he were only now grasping the reality of Mordecai's presence, David Mantel flung his arms round him and embraced him and kissed him and kept calling out his name again and again and again.

"Mordecai!" he cried, over and over again. "Mordecai! Alive! Alive!" Tears were streaming down his face.

Mordecai tried to force a smile. "Alive," he said. "After a fashion."

"God be thanked," said David Mantel. "You have come back."

"And the others?"

"The family?"

"Yes. The family?"

David Mantel spoke very quietly. "No one else has yet come back. I am trying to find out what has happened to them. But for the moment it is very difficult. There is too much confusion. Perhaps some have survived. We must pray and we must hope. You have come back, and I have come back. And perhaps they will also come back. We must wait and we must have patience. We must have trust in the Almighty."

"We have had too much trust," said Mordecai sharply. "We have had too much patience. We have waited too long."

"We must not give up. Especially not now."

"Why should we want to go on living? What point is there in life when so many have been killed and so much has been destroyed?" He felt inexpressibly weary. Nothing mattered anymore.

Suddenly all his strength drained from his body. The walls of the small, bare room began to close in on him, and then he himself seemed to be whirled about, ever more swiftly, until he seemed to be floating upwards and upwards, through the ceiling and out the room. Strange sounds assailed him, and then he heard someone calling his name, but from far, far away, and when he tried to answer, no sound came. He floated further and further away and all was dark and silent.

III

For five days the fever raged in him. From time to time he saw figures hovering above him as he lay on the hard, narrow bed. Sometimes it was the face of a man that he saw, sometimes that of a woman, but he could not make his eyes focus long enough to make out their features clearly before everything dissolved again, and his body floated off into space.

On the sixth day he heard someone call his name out clearly, and when he opened his eyes he saw a thin man whose sad, drawn face looked down at him.

"Mordecai!" said the man. "Mordecai! Can you see me?"

Mordecai had difficulty shaping the words he wanted. "I think— I see," he said at last, slowly.

"And do you know who I am?"

"You are—I think you are—you are—my uncle. My uncle David."

"Thank God, thank God," David Mantel cried out. "You have come back to us." Tears welled up in his eyes. He sobbed. "You have come home. You have come home."

Mordecai's eyes closed. He could not keep them in focus. He was very tired. But things did not dissolve, his body did not float off into space. After what seemed a long, long time he opened his eyes again. David Mantel had pulled a chair up to the bed and was sitting there, looking at him.

"Who else has come home?" Mordecai asked. He didn't have so much difficulty now shaping the words.

"You have come. We must be thankful for that."

"And the others? My mother? My father? My sister?"

A long silence. Then, his voice hardly audible, "No. Not yet."

"And your wife, my Aunt Rebecca? And your sons, my cousins?"

"Your aunt and your cousin Jonathan ...." His voice broke. Tears were streaming down his cheeks. "They will not come back. They—they have perished."

The words were barely whispers and yet their force was that of hammer blows.

"How—how do you know? How can you be sure?"

"I know. I am sure."

"And my cousin Pinchas?"

"Pinchas and I were taken away together. But then, in one of the camps, we were separated and lost each other. But perhaps God was merciful and he was spared. And perhaps some of the other members of our family also."

Mordecai seemed bereft of speech. What was there to say. But he had to speak. Like a child he craved reassurance. "Will they come back?" he cried out. "Will we find them?" There was desperation in the voice, but it was also a terrible cry for hope.

"I don't know," said David Mantel.

"Why am I alive? Why are you alive? Why did we come back?"

"Because it was willed."

"Who willed it?"

A long pause. Then David Mantel said quietly, "The Almighty."

Mordecai gave him a long, ironic look. "Do you really believe that?"

"I must."

"The great cosmic jokester," said Mordecai. "Do you really believe that he sits there in his heaven and plays a cruel game of chance with us? All a part of a great cosmic lottery?"

"It isn't for us to judge."

Mordecai raised himself on the bed and said angrily, "It is absolutely for us to judge. Who else can judge? Where did he hide during the great slaughter? Where was he, that almighty of yours? Where was he when we cried out to him?"

"I know all the questions. I have often asked them. But in the end I cannot judge Him. His ways are not our ways."

"No. That's not enough any more. If he is really there, he must answer. He must."

"There are signs of His Presence."

"There are more signs of his absence." Talking and concentrating had exhausted him. He let his head sink back into the pillow and closed his eyes.

After a while he heard footsteps out in the hallway, and then there was a knock on the door.

"That must be Rachel," said David Mantel. He rose to go to the door. "She has been here every day since you came."

"Rachel?"

"Yes. She came on the first morning to ask for you. But you were delirious. She said she met you the evening before, and told you where you could find me. Don't you remember?"

Mordecai tried to recall the events of that day. There was a peasant. He remembered that. Gargoyles laughed at him. There was rubble. And then there was a woman in a dark street. He remembered that also. "I think I remember," he said. "But I don't know what she looked like."

There was another timid knock on the door.

"She's a pleasant woman," said David Mantel, and went to open the door.

"How is he?" Mordecai heard her ask with apprehension in the voice.

"He is awake. He has come back to us."

When she came into the room and he saw her, he remembered the gaunt face. Only now, in the daylight, it seemed a strangely beautiful face, with dark eyes glowing and the dark-brown hair pulled into a tight knot. She looked younger than he thought he remembered her, perhaps in her late twenties.

She smiled at him and without saying anything she sat down at the foot of the bed.

"She sat with you for hours every day," said David Mantel. "She nursed you. And when I thought you might leave us, she would not give up hope, and so she gave me courage, too."

"I must thank you, then," said Mordecai, and held out his hand.

She took his hand. "You don't owe me anything," she said softly. "I was glad I could help." She put her hand on his forehead and then stroked his face, heavy with several days' growth of beard. "Your fever is almost gone," she said.

He nodded. He took her hand and held it for a long time. A warm feeling suffused him. He felt very tired, drained of energy, but also, for the first time in many months, curiously at peace.

He closed his eyes and felt himself dozing off. When he woke again, she was still there, watching over him, but David Mantel had left the room.

"You slept," she said.

"I didn't realize it," he answered. "How long have I been sleeping?"

"Over an hour. How do you feel?"

"Still tired. But much better. I think I will recover. I'm sure of it now."

"I always knew you would recover," she said.

"And will you stop coming now?"

"No, no," she said. "I'll come again …. If you want me to," she added quickly.

"Oh, yes. I want you to come …. You cared for me, even though I was a total stranger …. I'm all alone in the world. I came home and found no one. Except my uncle. But all the others …."

"I'm also alone," she said.

"Come back, then. And then you and I will be less alone." He held out his arms. She came close to him and he put his arms around her and drew her down and kissed her.

"As soon as I'm well again," he said after a while, "I'll have to leave this place."

"Where will you go?"

"I don't know. Except that I have to leave Europe. Europe is finished for me. I'll find some place. So long as it's far away. Where one can breathe. Where there isn't the stench of death everywhere."

"Yes."

"And you? What will you do?"

"I don't know. I—I have no plans. I live from day to day. I was pleased that I could come here and—and help you."

"Well, then, when I leave, perhaps you could come with me."

She was taken aback. "No, no," she cried. "How could I go with you? We don't even know each other."

"At least we're alive," he said. "We survived. And you looked after me. That's already something."

"Perhaps it's something. But it may be nothing."

"We'll see."

"We'll see," she echoed him. "One day at a time."

"But you will come again?"

"Oh, yes. Yes, I'll come again. As long as you want me to come."

"Tomorrow?"

"Yes."

"And the day after."

"Yes."

"And the day after that?"

"I'm not yet ready to look so far into the future." She smiled, but it was an enigmatic smile.

"Are you serious?"

"Of course. I've been hurt too often. So I have to learn to trust again, and hope again. One day at a time."

"All right," he said. "One day at a time." He stroked her face softly, and then drew her down and kissed her again.

"I must go now," she said. "And I'll come again tomorrow."

When she had gone, he lay for a long time without moving. He could still feel the warmth of her body. Perhaps I can pick up the pieces of my life, he thought. Perhaps I can find some reason to want to live again. The thought took him by surprise. It astonished him. It was miraculous how powerfully the will to live asserted itself.

He got out of bed. He felt weak and his legs were unsteady. He had to hold on to a chair. But he stood. His strength would return. And he knew that he would not allow himself to be defeated.

About the cover painting

Charles Comfort, "Dieppe Raid," 1946. Oil on canvas,
91.4 cm x 152.7 cm. Catalogue number 12276.
Copyright © Canadian War Museum; used by permission.

About Muriel Whitaker

A specialist in medieval literature and art, Muriel Whitaker is Professor
Emerita from the Department of English at the University of Alberta.
She is the author of *The Legends of King Arthur in Art* and the editor of
several volumes of Canadian short stories. Dr. Whitaker lives in
Edmonton, Alberta but spends her summers at her cottage near
Kamloops, British Columbia.

About Peter Stursburg

CBC war correspondent Peter Stursberg covered the landing of the
Canadians in Sicily on July 10, 1943. The only Canadian correspondent
to enter both Rome and Berlin with the Western Allies, Stursberg also
reported on the Italian Campaign, the invasion of southern France, the
crossing of the Rhine, and the liberation of Holland and Norway. For
many Canadians, his voice is synonymous with news of the Second
World War.